I0666965

HOLIDAYS AT
ROSELANDS

A SEQUEL TO ELSIE DINSMORE

MARTHA FINLEY

1st WORLD
LIBRARY
Literary Society

Holidays at Roselands

Martha Finley

© 1st World Library, 2006
PO Box 2211
Fairfield, IA 52556
www.1stworldlibrary.com
First Edition

LCCN: 2006936237

Softcover ISBN: 978-1-4218-3099-5
Hardcover ISBN: 978-1-4218-2999-9
eBook ISBN: 978-1-4218-3199-2

Purchase *"Holidays at Roselands"*
as a traditional bound book at:
www.1stWorldLibrary.com/purchase.asp?ISBN=978-1-4218-3099-5

1st World Library is a literary, educational organization
dedicated to:

- Creating a free internet library of downloadable ebooks

- Hosting writing competitions and offering book
  publishing scholarships.

Interested in more 1st World Library books?
contact: literacy@1stworldlibrary.com
Check us out at: www.1stworldlibrary.com

1st World Library Literary Society

Giving Back to the World

"If you want to work on the core problem, it's early school literacy."

- James Barksdale, former CEO of Netscape

"No skill is more crucial to the future of a child, or to a democratic and prosperous society, than literacy."

- Los Angeles Times

Literacy... means far more than learning how to read and write... The aim is to transmit... knowledge and promote social participation."

- UNESCO

"Literacy is not a luxury, it is a right and a responsibility. If our world is to meet the challenges of the twenty-first century we must harness the energy and creativity of all our citizens."

- President Bill Clinton

"Parents should be encouraged to read to their children, and teachers should be equipped with all available techniques for teaching literacy, so the varying needs and capacities of individual kids can be taken into account."

- Hugh Mackay

"Hope not sunshine every hour,
Fear not clouds will always lower."

—Burns.

CHAPTER I

"Oh Truth,
Thou art, whilst tenant in a noble breast,
A crown of crystal in an iv'ry chest."

Elsie felt in better spirits in the morning; her sleep had refreshed her, and she arose with a stronger confidence in the love of both her earthly and her heavenly Father.

She found her papa ready, and waiting for her. He took her in his arms and kissed her tenderly. "My precious little daughter," he said, "papa is very glad to see you looking so bright and cheerful this morning. I think something was wrong with my little girl last night. Why did she not come to papa with her trouble?"

"*Why* did you think I was in trouble, papa?" she asked, hiding her face on his breast.

"How could I think otherwise, when my little girl did not come to bid me good night, though she had not seen me since dinner; and when I went to give her a good-night kiss I found her pillow wet, and a tear on her cheek?"

"*Did* you come, papa?" she asked, looking up in glad surprise.

"I did. Now tell me what troubled you, my own one?"

"I am afraid you will be angry with me, papa," she said, almost under her breath.

"Not half so angry as if you refuse to give me your confidence. I would be glad to know that my little daughter had not a single thought or feeling concealed from me."

He paused a moment, looking down at the little blushing face, half hidden on his breast, then went on:

"Elsie, daughter, you are more precious to me than aught else in the wide world, and you need not fear that any other can ever take your place in my heart, or that I will make any connection that would render you unhappy. I want no one to love but my little girl; and you must not let the gossip of the servants disturb you."

Elsie looked up in unfeigned astonishment.

"Papa! you seem to know everything about me. Can you read my thoughts?"

"*Almost*, when I can see your face," he answered, smiling at her puzzled look. "I cannot quite, though; but I can put things together and make a pretty good guess, sometimes."

She lay still on his breast for a moment; then, raising her eyes timidly to his face again, she said in a half-hesitating way, "I am afraid it is very naughty in me, papa, but I can't help thinking that Miss Stevens is very disagreeable. I felt so that very first day, and I did not want to take a present from her, because it didn't seem exactly right when I didn't like her, but I couldn't refuse—she wouldn't let me—and I have tried to like her since, but I can't."

"Well, darling, I don't think I am just the proper person to reprove you for *that*," he replied, trying to look grave, "for I am afraid I am as naughty as you are. But we won't talk any more about her. See what I have for you this morning."

Martha Finley

He pointed to the table, where lay a pile of prettily bound books, which Elsie had not noticed until this moment. They were Abbot's works. Elsie had read several of his historical tales, and liked them very much; and her father could hardly have given a more acceptable present.

"I was sorry for your disappointment yesterday," he said, "but I hope these will make up for it, and they will give you a great deal of useful information, as well as amusement; while it could only be an injury to you to read that trashy book."

Elsie was turning over the books with eager delight.

"*Dear* papa, you are so kind and good to me," she said, laying them down to put her arms around his neck and kiss him. "I like these books very much, and I don't at all care to read that other one since you have told me you do not approve of it."

"That is my own darling child," said he, returning her caress, "your ready obedience deserved a reward. Now put on your hat, and we will take our walk."

Mr. Travilla joined them in the avenue, and his kind heart rejoiced to see how the clouds of care and sorrow had all passed away from his little friend's face, leaving it bright and beaming, as usual. Her father had one hand, and Mr. Travilla soon possessed himself of the other.

"I don't altogether like these company-days, when you have to be banished from the table, little Elsie," he remarked. "I cannot half enjoy my breakfast without your bright face to look at."

"I don't like them either, Mr. Travilla, because I see so little of papa. I haven't had a ride with him since the company came."

"You shall have one this afternoon, if nothing happens," said her father quickly. "What do you say, Travilla, to a ride on horseback with the four young ladies you took charge of yesterday, and myself?"

"Bravo! I shall be delighted to be of the party, if the ladies don't object; eh! Elsie, what do you think?" with a questioning look down into her glad face, "will they want me?"

"You needn't be a bit afraid, Mr. Travilla," laughed the little girl; "I like you next to papa, and I believe Lucy and the rest like you better."

"Oh! take care, Elsie; are you not afraid of hurting his feelings?"

"No danger, as long as *she* puts me first," Mr. Dinsmore said, bestowing a smile and loving glance on her.

Caroline Howard was in Elsie's room, waiting to show her bracelet, which had just been handed to her by her maid; Pomp having brought it from the city late the night before.

"Oh! Elsie, I am so glad you have come at last. I have been waiting for half an hour, I should think, to show you these," she said, as Elsie came in from her walk. "But how bright and merry you look; so different from last night! what ailed you then?"

"Never mind," replied Elsie, taking the bracelet from her hand, and examining it. "Oh! this is *very* pretty, Carry! the clasp is so beautiful, and they have braided the hair so nicely."

"Yes, I'm sure mamma will like it. But now that Christmas is gone, I think I will keep it for a New Year's gift. Wouldn't you, Elsie?"

"Yes, perhaps—but I want to tell you, Carry, what papa says. He and Mr. Travilla are going to take you, and Lucy, and Mary, and me, riding on horseback this afternoon. Don't you think it will be pleasant?"

"Oh, it will be *grand*!" exclaimed Carry. "Elsie, I think now that your papa is very kind; and do you know I like him very much, indeed; quite as well as I do Mr. Travilla, and I always liked *him*—he's so pleasant, and so funny, too, sometimes. But I must go and show my bracelet to Lucy. Hark! no, there's the bell, and I'll just leave it here until after breakfast."

Elsie opened a drawer and laid it carefully in, and they ran off to the nursery.

"Elsie," said her father, when they had finished the morning lessons, "there is to be a children's party to-night, at Mr. Carleton's, and I have an invitation for you. Would you like to go?"

"Do you wish me to go, papa?" she asked.

"Not unless *you* wish to do so, daughter," he said kindly. "I cannot go with you, as there are to be none but little people, and I never feel altogether comfortable in seeing my darling go from home without me; and you will, no doubt, be very late in returning and getting to bed, and I fear will feel badly to-morrow in consequence; but this once, at least, you shall just please yourself. All your little guests are going, and it would be dull and lonesome for you at home, I am afraid."

Elsie thought a moment.

"Dear papa, you are very kind," she said, "but if you please, I would much rather have you decide for me, because I am only a silly little girl, and you are so much older and wiser."

He smiled, and stroked her hair softly, but said nothing.

"Are you going to stay at home, papa?" she asked presently.

"Yes, daughter, I expect to spend the evening either in this room or the library, as I have letters to write."

"Oh, then, papa, please let me stay with you! I would like it *much* better than going to the party; will you, papa? please say yes."

"But you know I cannot talk to you, or let you talk; so that it will be very dull," he said, pushing back the curls from the fair forehead, and smiling down into the eager little face.

"Oh! but if you will only let me sit beside you and read one of my new books, I shall be quite contented, and sit as quiet as a little mouse, and not say one word without leave. Mayn't I, papa?"

"I said you should do as you pleased, darling, and I always love to have my pet near me."

"Oh, then I shall stay!" she cried, clapping her hands.

Then, with a happy little sigh, "It will be so nice," she said, "to have one of our quiet evenings again." And she knew, by her father's gratified look, that she had decided as he would have had her.

A servant put his head in at the door.

"Massa Horace, dere's a gen'leman in de library axin for to see you."

"Very well, Jim, tell him I will be there in a moment. Elsie, dear, put away your books, and go down to your little friends."

"Yes, papa, I will," she replied, as he went out and left her.

"How kind papa is to me, and how I do love him!" she murmured to herself as she placed the books carefully in the drawer where they belonged.

She found Lucy and Mary busily engaged in dressing a doll, and Carry deeply interested in a book. But several of the little

　　　　　　Martha Finley

ones were looking quite disconsolate.

"Oh, Elsie, do come and play with us," said Flora; "Enna won't play anything we like. We've been playing keeping house, but Enna will be mother all the time, and she scolds and whips us so much that we are all tired of it."

"Well, what shall we play?" asked Elsie, good-naturedly. "Will you build houses?"

"No, I'm tired of that, because Enna takes all the blocks," said another little girl. "She isn't at all polite to visitors, is she, Flora?"

"No," replied Flora, "and I don't *ever* mean to come to see her again."

"I don't care," retorted Enna, angrily, "and I don't take *all* the blocks, either."

"Well, *most* all, you do," said the other, "and it isn't polite."

"They're mine, and I'll have as many as I want; and I don't care if it *isn't* polite," Enna answered, with a pout that by no means improved her appearance.

"Will you play 'O sister, O Phebe?'" asked Elsie.

"No, no!" cried several little voices, "Enna always wants to be in the middle; and besides, Arthur always wants to play, and he will kiss us; and we don't like it."

Elsie was almost in despair; but Herbert, who was lying on a sofa, reading, suddenly shut his book, saying, "I tell you what, Elsie! tell us one of those nice fairy stories we all like so much!"

"Yes, do, do!" cried several of the little ones, clapping their hands.

So Elsie drew up a stool close to Herbert's sofa, and the little ones clustered around her, Enna insisting on having the best place for hearing; and for more than an hour she kept them quiet and interested; but was very glad when at last the maid came to take them out walking, thus leaving her at liberty to follow her own inclination.

"What are you going to do now, Elsie?" asked Caroline, closing her book.

"I am going down to the drawing-room to ask Aunt Adelaide to show me how to crochet this mitten for mammy," Elsie answered.

"Won't you come along, girls?"

"Yes, let's take our sewing down there," said Lucy, gathering up the bits of muslin and silk, and putting them in her work-box.

Elsie glanced hastily around as they entered, and gave a satisfied little sigh on perceiving that Miss Stevens was not in the room, and that her Aunt Adelaide was seated with her embroidery near one of the windows, while her papa sat near by, reading the morning paper.

The little girls soon established themselves in a group on the opposite side of Miss Adelaide's window, and she very good-naturedly gave Elsie the assistance she needed.

"Elsie," said Lucy, presently, in an undertone, "Carry has been showing us her bracelet, and I think it is beautiful; she won't tell whose hair it is—I guess it's her sister's, maybe—but I'm sure yours would make just as pretty a bracelet, and I want one for my mamma; won't you give me one of your curls to make it? you have so many that one would never be missed."

"No, Miss Lucy," said Mr. Dinsmore, looking at them over his paper, "you can't have one of my curls; I can't spare it."

Martha Finley

"I don't want one of *your* curls, Mr. Dinsmore," laughed Lucy, merrily. "I didn't ask for it. Your hair is very pretty, too, but it would be quite too short."

"I beg your pardon, Miss Lucy, if my ears deceived me," said he, with mock gravity, "but I was quite certain I heard you asking for one of my curls. Perhaps, though, you are not aware of the fact that my curls grow on two heads."

"I don't know what you mean, Mr. Dinsmore," replied Lucy, laughing again, "but it was one of Elsie's curls I asked for."

"Elsie doesn't own any," said he; "they all belong to me. I let her wear them, to be sure, but that is all; she has no right to give them away."

He turned to his paper again, and Elsie bent over her work, her face flushed, and her little hand trembling so that she could scarcely hold her needle.

"I'm afraid I ought to tell papa," she thought, "that I did give one of my curls away. I never thought about his caring, but I might have known, because when I wanted my hair cut last summer, he said they shouldn't one of them be touched. Oh! dear, why didn't I think of that? I am afraid he will be very much displeased."

"Don't tell him, then," whispered the tempter, "he is not likely ever to miss it."

"Nay, but it would be *wrong* to hide your fault," said conscience.

"I *will* tell him," she resolved.

"Wait till to-morrow, then," whispered the tempter again; "if you tell him now, very likely he will deprive you of your ride this afternoon, as a punishment."

So the struggle went on in the little breast while others were chatting and laughing around her, never suspecting what a battle the little girl was fighting within her own heart.

Presently Lucy jumped up. "Oh! I am so tired sewing; come, girls, let's put on our things, and take a run in the garden."

Carry and Mary readily assented.

"I must speak to papa first," Elsie said in a half whisper, "but don't wait for me."

She had spoken low, but not so low that his quick ear did not catch the sound. He had heard her, and laying his paper down on his knee, as the other little girls ran away, he turned half round and held out his hand, asking, with a smile, "Well, daughter, what is it? what have you to say to papa?"

She went to him at once, and he was surprised to see how she was trembling, and that her cheeks were flushed and her eyes full of tears.

"Why! what ails my darling?" he asked tenderly.

Adelaide had left the room a moment before, and there was no one near enough to hear.

"Please, papa, don't be very angry with me," she pleaded, speaking very low and hesitatingly. "I did not know you cared about my curls; I did not think about their belonging to you, and I did give one to Carry."

He was silent a moment, evidently surprised at her confession; then he said gently, "No, dearest, I will not be angry this time, and I feel sure you will not do so again, now you know that I *do* care."

"No, *indeed*, I will not, dear papa," she replied in a tone of intense relief. "But you are not going to punish me?" she

Martha Finley

asked, beginning to tremble again. "I was *so* afraid to tell you, lest you would say I should not have my ride this afternoon."

"Why, then, did you not put off your confession until after the ride?" he asked, looking searchingly into her face.

"I wanted to very much, papa," she said, looking down and blushing deeply, "but I knew it would be very wrong."

"My dear, conscientious little daughter," he said, taking her on his knee, "your father loves you better than ever for this new proof of your honesty and truthfulness. Deprive you of your ride? no, indeed, I feel far more like rewarding than punishing you. Ah! I had forgotten! I have something for you;" and he put his hand into his pocket and brought out a letter.

"Oh! it is from Miss Rose! dear, darling Miss Rose!" was Elsie's joyful exclamation, as he put it in her hand.

She made a movement as if to get down from his knee, but he detained her.

"Sit still and read it here, darling," he said, "I love to have you on my knee, and if there are any hard places I can help you."

"Thank you, papa; sometimes there are hard places—at least pretty hard for a little girl like me—though I think Miss Rose tries to write plainly because she knows that I cannot read writing as well as big people can."

She was eagerly tearing off the envelope while she answered him, and then settling herself comfortably she began to read.

He watched with deep interest the varying expression of her fine open countenance as she read. Once or twice she asked him to tell her a word, but the most of it she got through without any difficulty.

At last she had finished.

"It is such a nice letter, papa," she said as she folded it up, "and so good of Miss Rose to write to me again so soon."

"Are you not going to let *me* enjoy it, too?" he asked.

She put it into his hand instantly, saying, with a blush, "I did not know you would care to read it, papa."

"I am interested in all that gives either pleasure or pain to my little girl," he answered gently. "I wish to be a sharer in all her joys and sorrows."

Elsie watched him while he read, almost as intently as he had watched her; for she was anxious that he should be pleased with Miss Rose's letter.

It was a cheerful, pleasant letter, well suited to interest a child of Elsie's years; giving an account of home scenes; telling of her little brothers and sisters, their love for each other; the little gifts they had prepared in anticipation of Christmas, etc., etc.

At the close she made some allusion to Elsie's letters, and expressed her heartfelt sympathy in her little friend's happiness.

"I am so glad, my darling," she wrote, "that your father now loves you so dearly, and that you are so happy in his love. My heart ached for you in the bitter disappointment of your first meeting with him. It is true you never said that you were disappointed, but there was a tone of deep sadness in your dear little letter, the cause of which I—who knew so well how you had looked and longed for his return, and how your little heart yearned for his affection—could not fail to guess. But, dear child, while you thus rejoice in an *earthly* father's love, do not forget that you have a Father in Heaven, who claims the *first* place in your heart; and who is the giver of every good gift, not even excepting the precious love that now makes your young life so bright and happy. Keep close to Jesus, dear Elsie: His is the only *truly satisfying* love—the only one we can be certain

Martha Finley

will never fail us."

"Is it not a nice letter, papa?" asked the little girl, as he refolded and gave it to her again.

"Very nice, daughter," he answered, in an absent way. He looked very grave, and Elsie studied his countenance intently while, for some moments, he sat with his eyes bent thoughtfully upon the carpet. She feared that something in the letter had displeased him. But presently he looked at her with his usual affectionate smile, and laying his hand caressingly on her head, said, "Miss Allison seems to warn you not to trust too much to the permanence of my affection; but you need not fear that you will ever lose it, unless, indeed, you cease to be deserving of it. No, nor even then," he added, drawing her closer to him, "for even should you grow very naughty and troublesome, you would still be *my child*—a part of myself and of my lost Elsie, and therefore very dear to me."

"Ah! papa, how could I ever *bear* to lose your love? I think I should die," she said, dropping her head on his breast, with almost a sob. "Oh! if I am ever very, *very* naughty, papa, punish me as severely as you will; but oh, never, *never* quit *loving* me."

"Set your heart at rest, my darling," he said, tenderly, "there is no danger of such a thing. I could not do it, if I wished."

Ah! there came a time when Elsie had sore need of all the comfort the memory of those words could give.

"What are you going to wear to Isabel Carleton's party, to-night, Elsie?" asked Lucy, at the dinner table.

"Nothing," replied Elsie, with an arch smile, "I am not going, Lucy," she added.

"Not going! well, now, that is *too* bad," cried Lucy, indignantly. "I think it's really mean of your papa; he never lets you go anywhere."

"Oh, Lucy! he let me go to town with Carry the other day; he has let me stay up late two or three nights since you came; he is going to let me ride with the rest of you this afternoon, and he said that I might do just as I pleased about going to-night," Elsie summed up rather triumphantly, adding, in a very pleasant tone, "It is entirely my own choice to stay at home; so you see, Lucy, you must not blame my papa before you know."

Lucy looked a little ashamed, while Mary Leslie exclaimed:

"Your own choice, Elsie? why, how strange! don't you like parties?"

"Not nearly so well as a quiet evening with papa," replied Elsie, smiling.

"Well, you are a queer girl!" was Mary's comment, while Caroline expressed her disappointment and vainly endeavored to change Elsie's determination. The little girl was firm, because she felt sure she was doing right, and soon managed to change the subject of conversation to the pleasure nearest at hand—the ride they were to take immediately after dinner.

They were a merry party, and really enjoyed themselves about as much as they had expected; but they returned earlier than usual, as the gentlemen decided that the little ladies needed some time to rest before the evening entertainment.

Elsie assisted her young friends to dress for the party— generously offering to lend them any of her ornaments that they might fancy—saw them come down, one after another, full of mirth and eager expectation, and looking so pretty and graceful in their beautiful evening-dresses, heard their expressions of commiseration toward herself, and watched the last carriage roll away without a sigh or regret that she was left behind. And in another moment a graceful little figure glided quietly across the library, and sitting down on a stool at Mr.

Martha Finley

Dinsmore's feet, looked lovingly into his face with a pair of soft, dark eyes.

His pen was moving rapidly over the paper, but ere long there was a pause, and laying his hand caressingly on the curly head, he said, "How quiet my little girl is; but where is your book, daughter?"

"If you please, papa, I would rather answer Miss Rose's letter."

"You may," he said, "and if you want to stay with me, you may ring the bell and tell the servant to bring your writing desk here."

She joyfully availed herself of the permission, and soon her pen was vainly trying to keep pace with her father's. But presently his was thrown aside, and rising, he stood behind her chair, giving her directions how to sit, how to hold the pen, how to form this or that letter more correctly, guiding her hand, and commending her efforts to improve.

"There, you have spelled a word wrong, and I see you have one or two capitals where there should be a small letter; and that last sentence is not perfectly grammatical," he said. "You must let me correct it when you are done, and then you must copy it off more carefully."

Elsie looked very much mortified.

"Never mind, daughter," he said kindly, patting her cheek; "you do very well for a *little* girl; I dare say I made a great many more mistakes at your age, and I don't expect you to do better than I did."

"Oh, papa, the letters I sent you when you were away must have been full of blunders, I am afraid," she said, blushing deeply; "were you not very much ashamed of me? How could you bear to read them?"

"Ashamed of you, darling? No, indeed, neither of you nor them. I loved them all the better for the mistakes, because they showed how entirely your own they were; and I could not but be pleased with them when every line breathed such love to me. My little daughter's confidence and affection are worth more to me than the finest gold, or the most priceless jewels."

He bent down and kissed her fondly as he spoke; then, returning to his seat, bade her finish her letter and bring it to him when done.

He took up his pen, and Elsie collected her thoughts once more, worked busily and silently for another half hour, and then brought her sheet to him for inspection; presenting it with a timid, bashful air, "I am afraid it is very full of mistakes, papa," she said.

"Never mind, daughter," he answered, encouragingly; "I know that it takes a great deal of practice to make perfect, and it will be a great pleasure to me to see you improve."

He looked over it, pointed out the mistakes very kindly and gently, put the capitals in their proper places, corrected the punctuation, and showed her how one or two of her sentences might be improved.

Then, handing it back, he said, "You had better put it in your desk now, and leave the copying until to-morrow, as it will soon be your bedtime, and I want you on my knee until then."

Elsie's face grew very bright, and she hastened to do his bidding.

"And may I talk, papa?" she asked, as he pushed away his writing, wheeled his chair about toward the fire, and then took her on his knee.

"Yes," he said, smiling, "that is exactly what I want you to do. Tell me what you have been doing all day, and how you are enjoying your holidays; or talk to me of anything that pleases, or that troubles you. I love to be made the confidant of my little girl's joys and sorrows; and I want her always to feel that she is sure of papa's sympathy."

"I am so glad that I may tell you everything, my own papa," she answered, putting her arm around his neck, and laying her cheek to his. "I have enjoyed this day very much, because I have been with you nearly all the time; and then, I had that nice letter from Miss Rose, too."

"Yes, it was a very pleasant letter," he said; and then he asked her what she had been doing in those hours when she had not been with him; and she gave him an animated account of the occurrences of that and several of the preceding days, and told of some little accidents that had happened—amongst them that of the broken doll; and spoke of the sorrow it had caused her; but she did not blame either Flora or Enna, and concluded her narrative by saying that, "good, kind Mrs. Brown had mended it, so that it was almost as good as ever."

He listened with evident interest to all she said, expressed sympathy in her little trials, and gave her some good advice.

But at length he drew out his watch, and with an exclamation of surprise at the lateness of the hour, told her it was half an hour after her bedtime, kissed her good-night, and dismissed her to her room.

CHAPTER II

"There comes
Forever something between us and what
We deem our happiness."

BYRON'S SARDANAPALUS.

It was quite late when the young party returned, and the next day all were dull, and more than one peevish and fretful; so that Elsie, on whom fell, almost entirely, the burden of entertaining them, had quite a trying time.

She noticed at breakfast that Arthur seemed in an uncommonly bad humor, preserving a sullen and dogged silence, excepting once when a sly whisper from Harry Carrington drew from him an exclamation of fierce anger that almost frightened the children, but only made Harry laugh.

Presently after, as they were about dispersing, Arthur came to her side and whispered that he had something to say to her in private.

Elsie started and looked extremely annoyed, but said at once that he might come to her room, and that there they could be quite alone, as mammy would be down-stairs getting her breakfast.

She led the way and Arthur followed. He glanced hastily

Martha Finley

around on entering and then locked the door and stood with his back against it.

Elsie became very pale.

"You needn't be *afraid*" he said, sneeringly, "I'm not going to *hurt* you!"

"What do you want, Arthur? tell me quickly, please, because I must soon go to papa, and I have a lesson to look over first," she said, mildly.

"I want you to lend me some money," he replied, speaking in a rapid and determined manner; "I know you've got some, for I saw your purse the other day, and it hadn't less than five dollars in it, I'm sure, and that's just the sum I want."

"What do you want it for, Arthur?" she asked in a troubled voice.

"That's none of your business," he answered, fiercely. "I want the money; I *must* have it, and I'll pay it back next month, and that's all you need to know."

"No, Arthur," she said gently, but very firmly, "unless you tell me all about it, I cannot lend you a single cent, because papa has forbidden me to do so, and I cannot disobey him."

"Nonsense! that's nothing but an excuse because you don't choose to do me a favor," returned the boy angrily; "you weren't so particular about obeying last summer when he made you sit all the afternoon at the piano, because you didn't choose to play what he told you to."

"That was because it would have been breaking God's command; but this is very different," replied Elsie, mildly.

"Well, if you *must* know," said he, fiercely, "I want it to pay a debt; I've been owing Dick Percival a dollar or so for several weeks, and last night he won from me again, and he said if I didn't pay up he'd report me to papa, or Horace, and get the money from them; and I got off only by promising to let him have the full amount to-day; but my pocket money's all gone, and I can't get anything out of mamma, because she told me the last time I went to her, that she couldn't give me any more without papa finding out all about it. So you see there is nobody to help me but you, Elsie, for there's never any use in asking my sisters; they never have a cent to spare! Now be a good, obliging girl; come and let me have the money."

"Oh! Arthur, you've been gambling; how *could* you do so?" she exclaimed with a horrified look. "It is so *very* wicked! you'll go to ruin, Arthur, if you keep on in such bad ways; do go to grandpa and tell him all about it, and promise never to do so again, and I am sure he will forgive you, and pay your debts, and then you will feel a great deal happier."

"Tell papa, indeed; never! I'd *die* first! Elsie, you *must* lend me the money," he said, seizing her by the wrist.

"Let go of me, Arthur," she said, trying to free herself from his grasp. "You are stronger than I am, but you know if you hurt me, papa will be sure to find it out."

He threw her hand from him with a violence that made her stagger, and catch at the furniture to save herself from falling.

"Will you give me the money then?" he asked angrily.

"If I should do so, I would have to put it down in my expense book, and tell papa all about it, because he does not allow me to spend one cent without telling him just what it went for; and that would be much worse for you, Arthur, than to go and confess it yourself—a *great deal* worse, I am sure."

"You could manage it well enough, if you wanted to," said he, sullenly; "it would be an easy matter to add a few yards to the flannel, and a few pounds to the tobacco that you bought so

Martha Finley

much of for the old servants. Just give *me* your book, and I'll fix it in a minute, and he'll never find it out."

"Arthur!" she exclaimed, "I could *never* do such a wicked thing! I would not deceive papa so for any money; and even if I did he would be sure to find it out."

Some one tried the door.

Arthur put his hand on the lock; then, turning toward Elsie again, for an instant, shook his fist in her face, muttering, with an oath, that he would be revenged, and make her sorry for her refusal to the last day of her life. He then opened the door and went out, leaving poor Elsie pale, and trembling like a leaf.

The person, whoever it was, that had tried the door had gone away again, and Elsie had a few moments alone to recover herself, before Chloe came to tell her that her father could not have her with him that morning, as a gentleman had called on business.

And much as Elsie had always enjoyed that hour, she was almost glad of the respite, so fearful was she that her papa would see that something had agitated her, and insist upon knowing what it was. She was very much troubled that she had been made the repository of such a secret, and fearful that she ought to tell her father or grandfather, because it seemed so very important that Arthur should be stopped in his evil courses. But remembering that he had said that her assistance was his only hope for escaping detection, she at length decided that she need not speak about the matter to any one.

She had a trying time that day, endeavoring to keep the children amused; and her ingenuity and patience were taxed to the utmost to think of stories and games that would please them all.

It was still early in the afternoon when she seemed to have got quite to the end of her list. She was trying to amuse Enna's set, while her three companions and Herbert were taking care of themselves. They had sat down on the floor, and were playing jack-stones.

"Let us play jack-stones, too," said Flora. "I don't know how; but Elsie, you can teach me, can't you?"

"No, Flora, I cannot indeed, for papa says I must not play that game, because he does not like to have me sit down on the floor," replied Elsie. "We must try to think of something else."

"We needn't sit on the floor, need we? Couldn't we play it on the table?" asked Flora.

"I don't know; perhaps we could; but papa said I mustn't play it," replied Elsie, shaking her head doubtfully.

"But maybe he'd let you, if we don't sit on the floor," persisted the little girl.

Several other little ones joined their entreaties to Flora's, and at length Elsie said, "Well, I will go and ask papa; perhaps he may let me, if I tell him we are not going to sit on the floor."

She went to his dressing-room, but he was not there. Next she tried the library, and was more successful; he was in an easy chair by the fire, reading.

But now that she had found him, Elsie, remembering how often he had told her never to ask a second time to do what he had once forbidden, was more than half afraid to prefer her request, and very much inclined to go back without doing so.

But as she stood a moment irresolute, he looked up from his book, and seeing who it was, smiled and held out his hand.

She went to him then, and said timidly, "Papa, some of the little ones want me to play jack-stones, to teach them how; may I, if we don't sit on the floor?"

Martha Finley

"Elsie," he replied, in a tone of great displeasure, "it was only the other day that I positively forbade you to play that game, and, after all that I have said to you about not asking a second time, it surprises me very much that you would dare to do it. Go to my dressing-room, and shut yourself into the closet there."

Elsie burst into tears, as she turned to obey, then, hesitatingly, asked, "May I go down first, papa, and tell the children that I can't come to play with them?"

"Elsie!" he exclaimed, in his sternest tone; and not daring to utter another word, trembling and weeping, she hastened from the room, and shut herself up as he had bidden her.

The closet was large, and there was a stool she could sit on; but when she had shut the door, it was both dark and cold. It was a dismal place to be in, and poor Elsie wondered how long she would have to stay there.

It seemed a long, long time; so long that she began to think it must be night, and to fear that perhaps her papa had forgotten all about having sent her there, or that he considered her so very naughty as to deserve to stay there all night.

But at last she heard his step, and then he opened the door and called, "Elsie!"

"Yes, papa, I am here," she replied in a trembling voice, full of tears.

"Come to me," he said; and then, as he took her hand, "Why, how cold you are, child," he exclaimed; "I am really sorry you have been so long in that dismal place. I did not intend to punish you so severely, and should not have kept you there more than half an hour, at the *very longest*; but company came in, and I quite forgot you."

While speaking thus he had led her up to the fire and sat down with her on his knee. "My poor darling!" he said, "these little hands are very cold, let papa rub them; and are your feet cold too?"

"Yes sir," she replied, and he pulled off her shoes and stockings, and moving his chair closer to the fire, held her feet out toward the blaze, and rubbed them in his warm hands.

"You have been crying a good deal," he said, looking keenly into her face.

"Yes, papa," she replied, dropping her face on his breast and bursting into tears; "I thought you were going to leave me there all night."

"Did you? and were you afraid?"

"No, papa, not *afraid*, because I know you would be sleeping in the next room; and besides, God could take care of me as well in the closet as anywhere else. Is it getting night, papa, or morning?"

"It is beginning to grow dark," he said. "But tell me why you cried, if you were not afraid."

"Partly because I was uncomfortable, papa, but more because I was sorry I had been naughty, and displeased you, and afraid that I can never learn to be good."

"It is very strange," he remarked, "that you cannot learn not to ask to do what I have forbidden. I shall have to punish you every time you do it; for you *must* learn that no *means no*, and that you are never to coax or tease after papa has once said it. I love my little girl very dearly, and want to do all I can to make her happy, but I must have her entirely submissive and obedient to me. But stop crying now," he added, wiping her eyes with his handkerchief. "Kiss me, and tell me you are going to be a good girl, and I will forgive you this time."

Martha Finley

"I will try, papa," she said, holding up her face for the kiss; "and I would not have asked to play that, but the children begged me so, and I thought you only said I mustn't, because you didn't want me to sit on the floor; and we were going to try it on the table."

"Did I give that reason?" he asked gravely.

"No, papa," she replied, hanging her head.

"Then you had no right to think so. That *was one* reason, but not the *only* one. I have heard it said that that play enlarges the knuckles, and I don't choose to have these little hands of mine robbed of their beauty," he added, playfully raising them to his lips.

Elsie smiled faintly, then drew a deep sigh.

"Is it so very hard to give up jack-stones?" he asked.

"No, papa; I don't care anything about *that*, but I was just thinking how very naughty I must be growing; for you have had to punish me twice in one week; and then I have had such a hard day of it—it was so difficult to amuse the children. I think being up so late last night made them feel cross."

"Ah!" he said, in a sympathizing tone; "and had you all the burden of entertaining them? Where were Louise and Lora?"

"They are hardly ever with us, papa; we are too little to play with them, they say, and Enna won't do anything her little friends want her to, and"—she paused, and the color rushed over her face with the sudden thought—"I am afraid I am telling tales."

"And so they put upon you all the trouble of entertaining both your own company and theirs, eh? It is shameful! a downright imposition, and I shall not put up with it!" he exclaimed indignantly. "I shall speak to Lora and Louise, and tell them they must do their share of the work."

"Please, papa, *don't*," Elsie begged in a frightened tone. "I would a great deal rather just go on as we have been; they will be so vexed."

"And suppose they are! they shall not hurt you," he said, drawing her closer to him; "and they have no reason to be. I think the children will all want to go to bed early to-night," he added, "and then you can come here and sit by me while you copy your letter; shall you like that?"

"Very much, papa, thank you."

"Well, then we will put on the shoes and stockings again," he said pleasantly, "and then you must bathe your eyes, and go to your supper; and, as soon as the others retire, you may come back to me."

Elsie had to make haste, for the tea-bell rang almost immediately.

The others were just taking their places at the table when she entered the room, and thus, their attention being occupied with the business in hand, she escaped the battery of questions and looks of curiosity which she had feared.

Flora did turn round after a little, to ask: "Why didn't you come back, Elsie; wouldn't your papa let you play?" But Elsie's quiet "no" seemed to satisfy her, and she made no further remark about it.

As Mr. Dinsmore had expected, the children were all ready for bed directly after tea; and then Elsie went to him, and had another quiet evening, which she enjoyed so much that she thought it almost made up for all the troubles and trials of the day; for her father, feeling a little remorseful on account of her long imprisonment in the closet, was, if possible, even more than usually tender and affectionate in his manner toward her.

Martha Finley

The next morning Mr. Dinsmore found an opportunity to remonstrate with his sisters on their neglect of the little guests, but did it in such a way that they had no idea that Elsie had been complaining of them—as, indeed, she had not—but supposed that he had himself noticed their remissness; and feeling somewhat ashamed of their want of politeness, they went into the children's room after breakfast, and exerted themselves for an hour or two, for the entertainment of the little ones. It was but a spasmodic effort, however, and they soon grew weary of the exertion, and again let the burden fall upon Elsie. She did the best she could, poor child, but these were tiresome and trying days from that until New Year's.

One afternoon Mr. Horace Dinsmore was sitting in his own room, buried in an interesting book, when the door opened and closed again very quietly, and his little girl stole softly to his side, and laying her head on his shoulder, stood there without uttering a word.

For hours she had been exerting herself to the utmost to amuse the young guests, her efforts thwarted again and again by the petulance and unreasonableness of Walter and Enna; she had also borne much teasing from Arthur, and fault-finding from Mrs. Dinsmore, to whom Enna was continually carrying tales, until, at length, no longer able to endure it, she had stolen away to her father to seek for comfort.

"My little girl is tired," he said, passing his arm affectionately around her, and pressing his lips on her forehead.

She burst into tears, and sobbed quite violently.

"Why, what is it, darling? what troubles my own sweet child?" he asked, in a tone of mingled surprise and alarm, as he hastily laid aside his book and drew her to his knee.

"Nothing, papa; at least, nothing very bad; I believe I am very silly," she replied, trying to smile through her tears.

"It must have been something, Elsie," he said, very gravely; "something quite serious, I think, to affect you so; tell me what it was, daughter."

"Please don't ask me, papa," she begged imploringly.

"I hate concealments, Elsie, and shall be very much displeased if you try them with me," he answered, almost sternly.

"Dear papa, *don't* be angry," she pleaded, in a tremulous tone; "I don't want to have any concealments from you, but you know I ought not to tell tales. You won't *make* me do it?"

"Is that it?" he said, kissing her. "No, I shall not ask you to tell tales, but I am not going to have you abused by anybody, and shall take care to find out from some one else who it is that annoys you."

"Oh, papa, please don't trouble yourself about it. I do not mind it at all, now."

"But *I* do," replied her father, "and I shall take care that you are not annoyed in the same way again."

The tears rose in Elsie's eyes again, and she reproached herself severely for allowing her father to see how troubled she had been; but she said not another word, for she well knew from his look and tone that it would be worse than useless.

CHAPTER III

"Revenge, at first though sweet,
Bitter, ere long, back on itself recoils."

MILTON'S PARADISE LOST.

"'Tis easier for the generous to forgive,
Than for offence to ask it."

THOMSON'S EDMUND AND ELEONORA.

The last day of the old year had come; the afternoon was bright and warm for the season, and the little folks at Roselands were unanimously in favor of a long walk. They set out soon after dinner, all in high good humor except Arthur, who was moody and silent, occasionally casting an angry glance at Elsie, whom he had not yet forgiven for her refusal to lend him money; but no one seemed to notice it, and for some time nothing occurred to mar their enjoyment.

At length, some of the older ones, seeing that the sun was getting low, called to the others that it was time to return, and all turned their faces homeward, walking more soberly and silently along than at first, for they were beginning to feel somewhat fatigued.

They were climbing a steep hill. Elsie and Caroline Howard

reached the top first, Arthur and Harry Carrington being but a few steps behind.

Elsie stooped to pick up a pebble, and Arthur, darting quickly past her, managed to give her a push that sent her rolling down the bank. She gave one frightened cry as she fell, and the next instant was lying pale and motionless at the bottom.

All was now terror and confusion among the children; the little ones, who all loved Elsie dearly, began to scream and cry. Harry, Lucy, Carry, and Mary, rushed down the path again as fast as they could, and were soon standing pale and breathless beside the still form of their little companion. Carry was the only one who seemed to have any presence of mind. She sat down on the ground, and lifting Elsie's head, laid it on her lap, untied her bonnet-strings, and loosened her dress.

"Jim," she said to the black boy, who stood blubbering by her side, "run quickly for the doctor. And you, Harry Carrington, go for her father, as fast as you can. Lucy, crying so won't do any good. Haven't some of you a smelling-bottle about you?"

"Yes, yes, here, here! quick! quick! Oh, Carry, say she isn't dead!" cried Mary Leslie, diving into her pocket and bringing out a small bottle of smelling salts that some one had presented her as a Christmas gift.

"No, she is not dead, Mary; see, she is beginning to open her eyes," replied Carry, now bursting into tears herself.

But Elsie opened them only for an instant, moaned as if in great pain, and relapsed again into insensibility, so like death that Carry shuddered and trembled with fear.

They were not more than a quarter of a mile from the house, but it seemed almost an age to the anxious Carry before Mr. Dinsmore came; although it was in reality but a few moments, as Harry ran very fast, and Mr. Dinsmore sprang into the carriage—which was at the door, some of the party having just returned from a drive—the instant he heard the news, calling to Harry to accompany him, and bidding the coachman drive directly to the spot, with all speed.

The moment they were off he began questioning the boy closely as to the cause of the accident. Harry could not tell much about it. "She had fallen down the hill," he said, "but he did not see what made her fall."

"Was she much hurt?" Mr. Dinsmore asked, his voice trembling a little in spite of himself.

Harry "did not know, but feared she was pretty badly injured."

"Was she insensible?"

"Yes, she was when I left," Harry said.

Mr. Dinsmore leaned back in the carriage with a groan and did not speak again.

In another moment they had stopped, and flinging open the door, he sprang to the ground, and hurried toward the little group, who were still gathered about Elsie just as Harry had left them; some looking on with pale, frightened faces, others sobbing aloud. Walter was crying quite bitterly, and even Enna had the traces of tears on her cheeks. As for Arthur, he trembled and shuddered at the thought that he was perhaps already a murderer, and frightened and full of remorse, shrank behind the others as he saw his brother approach.

Elsie still lay with her head in Carry's lap.

Hastily pushing the others aside, Mr. Dinsmore stooped over her, sorrow and intense anxiety written in every line of his countenance.

Again Elsie opened her eyes, and smiled faintly as she saw him bending over her.

"My precious one," he murmured in a low, moved tone, as he gently lifted her in his arms; "are you much hurt? Are you in pain?"

"Yes, papa," she answered feebly.

"Where, darling?"

"My ankle, papa; it pains me terribly; and I think I must have hit my head, it hurts me so."

"How did she come to fall?" he asked, looking round upon the little group.

No one replied.

"Please, papa, don't ask," she pleaded in a faint voice.

He gave her a loving, pitying look, but paid no other heed to her remonstrance.

"Who was near her?" he asked, glancing sternly around the little circle.

"Arthur," said several voices.

Arthur quailed beneath the terrible glance of his brother's eye, as he turned it upon him, exclaiming bitterly: "Yes, I understand it all, now! I believe you will never be satisfied until you have killed her."

"Dear papa, please take me home, and don't scold poor Arthur," pleaded Elsie's sweet, gentle voice; "I am not so very badly hurt, and I am sure he is very sorry for me."

"Yes, darling," he said, "I will take you home and will try to do so without hurting you;" and nothing could exceed the tenderness with which he bore her to the carriage, supported her in his arms during the short ride, and on their arrival carried her up to her room and laid her down upon a sofa.

Jim had brought the doctor, and Mr. Dinsmore immediately requested him to make a careful examination of the child's injuries.

He did so, and reported a badly sprained ankle, and a slight bruise on the head; nothing more.

"Are you quite sure, doctor, that her spine has sustained no injury?" asked the father anxiously, adding, "there is scarcely anything I should so dread for her as that."

"None whatever," replied the physician confidently, and Mr. Dinsmore looked greatly relieved.

"My back does not hurt me at all, papa; I don't think I struck it," Elsie said, looking up lovingly into his face.

"How did you happen to fall, my dear?" asked the doctor.

"If you please, sir, I would rather not tell," she replied, while the color rushed over her face, and then instantly faded away again, leaving her deathly pale. She was suffering great pain, but bearing it bravely.

The doctor was dressing the injured ankle, and her father sat by the sofa holding her hand.

"You need not, darling," he answered, kissing her cheek.

"Thank you, papa," she said, gratefully, then whispered, "Won't you stay with me till tea-time, if you are not busy?"

"Yes, daughter, and all the evening, too; perhaps all night."

She looked her happiness and thanks, and the doctor praised her patience and fortitude; and having given directions concerning the treatment of the wounded limb, bade his little patient good-night, saying he would call again in the morning.

Mr. Dinsmore followed him to the door.

"That's a sweet child, Mr. Dinsmore," he remarked. "I don't know how any one could have the heart to injure her; but I think there has been foul play somewhere, and if she were mine I should certainly sift the matter to the bottom."

"That I shall, you may rest assured, sir; but tell me doctor, do you think her ankle very seriously injured?"

"Not permanently, I hope; indeed, I feel quite sure of it, if she is well taken care of, and not allowed to use it too soon; but these sprains are tedious things, and she will not be able to walk for some weeks. Good-night, sir; don't be too anxious, she will get over it in time, and you may be thankful it is nothing worse."

"I am, indeed, doctor," Mr. Dinsmore said, warmly grasping the hand the kind-hearted physician held out to him.

Everybody was asking what the doctor had said, and how much Elsie was injured, and Mr. Dinsmore stepped into the drawing-room a moment to answer their inquiries, and then hastened back to his child again.

She looked so glad to see him.

"My poor little pet," he said, pityingly, "you will have a sad New Year's Day, fastened down to your couch; but you shall have as much of my company as you wish."

"Shall I, papa?—then you will have to stay by me all day long."

"And so I will, dearest," he said, leaning fondly over her, and stroking back the hair from her forehead. "Are you in much pain now, darling?" he asked, as he noticed a slight contraction of her brow, and an almost deadly pallor around her mouth.

"Yes, papa, a good deal," she answered faintly; "and I feel so weak. Please take me in your arms, papa, I want to lay my head against you."

He raised her up gently, sat down on the end of the couch where her head had been, lifted her to his knee, and made Chloe place a pillow for the wounded limb to rest upon.

"There, darling, is that better?" he asked, soothingly, as she laid her head wearily down on his breast, and he folded his arms about her.

"Yes, papa; but, oh, it aches very much," she sighed.

"My poor little daughter! my poor little pet!" he said, in a deeply compassionate tone, "it is so hard to see you suffer; I would gladly take your pain and bear it for you if I could."

"Oh, no, dear papa, I would much rather bear it myself," she answered quickly.

The tea-bell rang, and Elsie half started up.

"Lie still, dearest," her father said. "I am in no hurry for my tea, so you shall have yours first, and I will hold you while you eat it. What will you have? You may ask for anything you want."

"I don't know, papa; whatever you please."

"Well, then, Aunt Chloe, go down and bring up whatever good things are there, and she can take her choice. Bring a cup of hot tea, too, I think it may do her good to-night."

"Thank you, dear papa, you are so kind," Elsie said, gratefully.

When the carriage had driven off with Mr. Dinsmore and Elsie, the rest of the young party at once turned their steps toward the house; Arthur skulking in the rear, and the others eagerly discussing the accident as they went.

"Arthur pushed her down, I am *sure* he did," said Lucy, positively. "I believe he hates her like poison, and he has been at her about something the several days past—I know it just by the way I've seen him look at her—yes, ever since the morning after the Carleton party. And now I remember I heard his voice talking angrily in her room that very morning. I went to get a book I had left in there, and when I tried the door it was locked, and I went away again directly."

"But what has that to do with Elsie's fall?" asked Mary Leslie.

"Why, don't you see that it shows there was some trouble between them, and that Arthur had a *motive* for pushing her down," returned Lucy, somewhat impatiently. "Really, Mary, you seem quite stupid sometimes."

Mary looked hurt.

"I don't know how any one could be so wicked and cruel; especially to such a dear, sweet little girl as Elsie," remarked Carry Howard.

"No, nor I," said Harry; "but the more I think about it the more certain I feel that Arthur did really push her down; for now I remember distinctly where she stood, and it seems to me she could not possibly have fallen of herself. Besides it was evident enough that Arthur felt guilty from the way he acted when Mr. Dinsmore came, and when he spoke to him. But perhaps he did not do it quite on purpose."

"Oh!" exclaimed Mary, "I do think I should be frightened to death if Mr. Dinsmore should look at me as he did at Arthur."

"Looks can't hurt," observed Harry, wisely; "but I wouldn't be in Arthur's shoes just now for considerable; because I'll venture to say Mr. Dinsmore will do something a good deal worse than *look*, before he is done with him."

When they reached the house Lucy went directly to her mamma's room. Herbert, who was more ailing than usual that day, lay on a sofa, while his mamma sat by his side, reading to him. They had not heard of the accident, and were quite startled by Lucy's excited manner.

"Oh, mamma!" she cried, jerking off her bonnet, and throwing herself down on a stool at her mother's feet, "we have had such a dreadful accident, or hardly an *accident* either, for I feel perfectly certain Arthur did it on purpose; and I just expect he'll kill her some day, the mean, wicked boy!" and she burst into tears. "If I were Mr. Dinsmore I'd have him put in jail, so I would," she sobbed.

"Lucy, my child, what *are* you talking about?" asked her mother with a look of mingled surprise and alarm, while Herbert started up asking, "Is it Elsie? Oh! Lucy, is she much hurt?"

"Yes," sobbed Lucy, "we all thought she was dead, it was so long before she spoke, or moved, or even opened her eyes."

Herbert was crying, too, now, as bitterly as his sister.

"But, Lucy dear," said her mother, wiping her eyes, "you haven't told us anything yet. Where did it happen? What did Arthur do? And where is poor little Elsie now?"

"Her papa brought her home, and Jim went for the doctor, and they're doing something with her now in her own room—for Pomp said Mr. Dinsmore carried her right up there! Oh I mamma, if you had seen him look at Arthur!"

"But what did Arthur do?" asked Herbert anxiously.

"He pushed her down that steep hill that you remember you were afraid to try to climb the other day; at least we all think he did."

"But surely, he did not do it intentionally," said Mrs. Carrington, "for why should he wish to harm such a sweet, gentle little creature as Elsie?"

"Oh! mamma," exclaimed Herbert, suddenly matching hold of her hand and he grew very pale, and almost gasped for breath.

"What is it, Herbert dear, what is it?" she asked in alarm; for he had fallen back on his pillow, and seemed almost ready to faint.

"Mamma," he said with a shudder, "mamma, I believe I know. Oh! why didn't I speak before, and, perhaps, poor little Elsie might have been saved all this."

"Why, Herbert, what can *you* know about it?" she asked in extreme surprise.

"I will tell you, mama, as well as I can," he said, "and then you must tell me what I ought to do. You know, mamma, I went out to walk with the rest the afternoon after that party at Mr. Carleton's; for if you remember, I had stayed at home the night before, and gone to bed very early, and so I felt pretty well and able to walk. But Elsie was not with us. I don't know where she could have been; she always thinks of my lameness, and walks slowly when I am along, but this time they all walked so fast that I soon grew very tired, indeed, with trying to keep up. So I sat down on a log to rest. Well, mamma, I had not been there very long when I heard voices near me, on the other side of some bushes, that, I suppose, must have prevented them from seeing me. One voice was Arthur's, but the other I didn't know. I didn't want to be listening, but I was too tired to move on; so I whistled a little, to let them know I was there; they didn't seem to care, though, but went on talking quite loud, so loud that I could not help hearing almost every word; and so I soon learned that Arthur owed Dick Percival a gambling debt—a debt of *honor*, they called it—and had sent this other boy, whom Arthur called Bob, to try to collect it. He reminded Arthur that he had promised to pay that day, and said Dick must have it to pay some debts of his own.

"Arthur acknowledged that he had promised, expecting to borrow the money from somebody. I didn't hear the name, and it never struck me until this moment who it was; but it must have been Elsie, for I recollect he said she wouldn't lend him anything without telling Horace all about it, and that, you know, is Mr. Dinsmore's name; and I have found out that Arthur is very much afraid of him; almost more than of his father, I think.

"He talked very angrily, saying he knew that was only an excuse, because she didn't wish to do him a favor, and he'd pay her for it some day. Then they talked about the debt again, and finally the boy agreed that Dick would wait until New Year's Day, when Arthur said he would receive his monthly allowance, and so would certainly be able to pay it.

"Now, mamma," concluded Herbert, "what ought I to do? Do you think it is my duty to tell Arthur's father?"

"Yes, Herbert, I do," said Mrs. Carrington, "because it is very important that he should know of his son's evil courses, that he may put a stop to them; and besides, if Arthur should escape punishment this time, Elsie may be in danger from him again. I am sorry it happened to be you rather than some other person who overheard the conversation; but it cannot be helped, and we must do our duty always, even though we find it difficult and disagreeable, and feel afraid that our motives may be misconstrued."

Herbert drew a deep sigh.

"Well, mamma, must I go just now, to tell him?" he asked, looking pale and troubled.

Mrs. Carrington seemed to be considering the matter for a moment.

"No, my dear," she said; "I think we had better wait a little. Probably Mr. Dinsmore will make an investigation, and perhaps he may be able to get at the truth without your assistance; and if not, as the mischief is already done, it will be time enough for your story to-morrow."

Herbert looked a good deal relieved, and just then they were summoned to tea.

The elder Mr. Dinsmore had been out all the afternoon, and not returning until just as the bell rang for tea, heard nothing of Elsie's injury until after he had taken his seat at the table.

The children had all reported that Arthur had pushed her down, and thus the story was told to his father. The old gentleman was very angry, for he had a great contempt for such cowardly deeds; and said before all the guests that if it were so, Arthur should be severely punished.

Mr. Horace Dinsmore came down as the rest were about leaving the table.

"I should like to have a few moments' conversation with you, Horace, when you have finished your tea," his father said, lingering behind the others.

"It is just what I wish, sir," replied his son; "I will be with you directly. Shall I find you in the library?"

"Yes. I hope the child was not hurt, Horace?" he added, inquiringly, stepping back again just as he had reached the door.

"Pretty badly, I am afraid," said Mr. Dinsmore, gravely; "she is suffering a good deal."

Mr. Dinsmore was not long at the table, for he was anxious to get back to his child; yet his father, whom he found striding back and forth across the library, in a nervous, excited way, hailed him with the impatient exclamation, "Come at last, Horace, I thought you would never have done eating."

Then throwing himself into a chair, "Well, what is to be done about this bad business?" he asked. "Is it true that Arthur had a hand in it?"

"I have not a doubt of it myself, sir," replied his son. "They all agree that he was close to her when she fell, and neither he nor she denies that he pushed her; she only begs not to be forced to speak, and he says nothing.

"And now, father, I have fully made up my mind that either that boy must be sent away to school, or I must take Elsie and make a home for her elsewhere."

"Why, Horace! that is a sudden resolution, is it not?"

"No, father, not so much as it seems. I have suspected, for some time past, that Elsie had a good deal to bear from Arthur and Enna—to say nothing of an older person, to whom Enna is continually carrying tales. Elsie is too generous to tell tales, too meek and patient to complain, and so it has been only very gradually that I have learned how much of petulance, tyranny, and injustice she has had to endure from those from whom she certainly had a right to expect common kindness, if not affection.

"Yesterday afternoon she came to me in such a state of nervous excitement as convinced me that something had gone very much amiss with her, but what it was I did not know, for she seemed unwilling to tell, and I would not force her to do so.

"However, by putting a few questions to some of the little guests, I have since learned enough to fill me with indignation at the treatment to which my child has been subjected, even during the last two weeks; and now the occurrences of this afternoon have put the finishing stroke to all this, and I cannot any longer feel that my child is safe where Arthur is. It is a great mercy that she escaped being killed or crippled for life," and he dropped his face into his hands and shuddered.

"Don't, Horace, my son," his father said kindly, laying his hand on his shoulder. "I don't like to see you give way so. It is not worth while troubling ourselves about what *might* have been, and we will take measures to prevent such occurrences in the future.

"But you mustn't think of leaving us to set up a separate establishment, unless you are intending to marry again, and I don't believe you are."

Mr. Dinsmore shook his head.

"Nothing of the kind," he said; "but I must protect my child; she has no one else to look to for protection, or sympathy, or love—my poor little one!—and it would be hard indeed if she could not have them from me."

"So it would, Horace, certainly. I am afraid we have none of us treated the poor little thing quite as kindly as we might, but I really was not aware that she had been so much abused, and shall certainly speak to Mrs. Dinsmore about it. And Arthur shall be sent away to school, as you have suggested. It is what I have been wanting to do for some time, for he is getting quite beyond Miss Day; but his mother has always opposed it, and I have foolishly given up to her for peace sake. I set my foot down now, however, and he *shall go*. He deserves it richly, the young rascal! such a base, cowardly act as to attack a little girl, big, strong boy that he is! I'm ashamed of him. You, Horace, were a wild, headstrong fellow, but I never knew you do a *mean* or *cowardly* thing; you were always above it."

"I hope so, indeed, sir. But now, to go back to the present business, do you not think it would be well to call all the young people together and have a thorough investigation of this affair? I have promised Elsie that she shall not be forced to speak, but I hope we may be able to learn from the others all

46   Martha Finley

that we need to know."

"Yes, yes, Horace, we will do so at once!" replied his father, ringing the bell. "They must be all through with their tea by this time, and we will invite them into the drawing-room, and cross-question them until we get to the bottom of the whole thing."

A servant answered the bell, and received directions to request—on his master's behalf—all the guests, both old and young, as well as every member of the family, to give their attendance in the drawing-room for a few moments.

"Stay, father," said Horace, "possibly Arthur might be induced to confess, and so spare himself and us the pain of a public exposure; had we not better send for him first?"

His father assented, and the servant was ordered to go in search of Arthur, and bring him to the library.

Arthur had been expecting such a summons, and had quite made up his mind what to do.

"Confess!" he said to himself; "no, indeed, I'll not! nobody but Elsie knows that I did it, and she'll never tell; so I'll stick to it that it was only an accident."

He came in with a look of sullen, dogged determination on his countenance, and stood before his father and brother with folded arms, and an air of injured innocence. He was careful, however, not to meet his brother's eye.

"Arthur," began his father, sternly, "this is shameful, cowardly behavior, utterly unworthy of a son of mine—this unprovoked assault upon a defenceless little girl. It has always been considered a cowardly act to attack one weaker than ourselves."

"I *didn't* do it! she slipped and fell of herself," replied the boy fiercely, speaking through his clenched teeth.

"Arthur," said his brother, in a calm, firm tone, "the alternative before you is a frank and full confession here in private, or a disgraceful, public exposure in the drawing-room. You had better confess, for I have not the least doubt of your guilty because I well know that Elsie would have asserted your innocence, had she been able to do so with truth."

"She *wouldn't*, she hates me," muttered the boy; "yes, and I hate her, too," he added, almost under his breath. But his brother's quick ear caught the words.

"Yes," he answered, bitterly; "you have given full proof of that; but *never*, while I live, shall you have another opportunity to wreak your hellish rage upon her."

But threats and persuasions were alike powerless to move Arthur's stubborn will; for, trusting to their supposed inability to prove his guilt, he persisted in denying it; and at length, much against his inclination, was forced to accompany his father and brother to the drawing-room, where the entire household was already assembled.

There was a good deal of excitement and whispering together, especially amongst the younger portion of the assembly, and many conjectures as to the cause of their being thus called together; nearly all giving it as their decided opinion that Elsie's accident had something to do with it.

Herbert was looking pale and nervous, and kept very close to his mamma, Harry Carrington and Carrie Howard were grave and thoughtful, while Lucy and Mary seemed restless and excited, and the lesser ones full of curiosity and expectation. There was quite a little buzz all over the room as the two gentlemen and Arthur entered, but it died away instantly, and was succeeded by an almost death-like stillness, broken the next moment by the elder Mr. Dinsmore's voice, as he briefly stated his object in thus calling them together, and earnestly requested any one present who could throw the least light on the subject, to speak.

He paused, and there was a moment of profound silence.

"Who was nearest to Elsie when she fell?" he asked; "can any one tell me?"

"Arthur, sir," replied several voices.

Another pause.

"Who else was near her?" he asked. "Miss Carrie Howard, I have noticed that you and Elsie are usually together; can you tell me if she could have fallen of herself? Were you near enough to see?"

Carrie answered reluctantly: "Yes, sir; I had stepped from her side at the moment she stooped to pick up something, and feel quite certain that she was not near enough to the edge to have fallen of herself."

"Thank you for your frank reply. And now, Master Harry Carrington, I think I heard some one say you were quite close to Arthur at the time of Elsie's fall; can you tell me what he did to her? You will confer a great favor by answering with equal frankness."

"I would much rather have been excused from saying anything, sir," replied Harry, coloring and looking as if he wished himself a thousand miles away; "but since you request it, I will own that I was close to Arthur, and think he must have pushed Elsie in springing past her, but it may have been only an accident."

"I fear not," said the old gentleman, looking sternly at his son. "And now, does any one know that Elsie had vexed Arthur in any way, or that he had any unkind feelings toward her?"

"Yes, papa," Walter spoke up suddenly. "I heard Arthur, the other day, talking very crossly about Elsie, and threatening to pay her for something; but I didn't understand what."

Mr. Dinsmore's frown was growing darker, and Arthur began to tremble and turn pale. He darted a fierce glance at Walter, but the little fellow did not see it.

"Does any one know what Elsie had done?" was the next question.

No one spoke, and Herbert fidgeted and grew very pale. Mr. Horace Dinsmore noticed it, and begged him if he knew anything to tell it at once; and Herbert reluctantly repeated what he had already told his mother of the conversation in the woods; and as he concluded, Lora drew a note from her pocket, which she handed to her father, saying that she had picked it up in the school-room, from a pile of rubbish which Arthur had carelessly thrown out of his desk.

Mr. Dinsmore took it, glanced hastily over the contents, and with a groan, exclaimed: "Is it possible!—a gambler already! Arthur, has it really come to this?

"Go to your room, sir," he added, sternly, "there to remain in solitary confinement until arrangement can be made to send you to school at a distance from the home which shall be no longer polluted by your presence; for you are unworthy to mingle with the rest of the family."

Arthur obeyed in sullen silence, and his father, following, turned the key upon him, and left him to solitude and his own reflections.

"Did my little daughter think papa had quite forgotten his promise?" asked Mr. Horace Dinsmore, as again he stood by Elsie's couch.

"No, papa," she said, raising her eyes to his face with a grateful, loving look; "it seemed very long, but I knew you would come as soon as you could, for I know you never break your word."

Her confidence pleased him very much, and with a very gratified look he asked whether he should sit by her side or take her again upon his knee.

"Take me on your knee again, if you please, papa," she said, "and then will you read a little to me? I would like it so much."

"I will do anything that will give my little girl pleasure," he replied, as he once more lifted her gently, and placed her in the desired position.

"What shall the book be?" he asked; "one of the new ones I bought you the other day?"

"Not that, to-night; if you please, papa; I would rather hear a little from an old book," she answered, with a sweet smile lighting up her little pale face; "won't you please read me the fifty-third chapter of Isaiah?"

"If you wish it, dearest; but I think something lively would be much better; more likely to cheer you up."

"No, dear papa; there is nothing cheers me up like the Bible, it is so sweet and comforting. I do so love to hear of Jesus, how he bore our griefs and carried our sorrows."

"You are a strange child," he said, "but you shall have whatever you want to-night. Hand me that Bible, Aunt Chloe, and set the light a little nearer."

Mr. Dinsmore was an uncommonly fine reader, and Elsie lay listening to that beautiful passage of Holy Writ, as one might listen to strains of the softest, sweetest music.

"Now, dear papa, the twenty-third of Luke, if you please," she said, when he had finished.

He turned to it, and read it without any remark.

As he closed the book and laid it aside, he saw that tears were trembling on the long, silken lashes that rested on the fair young cheek; for her eyes were closed, and but for those tell-tale drops he would have thought her sleeping.

"I feared it would make you sad, darling," he said, brushing them away, and kissing her fondly.

"No, dear papa, *oh, no!*" she answered, earnestly; "thank you very much for reading it; it has made me feel a great deal better."

"Why did you select those particular passages?" he asked, with some curiosity.

"Because, papa, they are all about Jesus, and tell how meekly and patiently he bore sorrow and suffering. Oh, papa, if I could only be like him! I am not much like him, but it makes it easier to forgive and to be patient, and kind, and gentle, when we read about him, how good he was, and how he forgave his murderers."

"You are thinking of Arthur," he said. "*I* shall find it very hard to forgive him; can *you* do so?"

"Yes, papa, I think I can. I have been praying for him, and have asked God to help me to forgive and love him."

"He has treated you very badly; I know all about it now."

And then, in answer to her surprised, inquiring look, he proceeded to give her an account of all that had taken place that evening in the library and drawing-room.

"And he hates me, papa," she said, mournfully, the tears filling her eyes; "why should he feel so? I have always tried to be kind to him."

"Yes, I know it," he replied, "you have often done him

kindnesses, and I know of no other cause for his enmity, unless it is that you have sometimes been obliged to bear witness against him."

"Yes, papa, on several occasions when he was putting all the blame of his naughty deeds on little Walter, or poor Jim."

"You were perfectly right," he said, caressing her; "and he will not have another opportunity to vent his spite upon you, as he is to be sent away to boarding-school immediately."

"Oh, papa!" she exclaimed, "I am so sorry for him, poor fellow! It must be so dismal to go off alone among strangers. Dear papa, *do* ask grandpa to forgive him, just this once; and I don't believe he will ever behave so again."

"No, daughter, I shall not do anything of the kind," he answered, decidedly. "I think it will be for Arthur's own good to be sent away, where he will not have his mother to spoil him by indulgence; and besides, I cannot feel that *you* are safe while he is about the house, and I consider it my first duty to take care of you; therefore, I have insisted upon its that either *he* must be sent away, or you and I must go and make a home for ourselves somewhere else."

"Oh, papa, how delightful that would be, to have a home of our own!" she exclaimed eagerly; "*will* you do it some day?"

"Should you like it so much?" he asked.

"Oh, yes, papa, so very, *very* much! When will you do it, papa?"

"I don't know, darling; some day, if we both live; perhaps when you are old enough to be my housekeeper."

"But that will be such a long, long time to wait, papa," she said—the eager, joyous expression fading away from her face, and the pale, wearied look coming back again.

"Perhaps we will not wait for that, darling; I did not say that we would," he replied, in a soothing tone, as he passed his hand caressingly over her hair and cheek.

Then he added, a little mischievously, "I think, possibly, I might induce Miss Stevens to keep house for us. Shall I ask her?"

"Oh, papa, no; that would spoil it all," she said, with a blush and a look of surprise; "and besides, I'm sure Miss Stevens would feel insulted if anybody should ask her to go out as housekeeper."

"No, I think not, if *I* asked her," laughed Mr. Dinsmore; "but you need not be alarmed; I have no notion of doing it.

"Now, daughter, I shall bathe your ankle with that liniment again, and put you in bed, and you must try to go to sleep."

"My prayers first, papa, you know," she replied, making an effort to get down upon the floor.

But he held her fast.

"No, daughter, you are not able to kneel to-night," he said, "and therefore it is not required; the posture makes but little difference, since God looks not at it, but at your heart."

"I know that, papa, but I ought to kneel if I can; and if I may, I would much rather try."

"No, I shall not allow you to do so; it would not be right," he replied decidedly; "you may say them here, while I have you in my arms, or after I have put you in bed."

"Then I will say them in my bed, papa," she answered submissively.

She was very patient and quiet while her father and nurse

dressed her ankle, and prepared her for bed, and when he had laid her in and covered her up, he sat down beside her and listened to the low, murmured words of her prayer.

"I think you prayed for me as well as for Arthur," he remarked when she had done; "what did you request for me?"

"I asked, as I always do, that you might love Jesus, papa, and be very happy, indeed, both in this world and the next."

"Thank you," he said, "but why are you so anxious that I should love him? It would not trouble *me* if *you* did not, so long as you loved and obeyed me."

A tear trickled down her cheek and fell upon the pillow as she answered, in a half tremulous tone: "Because I know, papa, that no one can go to heaven who does not love Jesus, nor ever be really happy anywhere, for the Bible says so. Papa, you always punish me when I am disobedient to you, and the Bible says God is our Father and will punish us if we do not obey him; and one of his commands is: Thou shalt love the Lord thy God; and in another place it says: Every one that loveth him that begat loveth him also that is begotten of him."

He did not reply, and his countenance was almost stern in its deep gravity.

Elsie feared she had displeased him.

"Dear papa," she said, stretching out her little hand to him, "I am afraid I have said things to you that I ought not; are you angry with me?"

"No, daughter," he replied, as he bent down and kissed her cheek; "but you must not talk any more to-night. I want you to shut your eyes and go to sleep."

She threw her arm around his neck and returned his caress, saying, "Good-night, dear, *dear* papa; I do love you *so* much;"

then turned away her face, shut her eyes, and in a few moments was sleeping sweetly.

The next morning quite a number of the little folks begged leave to go in after breakfast to see Elsie, and as she seemed much better—indeed, quite well, except that she could not put her foot to the floor—Mr. Dinsmore gave a ready consent.

They found Elsie dressed and lying upon a sofa, with the lame foot on a pillow. She seemed very glad to see them, looked as smiling and cheerful as if nothing ailed her; and to all their condolences replied that she did not mind it very much; she was doing nicely—papa and everybody else was so kind—and the doctor said he hoped she would be able to run about again in a few weeks.

They were all around her, talking and laughing in a very animated way, when Mr. Dinsmore came in, and going up to her couch, said, "Elsie, daughter, I have an errand to the city this morning; but, as I have promised to give you all you want of my company to-day, I will commission some one else to do it, if you are not willing to spare me for a couple of hours; do you think you could do without your papa that long? It shall be just as you say."

"You know I love dearly to have you by me, papa," she answered, smiling up into his face; "but I will be quite satisfied with whatever you do, because you always know best."

"Spoken like my own little girl," he said, patting her cheek. "Well, then I will leave these little folks to entertain you for a short time; and I think you will not be sorry, when I return, that you left it to me to do as I think best. Kiss papa good-bye, darling. Aunt Chloe, take good care of her, and don't let her be *fatigued* with company."

He turned to look at her again, as he reached the door, and Elsie gaily kissed her hand to him.

Before long, Chloe, seeing that her young charge was beginning to look weary, sent away all the little folks except Herbert, who, at Elsie's request, remained with her, and seated in her little rocking-chair, close by her side, did his best to amuse her and make her forget her pain, sometimes reading aloud to her, and sometimes stopping to talk.

Many an hour Elsie had spent by his couch of suffering, reading, talking or singing to him, and he rejoiced now in the opportunity afforded him to return some of her past kindness.

They had always been fond of each other's society, too, and the time passed so quickly and pleasantly that Mr. Dinsmore's return, only a very little sooner than he had promised, took them quite by surprise.

Herbert noticed that he had a bundle in his hand, and thinking it was probably some present for Elsie, and that they might like to be alone, slipped quietly away to his mamma's room.

"What is that, papa?" Elsie asked.

"A New Year's gift for my little girl," he answered, with a smile, as he laid it down by her side. "But I know you are tired lying there; so I will take you on my knee, and then you shall open it."

She looked quite as eager and interested as he could have wished, as he settled her comfortably on his knee, and laid the bundle in her lap. Her hands trembled with excitement and haste, as she untied the string, and with an exclamation of joyful surprise, brought to light a large and very beautiful wax doll.

"Oh, *papa*, how *pretty*!" she cried, in ecstasy. "And it is as large as a real, live baby, and has such a sweet, dear little face, and such pretty little hands, just like a real baby's—and the dearest little toes, too," she added, kissing them. "I love it already, the little dear! and how prettily it is dressed, too, like a little baby-girl."

He enjoyed her pleasure intensely.

"But you have not come to the bottom of your bundle yet," he said; "see here!" and he showed her quite a pile of remnants of beautiful lawns, muslins, silk, etc., which he had bought to be made up into clothing for the doll.

"I did not buy them ready made," he said, "because I thought you would enjoy making them yourself."

"Oh, how nice, papa. Yes, indeed, I shall enjoy it, and you are so *very* good and kind to me," she said, holding up her face for a kiss. "Now, with you beside me, and plenty to do making pretty things for this dear new dolly, I think I shall hardly mind at all having to stay in the house and keep still. I'll call her Rose, papa, mayn't I? for dear Miss Allison."

"Call it what you like, darling; it is all your own," he replied, laughing at the question.

"I'm its mother, ain't I?—and then you must be its grandfather!" she exclaimed, with a merry laugh, in which he joined her heartily.

"You ought to have some gray hairs, papa, like other grandfathers," she went on, running her fingers through his hair. "Do you know, papa, Carry Howard says she thinks it is so funny for me to have such a young father; she says you don't look a bit older than her brother Edward, who has just come home from college. How old are you, papa?"

"You are not quite nine, and I am just about eighteen years older; can you make that out now?"

"Twenty-seven," she answered, after a moment's thought; then, shaking her head a little, "that's pretty old, I think, after all. But I'm glad you haven't got gray hairs and wrinkles, like Carry's papa," she added, putting her arms around his neck, and laying her head down on his breast. "I think it is nice to have such a young, handsome father."

"I think it is very nice to have a dear little daughter to love me," he said, pressing her to his heart.

Elsie was eager to show her new doll to Carry and Lucy, and presently sent Chloe to invite them to pay her another visit.

"Bring Mary Leslie, too, mammy, if she will come; but be sure not to tell any of them what I have got," she said.

Chloe found them all three in the little back parlor, looking as if they did not know what to do with themselves, and Elsie's invitation was hailed with smiles and exclamations of delight.

They all admired the doll extremely, and Carry, who had a great taste for cutting and fitting, seized upon the pile of silks and muslins, exclaiming eagerly, that she should like no better fun than to help Elsie make some dresses.

"Oh, yes!" cried Lucy, "let us all help, for once in my life I'm tired to death of play, and I'd like to sit down quietly and work at these pretty things."

"I, too," said Mary, "if Elsie is willing to trust us not to spoil them,"

"Indeed, *I'll* not spoil them, Miss Mary; I've made more dolls' clothes than a few," remarked Carry, with a little toss of her head.

"I am not at all afraid to trust you, Carry, nor the others either," Elsie hastened to say; "and shall be very glad of your assistance."

Work-boxes were now quickly produced, and scissors and

thimbles set in motion.

Mr. Dinsmore withdrew to the other side of the room, and took up a book; thus relieving the little ladies from the constraint of his presence, while at the same time he could keep an eye upon Elsie, and see that she did not over-fatigue herself with company or work.

"What a nice time we have had," remarked Mary Leslie, folding up her work as the dinner-bell rang. "May we come back this afternoon, Elsie? I'd like to finish this apron, and I'm to go home to-morrow."

Mr. Dinsmore answered for his little girl, "When Elsie has had an hour to rest, Miss Mary, she will be glad to see you all again."

"Yes, do come, girls," Elsie added, "if you are not tired of work. I am sorry that you must go to-morrow, Mary. Carry and Lucy, *you* are not to leave us so soon, are you?"

"No," they both replied, "we stay till Saturday afternoon. And intend to make dolly two or three dresses before we go, if her mother will let us," Carry added, laughingly, as she put away her thimble and ran after the others.

All the guests left the next morning, excepting the Carringtons and Caroline Howard, and the house seemed very quiet—even in Elsie's room, where the little girls were sewing—while Harry and Herbert took turns in reading aloud; and in this way they passed the remainder of their visit very pleasantly, indeed.

Elsie felt her confinement more when Sabbath morning came, and she could not go to church, than she had at all before. Her father offered to stay at home with her, remarking that she must feel very lonely now that all her little mates were gone; but she begged him to go to church, saying that she could employ herself in reading while he was away, and that would keep her from being lonely, and then they could have all the afternoon and evening together. So he kissed her good-bye, and left her in Chloe's care.

She was sitting on his knee that evening; she had been singing hymns—he accompanying her sweet treble with his deep bass notes; then for a while she had talked to him in her own simple, childlike way, of what she had been reading in her Bible and the "Pilgrim's Progress," asking him a question now and then, which, with all his learning and worldly wisdom, he was scarcely as capable of answering as herself. But now she had been for some minutes sitting perfectly silent, her head resting upon his breast, and her eyes cast down, as if in deep thought,

He had been studying with some curiosity the expression of the little face, which was much graver than its wont, and at length he startled her from her reverie with the question, "What is my little girl thinking about?"

"I was thinking, papa, that if you will let me, I should like very much to give Arthur a nice present before he goes away. May I?"

"You may if you wish," he said, stroking her hair.

"Oh, thank you, papa," she answered joyously, "I was half afraid you would not let me; then, if you please, won't you, the next time you go to the city, buy the very handsomest pocket Bible you can find?—and then, if you will write his name and mine in it, and that it is a token of affection from me, I will be so much obliged to you, dear papa."

"I will do so, daughter, but I am afraid Arthur will not feel much gratitude to you for such a present."

"Perhaps he may like it pretty well, papa, if it is *very handsomely* bound," she said, rather doubtfully; "at any rate I should like to try. When does he go, papa?"

"Day after to-morrow, I believe."

"I wish he would come in for a few minutes to see me, and say good-bye; do you think he will, papa?"

"I am afraid not," replied her father, shaking his head; "however, I will ask him. But why do you wish to see him?"

"I want to tell him that I am not at all vexed or angry with him, and that I feel very sorry for him, because he is obliged to go away all alone amongst strangers, poor fellow!" she sighed.

"You need not waste any sympathy on him, my dear," said her father, "for I think he rather likes the idea of going off to school."

"Does he, papa? Why, how strange!" exclaimed the little girl, lost in astonishment.

As Mr. Dinsmore had predicted, Arthur utterly refused to go near Elsie; and, at first, seemed disposed to decline her gift; but at length, on Lora suggesting that he might require a Bible for some of his school exercises, he accepted it, as Elsie had thought he might, on account of the handsome binding.

Elsie was hurt and disappointed that he would not come to see her; she shed a few quiet tears over his refusal, because she thought it showed that he still disliked her, and then wrote him a little note, breathing forgiveness, sisterly affection, and regard for his welfare. But the note was not answered, and Arthur went away without showing any signs of sorrow for his unkind treatment of her; nor, indeed, for any of his bad conduct.

Miss Day had returned, and the rest of her pupils now resumed their studies; but Elsie was, of course, quite unable to attend in the school-room, as her ankle was not yet in a condition to be used in the least. Her father said nothing to her about lessons, but allowed her to amuse herself as she liked with reading, or working for the doll. She, however, was growing weary of play, and wanted to go back to her books.

"Papa," she said to him one morning, "I am quite well now, excepting my lameness, and you are with me a great deal every day, may I not learn my lessons and recite them to you?"

"Certainly, daughter, if you wish it," he replied, looking much pleased; "I shall consider it no trouble, but, on the contrary, a very great pleasure to teach you, if you learn your lessons well, as I am sure you will."

Elsie promised to be diligent, and from that day she went on with her studies as regularly as if she had been in school with the others.

She felt her confinement very much at times, and had a great longing for the time when she could again mount her pony, and take long rides and walks in the sweet fresh air; but she was not often lonely, for her papa managed to be with her a great deal, and she never cared for any other companion when he was by. Then, Mr. Travilla came in frequently to see her, and always brought a beautiful bouquet, or some fine fruit from his hot-house, or some other little nicety to tempt an invalid's appetite, or what she liked, even better still, a new book. Her aunts Adelaide and Lora, too, felt very kindly toward her, coming in occasionally to ask how she was, and to tell her what was going on in the house; and sometimes Walter brought his book to ask her to help him with his lessons, which she was always ready to do, and then he would sit and talk a while, telling her what had occurred in the school-room, or in their walks or rides, and expressing his regret on account of the accident that prevented her from joining them as usual.

Her doll, too, was a great source of amusement to her, and she valued it very highly, and was so extremely careful of it that she hardly felt willing to trust it out of her own hands, lest it should be broken. Especially was she annoyed when Enna, who was a very careless child, wished to take it; but it was a dangerous thing to refuse Enna's requests, except when Mr. Dinsmore was by, and so Elsie always endeavored to get the doll out of sight when she heard her coming.

But one unfortunate afternoon Enna came in quite unexpectedly, just as Elsie finished dressing it in a new suit, which she had completed only a few moments before.

"Oh, Elsie, how pretty it looks!" she cried. "Do let me take it on my lap a little while. I won't hurt it a bit."

Elsie reluctantly consented, begging her to be very careful, "because, Enna," she said, "you know if you should let it fall, it would certainly be broken."

"You needn't be afraid," replied Enna, pettishly, "I guess I can take care of a doll as well as you."

She drew up Elsie's little rocking-chair, as she spoke, and taking the doll from her, sat down with it in her arms.

Elsie watched nervously every movement she made, in momentary dread of a catastrophe.

They were alone in the room, Chloe having gone down to the kitchen on some errand.

For a few moments Enna was content to hold the doll quietly in her arms, rocking backwards and forwards, singing to it; but ere long she laid it down on her lap, and began fastening and unfastening its clothes, pulling off its shoes and stockings to look at its feet—dropping them on the floor, and stooping to pick them up again, at the same time holding the doll in such a careless manner that Elsie expected every instant to see it scattered in fragments on the floor.

In vain she remonstrated with Enna, and begged her to be more careful; it only vexed her and made her more reckless; and at length Elsie sprang from her couch and caught the doll, just in time to save it, but in so doing gave her ankle a terrible wrench.

She almost fainted with the pain, and Enna, frightened at her pale face, jumped up and ran out of the room, leaving her alone.

She had hardly strength to get back on to her couch; and when her father came in, a moment after, he found her holding her ankle in both hands, while the tears forced from her by the pain were streaming down over her pale cheeks.

"Why, my poor darling, what is it?" he exclaimed, in a tone of mingled surprise and alarm.

"Oh, papa," she sobbed, "Enna was going to let my doll fall, and I jumped to catch it, and hurt my ankle."

"And what did you do it for?" he said angrily. "I would rather have bought you a dozen such dolls than have had your ankle hurt again. It may cripple you for life, yet, if you are not more careful."

"Oh, papa, please don't scold me, please don't be so angry with me," she sobbed. "I didn't have a minute to think, and I won't do it again."

He made no reply, but busied himself in doing what he could to relieve her pain; and Chloe coming in at that moment, he reproved her sharply for leaving the child alone.

The old nurse took it very meekly, far more disturbed at seeing how her child was suffering than she could have been by the severest rebuke administered to herself. She silently assisted Mr. Dinsmore in his efforts to relieve her; and at length, as Elsie's tears ceased to flow, and the color began to come back to her cheeks, she asked, in a tone full of loving sympathy, "Is you better now, darlin'?"

"Yes, mammy, thank you; the pain is nearly all gone now," Elsie answered gently; and then the soft eyes were raised pleadingly to her father's face.

"I'm not angry with you, daughter," he replied, drawing her head down to his breast, and kissing her tenderly. "It was only my great love for my little girl that made me feel so vexed that she should have been hurt in trying to save a paltry toy."

After this Mr. Dinsmore gave orders that Enna should never be permitted to enter Elsie's room in his absence, and thus she was saved all further annoyance of that kind; and Chloe was careful never to leave her alone again until she was quite well, and able to run about. That, however, was not for several weeks longer, for this second injury had retarded her recovery a good deal; and she began to grow very weary, indeed, of her long confinement. At length, though, she was able to walk about her room a little, and her father had several times taken her out in the carriage, to get the fresh air, as he said.

It was Saturday afternoon. Elsie was sitting on her sofa, quietly working, while her nurse sat on the other side of the room, knitting busily, as usual.

"Oh, mammy!" exclaimed the little girl, with sigh, "it is such a long, long time since I have been to church. How I wish papa would let me go to-morrow! Do you think he would, if I should ask him?"

"Dunno, darlin'! I'se 'fraid not," replied the old woman, shaking her head doubtfully. "Massa Horace berry careful ob you, an' dat ankle not well yet."

"Oh! but, mammy, I wouldn't need to walk, excepting just across the church, for you know papa could carry me down to the carriage," said the little girl eagerly.

Mr. Dinsmore came in soon afterwards, and, greeting his little girl affectionately, sat down beside her, and, taking a newspaper from his pocket, began to read.

"Papa, mayn't I sit on your knee?" she asked softly, as he paused in his reading to turn his paper.

He smiled, and without speaking lifted her to the desired position, then went on reading.

She waited patiently until there was another slight pause; then asked in her most coaxing tone, "Papa, may I go to church to-morrow?"

"No," he said, decidedly, and she dared not say another word; but she was sadly disappointed, and the tears sprang to her eyes, and presently one rolled down and fell upon her lap.

He saw it, and giving her a glance of mingled surprise and displeasure, put her back upon the sofa again, and returned to his paper.

She burst into sobs and tears at that, and laying her head down upon the cushion, cried bitterly.

Her father took no notice for a little while; then said, very gravely, "Elsie, if you are crying because I have put you off my knee, that is not the way to get back again. I must have *cheerful* submission from my little girl, and it was precisely *because* you were crying that I put you down."

"Please take me again, papa, and I won't cry any more," she answered, wiping her eyes.

He took her in his arms again, and she nestled close to him, and laid her head down on his breast with a sigh of satisfaction.

"You *must* learn not to cry when I do not see fit to acquiesce in your wishes, my daughter," he said, stroking her hair. "I do not think you quite well enough yet to go to church; and to-morrow bids fair to be a stormy day. But I hope by next Sabbath you may be able to go."

Elsie tried to submit cheerfully to her father's decision, but she looked forward very anxiously all the week to the next Sabbath. When it came, to her great delight, she was permitted to attend church, and the next morning she took her place in the school-room again.

She was far from enjoying the change from her father's instruction to Miss Day's; yet Arthur's absence rendered her situation far more comfortable than it had formerly been, and she still continued several studies with her father, and spent many happy hours with him every day. And thus everything moved on quite smoothly with the little girl during the remainder of the winter.

CHAPTER IV

"Remember the Sabbath-day to keep it holy."

EXOD. 10:6.

"We ought to obey God rather than men."

ACTS 5:29.

"Dear papa, are you sick?" It was Elsie's sweet voice that asked the question in a tone of alarm. She had just finished her morning lessons, and coming into her father's room, had found him lying on the sofa, looking flushed and feverish.

"Yes, daughter," he said, "I have a severe headache, and some fever, I think. But don't be alarmed, my pet, 'tis nothing at all serious," he added in a more cheerful tone, taking both her little hands in his, and gazing fondly into the beautiful dark eyes, now filled with tears.

"You will let me be your little nurse, my own dear papa, will you not?" she asked coaxingly. "My I bring some cool water and bathe your head?"

"Yes, darling, you may," he said, releasing her hands.

Elsie stole softly out of the room, but was back again almost in a moment, followed by Chloe, bearing a pitcher of ice-water.

"Now, mammy, please bring a basin and napkin from the

dressing-room," she said, in a low tone, as the old nurse set down her burden. "And then you may darken the room a little. And shall I not tell her to send Jim or Jack for the doctor, papa?"

"It is hardly necessary, darling," he replied, with a faint smile.

"Oh! please, papa, my own dear, darling papa, do let me!" she entreated. "You know it cannot do any harm, and may do a great deal of good."

"Ah! well, child, do as you like," he replied with a weary sigh; "but the doctor will, no doubt, think me very foolish to be so easily frightened."

"Then, papa, I will tell him it was I, not you, who were frightened, and that you sent for him to please your silly little daughter," Elsie said, fondly laying her cheek to his, while he passed his arm around her, and pressed her to his side.

"Here are de tings, darlin'," said Chloe, setting down the basin, and filling it from the pitcher.

"That is right, you good old mammy. Now close the blinds, and then you may go and tell Jim to saddle a horse and ride after the doctor immediately."

Chloe left the room, and Elsie brought another pillow for her father, smoothed his hair, bathed his forehead, and then, drawing a low chair to the side of the sofa, sat down and fanned him gently and regularly.

"Why!" said he, in a gratified tone, "you are as nice a little nurse as anybody need ask for; you move about so gently, and seem to know just the right thing to do. How did you learn?"

"I have had bad headaches so often myself, papa, that I have found out what one wants at such times," replied the little girl, coloring with pleasure.

He closed his eyes and seemed to be sleeping, and Elsie almost held her breath, lest she should disturb him. But presently the dinner-bell rang, and, opening them again, he said, "Go down, my daughter, and get your dinner."

"I am not hungry, papa," she replied. "Please let me stay and wait on you. Won't you have something to eat?"

"No, my dear, I have no desire for food; and you see, Chloe is coming to take care of me; so I wish you to go down at once," he said in his decided tone, and Elsie instantly rose to obey.

"You may come back if you choose when you have eaten your dinner," he added kindly. "I love to have you here."

"Thank you, papa, I will," she answered, with a brightened countenance, as she left the room. She was soon in her place again by his side. He was sleeping—and taking the fan from Chloe's hand without speaking, she motioned her away, and resuming her seat, sat for an hour or more, fanning him in perfect silence.

The physician had come while the family were at dinner, and leaving some medicine, had gone again, saying he was in haste to visit another patient; and assuring Elsie, whom he met in the hall as he was going out, that he did not think her papa was going to be very ill. This assurance had comforted her very much, and she felt quite happy while sitting there watching her father's slumbers.

At length he opened his eyes, and smiling fondly on her, asked: "Does not my little girl want some play this afternoon? Your little hand must surely be very tired wielding that fan;" and taking it from her, he drew her head down to his breast and stroked her hair caressingly.

"No, my own papa, I would much rather stay with you, if you will let me," she answered eagerly.

"I am afraid I *ought* to be very determined, and send you out to take some exercise," he replied, playfully running his fingers through her curls; "but it is too pleasant to have you here, so you may stay if you like."

"Oh, thank you, dear papa! and will you let me wait on you? What can I do for you now?"

"You may bring that book that lies on the table there, and read to me. You need not learn any lessons for to-morrow, for I intend to keep you with me."

The next day, and the next, and for many succeeding ones, Mr. Dinsmore was quite too ill to leave his bed, and during all this time Elsie was his constant companion by day—except for an hour every afternoon, when he compelled her to go out and take some exercise in the open air—and she would have sat by his side at night, also, but he would by no means permit it.

"No, Elsie," he replied to her repeated entreaties, "you must go to bed every night at your usual hour, and stay there until your accustomed hour for rising. I will not have you deprived of your rest unless I am actually dying."

This was said in the determined tone that always silenced Elsie at once, and she submitted to his decision without another word, feeling very thankful that he kept her so constantly at his side through the day. She proved herself the best and most attentive of nurses, seeming to understand his wishes intuitively, and moving about so gently and quietly—never hurried, never impatient, never weary of attending to his wants. His eyes followed with fond delight her little figure as it flitted noiselessly about the room, now here, now there, arranging everything for his comfort; and often, as she returned to her station at his side, he would draw her down to him, and stroke her hair, or pat her cheek, or kiss the rosy lips, calling her by every fond, endearing name—rose-bud—his pet—his bird—his darling.

It was she who bathed his head with her cool, soft hands, in his paroxysms of fever, smoothed his hair, shook up his pillows, gave him his medicines, fanned him, and read or sang to him, in her clear sweet tones.

He was scarcely considered in danger, but his sickness was tedious, and would have seemed far more so without the companionship of his little daughter. Every day seemed to draw the ties of affection more closely between them; yet, fond as he was of her, he ever made her feel that his will was always to be law to her; and while he required nothing contrary to her conscience, she submitted without a murmur, both because she loved him so well that it was a pleasure to obey him, and also because she knew it was her duty to do so.

But, alas! duty was not always to be so easy and pleasant.

It was Sabbath morning. All the family had gone to church, excepting Elsie, who, as usual, sat by her papa's bedside. She had her Bible in her hand, and was reading aloud.

"There, Elsie, that will do now," he said, as she finished her chapter. "Go and get the book you were reading to me yesterday. I wish to hear the rest of it this morning."

Poor little Elsie! she rose to her feet, but stood irresolute. Her heart beat fast, her color came and went by turns, and her eyes filled with tears.

The book her father bade her read to him was simply a fictitious moral tale, without a particle of religious truth in it, and, Elsie's conscience told her, entirely unfit for Sabbath reading.

"Elsie!" exclaimed her father, in a tone of mingled reproof and surprise, "did you hear me?"

"Yes, papa," she murmured, in a low tone.

"Then go at once and get the book, as I bid you; it lies yonder on the dressing-table."

Elsie moved slowly across the room, her father looking after her somewhat impatiently.

"Come, Elsie, make haste," he said, as she laid her hand upon the book. "I think I never saw you move so slowly,"

Without replying she took it up and returned to the bedside. Then, as he caught sight of her face, and saw that her cheeks were pale and wet with tears, he exclaimed, "What, *crying*, Elsie! what ails you, my daughter? Are you ill, darling?"

His tone was one of tender solicitude, and accompanied with a caress, as he took her hand and drew her towards him.

"Oh, papa!" she sobbed, laying her head on the pillow beside him, "please do not ask me to read that book to-day."

He did not reply for a moment, and when he did, Elsie was startled by the change in his tone; it was so exceedingly stern and severe.

"Elsie," he said, "I do not *ask* you to read that book, I *command* you to do it, and what is more, *I intend to be obeyed.* Sit down at once and begin, and let me have no more of this perverseness."

"Dear papa," she answered in low, pleading, trembling tones, "I do not, *indeed*, I do not want to be perverse and disobedient, but I cannot break the Sabbath-day. *Please*, papa, let me finish it to-morrow."

"Elsie!" said he, in a tone a little less severe, but quite as determined, "I see that you think that because you gained your point in relation to that song that you will always be allowed to do as you like in such matters; but you are mistaken; I am *determined* to be obeyed this time. I would not by any means bid you do anything I considered wrong, but I can see no harm whatever in reading that book to-day; and certainly I, who have lived so much longer, am far more capable of judging in these matters than a little girl of your age. Why, my daughter, I have seen ministers reading worse books than that on the Sabbath."

"But, papa," she replied timidly, "you know the Bible says: 'They measuring themselves by themselves, and comparing themselves among themselves, are not wise;' and are we not just to do whatever God commands, without stopping to ask what other people do or say? for don't even the best people very often do wrong?"

"Very well; find me a text that says you are not to read such a book as this on the Sabbath, and I will let you wait until to-morrow."

Elsie hesitated. "I cannot find one that says just *that*, papa," she said, "but there is one that says we are not to think our own thoughts, nor speak our own words on the Sabbath; and does not that mean worldly thoughts and words? and is not that book full of such things, and only of such?"

"Nonsense!" he exclaimed, impatiently, "let me hear no more of such stuff! you are entirely too young and childish to attempt to reason on such subjects. Your place is simply to obey; are you going to do it?"

"Oh, papa!" she murmured, almost under her breath, "I cannot."

"Elsie," said he, in a tone of great anger, "I should certainly be greatly tempted to whip you into submission, had I the strength to do it."

Elsie answered only by her tears and sobs.

There was silence for a moment, and then her father said:

"Elsie, I expect from my daughter entire, unquestioning obedience, and until you are ready to render it, I shall cease to treat you as my child. I shall banish you from my presence, and my affections. This is the alternative I set before you. I will give you ten minutes to consider it. At the end of that time, if you are ready to obey me, well and good—if not, you will leave this room, not to enter it again until you are ready to acknowledge your fault, ask forgiveness, and promise implicit obedience in the future."

A low cry of utter despair broke from Elsie's lips, as she thus heard her sentence pronounced in tones of calm, stern determination; and, hiding her face on the bed, she sobbed convulsively.

Her father lifted his watch from a little stand by the bedside, and held it in his hand until the ten minutes expired.

"The time is up, Elsie," he said; "are you ready to obey me?"

"Oh, papa!" she sobbed, "I cannot do it."

"Very well, then," he said, coldly; "if neither your sense of duty, nor your affection for your sick father is strong enough to overcome your self-will, you know what you have to do. Leave the room at once, and send one of the servants to attend me. I will not have such a perverse, disobedient child in my presence."

She raised her head, and he was touched by the look of anguish on her face.

"My daughter," he said, drawing her to him, and pushing back the curls from her face, "this separation will be as painful to me as to you; yet I cannot yield my authority. I *must* have obedience from you. I ask again, will you obey me?"

He waited a moment for an answer; but Elsie's heart was too full for speech.

Martha Finley

Pushing her from him, he said: "Go! remember, whenever you are ready to comply with the conditions, you may return; but *not till then!*"

Elsie seized his hand in both of hers, and covered it with kisses and tears; then, without a word, turned and left the room.

He looked after her with a sigh, muttering to himself, "She has a spice of my own obstinacy in her nature; but I think a few days' banishment from me will bring her round. I am punishing myself quite as much, however, for it will be terribly hard to do without her."

Elsie hastened to her own room, almost distracted with grief; the blow had been so sudden, so unexpected, so terrible; for she could see no end to her banishment; unless, indeed, a change should take place in her father's feelings, and of that she had very little hope.

Flinging herself upon a couch, she wept long and bitterly. Her grief was deep and despairing, but there was no anger in it; on the contrary, her heart was filled with intense love to her father, who, she doubted not, was acting from a mistaken sense of duty; and she could scarcely bear the thought that now she should no longer be permitted to wait upon him, and attend to his comfort. She had sent a servant to him, but a servant could ill supply a daughter's place, and her heart ached to think how he would miss her sympathy and love.

An hour passed slowly away; the family returned from church, and the bell rang for dinner. But Elsie heeded it not; she had no desire for food, and still lay sobbing on her couch, till Chloe came to ask why she did not go down.

The faithful creature was much surprised and distressed at the state in which she found her child, and raising her in her arms tenderly, inquired into the cause of her grief.

Elsie told her in a few words, and Chloe, without finding any fault with Mr. Dinsmore, strove to comfort the sorrowing child, assuring her of her own unalterable affection, and talking to her of the love of Jesus, who would help her to bear every trial, and in his own good time remove it.

Elsie grew calmer as she listened to her nurse's words; her sobs and tears gradually ceased, and at length she allowed Chloe to bathe her face, and smooth her disordered hair and dress; but she refused to eat, and lay on her couch all the afternoon, with a very sad little face, a sob now and then bursting from her bosom, and a tear trickling down her cheek. When the tea-bell rang, she reluctantly yielded to Chloe's persuasions, and went down. But it was a sad, uncomfortable meal to her, for she soon perceived, from the cold and averted looks of the whole family, that the cause of her banishment from her papa's room was known. Even her Aunt Adelaide, who was usually so kind, now seemed determined to take no notice of her, and before the meal was half over, Enna, frowning at her across the table, exclaimed in a loud, angry tone, "Naughty, bad girl! Brother Horace ought to whip you!"

"That he ought," added her grandfather, severely, "if he had the strength to do it; but he is not likely to gain it, while worried with such a perverse, disobedient child."

Elsie could not swallow another mouthful, for the choking sensation in her throat; and it cost her a hard struggle to keep back the tears that seemed determined to force their way down her cheek at Enna's unkind speech; but the concluding sentence of her grandfather's remark caused her to start and tremble with fear on her father's account; yet she could not command her voice sufficiently to speak and ask if he were worse.

There was, indeed, a very unfavorable change in Mr. Dinsmore, and he was really more alarmingly ill than he had been at all. Elsie's resistance to his authority had excited him so much as to bring on a return of his fever; her absence fretted him, too, for no one else seemed to understand quite as well how to wait upon him; and besides, he was not altogether satisfied with himself; not entirely sure that the course he had adopted was the right one. Could he only have got rid of all doubts of the righteousness and justice of the sentence he had pronounced upon her, it would have been a great relief. He was very proud, a man of indomitable will, and very jealous of his authority; and between these on the one hand, and his love for his child and desire for her presence, on the other, a fierce struggle had been raging in his breast all the afternoon.

As soon as she dared leave the table Elsie stole out into the garden, there to indulge her grief, unseen by any but the eye of God.

She paced up and down her favorite walk, weeping and sobbing bitterly. Presently her attention was attracted by the galloping of a horse down the avenue, and raising her head, she saw that it was the physician, returning from a visit to her father. It was not his usual hour for calling, and she at once conjectured that her father was worse. Her first impulse was to hasten to him, but instantly came the recollection that he had banished her from his presence, and sinking down upon a bank, she burst into a fresh paroxysm of grief. It was so hard— so *very* hard—to know that he was ill and suffering, and not to be permitted to go to him.

At length she could bear it no longer, and springing up she hurried into the house, and gliding softly up the stairs, stationed herself at her papa's door, determined to intercept some one passing in or out, and inquire how he was.

She had not been long there when her Aunt Adelaide came out, looking troubled and anxious.

"Oh, Aunt Adelaide," cried the child in a hoarse whisper, catching her by the dress, "dear Aunt Adelaide, *do* tell me, is papa worse?"

"Yes, Elsie," she replied coldly, attempting to pass on; "he is much worse."

The little girl burst into an agony of tears.

"You may well cry, Elsie," remarked her aunt severely, "for it is all your fault, and if you are left an orphan, you may thank your own perverseness and obstinacy for it."

Putting both hands over her face, with a low cry of anguish, Elsie fell forward in a deep swoon.

Adelaide caught her ere she had quite reached the floor, and hastily loosening her dress, looked anxiously around for help; but none was at hand, and she dared not call aloud lest she should alarm her brother. So laying her gently down on the carpet, she went in search of Chloe, whom she found, as she had expected, in Elsie's room. In a few hurried words Adelaide made her understand what had occurred, and that Elsie must be removed without the slightest noise or disturbance.

Another moment and Chloe was at her darling's side, and raising her gently in her strong arms, she bore her quickly to her room, and laying her on a couch, proceeded to apply restoratives, murmuring the while, in low, pitiful tones, "De dear, precious lamb! it mos' breaks your ole mammy's heart to see you dis way."

It was long ere consciousness returned; so long that Adelaide, who stood by, gazing sorrowfully at the little wan face, and reproaching herself for her cruelty, trembled and grew pale with apprehension.

But at last, with a weary sigh, Elsie opened her eyes, and looked up, with a sad, bewildered expression, into the dusky face bent so anxiously over her, and then, with a feeling of intense relief, Adelaide slipped away to her own room, leaving them alone together.

"What is it, mammy? Oh, I know! I remember! Oh, mammy,

mammy! will my dear, precious papa die?" sobbed the poor little girl, throwing her arms around her nurse's neck.

"I hope not, darling" replied Chloe, soothingly. "Massa Horace am pretty sick, I know; but I tinks de good Lord spare him, if we pray."

"Oh, yes, yes, mammy, let us pray for him. Let us both pray very earnestly, and I am sure God will spare him, because he has *promised* to grant whatever two shall agree to ask."

They knelt down, and Chloe prayed in her broken way; and when she had finished, Elsie poured out such a prayer as comes only from a heart ready to break with its load of sorrow and care.

None but he who has tried it can tell what a blessed relief comes to those who thus "cast their care on Jesus." Elsie's burden was not less, but she no longer bore it alone; she had rolled it upon the Lord and he sustained her. She shed a few quiet tears after she had laid her head upon her pillow, but soon forgot all her sorrows in a deep, sweet sleep, that lasted until morning.

It was still early when she awoke and sprang up, with the intention of hastening, as usual, to her father's side; but alas! in another moment memory had recalled all the distressing events of the previous day, and, sinking back upon her pillow, she wept long and bitterly.

But at length she dried her tears, and, kneeling at the bedside, poured out her sorrows and supplications into the ear of her Saviour, and thus again grew calm and strong to endure.

As soon as she was dressed she went to her papa's door, hoping to see some one who could tell her how he was; but no one came, and she dared not venture in, and her intense anxiety had yet found no relief when the bell summoned the family to breakfast.

The same cold looks awaited her there as on the night before, and the poor child could scarcely eat, and was glad when the comfortless meal was over.

She followed Adelaide to Mr. Dinsmore's door, and begged her with tears and sobs to ask her papa to allow her to come to him, if it was only for one moment, just to look at him, and then go away again.

Adelaide was touched by her evident anxiety and distress, and said, almost kindly, as she laid her hand on the handle of the door, "Well, Elsie, I will ask him; but I have no idea that it will be of any use, unless you will give up your foolish obstinacy."

Elsie stood outside waiting with a beating heart, and though her aunt was really gone but a moment, it seemed a long time to her ere the door again opened.

She looked up eagerly, and read the answer in Adelaide's face, ere she heard the coldly spoken, stern message—

"Your papa says you very well know the conditions on which you will be admitted to his presence, and that they are as unalterable as the laws of the Medes and Persians."

The tears gushed from Elsie's eyes, and she turned away with a gesture of despair.

"Elsie," said her aunt, "let me advise you to give up at once; for I am perfectly certain you never can conquer your father."

"Oh, Aunt Adelaide! that is not what I want," murmured the child, in low, broken accents.

But Adelaide went on without noticing the interruption—

"He is worse, and growing worse all the time, Elsie; his fever has been very high ever since yesterday afternoon—and we all know that it is nothing but your misconduct that has caused this relapse."

Elsie could bear no more, but rushing away to her own room, and locking herself in, she gave way without restraint to her feelings of distress and anguish.

Knowing that she was not expected in the school-room—as she had paid no attention to study since the beginning of her father's illness—she did not leave her room again until dinner-time.

She was on her way to the dining-room, when her Aunt Adelaide, passing her in the hall, caught hold of her, saying, "Elsie, your papa is so ill that the doctor trembles for his life; he says he is certain that he has something on his mind that is distressing him and causing this alarming change, and unless it is removed he fears he will never be any better. Elsie, *you know what that something is.*"

Elsie stood as if turned to stone, while Adelaide, letting go her arm, moved quickly away, leaving her alone, stunned, bewildered, terrified by the suddenness of the dreadful announcement.

She could not think or reason; she could only press her hands to her temples, in the vain endeavor to still their wild throbbing; then, turning back to her own room again, she threw herself upon her knees, and, resting her head against the bed, gave vent to her over-wrought feelings in such groans of anguish as seldom come from the heart of one so young. At first she could neither weep nor pray; but at length tears came to her relief, and she poured out agonizing supplications "that her dear, *dear* papa might be spared, at least, until he had learned to love Jesus, and was fit to go to heaven."

She felt as though her heart would break at the very thought of being separated from him forever in this world, but even that was as nothing compared to the more terrible fear of not meeting him in another.

That was a long, sad afternoon to the poor child; the longest and saddest she had ever known. Chloe now and then brought her word how her father was, but no one else came near her to speak a word of comfort or hope. Towards evening they had given up almost all hope; he had ceased to recognize any one, and one after another, parents, brother, sisters, and servants, had been permitted to take a last look—all but little Elsie, his own and only child—the one nearest and dearest to him, and to whom he was all the world—she alone was forbidden to come. She had begged and plead, in tones that might have melted a heart of stone, to be permitted to see his face once more in life; but Mrs. Dinsmore, who had taken the direction of everything, said, "No, her father has forbidden it, and she shall not come unless she expresses her willingness to comply with his conditions."

Adelaide had then ventured a plea in her behalf, but the reply was: "I don't pity her at all; it is all her own doing."

"So much the harder is it for her to bear, I presume," urged Adelaide.

"There, Adelaide, that will do now! Let me hear no more about it," replied her lady mother, and there the matter dropped.

Poor little Elsie tried to be submissive and forgiving, but she could not help feeling it terribly hard and cruel, and almost more than she could bear, thus to be kept away from her sick and dying father.

It was long ere sleep visited her weary eyes that night; hour after hour she lay on her pillow, pouring out prayers and tears on his behalf, until at length, completely worn out with sorrow, she fell into a deep and heavy slumber, from which she waked to find the morning sun streaming in at the windows, and Chloe standing gazing down upon her with a very happy face.

She started up from her pillow, asking eagerly, "What is it, mammy? Oh! what is it? is my papa better?"

"Yes, darling Massa Horace much better dis mornin'; de doctor say 'he gwine git well now for sartin, if he don't git worse again.'"

"Oh, mammy! It seems too good to be true! Oh, how very, very good God has been to me!" cried the little girl, weeping for very joy.

For a moment, in the intensity of her happiness, she forgot that she was still in disgrace and banishment—forgot everything but the joyful fact that her father was spared to her. But, oh! she could not forget it long. The bitter recollection soon returned, to damp her joy and fill her with sad forebodings.

CHAPTER V

"I'll do whate'er thou wilt, I'll be silent;
But oh! a reined tongue, and a bursting heart,
Are hard at once to bear."

JOANNA BAILLIE'S BASIL.

Mr. Dinsmore's recovery was not very rapid. It was several weeks after he was pronounced out of danger ere he was able to leave his room; and then he came down looking so altered, so pale, and thin, and weak, that it almost broke his little daughter's heart to look at him.

Very sad and lonely weeks those had been to her, poor child! She was never once permitted to see him, and the whole family treated her with marked coldness and neglect. She had returned to her duties in the school-room—her father having sent her a command to that effect, as soon as he was sufficiently recovered to think of her—and she tried to attend faithfully to her studies, but more than once Miss Day had seen the tears dropping upon her book or slate, and reproved her sharply for not giving her mind to her lessons, and for indulging in what she called her "babyish propensities."

Mr. Dinsmore made his first appearance in the family circle one morning at breakfast, a servant assisting him down stairs and seating him in an easy-chair at the table, just as the others were taking their places.

Martha Finley

Warm congratulations were showered upon him from all sides. Enna ran up to him, exclaiming, "I'm *so* glad to see you down again, brother Horace;" and was rewarded with a smile and a kiss; while poor little Elsie, who had been directed, she knew not why, to take her old seat opposite to his, was unable to utter a word, but stood with one hand on the back of her chair, pale and trembling with emotion, watching him with eyes so blinded by tears that she could scarcely see. But no one seemed to notice her, and her father did not once turn his eyes that way.

She thought of the morning when she had first met him there, her poor little heart hungering so for his love; and it seemed as if she had gone back again to that time; and yet it was worse; for now she had learned to love him with an intensity of affection she had then never known, and having tasted the sweetness of his love, her sense of suffering at its loss was proportionally great; and utterly unable to control her feelings, she silently left the room to seek some place where she might give her bursting heart the relief of tears, with none to observe or reprove her.

Elsie had a rare plant, the gift of a friend, which she had long been tending with great care, and which had blossomed that morning for the first time.

The flower was beautiful and very fragrant, and as the little girl stood gazing upon it with delighted eyes, while awaiting the summons to breakfast, she had said to Chloe, "Oh! how I should like papa to see it! He is so fond of flowers, and has been, so anxious for this one to bloom."

But a deep sigh followed as she thought what a long, long time it was likely to be before her father would again enter her room, or permit her to go into his. He had not, however, forbidden her to speak to him, and the thought struck her that, if he should be able to leave his room before the flower had faded, so that she could see and speak to him, she might pluck it off and present it to him.

She thought of it again, while weeping alone in her room, and a faint hope sprang up in her heart that the little gift might open the way for a reconciliation. But she must wait and watch for an opportunity to see him alone; for she could not, in the present state of affairs, think of addressing him before a third person.

The opportunity came almost sooner than she had dared to hope, for, on passing the library door just after the morning lessons were over, she saw him sitting there alone; and trembling between hope and fear, she hurried at once to her room, plucked the beautiful blossom from its stem, and with it in her hand hastened to the library.

She moved noiselessly across the thickly carpeted floor, and her papa, who was reading, did not seem to be aware of her approach, until she was close at his side. He then raised his head and looked at her with an expression of surprise on his countenance.

"Dear papa," said the little girl, in faltering accents, as she presented the flower, "my plant is bloomed at last; will you accept this first blossom as a token of affection from your little daughter?"

Her pleading eyes were fixed upon his face, and ere she had finished her sentence, she was trembling violently at the dark frown she saw gathering There.

"Elsie," said he, in the cold, stern tone she so much dreaded, "I am sorry you have broken your flower. I cannot divine your motive—affection for me it cannot be; for that such a feeling exists in the breast of a little girl, who not only could refuse her sick father the very small favor of reading to him, but would rather see him *die* than give up her own self-will, I cannot believe. No, Elsie, take it away; I can receive no gifts nor tokens of affection from a rebellious, disobedient child."

The flower had fallen upon the floor, and Elsie stood in an

attitude of utter despair, her head bent down upon her breast, and her hands hanging listlessly at her side. For an instant she stood thus, and then, with a sudden revulsion of feeling, she sank down on her knees beside her father's chair, and seizing his hand in both of hers, pressed it to her heart, and then to her lips, covering it with kisses and tears, while great bursting sobs shook her whole frame.

"Oh, papa! dear, *dear* papa! I *do love* you! indeed, *indeed* I do. Oh, how could you say such cruel words to me?" she sobbed.

"Hush!" he said, withdrawing his hand. "I will have nothing but the truth from you, and 'actions speak louder than words.' Get up immediately, and dry your tears. Miss Day tells me that you are ruining your eyes by continual crying; and if I hear any more such complaints, I shall punish you severely. I will not allow it at all, for you have nothing whatever to make you unhappy but your own misconduct. Just as soon as you are ready to submit to my authority, you will find yourself treated with the same indulgence and affection as formerly; but remember, *not till* then!"

His words were like daggers to the affectionate, sensitive child. Had he stabbed her to the heart he could not have hurt her more.

"Oh, papa!" she murmured in heart-broken accents, as in obedience to his command she rose to her feet, struggling hard to keep back the tears he had forbidden her to shed.

But her emotion did not seem to move him. Her conduct during his severe illness had been so misrepresented to him, that at times he was wellnigh convinced that her seeming affection was all hypocrisy, and that she really regarded him only in the light of a tyrant, from whose authority she would be glad to escape in any way.

"Pick up your flower and leave the room," he said. "I have no desire for your company until you can learn to obey as you ought."

Silently and mechanically Elsie obeyed him, and hastening to her own room again, threw herself into her nurse's arms, weeping as though she would weep her very life away.

Chloe asked no questions as to the cause of her emotion—which the flower in her hand, and the remembrance of the morning's conversation, sufficiently explained—but tried in every way to soothe and encourage her to hope for future reconciliation.

For some moments her efforts seemed to be quite unavailing; but suddenly Elsie raised her head, and wiping away her tears, said, with a convulsive sob, "Oh! I am doing wrong again, for papa has forbidden me to cry so much, and I must try to obey him. But, oh!" she exclaimed, dropping her head on her nurse's shoulder, with a fresh burst of tears, "how can I help it, when my heart is bursting?"

"Jesus will help you, darlin'," replied Chloe, tenderly. "He always helps his chillens to bear all dere troubles an' do all dere duties, an' never leaves nor forsakes dem. But you must try, darlin', to mind Massa Horace, kase he is your own papa; an' de Bible says, 'Chillen, obey your parents.'"

"Yes, mammy, I know I ought, and I *will* try," said the little girl, raising her head and wiping her eyes; "but, mammy, you must pray for me, for it will be very, very difficult."

Elsie had never been an eye-servant, but had always conscientiously obeyed her father, whether present or absent, and henceforward she constantly struggled to restrain her feelings, and even in solitude denied her bursting heart the relief of tears; though it was not always she could do this, for she was but young in the school of affliction, and often, in spite of every effort, grief would have its way, and she was ready to sink beneath her heavy weight of sorrow. Elsie had learned from God's holy word, that "affliction cometh not forth of the dust, neither doth trouble spring out of the ground;" and she soon set herself diligently to work to find out why this bitter trial had been sent her.

Her little Bible had never been suffered to lie a single day unused, nor had morning or evening ever failed to find her in her closet; she had neglected none of the forms of religion, and her devotions had been far from heartless; yet she discovered with pain that she had of late spent less time, and found less of her enjoyment in these duties than formerly; that she had been, too much engrossed by an earthly love, and needed this trial to bring her nearer to her Saviour, and teach her again to seek all her happiness in "looking unto him." And now the hours that she had been wont to pass in her father's society were usually spent in her own room, alone with her Bible and her God, and there she found that sweet peace and joy which the world can neither give nor take away; and thus she gathered strength to bear her troubles and crosses with heavenly meekness and patience; and she had indeed great need of a strength not her own, for every day, and almost every hour brought with it its own peculiar trial.

No one but the servants—who still loved her dearly—treated her with kindness; but coldness and neglect were the least she had to bear. She was constantly reminded, even by Walter and Enna, that she was stubborn and disobedient, and there was so little pleasure in her walks and rides, either when taken alone or in company with them, that she gradually gave them up almost entirely—until one day, her father's attention being called to it, by a remark of Mrs. Dinsmore's, "that it was no wonder the child was growing thin and pale, for she did not take exercise enough to keep her in health," he called her to him, reprimanded her severely, and laid his commands upon her "to take a walk and ride every day, when the weather would at all permit, but never dare to go alone farther than into the garden."

Elsie answered with meek submission, promising obedience; and then turned quickly away to hide the emotion that was swelling in her breast.

The change in her father was the bitterest part of her trial; she had so revelled in his affection, and now it seemed to be all withdrawn from her; and from the fond, indulgent parent, Mr. Dinsmore seemed suddenly to have changed to the cold, pitiless tyrant. He now seldom took any notice of his little daughter, and never addressed her unless it were to utter a rebuke, a threat, a prohibition, or command, in tones of harshness and severity.

Elsie bore it with all the meekness and patience of a martyr, but ere long her health began to suffer; she grew weak and nervous, and would start and tremble, and change color at the very sound of her father's step or voice—those sounds which she had once so loved to hear—and the little face became thin and pale, and an expression of deep and touching sadness settled down upon it.

Love was as necessary to Elsie's health and happiness as sunshine to the flowers, and even as the keen winds and biting frosts of winter wilt and wither the tender blossoms, so did all this coldness and severity, the gentle, sensitive spirit of the little child.

Mr. Travilla had called several times during the early part of Mr. Dinsmore's illness, while Elsie had been his nurse, and she sometimes wondered that she had seen nothing of him during all these sorrowful weeks; but the truth was, Mr. Travilla had been absent from home, and knew nothing of all that had been going on at Roselands. As soon, however, as he returned, and heard how ill his friend had been, he called to express his sympathy, and congratulate him on his recovery.

He found Mr. Dinsmore seated in an easy-chair in the library, still looking weak and ill, and more depressed in spirits than he had ever seen him.

"Ah! Dinsmore, my dear fellow, I hear you have been very ill;

and, indeed, I must say you are looking far from well yet," Travilla exclaimed in his cheerful, hearty way, shaking his friend's hand warmly. "I think my little friend, Elsie, has deserted her post almost too soon; but I suppose you have sent her back to her lessons again," he remarked, glancing around as if in search of her.

"I have no need of nursing now," replied Mr. Dinsmore, with a sad sort of smile. "I am able to ride, and even to walk out, and shall, I hope, soon be quite myself again."

He then introduced another topic of conversation, and they chatted for some time.

At length Mr. Travilla drew out his watch.

"I see it is past school-hours," he said; "might I see my little friend? I have brought a little gift for her, and should like to present it in person."

Mr. Dinsmore had become quite animated and cheerful during their previous conversation, but a great change came over his face while Mr. Travilla was making his request, and the expression of his countenance was very cold and stern, as he replied, "I thank you, Travilla, on her behalf; but, if you please, I would much prefer your not giving her anything at present, for, I am sorry to say, Elsie has been very stubborn and rebellious of late, and is quite undeserving of any indulgence."

Mr. Travilla looked exceedingly astonished. "Is it *possible!*" he exclaimed. "Really, I have had such an exalted opinion of Elsie's goodness, that I could not have credited such a charge from any one but her father."

"No, nor could I," replied Mr. Dinsmore, leaning his head upon his hand with a heavy sigh; "but it is as I tell you, and you see now that I have some cause for the depression of spirits upon which you have been rallying me. Travilla, I love that child as I have never loved another earthly thing except her mother, and it cuts me to the quick to have her rebel as she has been doing for the last five weeks; it is almost more than I can bear in my present weak state. I thought she loved me devotedly, but it seems I was mistaken, for surely obedience is the best test of love, and she refuses me that."

He paused for a moment, apparently quite overcome by his feelings, then went on; "I have been compelled to banish her from my presence, but, alas! I find I cannot tear her from my heart, and I miss her every moment."

Mr. Travilla looked very much concerned. "I am sorry, indeed," he said, "to hear such an account of my little friend; but her love for you I cannot doubt, and we will hope that she will soon return to her duty."

"Thank you, Travilla; I am always sure of your sympathy in any kind of trouble," replied Mr. Dinsmore, trying to speak cheerfully; "but we will leave this disagreeable subject, and talk of something else."

In a few moments Mr. Travilla rose to take leave, declining Mr. Dinsmore's urgent invitation to remain to dinner, but promising to come again before long and stay a day or two. His kind heart was really pained to learn that there was again a misunderstanding between his little friend—as he had been in the habit of calling Elsie—and her father; and as he rode home silently pondering the matter, he determined that he would very soon fulfil his promise of paying a longer visit, for he could not refrain from indulging a faint hope that he might be able to accomplish something as mediator between them.

A few days after this, Elsie was passing down the hall. The doors and windows were all open, for it was a warm spring day, and as she passed the drawing-room door, she paused a moment and looked in. Her father sat reading near one of the windows, and her eyes were riveted upon his face. He was still pale from his recent illness; and his face had a troubled, care-worn look, very different from its usual expression.

Oh! what a *longing* desire came over the little girl at that sight, to go to him and say that she was sorry for all the past, and that in the future she would be and do everything that he asked. She burst into tears and turned hastily away. She was hurrying out to the garden, but at the door she encountered her aunt Adelaide.

"What is the matter, Elsie?" she asked, putting her hand on the child's shoulder and forcibly detaining her.

"Oh! Aunt Adelaide," sobbed the little girl, "papa looks so ill and sad."

"And no wonder, Elsie," replied her aunt severely; "*you* are quite enough to make him sad, and ill, too, with your perverse, obstinate ways. You have yourself to thank for it all, for it is just that, and nothing else, that ails him."

She turned away as she spoke, and poor Elsie, wringing her hands in an agony of grief, darted down the garden-walk to her favorite arbor.

Her eyes were so blinded by tears that she did not see that Mr. Travilla was sitting there, until she was close beside him.

She turned then, and would have run away again, but he caught her by the dress, and drawing her gently toward him, said in a mild, soothing tone—

"Don't run away from me, my poor little friend, but tell me the cause of your sorrow, and who knows but I may be able to assist you."

Elsie shook her head mournfully, but allowed him, to set her on his knee, and put his arm around her.

"My poor child! my poor, dear little girl!" he said, wiping away her tears, and kissing her very much as her father had been in the habit of doing.

It reminded her of him and his lost love, and caused a fresh burst of tears and sobs.

"Poor child!" said Mr. Travilla again, "is there nothing I can do for you? Will you not tell me the cause of your grief?"

"Oh, Mr. Travilla!" she sobbed, "papa is very much displeased with me, and he looks so sad and ill, it almost breaks my heart."

"And why is he displeased with you, my dear? If you have done wrong and are sorry for your fault, I am sure you have only to confess it, and ask forgiveness, and all will be right again," he said kindly, drawing her head down upon his breast, and smoothing back the curls from her flushed and tear-stained face.

Elsie made no reply, and he went on—

"When we have done wrong, my dear little girl—as we do all sometimes—it is much more noble to acknowledge it and ask pardon, than to try to hide our faults; and you know, dear little Elsie," he added in a graver tone, "that the Bible teaches us that children must obey their parents."

"Yes, Mr. Travilla," she answered, "I know that the Bible says: 'He that covereth his sins shall not prosper,' and I know it tells me to obey my father; and I do think I am willing to confess my faults, and I do try to obey papa in everything that is right; but sometimes he bids me disobey God; and you know the Bible says: 'We ought to obey God rather than men.'"

"I am afraid, my dear," said Mr. Travilla gently, "that you are perhaps a little too much inclined to judge for yourself about right and wrong. You must remember that you are but a very little girl yet, and that your father is very much older and wiser; and therefore I should say it would be much safer to leave it to him to decide these matters. Besides, if he *bids* you do thus and so, I think all the responsibility of the wrong—supposing there *is* any—will rest with *him*, and *he*, not *you*, will have to account for it."

"Oh! no, Mr. Travilla," replied the little girl earnestly, "my Bible teaches me better than that; for it says: '*Every one* of us shall give account of *himself* to God;' and in another place: 'The soul that sinneth *it* shall die.' So I know that *I*, and not papa, nor any one else, will have to give account for *my* sins."

"I see it will never do for me to try to quote Scripture to you," he remarked, looking rather discomfited; "for you know a great deal more about it than I do. But I am very anxious to see you and your father friends again, for I cannot bear to see you both looking so unhappy.

"You have a good father, Elsie, and one that you may well be proud of—for a more high-minded, honorable gentleman cannot be found anywhere; and I am quite sure he would never require you to do anything very wrong. Have you any objection, my dear, to telling me what it is?"

"He bade me read to him, one Sabbath-day, a book which was only fit for week-day reading, because it had nothing at all in it about God, or being good—and I could not do that; and now he says I must say I am sorry I refused to obey him that time, and promise always to do exactly as he bids me in future," replied Elsie, weeping; "and oh! Mr. Travilla, I cannot do that. I cannot say I am sorry I did not disobey God, nor that I will disobey him in future, if papa bids me."

"But if that was a sin, Elsie, it was surely a very *little* one; I don't think God would be very angry with you for anything so small as that," he said very gravely.

"Mr. Travilla," Elsie replied in a tone of deep solemnity, "it is written, 'Cursed is every one that continueth not in *all* things which are written in the book of the law to do them;' *that* is in the Bible; and the catechism says: '*Every sin* deserveth the wrath and curse of God!' And oh! Mr. Travilla," she added in a tone of anguish, "if you knew how *hard* it is for me to keep from giving up, and doing what my conscience says is wrong, you wouldn't try to persuade me to do it."

Mr. Travilla knew not what to say; he was both perplexed and distressed.

But just at that moment a step was heard coming down the path. Elsie recognized it instantly, and began to tremble, and the next moment her father entered the arbor.

Mr. Dinsmore felt a pang of jealousy at seeing his little girl in Travilla's arms, which he would have been ashamed to acknowledge to himself, but it caused his tone to be even more than usually stern and severe as he hastily inquired, "What are you doing here, Elsie—crying again, after all I have said to you? Go to your room this moment, and stay there until you can show a cheerful face!"

Mr. Travilla set her down, and she obeyed without a word, not even daring to look at her father.

There was a moment of embarrassing silence after she had gone.

Then Travilla said, "It seems Elsie stumbled upon me here quite unexpectedly, and I detained her somewhat against her will, I believe, and have been doing my best to persuade her that she ought to be entirely submissive to you."

Mr. Dinsmore looked interested, but replied with a sigh, "I fear you did not succeed; she is sadly obstinate, and I begin to fear I shall have to use great severity before I can conquer her."

Mr. Travilla hesitated a moment, then said, "I am afraid, Dinsmore, that she has the right of it; she quoted Scripture to me till I really had no more to say."

Mr. Dinsmore looked displeased.

"*I* should think," he said almost haughtily, "that the fifth commandment would be answer enough to any argument she could bring to excuse her disobedience."

"We do not all see alike, Dinsmore," remarked his friend, "and though I do not say that you are wrong, I must acknowledge that were I in your place, I should do differently, because I should fear that the child was acting from *principle* rather than self-will or obstinacy."

"*Give up* to her, Travilla? never! It astonishes me that you could suggest such a thing!" exclaimed Mr. Dinsmore with almost fierce determination. "No, I *will* conquer her! I will break *her will*, though in doing so I break my own heart."

"And *hers*, too," murmured Travilla in a low, sad tone, more as if thinking aloud than answering his friend.

Mr. Dinsmore started. "No, no," he said hurriedly, "there is no danger of *that*; else she would certainly have given up long ago."

Travilla shook his head, but made no reply; and presently Mr. Dinsmore rose and led the way to the house.

CHAPTER VI

"The storm of grief bears hard upon her youth,
And bends her, like a drooping flower, to earth."

ROWE'S FAIR PENITENT.

"You are not looking quite well yet, Mr. Dinsmore," remarked a lady visitor, who called one day to see the family; "and your little daughter, I think, looks as if she, too, had been ill; she is very thin, and seems to have entirely lost her bright color."

Elsie had just left the room a moment before the remark was made.

Mr. Dinsmore started slightly.

"I believe she *is* a little pale," he replied in a tone of annoyance; "but as she makes no complaint, I do not think there can be anything seriously amiss."

"Perhaps not," said the lady indifferently; "but if she were *my* child I should be afraid she was going into a decline."

"Really, Mrs. Grey, I don't know what should put such a notion into your head!" exclaimed Mrs. Dinsmore, "for I assure you Elsie has always been a perfectly healthy child since I have known her."

"Ah! well; it was but the thought of a moment," replied Mrs. Grey, rising to take leave, "and I am glad to hear there is no ground for fear, for Elsie is certainly a very sweet little girl."

Mr. Dinsmore handed Mrs. Grey to her carriage, and re-entering the house went into the little back parlor where Elsie, the only other occupant of the room, sat reading, in the corner of the sofa.

He did not speak to her, but began pacing back and forth across the floor. Mrs. Grey's words had alarmed him; he could not forget them, and whenever in his walk his face was turned towards his child, he bent his eyes upon her with a keen, searching gaze; and he was surprised that he had not before noticed how thin, and pale, and careworn that little face had grown.

"Elsie," he said suddenly, pausing in his walk.

The child started and colored, as she raised her eyes from the book to his face, asking, in a half tremulous tone, "What, papa?"

"Put down your book and come to me," he replied, seating himself.

His tone lacked its usual harshness, yet the little girl came to him trembling so that she could scarcely stand.

It displeased him.

"Elsie," he said, as he took her hand and drew her in between his knees, "why do you always start and change color when I speak to you? and why are you trembling now as if you were venturing into the lion's jaws?—are you afraid of me?—speak!"

"Yes, papa," she replied, the tears rolling down her cheeks, "you always speak so sternly to me now, that I cannot help feeling frightened."

"Well, I didn't intend to be stern this time," he said more gently than he had spoken to her for a long while; "but tell me, my daughter, are you quite well?—you are growing very pale and thin, and I want to know if anything ails you."

"Nothing, papa, but—" the rest of her sentence was lost in a burst of tears.

"But what?" he asked almost kindly.

"Oh, papa! you know! I want your love. *How can I live without it?*"

"You need not, Elsie," he answered very gravely, "you have only to bow that stubborn will of yours, to have all the love and all the caresses you can ask for."

Wiping her eyes, she looked up beseechingly into his face, asking, in pleading tones, "*Dear* papa, won't you give me one kiss—just *one?* Think how long I have been without one."

"Elsie, say 'I am sorry, papa, that I refused to obey you on that Sabbath-day; will you please to forgive me? and I will always be obedient in future,' That is all I require. Say it, and you will be at once entirely restored to favor."

"I am *very sorry*, dear papa, for *all* the naughty things I have ever done, and I will always try to obey you, if you do not bid me break God's commandments," she answered in a low, tremulous tone.

"That will not do, Elsie; it is not what I bid you say. I will have no *if* in the matter; nothing but *implicit, unconditional* obedience," he said in a tone of severity.

He paused for a reply, but receiving none, continued: "I see you are still stubborn, and I shall be compelled to take severe measures to subdue you. I do not yet know what they will be, but one thing is certain—I will not keep a rebellious child in my sight; there are boarding-schools where children can be sent who are unworthy to enjoy the privileges and comforts of home."

"Oh, papa! dear, *dear* papa, don't send me away from you! I should die!" she cried in accents of terror and despair, throwing her arms around his neck and clinging to him with a convulsive grasp. "Punish me in any other way you choose; but oh! *don't* send me where I cannot see you."

He gently disengaged her arms, and without returning her caress, said gravely, and almost sadly, "Go now to your room. I have not yet decided what course to take, but you have only to submit, to escape *all* punishment."

Elsie retired, weeping bitterly, passing Adelaide as she went out.

"What is the matter now?" asked Adelaide of her brother, who was striding impatiently up and down the room.

"Nothing but the old story," he replied; "she is the most stubborn child I ever saw. Strange!" he added musingly, "I once thought her rather *too* yielding. Adelaide," he said, sitting down by his sister, and leaning his head upon his hand, with a deep-drawn sigh, "I am *terribly* perplexed! This estrangement is killing us both. Have you noticed how thin and pale she is growing? It distresses me to see it; but what can I do?—give up to her I cannot; it is not once to be thought of. I am sorry I ever began the struggle, but since it *is* begun she *must* and *shall* submit; and it has really become a serious question with me, whether it would not be the truest kindness just to conquer her thoroughly and at once, by an appeal to the rod."

"Oh no, Horace, don't! don't think of such a thing, I beg of you!" exclaimed Adelaide, with tears in her eyes; "such a delicate, sensitive little creature as she is, I do believe it would quite break her heart to be subjected to so ignominious a punishment; surely you could adopt some other measure less revolting to one's feelings, and yet perhaps quite as effectual. I couldn't *bear* to have you do it. I would try everything else first."

"I assure you, Adelaide, it would be *exceedingly* painful to my feelings," he said, "and yet so anxious am I to subdue Elsie, and end this trying state of affairs, that were I certain of gaining my point, even by great severity, I would not hesitate a moment, but I am very doubtful whether she could be conquered in that way, and I would not like to undertake it unless I could carry it through. I hinted at a boarding-school, which seemed to alarm her very much; but I shall not try it, at least not yet, for she is my only child, and I still love her too well to give her up to the tender mercies of strangers. Ah! you don't know how strongly I was tempted to give her a kiss, just now, when she begged so hard for it. But what *shall* I do with her, Adelaide?—have you no suggestion to make?"

"Indeed, I don't know what to say, Horace; I shouldn't like to give up to her, if I were you; it does seem as if you ought to conquer her, and if you don't do it now, I do not believe you ever will."

"Yes, that is just it," he said. "I have sometimes felt sorry for having begun the struggle, and yet perhaps it is just as well, since it must have come sooner or later. Ten years hence I shall want to take her occasionally to the theatre or opera, or perhaps now and then to a ball, and unless I can eradicate these ridiculously strict notions she has got into her head, she will be sure to rebel then, when she will be rather too old to punish, at least in the same way in which I might punish her now."

"A thought has just struck me, Horace," said Adelaide suddenly.

"Well, what is it?" he asked.

Adelaide hesitated. She felt some little sympathy for Elsie, and did not quite like to propose a measure which she knew would give her great pain; but at length she said, in a half-regretful tone—

"I think, Horace, that Aunt Chloe upholds Elsie in her obstinacy, and makes her think herself a martyr to principle, for you know she has the same strange notions, which they both learned from the old housekeeper, Mrs. Murray, who was an old-fashioned Presbyterian, of the strictest sort; and now, as Elsie is still so young, it seems to me it might be *possible* to change her views, if she were entirely removed from all such influences. But take notice, Horace, I do not advise it, for I know it would wellnigh break both their hearts."

For a moment Mr. Dinsmore seemed lost in thought. Then he spoke:

"That is a wise suggestion, Adelaide. I thank you for it, and shall certainly take it into consideration. Yet it is a measure I feel loth to adopt, for Chloe has been a most faithful creature. I feel that I owe her a debt of gratitude for the excellent care she has taken of Elsie, and of her mother before her, and as you say, I fear it would wellnigh break both their hearts. But if less severe measures fail, I shall feel compelled to try it, for I am more anxious than I can tell you to bring Elsie to unconditional obedience."

"Here is a letter for you, Elsie," said her grandfather, the next morning, at the breakfast-table. "Here, Pomp"—to the servant—"hand this to Miss Elsie."

The child's eyes sparkled with pleasure, and she held out her hand eagerly to take it.

But her father interfered.

"No, Pomp," he said, "bring it to me; and remember, in future, that *I* am to receive *all* Miss Elsie's letters."

Elsie relinquished it instantly, without a word of remonstrance, but her heart was so full that she could not eat another morsel; and in spite of all her efforts the tears would come into her eyes, as she saw her father deliberately open and read the letter, and then refold and put it into his pocket. He looked at her as he did so, and seeing the tears rolling down her cheeks, sternly bade her leave the room,

She obeyed, feeling more angry and rebellious toward him than she ever had before. It seemed so cruel and unjust to deprive her of her own letters; one of Miss Rose's—as she knew it must be, for she had no other correspondent—which never contained anything but what was good, and kind, and comforting. They were always a great treat to the little girl, and she had been longer than usual without one, and had been looking longingly for it every day for several weeks past; for sad and lonely as her days now were, she felt very keenly the need of her friend's sympathy and love; and now to have this letter taken from her just as she laid her hand upon it, seemed a disappointment almost too great to be endured. She had a hard struggle with herself before she could put away entirely her feelings of anger and impatience.

"Oh! this is not honoring papa," she said to herself; "he may have good reasons for what he has done; and as *I* belong to him, he certainly has a sort of right to everything that is mine. I will try to be submissive, and wait patiently until he sees fit to give me my letter, as perhaps he will, some time."

All the morning the thought of her letter was scarcely out of her mind, and as soon as she was released from school duties, and dressed for dinner, she went down to the drawing-room, hoping that her father might be there, and that he would give it to her.

But he was not in, and when he came, brought a number of strangers with him, who remained until after tea; so that all the afternoon passed away without affording her an opportunity to speak to him. But, to her great joy, the visitors all left early in the evening, excepting a very mild, pleasant-looking, elderly gentleman, who had settled himself in the portico, with Enna on his knees.

Elsie was watching her fathers movements, and was not sorry to see him, after the departure of his guests, return to the drawing-room, and take up the evening paper.

No one else was at that end of the room, so now, at last, she might speak to him without fear of being overheard. She was glad, too, that his back was towards her, for she had grown very timid about approaching him of late. She stole softly up to the back of his chair, and stood there for some moments without speaking; her heart beat so fast with mingled hope and fear, that it seemed impossible to command her voice.

But at last, coming to his side, she said, in a tone so low and tremulous as to be almost inaudible, "Papa."

"Well, Elsie, what do you want?" he asked, with his eyes still on the paper.

"Dear papa, I do so want to see Miss Rose's letter; won't you please give it to me?"

She waited a moment for a reply; then asked again, "May I not have it, papa?"

"Yes, Elsie, you may have *that*, and *everything* else you want, just as soon as you show yourself a submissive, obedient child."

Tears gathered in Elsie's eyes, but she resolutely forced them back, and made one more appeal. "*Dear* papa," she said, in pleading, tearful tones, "you don't know how I have looked and longed for that letter; and I *do want* it so *very* much; won't you let me see it just for a few moments?"

"You have your answer, Elsie," he said coldly; "and it is the only one I have to give you."

Elsie turned and walked away, silently crying as she went.

But ere she had reached the door he called her back, and looking sternly at her, as she again stood trembling and weeping at his side, "Remember," he said, "that from this time forth, I forbid you to write or receive any letters which do not pass through my hands, and I shall not allow you to correspond with Miss Allison, or any one else, indeed, until you become a more dutiful child."

"Oh, papa! what will Miss Allison think if I don't answer her letter?" exclaimed Elsie, weeping bitterly.

"I shall wait a few weeks," he said, "to see if you are going to be a better girl, and then, if you remain stubborn, I shall write to her myself, and tell her that I have stopped the correspondence, and my reasons for doing so."

"Oh, papa! *dear* papa! *please* don't do that!" cried the little girl in great distress. "I am afraid if you do she will never love me any more, for she will think me such a very bad child."

"If she does, she will only have a just opinion of you," replied her father coldly; "and *all* your friends will soon cease to love you, if you continue to show such a wilful temper; my patience is almost worn out, Elsie, and I shall try some very severe measures before long, unless you see proper to submit. Go now to your own room; I do not wish to see you again to-night."

"Good-night, papa," sobbed the little girl, as she turned to obey him.

"Elsie, my daughter," he said, suddenly seizing her hand, and drawing her to his side, "why will you not give up this strange wilfulness, and let your papa have his own darling again? I love you dearly, my child, and it pains me more than I can express to see you so unhappy," he added, gently pushing back the curls from the little tear-stained face upturned to his.

Martha Finley

His tone had all the old fondness, and Elsie's heart thrilled at the very sound; his look, too, was tender and affectionate, and throwing down his paper he lifted her to his knee, and passed his arm around her waist.

Elsie laid her head against his breast, as was her wont before their unhappy estrangement, while he passed his hand caressingly over her curls.

"Speak, my daughter," he said in a low tone, full of tenderness; "speak, and tell papa that he has his own dutiful little daughter again. His heart aches to receive her; must he do without her still?"

The temptation to yield was very strong. She loved him, oh, how dearly! Could she bear to go on making him unhappy? And it was such *rest*—such *joy*—thus once more to feel herself folded to his heart, and hear his dear voice speaking to her in loving, tender tones. Can it be wondered at that for a moment Elsie wavered? On the one hand she saw her father's fond affection, indulgent kindness, and loving caresses; on the other, banishment from his love, perhaps from home, cold, stern, harsh words and looks; and what more might be meant by the very severe measures threatened, she trembled to think.

For a moment she was silent, for a mighty struggle was going on in her heart. It was hard, *very* hard, to give up her father's love. But the love of Jesus!—ah, that was more precious still!

The struggle was past.

"Papa," she said, raising an earnest, tearful little face to his, and speaking in tones tremulous with emotion, "dear, *dear* papa, I do love you so very, *very* much, and I do want to be to you a good, obedient child; but, papa, Jesus says, 'He that loveth father or mother more than me, is not worthy of me,' and I must love Jesus best, and keep *his* commandments *always*. But you bid me say that I am sorry I refused to break them; and that I will yield implicit obedience to you, even though you should command me to disobey him. Oh, papa, I cannot do *that*, even though you should never love me again; even though you should put me to death."

The cold, stern expression had returned to his face before she had half finished, and putting her off his knee, he said, in his severest tone, "Go, disobedient, rebellious child! How often have I told you that you are too young to judge of such matters, and must leave all that to me, your father and natural guardian, whom the Bible itself commands you to obey. I will find means to conquer you yet, Elsie. If affection and mild measures will not do it, severity shall."

He rose and walked hastily up and down the floor, excited and angry, while poor Elsie went weeping from the room.

"Is that one of your sisters, my dear?" asked the old gentleman of Enna, as he saw the sobbing Elsie pass through the hall, on her way up-stairs.

"No; that is brother Horace's daughter," replied Enna scornfully; "she is a real naughty girl, and won't mind her papa at all."

"Ah!" said the old gentleman gravely, "I am sorry to hear it; but I hope you will always obey your papa."

"Indeed, my papa lets me do *just* as I please," said Enna, with a little toss of her head. "*I* don't have to mind anybody."

"Ah! then I consider you a very unfortunate child," remarked the old gentleman, still more gravely; "for it is by no means good for a little one like you to have too much of her own way."

Mr. Grier—for that was the old gentleman's name—had been much interested in the little Elsie's appearance. He had noticed the look of sadness on her fair young face, and conjectured, from something in the manner of the rest of the family toward her, that she was in disgrace; yet he was sure there was no stubbornness or self-will in the expression of that meek and gentle countenance. He began to suspect that some injustice had been done the little girl, and determined to watch and see if she were indeed the naughty child she was represented to be, and if he found her as good as he was inclined to believe, to try to gain her confidence, and see if he could help her out of her troubles.

But Elsie did not come down again that evening, and though he saw her at the breakfast-table the next morning, she slipped away so immediately after the conclusion of the meal, that he had no opportunity to speak to her; and at dinner it was just the same.

But in the afternoon, seeing her walk out alone, he put on his hat and followed at a little distance. She was going toward the quarter, and he presently saw her enter a cabin where, he had been told, a poor old colored woman was lying ill, perhaps on her death-bed.

Very quietly he drew near the door of the hut, and seating himself on a low bench on the outside, found that he could both see and hear all that was going on without himself being perceived, as Elsie had her back to the door, and poor old Dinah was blind.

"I have come to read to you again, Aunt Dinah," said the little girl, in her sweet, gentle tones.

"Tank you, my young missus; you is bery kind," replied the old woman feebly.

Elsie had already opened her little Bible, and in the same sweet, gentle voice in which she had spoken, she now read aloud the third chapter of St. John's gospel.

When she had finished reading the sixteenth verse—"God so loved the world that he gave his only begotten Son, that whosoever believeth in him should not perish, but have everlasting life,"—she paused and exclaimed, "Oh! Aunt Dinah, is not that beautiful? Does it not make you glad? You see it does not say whosoever is good and holy, or whosoever has not sinned, but it is whosoever believes in Jesus, the only begotten Son of God. If it was only the good, Aunt Dinah, you and I could never hope to be saved, because we are both great sinners."

"Not you, Miss Elsie! not you, darlin'," interrupted the old woman; "ole Dinah's a great sinner, she knows dat well nuff—but you, darlin', you never did nuffin bad."

"Yes, Dinah," said the little voice in saddened tones, "I have a very wicked heart, and have been a sinner all my life; but I know that Jesus died to save sinners, and that whosoever believes in him shall have eternal life, and I do believe, and I want you to believe, and then you, too, will be saved."

"Did de good Lord Jesus die for poor ole Dinah, Miss Elsie?" she asked eagerly.

"Yes, Aunt Dinah, if you will believe in him; it says for *whosoever believeth.*"

"Ole Dinah dunno how to believe, chile; can't do it nohow."

"You must ask God to teach you, Dinah," replied the little girl earnestly, "for the Bible says 'faith'—that means believing—'is the gift of God.'"

"You don't mean *dat*, Miss Elsie! You don't mean dat God will save poor ole Dinah, an' gib her hebben, an' all for nuffin?" she inquired, raising herself on her elbow in her eagerness.

"Yes, Dinah; God says without money and without price; can't you believe him? Suppose I should come and put a hundred dollars in your hand, saying, 'Here, Aunt Dinah, I *give* you this; you are old, and sick, and poor, and I know you can do nothing to earn it, but it is a *free* gift, just *take* it and it is yours;' wouldn't you believe me, and take it?"

"'*Deed* I would, Miss Elsie, kase you nebber tole nuffin but de truff."

"Well, then, can't you believe God when he says that he will save you? Can't you believe Jesus when he says, 'I *give* unto them eternal life'?"

"Yes, yes, Miss Elsie! I do b'lieve; read de blessed words again, darlin'."

Elsie read the verse again, and then finished the Chapter. Then closing the book, she asked softly,

"Shall we pray, now, Aunt Dinah?"

Dinah gave an eager assent; and Elsie, kneeling down by the bedside, prayed in simple, childlike words that Jesus would reveal himself to poor old Dinah, as *her* Saviour; that the Holy Spirit would be her sanctifier and comforter, working faith in her, and thereby uniting her to Christ; that God would adopt her into his family, and be her God and portion forever; and that Jesus would be her shepherd, so that she need fear no evil, even though called to pass through the dark valley of the shadow of death.

"Amen!" was Dinah's fervent response to each of the petitions.

"De good Lord bless you, darlin'," she said, taking Elsie's little white hand in hers, and pressing it to her lips; "de good Lord bless an' keep you, an' nebber let trouble come near you. You knows nuffin 'bout trouble now, for you's young, an' handsome, an' rich, an' good; an' Massa Horace, he doats on you; no, *you* knows nuffin 'bout trouble, but ole Dinah does, kase she's ole, an' sick, an' full ob aches and pains."

"Yes, Aunt Dinah, and I am very sorry for you; but remember, if you believe in Jesus, you will soon go to heaven, where you will never be sick or in pain any more. But, Dinah,"—and the little voice grew very mournful—"we cannot always know when others are in trouble; and I want you to pray for me that I may always have strength to do right."

"I will, darlin', 'deed I will," said Dinah earnestly, kissing the little hand again ere she released it.

As Elsie ceased speaking, Mr. Grier slipped quietly away, and continued his walk. From what he had just seen and heard, he felt fully convinced that Elsie was not the wicked, disobedient child Enna had represented her to be; yet he knew that Enna was not alone in her opinion, since it was very evident that Elsie was in disgrace with the whole family—her father especially—and that she was very unhappy. He felt his heart drawn out in sympathy for the child, and longed to be able to assist her in regaining her father's favor, yet he knew not how to do it, for how was he to learn the facts in the case without seeming to pry into the family secrets of his kind entertainers? But there was one comfort he could do for her—what she had so earnestly asked of Dinah—and he would. As he came to this resolution he turned about and began to retrace his steps toward the house. To his surprise and pleasure, upon turning around a thicket, he came suddenly upon Elsie herself, seated upon a bench under a tree, bending over her little Bible, which lay open on her lap, and upon which her quiet tears were dropping, one by one.

She did not seem aware of his presence, and he stood a moment gazing compassionately upon her, ere he spoke.

"My dear little girl, what is the matter?" he asked in a gentle tone, full of sympathy and kindness, seating himself by her side.

Elsie started, and raising her head, hastily brushed away her tears.

"Good evening, sir," she said, blushing painfully, "I did not know you were here."

"You must excuse my seeming intrusion," replied the old gentleman, taking her hand in his. "I came upon you unawares, not knowing you were here; but now that we have met, will you not tell me the cause of your grief? Perhaps I may be able to assist you."

"No, sir," she said, "you could not do anything for me; but I thank you very much for your kindness."

"I think," said he, after a moment's pause, "that I know something of your trouble; you have offended your father; is it not so, my dear?"

Elsie answered only by her tears, and he went on.

Laying his hand upon the Bible, "Submission to parents, my dear child," he said, "you know is enjoined in this blessed book; children are here commanded to honor and obey their father and mother; it is *God's* command, and if you love his holy word, you will obey its precepts. Surely your father will forgive, and receive you into favor, if you show yourself penitent and submissive?"

"I love my papa very, *very* dearly," replied Elsie, weeping, "and I do want to obey him; but he does not love Jesus, and sometimes he bids me break God's commandments, and then I cannot obey him."

"Is that it, my poor child?" said her friend pityingly. "Then you are right in not obeying; but be *very sure* that your father's commands *are* opposed to those of God, before you refuse obedience; and be very careful to obey him in all things in which you can conscientiously do so."

"I do try, sir," replied Elsie meekly.

"Then be comforted, my dear little girl. God has surely sent you this trial for some wise and kind purpose, and in his own good time he will remove it. Only be patient and submissive. He can change your father's heart, and for that you and I will both pray."

Elsie looked her thanks as they rose to return to the house, but her heart was too full for speech, and she walked silently along beside her new friend, who continued to speak words of comfort and encouragement to her, until they reached the door, where he bade her good-by, saying that he was sorry he was not likely to see her again, as he must leave Roselands that afternoon, but promising not to forget her in his prayers.

When Elsie reached her room, Chloe told her her father had sent word that she was to come to him as soon as she returned from her walk, and that she would find him in his dressing-room.

Chloe had taken off the little girl's hat and smoothed her hair ere she delivered the message, and with a beating heart Elsie proceeded immediately to obey it.

In answer to her timid knock, her father himself opened the door.

"Mammy told me that you wanted me, papa," she said in a tremulous voice, and looking up timidly into his face.

"Yes, I sent for you; come in," he replied; and taking her by the hand he led her forward to the arm-chair from which he had just risen, where he again seated himself, making her stand before him very much like a culprit in the presence of her judge.

There was a moment's pause, in which Elsie stood with her head bent down and her eyes upon the carpet, trembling with apprehension, and not knowing what new trial might be in store for her. Then she ventured to look at her father.

His face was sad and distressed, but very stern.

"Elsie," he began at length, speaking in slow, measured tones, "I told you last evening that should you still persist in your resistance to my authority, I should feel compelled to take severe measures with you. I have now decided what those measures are to be. Henceforth, so long as you continue rebellious, you are to be banished entirely from the family circle; your meals must be taken in your own apartment, and though I shall not reduce your fare to bread and water, it will be very plain—no sweetmeats—no luxuries of any kind. I shall also deprive you entirely of pocket-money, and of all books excepting your Bible and school-books, and forbid you either to pay or receive any visits, telling all who inquire for you, why you cannot be seen. You are also to understand that I forbid you to enter any apartment in the house excepting your own and the school-room—unless by my express permission—and never to go out at all, even to the garden, excepting to take your daily exercise, accompanied always and only by a servant. You are to go on with your studies as usual, but need not expect to be spoken to by any one but your teacher, as I shall request the others to hold no communication with you. This is your sentence. It goes into effect this very hour, but becomes null and void the moment you come to me with acknowledgments of penitence for the past, and promises of implicit obedience for the future."

Elsie stood like a statue; her hands clasped, and her eyes fixed upon the floor. She had grown very pale while her father was speaking, and there was a slight quivering of the eyelids and of the muscles of the mouth, but she showed no other sign of emotion.

"Did you hear me, Elsie?" he asked.

"Yes, papa," she murmured, in a tone so low it scarcely reached his ear.

"Well, have you anything to say for yourself before I send you back to your room?" he asked in a somewhat softened tone.

He felt a little alarmed at the child's unnatural calmness; but it was all gone in a moment. Sinking upon her knees she burst into a fit of passionate weeping. "Oh! papa, papa!" she sobbed, raising her streaming eyes to his face, "will you never, *never* love me any more?—must I never come near you, or speak to you again?"

He was much moved.

"I did not say *that*, Elsie," he replied. "I hope most sincerely that you *will* come to me before long with the confessions and promises I require; and then, as I have told you so often, I will take you to my heart again, as fully as ever. Will you not do it at once, and spare me the painful necessity of putting my sentence into execution?" he asked, raising her gently, and drawing her to his side.

"Dear papa, you know I cannot," she sobbed.

"Then return at once to your room; my sentence must be enforced, though it break both your heart and mine, for I *will* be obeyed. *Go!*" he said, sternly putting her from him. And weeping and sobbing, feeling like a homeless, friendless outcast from society, Elsie went back to her room.

The next two or three weeks were very sad and dreary ones to the poor little girl. Her father's sentence was rigidly enforced; she scarcely ever saw him excepting at a distance, and when once or twice he passed her in going in and out, he neither looked at nor spoke to her. Miss Day treated her with all her former severity and injustice, and no one else but the servants ever addressed her.

She went out every day for an hour or two, in obedience to her father's command, but her walks and rides were sad and lonely; and during the rest of the day she felt like a prisoner, for she dared not venture even into the garden, where she had always been in the habit of passing the greater part of her leisure hours, in the summer season.

But debarred from all other pleasures, Elsie read her Bible more and more constantly, and with ever increasing delight; it was more than meat and drink to her; she there found consolation under every affliction, a solace for every sorrow. Her trial was a heavy one; her little heart often ached sadly with its intense longing for an earthly father's love and favor; yet in the midst of it all, she was conscious of a deep, abiding peace, flowing from a sweet sense of pardoned sin, and a consciousness of a Saviour's love.

At first Elsie greatly feared that she would not be allowed to attend church, as usual, on the Sabbath. But Mr. Dinsmore did not care to excite too much remark, and so, as Elsie had always been very regular in her attendance, to her great joy she was still permitted to go.

No one spoke to her, however, or seemed to take the least notice of her; but she sat by her father's side, as usual, both in the carriage and in the pew, and there was some pleasure even in that, though she scarcely dared even to lift her eyes to his face. Once during the sermon, on the third Sabbath after their last interview, she ventured to do so, and was so overcome by the sight of his pale, haggard looks, that utterly unable to control her emotion, she burst into tears, and almost sobbed aloud.

"Elsie," he said, bending down, and speaking in a stern whisper, "you *must control* yourself."

And with a mighty effort she swallowed down her tears and sobs.

He took no further notice of her until they were again at their own door, when, lifting her from the carriage, he took her by the hand and led her to his own room. Shutting the door, he said sternly, "Elsie, what did you mean by behaving so in church? I was ashamed of you."

"I could not help it, papa; indeed I could not," replied the little girl, again bursting into tears.

"What were you crying about? tell me at once," he said, sitting down and taking off her bonnet, while she stood trembling before him.

"Oh, papa! dear, *dear* papa!" she cried, suddenly throwing her arms round his neck, and laying her cheek to his; "I love you so much, that when I looked at you, and saw how pale and thin you were, I couldn't help crying."

"I do not understand, nor want such love, Elsie," he said gravely, putting her from him; "it is not the right kind, or it would lead you to be docile and obedient. You certainly deserve punishment for your behavior this morning, and I am much inclined to say that you shall not go to church again for some time."

"Please, papa, don't say that," she replied tearfully; "I will try never to do so again."

"Well," he replied, after a moment's reflection, "I shall punish you to-day by depriving you of your dinner, and if you repeat the offence I shall whip you."

Elsie's little face flushed crimson.

"I know it is an ignominious punishment, Elsie," said her father, "and I feel very loth to try it with you, but I greatly fear I shall be compelled to do so before I can subdue your rebellious spirit; it will be the *very last* resort, however. Go now to your room."

This last threat might almost be said to have given Elsie a new dread; for though his words on several former occasions had seemed to imply something of the sort, she had always put away the thought as that of something too dreadful to happen. But now he had spoken plainly, and the trial to her seemed inevitable, for she could never give the required promise, and she knew, too, that he prided himself on keeping his word, to the very letter.

Poor little girl! she felt very much like a martyr in prospect of torture or the stake. For a time she was in deep distress; but she carried *this* trouble, like all the rest, to her Saviour, and found relief; many precious, comforting texts being brought to her mind: "The king's heart is in the hand of the Lord as the rivers of water: he turneth it whithersoever he will." "My grace is sufficient for thee." "As thy days, so shall thy strength be." These, and others of a like import, came to her remembrance in this hour of fear and dread, and assured her that her heavenly Father would either save her from that trial, or give her strength to endure it; and she grew calm and peaceful again.

"The name of the Lord is a strong tower; the righteous runneth into it and is safe."

CHAPTER VII

"Alone! alone! how drear it is
Always to be alone!"

WILLES.

It was only a few days after Adelaide had suggested to her brother the propriety of separating Elsie from her nurse, that he had the offer of a very fine estate in the immediate neighborhood of his father's plantation.

Mr. Granville, the present owner, was about removing to a distant part of the country, and having become somewhat reduced in circumstances, was anxious to sell, and as the place suited Mr. Dinsmore exactly, they were not long in coming to an arrangement, satisfactory to both, by which it passed into his hands.

Horace Dinsmore had inherited a large fortune from his mother, and having plenty of money at his command, he immediately set about making sundry improvements upon his new purchase; laying out the grounds, and repairing and enlarging the already fine old mansion, adding all the modern conveniences, and furnishing it in the most tasteful and elegant style.

And so "Rumor, with her thousand tongues," soon had it noised abroad that he was about to bring home a second wife,

Martha Finley

and to that cause many attributed Elsie's pale and altered looks.

Such, however, was not Mr. Dinsmore's intention.

"I must have a housekeeper," he said to Adelaide. "I shall send Chloe there. She will do very well for the present, and it will give me the opportunity I desire of separating her from Elsie, while in the meantime I can be looking out for a better."

"But you are not going to leave us yourself, Horace?" said his sister inquiringly.

"Not immediately, Adelaide; I intend to end this controversy with Elsie first, and I indulge the hope that the prospect of sharing such a home with me as soon as she submits, will go far towards subduing her."

Mr. Dinsmore shrank from the thought of Elsie's grief, if forced to part from her nurse; but he was not a man to let his own feelings, or those of others, prevent him from carrying out any purpose he had formed, if, as in this case, he could persuade himself that he was doing right. And so—all his arrangements being now made—the very morning after his late interview with Elsie, Chloe was summoned to his presence.

He informed her of his purchase, and that it was his intention to send her there to take charge of his house and servants, for the present.

Chloe, who was both extremely surprised and highly flattered by this proof of her young master's confidence, looked very much delighted, as, with a low courtesy, she expressed her thanks, and her willingness to undertake the charge. But a sudden thought struck her, and she asked anxiously if "her child" was to go with her.

Mr. Dinsmore said "*No*," very decidedly; and when Chloe told him that that being the case, she would much rather stay where she was, if he would let her, he said she could not have any choice in the matter; *she* must go, and Elsie must stay.

Chloe burst into an agony of tears and sobs, begging to know why she was to be separated from the child she had loved and cherished ever since her birth; the child committed to her charge by her dying mother? What had she done to so displease her master, that he had determined to subject her to such a bitter trial?

Mr. Dinsmore was a good deal moved by her grief, but still not to be turned from his purpose. He merely waited until she had grown somewhat calmer, and then, in a tone of great kindness, but with much firmness and decision, replied, "that he was not angry with her; that he knew she had been very faithful in her kind care of his wife and child, and he should always take care of her, and see that she was made comfortable as long as she lived; but, for reasons which he did not think necessary to explain, he considered it best to separate her from Elsie for a time; he knew it would be hard for them both, but it *must* be done, and tears and entreaties would be utterly useless; she must prepare to go to her new home that very afternoon."

So saying he dismissed her, and she went back to Elsie's room wellnigh heart-broken; and there the little girl found her when she came in from school duties, sitting beside the trunk she had just finished packing, crying and sobbing as she had never seen her before.

"Oh, mammy, mammy! what *is* the matter? *dear* old mammy, what ails you?" she asked, running to her, and throwing her arms around her neck.

Chloe clasped her to her breast, sobbing out that she must leave her. "Massa Horace was going to send her away from her precious child."

Elsie was fairly stunned by the announcement, and for a moment could not speak one word. To be separated from her beloved nurse who had always taken care of her!—who seemed almost necessary to her existence. It was such a calamity as even her worst fears had never suggested, for they never had been parted, even for a single day; but wherever the little girl went, if to stay more than a few hours, her faithful attendant had always accompanied her, and she had never thought of the possibility of doing without her.

She unclasped her arms from Chloe's neck, disengaging herself from her loving grasp, stood for a moment motionless and silent; then, suddenly sinking down upon her nurse's lap, again wound her arms about her neck, and hid her face on her bosom, sobbing wildly: "Oh, mammy, mammy! you shall not go! Stay with me, mammy! I've nobody to love me now but you, and my heart will break if you leave me. Oh, mammy, say that you won't go!"

Chloe could not speak, but she took the little form again in her arms, and pressed it to her bosom in a close and fond embrace, while they mingled their tears and sobs together.

But Elsie started up suddenly.

"I will go to papa!" she exclaimed; "I will beg him on my knees to let you stay! I will tell him it will kill me to be parted from my dear old mammy."

"'Tain't no use, darlin'! Massa Horace, he say I *must* go; an' you know what dat means, well as I do," said Chloe, shaking her head mournfully; "he won't let me stay, nohow."

"But I must try, mammy," Elsie answered, moving toward the door. "I think papa loves me a little yet, and maybe he will listen."

But she met a servant in the hall who told her that her father had gone out, and that she heard him say he would not return before tea-time.

And Chloe was to go directly after dinner; so there was no hope of a reprieve, nothing to do but submit as best they might to the sad necessity of parting; and Elsie went back to her room again, to spend the little time that remained in her nurse's arms, sobbing out her bitter grief upon her breast. It was indeed a hard, hard trial to them both; yet neither uttered one angry or complaining word against Mr. Dinsmore.

Fanny, one of the maids, brought up Elsie's dinner, but she could not eat. Chloe's appetite, too, had failed entirely; so they remained locked in each other's embrace until Jim came to the door to tell Chloe the carriage was waiting which was to convey her to her new home.

Once more she strained her nursling to her breast, sobbing out the words: "Good-by, darlin'! de good Lord bless an' keep you forebber an' ebber, an' nebber leave you alone."

"Oh, mammy, mammy, don't leave me!" almost shrieked the child, clinging to her with a convulsive grasp.

"Don't now, darlin'! don't go for to break dis ole heart! You knows I *must* go," said Chloe, gently disengaging herself. "We'll ask de Lord to bring us together again soon, dear chile, an' I think he will 'fore long," she whispered in Elsie's ear; and with another fond caress she left her all drowned in tears, and half fainting with grief.

An hour might have passed—it seemed longer than that to Elsie—when the door opened, and she started up from the sofa, where she had flung herself in the first abandonment of her sorrow. But it was only Fanny, come to tell her that Jim had brought her horse to the door, and to prepare her for her ride.

She quietly submitted to being dressed; but, ah! how strange it seemed to have any other than Chloe's hands busy about her!

It swelled her young heart wellnigh to bursting, though Fanny, who evidently understood her business well, was very kind and attentive, and full of unobtrusive sympathy and love for her young charge.

The brisk ride in the fresh air did Elsie good, and she returned quite calm and composed, though still very sad.

Fanny was in waiting to arrange her dress again, and when that was done, went down to bring up her supper. It was more tempting than usual, but Elsie turned from it with loathing.

"Do, Miss Elsie, *please* do try to eat a little," urged Fanny, with tears in her eyes. "What will Massa Horace say if he axes me 'bout your eatin' an' I'm 'bliged to tell him you didn't eat never a mouthful of dinner, an' likewise not the first crumb of your supper?"

That, as Fanny well knew, was a powerful argument with Elsie, who, dreading nothing so much as her father's displeasure, which was sure to be excited by such a report of her conduct, sat down at once and did her best to make a substantial meal.

Fanny was not more than half satisfied with the result of her efforts; but seeing it was useless to press her any further, silently cleared away the tea-things and carried them downstairs, and Elsie was left alone.

Alone! She looked around upon the familiar furniture with a strange feeling of desolation; an over-powering sense of loneliness came over her; she missed the dear face that had been familiar to her from her earliest infancy, and had ever looked so lovingly upon her; the kind arms wont to fold her in a fond embrace to that heart ever beating with such true, unalterable affection for her; that breast, where she might ever lean her aching head, and pour out all her sorrows, sure of sympathy and comfort.

She could not stay there, but passing quickly out on to the

balcony upon which the windows of her room opened, she stood leaning against the railing, her head resting upon the top of it, and the silent tears dropping one by one upon the floor.

"Oh, mammy, mammy!" she murmured half aloud, "why did you leave your poor heart-broken child? How can I live without you—without any one to love me?"

"Elsie," said Mr. Dinsmore's voice, close at her side, "I suppose you think me a very cruel father thus to separate you from your nurse. Is it not so?"

"Papa, dear papa, don't say that," she cried with a burst of sobs and tears, as she turned hastily round, and taking his hand in both of hers, looked up pleadingly into his face. "I know you have a right to do it, papa; I know I belong to you, and you have a right to do as you will with me, and I will try to submit without murmuring, but I cannot help feeling sad, and shedding some tears."

"I am not blaming you for crying now; it is quite excusable under the circumstances," he replied in a slightly softened tone, adding, "I take no pleasure in causing you sorrow, Elsie; and though I have sent away your nurse, I have provided you with another servant, who will, I think, be respectful and kind, and attentive to all your wishes. If she is not, you have only to complain to me, and she shall be at once removed, and her place supplied by another. And I have good reasons for what I am doing. You have resisted my authority for a long time now, and I must try the effect of placing you under new influences. I fear Chloe has, at least tacitly, encouraged you in your rebellion, and therefore I intend to keep you apart until you have learned to be submissive and obedient."

"Dear papa," replied the little girl meekly, "you wrong poor mammy, if you think she would ever uphold me in disobedience to you; for on the contrary, she has always told me that I ought, on all occasions, to yield a ready and cheerful obedience to every command, or even *wish* of yours, unless it was contrary to the word of God."

"There! that is just it!" said he, interrupting her with a frown; "she and Mrs. Murray have brought you up to believe that you and they are wiser and more capable of interpreting the Bible, and deciding questions of right and wrong, than your father; and that is precisely the notion that I am determined to get out of your head."

She opened her lips to reply, but bidding her be silent, he turned to leave her; but she clung to him, looking beseechingly up into his face.

"Well," he said, "what is it—what do you want?"

She struggled for utterance.

"Oh, papa!" she sobbed, "I feel so sad and lonely to-night—will you not sit down a little while and take me on your knee?—my heart aches so to lay my head against you just for one moment. Oh, papa, dear papa, will you not let me—will you not kiss me once, *just once?* You know I am all alone!—*all alone!*"

He could not resist her pleading looks and piteous accents. A tear trembled in his eye, and hastily seating himself, he drew her to his knee, folded her for an instant in his arms, laid her head against his breast, kissed her lips, her brow, her cheek; and then putting her from him, without speaking a word, walked quickly away.

Elsie stood for a moment where he had left her, then sinking on her knees before the sofa, whence he had just risen, she laid her head down upon it, weeping and sobbing most bitterly, "Oh! papa, papa! oh, mammy, mammy, dear, dear mammy! you are all gone, all gone! and I am alone! alone! all alone!—nobody to love me—nobody to speak to me. Oh, mammy! Oh, papa! come back, come back to me—to your poor little Elsie, for my heart is breaking."

Alas! that caress, so earnestly pleaded for, had only by contrast increased her sense of loneliness and desolation. But in the midst of her bitter grief a loving, gentle voice came to her ear, whispering in sweetest tones, "*I* will *never* leave thee, nor forsake thee." "When thy father and thy mother forsake thee, I, the Lord, will take thee up." "I will deliver thee in six troubles; yea, in seven there shall no evil touch thee." And the sobs were hushed—the tears flowed more quietly, until at length they ceased altogether, and the little sorrowing one fell asleep.

"As one whom his mother comforteth, so will I comfort you; and ye shall be comforted."

CHAPTER VIII

"No future hour can rend my heart like this,
Save that which breaks it."

MATURIN'S BERTRAM.

"Unless thy law had been my delight, I should then have
perished in mine affliction."

PSALM 119: 92.

Elsie was sitting alone in her room when there came a light tap
on the door, immediately followed, much to the little girl's
surprise, by the entrance of her Aunt Adelaide, who shut and
locked the door behind her, saying, "I am glad you are quite
alone; though, indeed, I suppose that is almost always the case
now-a-days. I see," she continued, seating herself by the side of
the astonished child, "that you are wondering what has
brought me to visit you, to whom I have not spoken for so
many weeks; but I will tell you. I come from a sincere desire to
do you a kindness, Elsie; for, though I don't know how to
understand nor excuse your obstinacy, and heartily approve of
your father's determination to conquer you, I must say that I
think he is unnecessarily harsh and severe in some of his
measures—"

"Please don't, Aunt Adelaide," Elsie interrupted, in a pleading
voice, "please don't speak so of papa to me; for you know I

ought not to hear it."

"Pooh! nonsense!" said Adelaide, "it is very naughty in you to interrupt me; but, as I was about to remark, I don't see any use in your being forbidden to correspond with Miss Allison, because her letters could not possibly do you any harm, but rather the contrary, for she is goodness itself—and so I have brought you a letter from her which has just come enclosed in one to me."

She took it from her pocket as she spoke, and handed it to Elsie.

The little girl looked longingly at it, but made no movement to take it.

"Thank you, Aunt Adelaide, you are very kind indeed," she said, with tears in her eyes, "and I should dearly love to read it; but I cannot touch it without papa's permission."

"Why, you silly child! he will never know anything about it," exclaimed her aunt quickly. "*I* shall never breathe a word to him, nor to anybody else, and, of course, you will not tell on yourself; and if you are afraid the letter might by some mischance fall into his hands, just destroy it as soon as you have read it."

"Dear Aunt Adelaide, please take it away and don't tempt me any more, for I want it so very much I am afraid I shall take it if you do, and that would be so very wrong," said Elsie, turning away her head.

"I presume you are afraid to trust me; you needn't be, though," replied Adelaide, in a half offended tone. "Horace will never learn it from me, and there is no possible danger of his ever finding it out in any other way, for I shall write to Rose at once, warning her not to send you any more letters at present."

"I am not at all afraid to trust you, Aunt Adelaide, nor do I think there is any danger of papa's finding it out," Elsie answered earnestly; "but I should know it myself, and God would know it, too, and you know he has commanded me to obey my father in everything that is not wrong; and I *must* obey him, no matter how hard it is."

"Well, you are a strange child," said Adelaide, as she returned the letter to her pocket and rose to leave the room; "such a compound of obedience and disobedience I don't pretend to understand."

Elsie was beginning to explain, but Adelaide stopped her, saying she had no time to listen, and hastily quitted the room.

Elsie brushed away a tear and took up her book again—for she had been engaged in preparing a lesson for the next day, when interrupted by this unexpected visit from her aunt.

Adelaide went directly to her brother's door, and receiving an invitation to enter in answer to her knock, was the next instant standing by his side, with Miss Allison's letter in her hand.

"I've come, Horace," she said in a lively tone, "to seek from you a reward of virtue in a certain little friend of mine; and because you alone can bestow it, I come to you on her behalf, even at the expense of having to confess a sin of my own."

"Well, take a seat, won't you?" he said good-humoredly, laying down his book and handing her a chair, "and then speak out at once, and tell me what you mean by all this nonsense."

"First for my own confession then," she answered laughingly, accepting the offered seat. "I received a letter this morning from my friend, Rose Allison, enclosing one to your little Elsie."

He began to listen with close attention, while a slight frown gathered on his brow.

"Now, Horace," his sister went on, "though I approve in the main of your management of that child—which, by the way, I presume, is not of the least consequence to you—yet I must say I have thought it right hard you should deprive her of Rose's letters. So I carried this one, and offered it to her, assuring her that you should never know anything about it; but what do you think?—the little goose actually refused to touch it without papa's permission. She *must* obey him, she said, no matter how hard it was, whenever he did not bid her do anything wrong. And now, Horace," she concluded, "I want you to give me the pleasure of carrying this letter to her, with your permission to read it. I'm sure she deserves it."

"Perhaps so; but I am sure *you* don't, Adelaide, after tampering with the child's conscience in that manner. You may send her to me, though, if you will," he said, holding out his hand for the letter. "But are you quite sure that she really wanted to see it, and felt assured that she might do so without my knowledge?"

"Perfectly certain of it," replied his sister confidently.

They chatted for a few moments longer; Adelaide praising Elsie, and persuading him to treat her with more indulgence; and he, much pleased with this proof of her dutifulness, half promising to do so; and then Adelaide went back to her room, despatching a servant on her way to tell Elsie that her papa desired to see her immediately.

Elsie received the message with profound alarm; for not dreaming of the true cause, her fears at once suggested that he probably intended putting his late threat into execution. She spent one moment in earnest prayer for strength to bear her trial, and then hastened, pale and trembling, to his presence.

How great, then, was her surprise to see him, as she entered, hold out his hand with a smile, saying, in the kindest tone, "Come here to me, my daughter!"

She obeyed, gazing wonderingly into his face.

He drew her to him; lifted her to his knee; folded her in his arms, and kissed her tenderly. He had not bestowed such a loving caress upon her—nor indeed ever kissed her at all, excepting on the evening after Chloe's departure—since that unhappy scene in his sick-room; and Elsie, scarcely able to believe she was awake, and not dreaming, hid her face on his breast, and wept for joy.

"Your aunt has been here telling me what passed between you this afternoon," said he, repeating his caress, "and I am much pleased with this proof of your obedience; and as a reward I will give you permission, not only to read the letter she offered you, but also the one I retained. And I will allow you to write to Miss Allison once, in answer to them, the letter passing through my hands. I have also promised, at your aunt's solicitation, to remove some of the restrictions I have placed upon you, and I now give you the same liberty to go about the house and grounds which you formerly enjoyed. Your books and toys shall also be returned to you, and you may take your meals with the family whenever you choose."

"Thank you, papa, you are very kind," replied the little girl; but her heart sank, for she understood from his words that she was not restored to favor as she had for a moment fondly imagined.

Neither spoke again for some moments. Each felt that this delightful reunion—for it was delightful to both—this enjoyment of the interchange of mutual affection, could not last.

Silent caresses, mingled with sobs and tears on Elsie's part, passed between them; and at length Mr. Dinsmore said, "Elsie, my daughter, I hope you are now ready to make the confession and promises I require?"

"Oh, papa! dear papa!" she said, looking up into his face with the tears streaming down her own, "have I not been punished enough for that? and can you not just punish me whenever I disobey you, without requiring any promise?"

"Stubborn yet, Elsie," he answered with a frown. "No; as I have told you before, my word is as the law of the Medes and Persians, which altered not. I have required the confession and promise, and *you must make them.*"

He set her down, but she lingered a moment. "Once more, Elsie, I ask you," he said, "will you obey?"

She shook her head; she could not speak.

"Then go," said her father. "I have given you the last caress I ever shall, until you submit."

He put the letters into her hand as he spoke, and motioned her to be gone; and Elsie fled away to her own room, to throw herself upon the bed, and weep and groan in intense mental anguish.

She cared not for the letters now; they lay neglected on the floor, where they had fallen unheeded from her hand. The gloom on her pathway seemed all the darker for that bright but momentary gleam of sunshine. So dark was the cloud that overshadowed her that for the time she seemed to have lost all hope, and to be able to think of nothing but the apparent impossibility of ever regaining her place in her father's heart. His last words rang in her ears.

"Oh! papa, papa! my own papa!" she sobbed, "will you never love me again? never kiss me, or call me pet names? Oh, *how can* I bear it! how can I ever live without your love?"

Her nerves, already weakened by months of mental suffering, could hardly bear the strain; and when Fanny came into the room, an hour or two later, she was quite frightened to find her young charge lying on the bed, holding her head with both hands and groaning, and speechless with pain.

"What's de matter darlin'?" she asked; but Elsie only answered with a moan; and Fanny, in great alarm, hastened to Mr. Dinsmore's room, and startled him with the exclamation: "Oh, Massa Horace, make haste for come to de chile! she gwine die for sartain, if you don't do sumfin mighty quick!"

"Why, what ails her, Fanny?" he asked, following the servant with all speed.

"Dunno, Massa; but I'se sure she's berry ill," was Fanny's reply, as she opened the door of Elsie's room, and stepped back to allow her master to pass in first.

One glance at Elsie's face was enough to convince him that there was some ground for her attendant's alarm. It was ghastly with its deadly pallor and the dark circles round the eyes, and wore an expression of intense pain.

He proceeded at once to apply remedies, and remained beside her until they had so far taken effect that she was able to speak, and looked quite like herself again.

"Elsie!" he said in a grave, firm tone, as he placed her more comfortably on her pillow, "this attack has been brought on by violent crying; you must not indulge yourself in that way again."

"I could not help it, papa," she replied, lifting her pleading eyes to his face.

"You *must* help it in future, Elsie," he said sternly.

Tears sprang to her eyes, but she struggled to keep them back.

He turned to leave her, but she caught his hand, and looked so beseechingly in his face, that he stopped and asked in a softened tone, "What is it, my daughter?"

"Oh, papa!" she murmured in low, tremulous accents, "love me a little."

"I do love you, Elsie," he replied gravely, and almost sadly, as he bent over her and laid his hand upon her forehead. "I love you only too well, else I should have sent my stubborn little daughter away from me long ere this."

"Then, papa, kiss me; just *once*, dear papa!" she pleaded, raising her tearful eyes to his face.

"No, Elsie, not *once* until you are entirely submissive. This state of things is as painful to me as it into you, my daughter; but I cannot yield my authority, and I hope you will soon see that it is best for you to give up your self-will."

So saying, he turned away and left her alone; alone with that weary home-sickness of the heart, and the tears dropping silently down upon her pillow.

Horace Dinsmore went back to his own room, where he spent the next half hour in pacing rapidly to and fro, with folded arms and contracted brow.

"Strange!" he muttered, "that she is *so hard* to conquer. I never imagined that she could be so stubborn. One thing is certain," he added, heaving a deep sigh; "we must separate for a time, or I shall be in danger of yielding; for it is no easy matter to resist her tearful pleadings, backed as they are by the yearning affection of my own heart. How I love the perverse little thing! Truly she has wound herself around my very heart-strings. But I *must* get these absurd notions out of her head, or I shall never have any comfort with her; and if I yield *now*, I may as well just give that up entirely; besides, I have *said* it; and *I will* have her to understand that my word is law."

And with another heavy sigh he threw himself upon the sofa, where he lay in deep thought for some moments; then, suddenly springing up, he rang the bell for his servant.

"John," he said, as the man appeared in answer to his summons, "I shall leave for the North to-morrow morning. See that my trunk is packed, and everything in readiness. You are to go with me, of course."

"Yes, Massa, I'll 'tend to it," replied John, bowing, and retiring with a grin of satisfaction on his face. "Berry glad," he chuckled to himself, as he hurried away to tell the news in the kitchen, "*berry* glad dat young Massa's got tired ob dis dull ole place at last. Wonder if little Miss Elsie gwine along."

Elsie rose the next morning feeling very weak, and looking pale and sad: and not caring to avail herself of her father's permission to join the family, she took her breakfast in her own room, as usual. She was on her way to the school-room soon afterwards, when, seeing her papa's man carrying out his trunk, she stopped and inquired in a tone of alarm—

"Why, John! is papa going away?"

"Yes, Miss Elsie; but ain't you gwine along? I s'posed you was."

"No, John," she answered faintly, leaning against the wall for support; "but where is papa going?"

"Up North, Miss Elsie; dunno no more 'bout it; better ask Massa Horace hisself," replied the servant, looking compassionately at her pale face, and eyes brimful of tears.

Mr. Dinsmore himself appeared at this moment, and Elsie, starting forward with clasped hands, and the tears running down her cheeks, looked piteously up into his face, exclaiming, "Oh, papa, dear are you going away, and without me?"

Without replying, he took her by the hand, and turning back into his room again, shut the door, sat down, and lifted her to his knee. His face was very pale and sad, too, but withal wore an expression of firm determination.

Elsie laid her head on his shoulder, and sobbed out her tears and entreaties that he would not leave her.

"It depends entirely upon yourself, Elsie," he said presently. "I gave you warning some time since that I would not keep a rebellious child in my sight; and while you continue such, either you or I must be banished from home, and I prefer to exile myself rather than you; but a submissive child I will not leave. It is not yet too late; you have only to yield to my requirements, and I will stay at home, or delay my journey for a few days, and take you with me. But if you prefer separation from me to giving up your own self-will, you have no one to blame but yourself."

He waited a moment, then said: "Once more I ask you, Elsie, will you obey me?"

"Oh, papa, always, if—"

"Hush!" he said sternly; "you *know* that will not do;" and setting her down, he rose to go.

But she clung to him with desperate energy. "Oh, papa," she sobbed, "when will you come back?"

"That depends upon *you*, Elsie," he said. "Whenever my little daughter writes to me the words I have so vainly endeavored to induce her to speak, that *very day*, if possible, I will start for home."

He laid his hand on the handle of the door as he spoke.

But clinging to him, and looking up beseechingly into his face, she pleaded, in piteous tones, amid her bitter sobs and tears, "Papa, dear, *dear* papa, kiss me once before you go; just *once*, papa; perhaps you may never come back—perhaps I may die. Oh, papa, papa! will you go away without kissing me?—me, your own little daughter, that you used to love so dearly? Oh, papa, my heart will break!"

His own eyes filled with tears, and he stooped as if to give her the coveted caress, but hastily drawing back again, said with much of his accustomed sternness—

"No, Elsie, I cannot break my word; and if you are determined to break your own heart and mine by your stubbornness, on your own head be the consequences,"

And putting her forcibly aside, he opened the door and went out, while, with a cry of despair, she sank half-fainting upon the floor.

She was roused ere long by the sound of a carriage driving up to the door, and the thought flashed upon her, "He is not gone yet, and I may see him once more;" and springing to her feet, she ran downstairs, to find the rest of the family in the hall, taking leave of her father.

He was just stooping to give Enna a farewell kiss, as his little daughter came up. He did not seem to notice her, but was turning away, when Enna said, "Here is Elsie; aren't you going to kiss *her* before you go?"

He turned round again, to see those soft, hazel eyes, with their mournful, pleading gaze, fixed upon his face. He never forgot that look; it haunted him all his life.

He stood for an instant looking down upon her, while that mute, appealing glance still met his, and she ventured to take his hand in both of hers and press it to her lips.

But he turned resolutely away, saying, in his calm, cold tone, "No! Elsie is a stubborn, disobedient child. I have no caress for her."

A moan of heart-breaking anguish burst from Elsie's pale and trembling lips; and covering her face with her hands, she sank down upon the door-step, vainly struggling to suppress the bitter, choking sobs that shook her whole frame.

But her father was already in the carriage, and hearing it begin to move, she hastily dashed away her tears, and strained her eyes to catch the last glimpse of it, as it whirled away down the avenue.

It was quite gone; and she rose up and sadly re-entered the house.

"I don't pity her at all," she heard her grandfather say, "for it is all her own fault, and serves her just right."

But so utterly crushed and heart-broken was she already, that the cruel words fell quite unheeded upon her ear.

She went directly to her father's deserted room, and shutting herself in, tottered to the bed, and laying her face on the pillow where his head had rested a few hours before, clasped her arms around it, and wetted it with her tears, moaning sadly to herself the while, "Oh, *papa*, my own dear, darling papa! I shall never, *never* see you again! Oh, how can I live without you? who is there to love me now? Oh, papa, papa, will you never, never come back to me? Papa, papa, my heart is breaking! I shall die."

From that time the little Elsie drooped and pined, growing paler and thinner day by day—her step more languid, and her eye more dim—till no one could have recognized in her the bright, rosy, joyous child, full of health and happiness, that she had been six months before. She went about the house like a shadow, scarcely ever speaking or being spoken to. She made no complaint, and seldom shed tears now; but seemed to have lost her interest in everything and to be sinking into a kind of apathy.

"I wish," said Mrs. Dinsmore one day, as Elsie passed out into the garden, "that Horace had sent that child to boarding-school, and stayed at home himself. Your father says he needs him, and as to her—she has grown so melancholy of late, it is enough to give one the vapors just to look at her."

"I am beginning to feel troubled about her," replied Adelaide, to whom the remark had been addressed; "she seems to be losing flesh, and strength, too, so fast. The other day I went into her room, and found Fanny crying heartily over a dress of Elsie's which she was altering. 'Oh! Miss Adelaide,' she sobbed, 'the chile gwine die for sartain!' 'Why no, Fanny,' I said, 'what makes you think so? she is not sick.' But she shook her head, saying, 'Just look a here, Miss Adelaide,' showing me how much she was obliged to take the dress in to make it fit, and then she told me Elsie had grown so weak that the least exertion overcame her. I think I must write to Horace."

"Oh, nonsense, Adelaide!" said her mother, "I wouldn't trouble him about it. Children are very apt to grow thin and languid during the hot weather, and I suppose fretting after him makes it affect her rather more than usual; and just now in the holidays she has nothing else to occupy her thoughts. She will do well enough."

So Adelaide's fears were relieved, and she delayed writing, thinking that her mother surely knew best.

Mrs. Travilla sat in her cool, shady parlor, quietly knitting. She was alone, but the glance she occasionally sent from the window seemed to say that she was expecting some one.

"Edward is unusually late to-day," she murmured half aloud. "But there he is at last," she added, as her son appeared, riding slowly up the avenue. He dismounted and entered the house, and in another moment had thrown himself down upon the sofa, by her side. She looked at him uneasily; for with the quick ear of affection she had noticed that his step lacked its accustomed elasticity, and his voice its cheerful, hearty tones. His orders to the servant who came to take his horse had been given in a lower and more subdued key than usual, and his greeting to herself, though perfectly kind and respectful, was grave and absent in manner; and now his thoughts seemed far away, and the expression of his countenance was sad and troubled.

"What ails you, Edward—is anything wrong, my son?" she asked, laying her hand on his shoulder, and looking into his face with her loving, motherly eyes.

"Nothing with *me* mother," he answered affectionately; "but," he added, with a deep-drawn sigh, "I am sorely troubled about my little friend. I called at Roselands this afternoon, and learned that Horace Dinsmore has gone North—to be absent nobody knows how long—leaving her at home. He has been gone nearly a week, and the child is—heart-broken."

"Poor darling! is she really so much distressed about it, Edward?" his mother asked, taking off her spectacles to wipe them, for they had suddenly grown dim. "You saw her, I suppose?"

"Yes, for a moment," he said, struggling to control his feelings. "Mother, you would hardly know her for the child she was six months ago! she is so changed, so thin and pale—but that is not the worst; she seems to have lost all her life and animation. I felt as though it would be a relief even to see her cry. When I spoke to her she smiled, it is true; but ah! such a sad, hopeless, dreary sort of smile—it was far more touching than tears, and then she turned away, as if she had scarcely heard or understood what I said. Mother, you must go to her; she needs just the sort of comfort you understand so well how to give, but which I know nothing about. You will go, mother, will you not?"

"Gladly, Edward! I would go this moment, if I thought I would be permitted to see her, and could do her any good."

"I hardly think," said her son, "that even Mrs. Dinsmore would refuse you the privilege of a private interview with the child should you request it, mother; but, no doubt, it would be much pleasanter for all parties if we could go when Elsie is at home alone; and fortunately such will be the case to-morrow, for, as I accidentally learned, the whole family, with the exception of Elsie and the servants, are expecting to spend the day abroad. So if it suits you, mother, we will drive over in the morning."

Mrs. Travilla expressed her readiness to do so; and about the middle of the forenoon of the next day their carriage might have been seen turning into the avenue at Roselands.

Pomp came out to receive the visitors. "Berry sorry, Massa and Missus," he said, making his best bow to them as they alighted from the carriage, "dat de family am all from home with the single 'ception of little Miss Elsie. But if you will be pleased to walk into the drawin'-room, an' rest yourselves, I will call for suitable refreshments, and Fanny shall be instantly despatched to bring de young lady down."

"No, thank you, Pomp," replied Mr. Travilla pleasantly, "we are not at all in want of refreshments, and my mother would prefer seeing Miss Elsie in her own room. I will step into the drawing-room, mother, until you come down again," he added in an undertone to her.

Pomp was about to lead the way, but Mrs. Travilla gently put him aside, saying that she would prefer to go alone, and had no need of a guide.

She found the door of Elsie's room standing wide to admit the air—for the weather was now growing very warm indeed—and looking in, she perceived the little girl half reclining upon a sofa, her head resting on the arm, her hands clasped in her lap, and her sad, dreamy eyes, tearless and dry, gazing mournfully into vacancy, as though her thoughts were far away, following the wanderings of her absent father. She seemed to have been reading, or trying to read, but the book had fallen from her hand, and lay unheeded on the floor.

Mrs. Travilla, stood for several minutes gazing with tearful eyes at the melancholy little figure, marking with an aching heart the ravages that sorrow had already made in the wan child face; then stealing softly in, sat down by her side, and took the little forlorn one into her kind motherly embrace, laying the weary little head down on her breast.

Elsie did not speak, but merely raised her eyes for an instant to Mrs. Travilla's face, with the dreary smile her son had spoken of, and then dropped them again with a sigh that was half a sob.

Mrs. Travilla pressed her quivering lips on the child's forehead, and a scalding tear fell on her cheek.

Elsie started, and again raising her mournful eyes, said, in a husky whisper, "Don't, dear Mrs. Travilla *don't* cry. I never *cry* now."

"And why not, darling? Tears are often a blessed relief to an aching heart, and I think it would do you good; these dry eyes need it."

"No—no—I *cannot*; they are all dried up—and it is well, for they always displeased my papa,"

There was a dreary hopelessness in her tone, and in the mournful shake of her head, that was very touching.

Mrs. Travilla sighed, and pressed the little form closer to her heart.

"Elsie, dear," she said, "you must not give way to despair. Your troubles have not come by chance; you know, darling, who has sent them; and remember, it is those whom the Lord *loveth* he chasteneth, and he will not *always* chide, neither will he keep his anger forever."

"Is he angry with me?" she asked fearfully.

"No, dearest, it is all sent in *love*; we cannot see the reason now, but one day we shall—when we get home to our Father's house, for then everything will be made plain; it may be, Elsie dear, that you, by your steady adherence to the right, are to be made the honored instrument in bringing your father to a saving knowledge of Christ. You would be willing to suffer a great deal for that, dear child, would you not? even all you are suffering now?"

"Ah, yes, indeed!" she said earnestly, clasping her hands together; "but I am afraid it is *not that*! I am afraid it is because I loved my papa *too* well, my dear, *dear* papa—and God is angry with me—and now I shall never, never see him again,"

She groaned aloud, and covered her face with her hands; and now the tears fell like rain, and her whole frame shook with convulsive sobs.

Mrs. Travilla hailed this outburst of grief with deep thankfulness, knowing that it was far better for her than that unnatural apathy, and that when the first violence of the storm had subsided, the aching heart would find itself relieved of half its load.

She gently soothed the little weeper until she began to grow calm again, and the sobs were almost hushed, and the tears fell softly and quietly.

Then she said, in low, tender tones, "Yes, my darling, you will see him again; I feel quite sure of it. God is the hearer of prayer, and he will hear yours for your dear father."

"And will he send my papa hack to me I oh, will he come *soon*? do you think he will, dear Mrs. Travilla?" she asked eagerly.

"I don't know, darling; I cannot tell *that*; but one thing we do know, that it is *all* in God's hands, and he will do just what is best both for you and your father. He may see fit to restore you to each other in a few weeks or months, and I hope and trust he will; but however *that* may be, darling, remember the words of the Lord Jesus, how he said, 'Your Father knoweth that ye have *need* of *all* these things.' He will not send you any unnecessary trial, nor allow you to suffer one pang that you do not need. It may be that he saw you were loving your earthly father too well, and has removed him from you for a time, that thus he may draw you nearer to himself; but never doubt for one moment, dear one, that it is all done in *love*. 'As many as I *love*, I rebuke and chasten.' They are the dear Saviour's own words."

When Mrs. Travilla at length rose to go, Elsie clung to her tearfully, entreating that she would stay a little longer.

"I will, dear child, since you wish it so much," said the lady, resuming her seat, "and I will come again very soon, if you think there will be no objection. But, Elsie, dear, can you not come to Ion, and spend the rest of your holidays with us? Both Edward and I would be delighted to have you, and I think we could make you happier than you are here."

"I cannot tell you how very much I should like it, dear Mrs. Travilla, but it is quite impossible," Elsie answered, with a sorrowful shake of the head. "I am not allowed to pay or receive visits any more; papa forbade it some time ago."

"Ah, indeed! I am very sorry, dear, for I fear that cuts me off from visiting you," said Mrs. Travilla, looking much disappointed. "However," she added more cheerfully, "I will get my son to write to your papa, and perhaps he may give you permission to visit us."

"No, ma'am, I cannot hope that he will," replied Elsie sadly; "papa never breaks his word or changes his mind."

"Ah! well, dear child," said her friend tenderly, "there is one precious blessing of which no one can deprive you—the presence and love of your Saviour; and if you have that, no one can make you wholly miserable. And now, dear child, I must go," she added, again clasping the little girl to her heart, and kissing her many times. "God bless and keep you, darling, till we meet again, and we will hope that time will come ere long."

Mr. Travilla was waiting to hand his mother into the carriage.

Neither of them spoke until they had fairly left Roselands behind them, but then he turned to her with an anxious, inquiring look, to which she replied:

"Yes, I found her in just the state you described, poor darling! but I think I left her a little happier; or rather, I should say, a little less wretched than I found her. Edward, Horace Dinsmore does not know what he is doing; that child's heart is breaking."

He gave an assenting nod, and turned away to hide his emotion.

"Can you not write to him, Edward, and describe the state she is in, and beg him, if he will not come home, at least to permit us to take her to Ion for a few weeks?" she asked, laying her hand on his arm.

"I will do so, mother, if you think it best," Mr. Travilla replied; "but I think I know Horace Dinsmore better than you do, and that such a proceeding would do more harm than good. He is very jealous of anything that looks like interference, especially between him and his child, and I fear it would only irritate him, and make him, if possible, still more determined. Were I asked to describe his character in a few words, I should say he is a man of indomitable will."

"Well, my son, perhaps you are right," said his mother, heaving a deep sigh; "and if so, I can see nothing more we can do but pray for the little girl."

Mrs. Travilla was right in thinking that her visit had done Elsie good; it had roused her out of the torpor of grief into which she had sunk; it had raised her from the depths of despair, and shown her the beacon light of hope still shining in the distance.

This last blow had come with such crushing weight that there had seemed to be no room left in her heart for a thought of comfort; but now her kind friend had reminded her of the precious promises, and the tender love that were still hers; love far exceeding that of any earthly parent—love that was able even to bring light out of all this thick darkness; love which was guiding and controlling all the events of her life, and would never allow her to suffer one unnecessary pang, but would remove the trial as soon as its needed work was done; and she was now no longer altogether comfortless.

When Mrs. Travilla had left, she took up her Bible—that precious little volume, her never-failing comforter—and in turning over its leaves her eye fell upon these words: "Unto you it is given in the behalf of Christ, not only to believe on him, but also to suffer for his sake."

They sent a thrill of joy to her heart; for was not *she* suffering for *his* sake? was it not because she loved him too well to disobey his commands, even to please her dearly beloved earthly father, that she was thus deprived of one privilege, and one comfort after another, and subjected to trials that wrung her very heart?

Yes, it was because she loved Jesus. She was bearing suffering for his dear sake, and here she was taught that even to be permitted to *suffer* for him, was a privilege. And she remembered, too, that in another place it is written: "If we *suffer*, we shall also reign with him."

Ah! those are tears of joy and thankfulness that are falling now. She has grown calm and peaceful, even happy, for the time, in the midst of all her sorrow.

CHAPTER IX

"Heaven oft in mercy smites, e'en when the blow
Severest is."

JOANNA BAILLIE'S ORRA.

"The heart knoweth his own bitterness."

PROV. 14:10.

But only a few days after Mrs. Travilla's visit, an event occurred, which, by exciting Elsie's sympathy for the sorrows of another, and thus preventing her from dwelling so constantly upon her own, was of great benefit to her.

Adelaide received a letter bringing tidings of the death of one who had been very dear to her. The blow was very sudden—entirely unexpected—and the poor girl was overwhelmed with grief, made all the harder to endure by the want of sympathy in her family.

Her parents had indeed given their consent to the contemplated union, but because the gentleman, though honorable, intelligent, educated and talented, was neither rich nor high-born, they had never very heartily approved of the connection, and were evidently rather relieved than afflicted by his death.

Elsie was the only one who really felt deeply for her aunt; and her silent, unobtrusive sympathy was very grateful.

The little girl seemed almost to forget her own sorrows, for the time, in trying to relieve those of her bereaved aunt. Elsie knew—and this made her sympathy far deeper and more heartfelt—that Adelaide had no consolation in her sore distress, but such miserable comfort as may be found in the things of earth. She had no compassionate Saviour to whom to carry her sorrows, but must bear them all alone; and while Elsie was permitted to walk in the light of his countenance, and to her ear there ever came the soft whispers of his love— "Fear not: thou art mine"—"*I* have loved thee with an *everlasting* love"—"*I* will *never* leave thee nor forsake thee," to Adelaide all was darkness and silence.

At first Elsie's sympathy was shown in various little kind offices; sitting for hours beside her aunt's couch, gently fanning her, handing her a drink of cold water, bringing her sweet-scented flowers, and anticipating every want. But at last she ventured to speak.

"Dear Aunt Adelaide," she whispered, "I am so sorry for you. I wish I knew how to comfort you."

"Oh, Elsie!" sobbed the mourner, "there is no comfort for me, I have lost my dearest treasure—my all—and no one cares."

"Dear Aunt Adelaide," replied the child timidly, "it is true I am only a little girl, but I do care very much for your grief; and surely your papa and mamma are very sorry for you."

Adelaide shook her head mournfully. "They are more glad than sorry," she said, bursting into tears.

"Well, dear aunty," said Elsie softly, "there is One who does feel for you, and who is able to comfort you if you will only go to him. One who loved you so well that he died to save you."

"No, no, Elsie! not me! He cannot care for me! He cannot love me, or he would never have taken away my Ernest," she sobbed.

"Dear Aunt Adelaide," said Elsie's low, sweet voice, "we cannot always tell what is best for us, and will make us happiest in the end.

"I remember once when I was a very little child, I was walking with mammy in a part of my guardian's grounds where we seldom went. I was running on before her, and I found a bush with some most beautiful red berries; they looked delicious, and I hastily gathered some, and was just putting them to my mouth when mammy, seeing what I was about, suddenly sprang forward, snatched them out of my hand, threw them on the ground, and tramped upon them; and then tearing up the bushes treated them in the same manner, while I stood by crying and calling her a naughty, cross mammy, to take my nice berries from me."

"Well," asked Adelaide, as the little girl paused in her narrative, "what do you mean by your story? You haven't finished it, but, of course, the berries were poisonous."

"Yes," said Elsie; "and mammy was wiser than I, and knew that what I so earnestly coveted would do me great injury."

"And now for the application," said Adelaide, interrupting her; "you mean that just as mammy was wiser than you, and took your treasure from you in kindness, so God is wise and kind in taking mine from me; but ah! Elsie, the analogy will not hold good; for my good, wise, kind Ernest could never have harmed me as the poisonous berries would you. No, no, no, he always did me good!" she cried with a passionate burst of grief.

Elsie waited until she grew calm again, and then said gently, "The Bible says, dear aunty, that God 'does not willingly afflict nor grieve the children of men.' Perhaps he saw that you loved your friend too well, and would never give your heart to Jesus unless he took him away, and so you could only live with him for a little while in this world. But now he has taken him to heaven, I hope—for Lora told me Mr. St. Clair was a Christian—and if you will only come to Jesus and take him for your Saviour, you can look forward to spending a happy eternity there with your friend.

"So, dear Aunt Adelaide, may we not believe that God, who is infinitely wise, and good, and kind, has sent you this great sorrow in love and compassion?"

Adelaide's only answer was a gentle pressure of the little hand she held, accompanied by a flood of tears. But after that she seemed to love Elsie better than, she ever had before, and to want her always by her side, often asking her to read a chapter in the Bible, a request with which the little girl always complied most gladly.

Adelaide was very silent, burying her thoughts almost entirely in her own bosom; but it was evident that the blessed teachings of the holy book were not altogether lost upon her, for the extreme violence of her grief gradually abated, and the expression of her countenance, though still sad, became gentle and patient.

And could Elsie thus minister consolation to another, and yet find no lessening of her own burden of sorrow? Assuredly not.

She could not repeat to her aunt the many sweet and precious promises of God's holy word, without having them brought home to her own heart with renewed power; she could not preach Jesus to another without finding him still nearer and dearer to her own soul; and though there were yet times when she was almost overwhelmed with grief, she could truly say that the "consolations of God were not small with her." There was often a weary, weary aching at her heart—such an unutterable longing for her father's love and favor as would send her weeping to her knees to plead long and earnestly that this trial might be removed; yet she well knew who had sent it, and was satisfied that it was one of the "*all* things which shall work together for good to them that love God," and she was at length enabled to say in reference to it: "Thy will, not mine, be done," and to bear her cross with patient submission.

But ah! there was many a bitter struggle, first! She had many sad and lonely hours; and there were times when the yearning of the poor little heart for her father's presence, and her father's love, was almost more than weak human nature could endure.

Sometimes she would walk her room, wringing her hands and weeping bitterly.

"Oh, papa! papa!" she would exclaim, again and again, "how can I bear it? how *can* I bear it? will you never, never come back? will you never, never love me again?"

And then would come up the memory of his words on that sad, sad day, when he left her—"Whenever my little daughter writes to me the words I have so vainly endeavored to induce her to speak, that very day, if possible, I will start for home"— and the thought that it was in her power to recall him at any time; it was but to write a few words and send them to him, and soon he would be with her—he would take her to his heart again, and this terrible trial would be over.

The temptation was fearfully strong; the struggle often long and terrible; and this fierce battle had to be fought again and again, and once the victory had wellnigh been lost.

She had struggled long; again and again had she resolved that she would not, could not, *dare* not yield! but vainly she strove to put away the sense of that weary, aching void in her heart— that longing, yearning desire for her father's love.

"I cannot bear it! oh, I *cannot* bear it!" she exclaimed, at length; and seizing a pen, she wrote hastily, and with trembling fingers, while the hot, blinding tears dropped thick and fast upon the paper—"Papa, come back! oh, come to me, and I will be and do all you ask, all you require."

But the pen dropped from her fingers, and she bowed her face upon her clasped hands with a cry of bitter anguish.

"How can I do this great wickedness and sin against God?" The words darted through her mind like a flash of lightning, and then the words of Jesus seemed to come to her ear in solemn tones: "He that loveth father and mother more than me, is not worthy of me!"

"What have I done?" she cried. "Has it come to this, that I must choose between my father and my Saviour? and *can* I give up the love of Jesus? oh, never, *never!*—

'Jesus, I my cross have taken
All to leave and follow thee.'"

she repeated, half aloud, with clasped hands, and an upward glance of her tearful eyes. Then, tearing into fragments what she had just written, she fell on her knees and prayed earnestly for pardon, and for strength to resist temptation, and to be "faithful unto death," that she might "receive the crown of life."

When Elsie rapped at her aunt's dressing-room door the next morning, no answer was returned, and after waiting a moment, she softly opened it, and entered, expecting to find her aunt sleeping. But no, though extended upon a couch, Adelaide was not sleeping, but lay with her face buried in the pillows, sobbing violently.

Elsie's eyes filled with tears, and softly approaching the mourner, she attempted to soothe her grief with words of gentle, loving sympathy.

"Oh! Elsie, you cannot feel for me; it is impossible!" exclaimed her aunt passionately. "*You* have never known sorrow to be compared to mine! You have never loved, and lost—you have known none but mere childish griefs."

"The heart knoweth his own bitterness!" thought Elsie, silent tears stealing down her cheeks, and her breast heaving with emotion.

"Dear Aunt Adelaide," she said in tremulous tones, "*I* think I *can* feel for you. Have I not known *some* sorrow? Is it nothing that I have pined all my life long for a mother's love? nothing to have been separated from the dear nurse, who had almost supplied her place? Oh, Aunt Adelaide!" she continued, with a burst of uncontrollable anguish, "is it nothing, *nothing* to be separated from my beloved father, my dear, only parent, whom I love better than my life—to be refused even a parting caress—to live month after month, and year after year under his frown—and to fear that his love may be lost to me forever? Oh! papa, papa, will you never, *never* love me again?" she cried, sinking on her knees, and covering her face with her hands, while the tears trickled fast between the slender fingers.

Her aunt's presence was for the moment entirely forgotten, and she was alone with her bitter grief.

Adelaide looked at her with a good deal of surprise. She had never before seen her give way to such a burst of sorrow, for Elsie was usually calm in the presence of others.

"Poor child!" she said, drawing the little girl towards her, and gently pushing back the hair from her forehead, "I should not have said that; you have your own troubles, I know; hard enough to bear, too. I think Horace is really cruel, and if I were you, Elsie, I would just give up loving him entirely, and never care for his absence or his displeasure."

"Oh, Aunt Adelaide! not love my own dear papa? I *must* love him! I could not help it if I would—no, not even if he were going to kill me; and please don't blame him; he does not mean to be cruel. But oh! if he would only love me!" sobbed the little girl.

"I am sure he does, Elsie, if that is any comfort; here is a letter from him; he speaks of you in the postscript; you may take it to your room and read it, if you like," replied her aunt, putting a letter into Elsie's hand. "Go now, child, and see if you can extract any comfort from it."

Elsie replied with a gush of tears and a kiss of thanks, for her little heart was much too full for speech. Clasping the precious letter tightly in her hand, she hastened to her own room and locked herself in. Then drawing it from the envelope, she kissed the well-known characters again and again, dashing away the blinding tears ere she could see to read.

It was short; merely a letter of condolence to Adelaide, expressing a brother's sympathy in her sorrow; but the postscript sent one ray of joy to the little sad heart of his daughter.

"Is Elsie well? I cannot altogether banish a feeling of anxiety regarding her health, for she was looking pale and thin when I left home. I trust to *you*, my dear sister, to send *immediately* for a physician, and also to write at once should she show any symptoms of disease. Remember she is my *only* and darling child—very near and dear to me still, in spite of the sad estrangement between us."

"Ah! then papa has not forgotten me! he does love me still—he calls me his darling child," murmured the little girl, dropping her tears upon the paper. "Oh, how glad, how glad I am! surely he will come back to me some day;" and she felt that she would be very willing to be sick if that would hasten his return.

CHAPTER X

"In this wild world the fondest and the best
Are the most tried, most troubled, and distress'd."

CRABBE.

It was about a week after this that Elsie's grandfather handed her a letter directed to her in her father's handwriting, and the little girl rushed away to her room with it, her heart beating wildly between hope and fear. Her hand trembled so that she could scarcely tear it open, and her eyes were so dimmed with tears that it was some moments before she could read a line.

It was kind, yes, even affectionate, and in some parts tender. But ah! it has brought no comfort to the little girl! else why does she finish with a burst of tears and sobs, and sinking upon her knees, hide her face in her hands, crying with a bitter, wailing cry, "Oh, papa! papa! papa!"

He told her of the estate he had purchased, and the improvements he had been making; of a suite of rooms he had had prepared and furnished expressly for her, close to his own apartments—and of the pleasant home he hoped they would have there together, promising to dispense with a governess and teach her himself, for that he knew she would greatly prefer.

He drew a bright picture of the peaceful, happy life they might lead; but finished by telling her that the condition was entire, unconditional submission on her part, and the alternative a boarding-school, at a distance from home and friends.

He had, on separating her from her nurse, forbidden her to hold any communication with her, or even to ride in the direction of the Oaks—as his estate was called—and Elsie had scrupulously obeyed him; but now he bade her go and see the lovely home and beautiful apartments he had prepared for her, and judge for herself of the happiness she might enjoy there—loved, and caressed, and taught by him—and then decide.

"If she were ready to give up her wilfulness," he wrote, "she might answer him immediately; and he would then return and their new home should receive them, and their new life begin at once. But if she were still inclined to be stubborn and rebellious, she must take a month to consider, ere he would receive her reply."

Ah! to little Elsie it was a most enchanting picture he had drawn. To live in her father's house—his own home and hers—to be his constant and loved companion—to exchange Miss Day's teaching for his—to walk, to ride, to sit with him—in a word, to live in the sunshine of his love—oh, it would be paradise upon earth!

And then the alternative! Oh, how dreadful seemed to the shrinking, sensitive child, the very thought of being sent away amongst entire strangers, who could not be expected to care for her, or love her; who would have no sympathy with her highest hopes and desires, and instead of assisting her to walk in the narrow way, would strive to turn her feet aside into the paths of worldly conformity and sin: for, alas! she well knew it was only to the care of such persons her father would be likely to commit her, wishing, as he did, to root out of her mind what he was pleased to call the "narrow prejudices of her unfortunate early training." Poor child! she shrank from it in terror and dismay.

But should she choose that which her poor, hungry heart so yearned for—the home with her father—she must pledge herself to take as her rule of faith and practice, *not* God's holy word, which had hitherto been her guide-book, but her father's wishes and commands, which she well knew would often be entirely opposed to its teachings.

It was indeed a hard choice; but Elsie could not hesitate where the path of duty was so plain. She seemed to hear a voice saying to her: "This is the way, walk ye in it." "We ought to obey God rather than men."

"Ah!" she murmured, "I *cannot* do this great wickedness and sin against God, for if my earthly father's frown is so dreadful, so *very* hard to bear, how much worse would be my heavenly Father's? But, oh, that boarding-school! How can I ever endure its trials and temptations? I am so weak and sinful! Ah! if papa would but spare me this trial—if he would only let me stay at home—but he will not—for he has *said* I must go, and never breaks his word;" and again her tears fell fast, but she dashed them away and took up her Bible.

It opened at the fiftieth chapter of Isaiah, and her eye fell upon these words: "For the Lord God will help me: therefore shall I not be confounded: therefore have I set my face like a flint, and I know that I shall not be ashamed. Who is among you that feareth the Lord, that obeyeth the voice of his servant, that walketh in darkness and hath no light? let him trust in the name of the Lord, and stay upon his God."

Ah! here was comfort. "The Lord God will help me!" she repeated; and bowing her face over the holy book she gave thanks for the precious promise, and earnestly, tearfully pleaded that it might be fulfilled unto her.

Then rising from her knees, she bathed her eyes and rang for Fanny to prepare her for her ride. It was the usual hour for it, her horse was already at the door, and very soon the little girl might have been seen galloping up the road towards the Oaks, quite alone, excepting that Jim, her constant attendant, rode some yards in the rear.

It was a pleasant summer morning; there had been just rain enough the night before to cool the air and lay the dust, and everything was looking fresh and beautiful—and had the little Elsie's heart been as light and free from care as would have seemed natural to one of her age, she would no doubt have enjoyed her ride extremely. It was but a short one, and the place well known to her, for she had often passed it, though she had never yet been in the grounds.

In a few moments she reached the gate, and Jim having dismounted and opened it for her, she rode leisurely up a broad, gravelled carriage-way, which wound about through the grounds, giving the traveller a number of beautiful views ere he reached the house, a large building of dark-gray stone, which stood so far back, and was so entirely hidden by trees and shrubbery, as to be quite invisible from the highway. Now the road was shaded on either hand by large trees, their branches almost meeting overhead, and anon, an opening in their ranks afforded a glimpse of some charming little valley, some sequestered nook amongst the hills, some grassy meadow, or field of golden wheat, or a far-off view of the sea.

"Oh, how lovely!" murmured the little girl, dropping the reins on her horse's neck and gazing about her with eyes now sparkling with pleasure, now dimmed with tears; for, alas! these lovely scenes were not for her; at least not now, and it might be, never; and her heart was very sad.

At length she reached the house. Chloe met her at the door, and clasped her to her bosom with tears of joy and thankfulness.

"Bless de Lord for his goodness in sendin' my chile back to her ole mammy again," she said; "I'se so glad, darlin', so berry glad!"

And as she spoke she drew the little girl into a pleasant room, fitted up with books and pictures, couches and easy-chairs and tables, with every convenience for writing, drawing, etc.

"Dis am Massa Horace's study," she said, in answer to the eager, inquiring glance Elsie sent round the room, while she removed her hat and habit, and seated her in one of the softly-cushioned chairs; "an' de next room is your own little sittin' room, an' jes de prettiest ever was seen, your ole mammy tinks; and now dat she's got her chile back again she'll be as happy as de day am long."

"Oh, mammy," sobbed the child, "I am not to stay."

Chloe's look of delight changed to one of blank dismay.

"But you are comin' soon, darlin'?" she said inquiringly. "I tink Massa Horace 'tends to be here 'fore long, sartain, kase he's had de whole house fixed up so fine; an' I'se sure he never take so much trouble, an' spend such loads ob money fixin' up such pretty rooms for you, ef he didn't love you dearly, an' 'tend to have you here 'long with himself."

Elsie shook her head sorrowfully. "No, mammy, he says not unless I give up my wilfulness, and promise to do exactly as he bids me; and if I will not do that, I am to be sent away to boarding-school."

The last words came with a great sob, as she flung herself into Chloe's outstretched arms, and hid her face on her bosom.

"Poor darlin'! poor little pet!" murmured the nurse, hugging her tight, while her own tears fell in great drops on the golden curls. "I thought your troubles were all over. I s'posed Massa Horace had found out you wasn't bad after all, an' was comin' right home to live with you in dis beautiful place. But dere, don't, don't you go for to break your little heart 'bout it, dear; I'se sure de good Lord make um all come right in de end."

Elsie made no reply, and for a little while they mingled their tears in silence. Then she raised her head, and gently releasing herself from Chloe's embrace, said, "Now, mammy, I must go all about and see everything, for that was papa's command."

Chloe silently led the way through halls, parlors, drawing-room, library, dining, sitting and bed-rooms, servants' apartments, kitchen, pantry, and all; then out into the grounds, visiting in turn vegetable and flower gardens, lawn, hot-houses and grapery; and finally, bringing the little girl back to her papa's study, she led her from there into his bed-room and dressing-room, and then to her own apartments, which she had reserved to the last. These were three—bed-room, sitting-room, and dressing-room—all beautifully furnished with every comfort and convenience.

Elsie had gazed on all with a yearning heart, and eyes constantly swimming in tears. "Ah! mammy," she exclaimed more than once, "what a lovely, *lovely* home! how happy we might be here!"

The sight of her father's rooms and her own affected her the most, and the tears fell fast as she passed slowly from one to another. Her own little sitting-room was the last; and here sinking down in an easy-chair, she gazed about her silently and tearfully. On one side the windows looked out upon a beautiful flower-garden, while beyond were hills and woods; on the other, glass doors opened out upon a grassy lawn, shaded by large trees, and beyond, far away in the distance, rolled the blue sea; all around her she saw the evidences of a father's thoughtful love; a beautiful piano, a harp, a small work-table, well furnished with every requisite; books, drawing materials—everything to give pleasure and employment; while luxurious couches and easy-chairs invited to rest and repose. Several rare pictures, too, adorned the walls.

Elsie was very fond of paintings, and when she had gazed her fill upon the lovely landscape without, she turned from one of these to another with interest and pleasure; but one was covered, and she was in the act of raising her hand to draw aside the curtain, when her nurse stopped her, saying, "Not now, darlin', try de piano first."

She opened the instrument as she spoke, and Elsie, running her fingers over the keys, remarked that it was the sweetest-toned she had ever heard.

Chloe begged her to play, urging her request on the plea that it was so very long since she had heard her, and she might not have another opportunity soon.

Just at that instant a little bird on a tree near the door poured forth his joy in a gush of glad melody, and Elsie, again running her fingers lightly over the keys, sang with touching sweetness and pathos—

> "Ye banks an' braes o' bonny Doon,
> How can ye look sae bright an' fair?
> How can you sing, ye little bird,
> An' I sae weary, full of care?" etc.

The words seemed to come from her very heart, and her voice, though sweet and clear, was full of tears.

Chloe sobbed aloud, and Elsie, looking lovingly at her, said softly, "Don't, dear mammy! I will sing a better one;" and she played and sang—

"He doeth all things well."

Then rising, she closed the instrument, saying, "Now, mammy, let me see the picture."

Chloe then drew aside the curtain; and Elsie, with clasped hands and streaming eyes, stood for many minutes gazing upon a life-sized and speaking portrait of her father.

"Papa! papa!" she sobbed, "my own darling, precious papa!

Oh! could you but know how dearly your little Elsie loves you!"

"Don't now, darlin'! don't take on so dreadful! It jes breaks your ole mammy's heart to see her chile so 'stressed," Chloe said, passing her arm around the little girl's waist, and laying her head on her bosom.

"Oh, mammy, will he ever smile on me again? Shall I ever live with him in this dear home?" sobbed the poor child. "Oh! it is hard, hard to give it all up—to have papa always displeased with me. Oh, mammy, there is such a weary aching at my heart—is it *never* to be satisfied?"

"My poor, poor chile! my poor little pet, I'se *sure* it'll all come right by-an'-by," replied Chloe soothingly, as soon as emotion would suffer her to speak. "You know it is de Lord that sends all our 'flictions, an' you must 'member de pretty words you was jes a singin', 'He doeth *all* things well.' He says, 'What I do thou knowest not now, but thou shalt know here after.' De great God can change your father's heart, and 'cline him to 'spect your principles, and I *do* blieve he will do it."

Elsie sobbed out her dread of the boarding-school, with its loneliness and its temptations.

"Now don't you go for to be 'fraid of all dat, darlin'," replied her nurse. "Has you forgotten how it says in de good book, 'Lo, I am with you *always*, even unto the end of the world'? an' if *he* is with you, who can hurt you? Jes *nobody*."

A text came to Elsie's mind: "The eternal God is thy refuge, and underneath are the everlasting arms!" and lifting her head, she dashed away her tears.

"No," she said, "I will *not* be afraid; at least I will *try* not to be. 'The Lord is my light and my salvation; whom shall I fear? the Lord is the strength of my life; of whom shall I be afraid?' But, oh! mammy, I must go now, and I feel as if I were saying farewell to you and this sweet home forever; as if I were never to live in these pretty rooms—never to see them again."

"Hush! hush, darlin'! 'tain't never best to borrow trouble, an' I'se sure you'll come back one ob dese days," replied Chloe, forcing herself to speak cheerfully, though her heart ached as she looked into the soft, hazel eyes, all dimmed with tears, and marked how thin and pale the dear little face had grown.

Elsie was passing around the room again, taking a farewell look at each picture and piece of furniture; then she stood a moment gazing out over the lawn, to the rolling sea beyond.

She was murmuring something to herself, and Chloe started as her ear faintly caught the words: "In my Father's house are many mansions."

"Mammy!" said the child, suddenly turning and taking her hand, "look yonder!" and she pointed with her finger. "Do you see that beautiful, tall tree that casts such a thick shade? I want to be buried right there, where papa can see my grave when he sits in here, and think that I am with him yet. When I am gone, mammy, you must tell him that I told you this. It would be so pleasant to be there—it is such a lovely spot, and the distant murmur of the sea seems like a lullaby to sing the weary one to rest." She added, dreamily, "I would like to lie down there now."

"Why, what you talkin' 'bout, Miss Elsie? My chile musn't say such tings!" exclaimed Chloe in great alarm. "Your ole mammy 'spects to die long 'nough 'fore you do. You's berry young, an? 'tain't worth while to begin talkin' 'bout dyin' yet."

Elsie smiled sadly.

"But you know, mammy," she said, "that death often comes to the youngest. Mamma died young, and so may I. I am afraid it isn't right, but sometimes I am so sad and weary that I cannot help longing very much to die, and go to be with her and with

Jesus; for they would always love me, and I should never be lonely any more. Oh! mammy, mammy, must we part?—shall I ever see you again?" she cried, throwing herself into her nurse's arms.

"God bless an' keep you, darlin'!" Chloe said, folding her to her heart; "de good Lord take care ob my precious lamb, an' bring her back to her ole mammy again, 'fore long."

Elsie shut herself into her own room on her return to Roselands, and was not seen again that day by any one but her maid, until just at dusk Adelaide rapped softly at her door.

Elsie's voice, in a low, tremulous tone, answered, "Come in," and Adelaide entered.

The little girl was just in the act of closing her writing-desk, and her aunt thought she had been weeping, but the light was so uncertain that she might have been mistaken.

"My poor darling!" she said in low, pitiful accents, as, passing her arm around the child's waist, she drew her down to a seat beside herself upon the sofa.

Elsie did not speak, but dropping her head upon Adelaide's shoulder, burst into tears.

"My poor child! don't cry so; better days will come," said her aunt soothingly, running her fingers through Elsie's soft curls.

"I know what has been the trial of to-day," she continued, still using the same gentle, caressing tone, "for I, too, had a letter from your papa, in which he told me what he had said to you. You have been to see your new home. I have seen it several times and think it very lovely, and some day I hope and expect you and your papa will be very happy there."

Elsie shook her head sorrowfully.

"Not *now*, I know," said Adelaide, "for I have no need to ask what your decision has been; but I am hoping and praying that God may work the same change in your father's views and feelings which has been lately wrought in mine; and then he will love you all the better for your steadfast determination to obey God rather than man."

"Oh, Aunt Adelaide! will it *ever* be?" sighed the poor child; "the time seems so very long! It is so dreadful to live without my papa's love!"

"He does love you, Elsie, and I really think he suffers nearly as much as you do; but he thinks he is right in what he requires of you, and he is so very determined, and so anxious to make a gay, fashionable woman of you—cure you of those absurd, puritanical notions, as he expresses it—that I fear he will never relent until his heart is changed; but God is able to do that."

"Oh, Aunt Adelaide!" said the little girl mournfully, "pray for me, that I may be enabled to wait patiently until that time shall come, and never permitted to indulge rebellious feelings towards papa."

Adelaide kissed her softly. "Poor child!" she whispered, "it is a hard trial; but try, dearest, to remember who sends it."

She was silent a moment; then said, reluctantly, "Elsie, your papa has entrusted me with a message to you, which I was to deliver after your visit to the Oaks, unless you had then come to the resolution to comply with his wishes, or rather, his commands."

She paused, and Elsie, trembling, and almost holding her breath, asked fearfully, "What is it, Aunt Adelaide?"

"Poor darling!" murmured Adelaide, clasping the little form more closely, and pressing her lips to the fair brow; "I wish I could save you from it. He says that if you continue obdurate, he has quite determined to send you to a convent to be educated."

As Adelaide made this announcement, she pitied the child from the bottom of her heart; for she knew that much of Elsie's reading had been on the subject of Popery and Papal institutions; that she had pored over histories of the terrible tortures of the Inquisition and stories of martyrs and captive nuns, until she had imbibed an intense horror and dread of everything connected with that form of error and superstition. Yet, knowing all this, Adelaide was hardly prepared for the effect of her communication.

"Oh, Aunt Adelaide!" almost shrieked the little girl, throwing her arms around her aunt's neck, and clinging to her, as if in mortal terror, "Save me! save me! Oh! tell papa I would rather he would kill me at once, than send me to such a place."

And she wept and sobbed, and wrung her hands in such grief and terror, that Adelaide grew absolutely frightened.

"They will not dare to hurt you, Elsie," she hastened to say.

"Oh, they will! they will!—they will try to make me go to mass, and pray to the Virgin, and bow to the crucifixes; and when I refuse, they will put me in a dungeon and torture me."

"Oh, no, child," replied Adelaide soothingly, "they will not *dare* to do so to *you*, because you will not be a nun, but only a boarder, and your papa would be sure to find it all out."

"No, no!" sobbed the little girl, "they will hide me from papa when he comes, and tell him that I want to take the veil, and refuse to see him; or else they will say that I am dead and buried. Oh, Aunt Adelaide, beg him not to put me there! I shall go crazy! I feel as if I were going crazy now!" and she put her hand to her head.

"Poor, poor child!" said Adelaide, weeping. "I wish it was in my power to help you. I would once have advised you to submit to all your father requires. I cannot do that now, but I will return some of your lessons to me. It is God, my poor darling, who sends you this trial, and he will give you strength according to your day. *He* will be with you, wherever you are, even should it be in a convent; for you know he says: '*I* will *never* leave thee, nor forsake thee;' and 'not a hair of your head shall fall to the ground without your Father.'"

"Yes, I know! I know!" Elsie answered, again pressing her hands to her head; "but I cannot think, and everything seems so dreadful."

Adelaide was much alarmed, for Elsie looked quite wild for a moment; but after staying with her for a considerable time, saying all she could to soothe and comfort her—reminding her that it would be some weeks ere the plan could be carried out, and that in that time something might occur to change her father's mind, she left her, though still in deep distress, apparently calm and composed.

CHAPTER XI

"In vain she seeks to close her weary eyes,
Those eyes still swim incessantly in tears—
Hope in her cheerless bosom fading dies,
Distracted by a thousand cruel fears,
While banish'd from his love forever she appears."

MRS. TIGHE'S PSYCHE.

When thus alone the little Elsie fell upon her knees, weeping and sobbing. "Oh!" she groaned, "I cannot, *cannot* bear it!"

Then she thought of the agony in the garden, and that bitter cry, "Father, if it be possible, let this cup pass from me!" followed by the submissive prayer, "If this cup may not pass from me except I drink it, thy will, not mine be done."

She opened her Bible and read of his sufferings, so meekly and patiently borne, without a single murmur or complaint; borne by One who was free from all stain of sin; born not for himself, but for others; sufferings to which her own were not for a moment to be compared; and then she prayed that she might bear the image of Jesus; that like him she might be enabled to yield a perfect submission to her heavenly Father's will, and to endure with patience and meekness whatever trial he might see fit to appoint her.

Elsie was far from well, and for many long hours after she had sought her pillow she lay tossing restlessly from side to side in mental and physical pain, her temples throbbing, and her heart aching with its intense longing for the love that now seemed farther from her than ever. And thought—troubled, anxious, distracting thought—was busy in her brain; all the stories of martyrs and captive nuns which she had ever read—all the descriptions of the horrible tortures inflicted by Rome upon her wretched victims, came vividly to her recollection, and when at length she fell asleep, it was but to wake again, trembling with fright from a dream that she was in the dungeons of the Inquisition.

Then again she slept, but only to dream of new horrors which seemed terribly real even when she awoke; and thus, between sleeping and waking, the hours dragged slowly along, until at last the day dawned, after what had seemed to the little girl the longest night she had ever known.

Her maid came in at the usual hour, and was surprised and alarmed to find her young mistress still in bed, with cheeks burning and eyes sparkling with fever, and talking in a wild, incoherent manner.

Rushing out of the room, Fanny hastened in search of Miss Adelaide, who, she had long since discovered, was the only one of the family that cared for Elsie; and in a few moments the young aunt was standing at the bedside, looking with tearful eyes at the little sufferer.

"Oh, Miss Adelaide!" whispered the girl, "I tink she's *berry* sick; shan't we send for de doctah?"

"Yes, tell Jim to go for him *immediately*, and to stop on his way back and tell Aunt Chloe that she is wanted here just as soon as she can possibly come," replied Adelaide quickly, and then she set herself to work to make the child as comfortable as possible, remaining beside her until Chloe came to take her place, which was in less than an hour after she had received the summons, and just as the breakfast-bell rang at Roselands.

"So Elsie has taken a fever, and there is no knowing what it is, or whether it is contagious or not," remarked Mrs. Dinsmore. "It is really fortunate that we were just going away for our summer trip. I shall take all the children now, and we will start this very day; what a good thing it is that Elsie has kept her room so constantly of late! Can you pack in time for the afternoon train, Adelaide?"

"I shall not go now, mamma," replied Adelaide quietly.

"Why not?" asked her mother in a tone of surprise.

"Because I prefer to stay with Elsie."

"What absurd folly!" exclaimed Mrs. Dinsmore. "Aunt Chloe will do everything that is necessary, and you don't know to what infection you may be exposing yourself."

"I don't think there is any danger, mamma; and if Elsie should be very ill Aunt Chloe will need assistance; and I am not willing to leave Horace's child to the care of servants. Elsie has been a great comfort to me in my sorrow," she added, with tears in her eyes, "and I will not forsake her now; and you know, mamma, it is no self-denial, for I have no heart for gayety. I would *much* rather stay."

"Certainly; stay if you like," answered her father, speaking for the first time. "I do not imagine that Elsie's disease is contagious; she has doubtless worried herself sick, and it would not look well to the neighbors for us all to run away and leave the child so ill. Ah! there is the doctor, and we will have his opinion," he exclaimed, as through the half-open door he caught a glimpse of the family physician descending the stairs. "Ask him in to breakfast, Pomp. Good-morning, doctor! how do you find your patient?"

"I think her quite a sick child, sir, though of the precise nature of her disease I am not yet able to form a decided opinion," replied the physician, accepting the offered seat at the table.

"Is it anything contagious?" inquired Mrs. Dinsmore anxiously.

"I cannot yet say certainly, madam, but I think not."

"Shall we send for Horace? that is, would you advise it?" asked Mr. Dinsmore hesitatingly.

"Oh, no," was the reply; "not until we have had more time to judge whether she is likely to be very ill; it may prove but a slight attack."

"I shall write this very day," was Adelaide's mental resolve, though she said nothing.

Mrs. Dinsmore hurried her preparations, and the middle of the afternoon found Adelaide and Elsie sole occupants of the house, with the exception of the servants. Adelaide watched the carriage as it rolled away, and then, with feelings of sadness and desolation, and a mind filled with anxious forebodings, returned to her station at Elsie's bedside.

The child was tossing about, moaning, and talking incoherently, and Adelaide sighed deeply at the thought that this was perhaps but the beginning of a long and serious illness, while she was painfully conscious of her own inexperience and want of skill in nursing.

"Oh!" she exclaimed half aloud, "if I only had some kind, experienced friend to advise and assist me, what a blessed relief it would be!"

There was a sound of carriage-wheels on the gravel walk below, and hastily turning to Chloe, she said, "Go down and tell them I must be excused. I cannot see visitors while my little niece is so very ill."

Chloe went, but returned almost immediately, followed by Mrs. Travilla.

With a half-smothered exclamation of delight, Adelaide threw herself into the kind, motherly arms extended to receive her, and burst into tears. Mrs. Travilla let them have their way for a moment, while she stroked her hair caressingly, and murmured a few soothing words. Then she said, softly, "Edward called at the gate this morning, and learned all about it; and I knew you were but young, and would feel lonely and anxious, and I love the dear child as if she were my own, and so I have come to stay and help you nurse her, if you will let me."

"*Let* you! dear Mrs. Travilla; I can never repay your kindness."

Mrs. Travilla only smiled, and pressed the hand she held; and then quietly laying aside her bonnet and shawl, took up her post at the bedside, with the air of one quite at home, and intending to be useful.

"It is such an inexpressible relief to see you sitting there," whispered Adelaide. "You don't know what a load you have taken off my mind."

But before Mrs. Travilla could reply, Elsie started up in the bed, with a wild outcry: "Oh, don't, papa! don't send me there! They will kill me! they will torture me! Oh, let me stay at home with you, and I will be very good."

Mrs. Travilla spoke soothingly to her, and persuaded her to lie down again.

Elsie looked at her quite rationally, and holding out her hand, with a faint smile, said: "Thank you, Mrs. Travilla; you are very kind to come to see me; I am very sick; my head hurts me so;" and she put her hand up to it, while again her eyes rolled wildly, and she shrieked out, "Oh, Aunt Adelaide! save me! save me! don't let them take me away to that dreadful place! Must I go now? to-day?" she asked in piteous accents. "Oh! I don't want to go!" and she clung shuddering to her aunt, who was bending over her, with eyes swimming in tears.

"No, darling, no," she said, "no one shall take you away; nobody shall hurt you." Then in answer to Mrs. Travilla's inquiring look, she explained, speaking in an undertone: "He had decided to place her in a convent, to complete her education. I told her of it last night," she added mournfully, "as he requested, and I very much fear that the fright and terror she suffered on that account have helped to bring on this attack."

"Poor, dear, precious lamb!" sighed Chloe, who stood at the foot of the bed, gazing sadly at her nursling, and wiping away tear after tear, as they chased each other down her sable cheek. "I wish Massa Horace could see her now. I'se sure he nebber say such cruel tings no more."

"He ought surely to be here! You have sent for him, Adelaide?" Mrs. Travilla said inquiringly. "She is very ill, and it is of great importance that her mind should be set at rest, if indeed it *can* be done at present."

"I wrote this morning," Adelaide said, "and I shall write every day until he comes."

Elsie caught the words, and turning with an eager look to her aunt, she again spoke quite rationally, "Are you writing to papa, Aunt Adelaide?" she asked. "Oh! *beg* him to come home soon, *very* soon; tell him I want to see him once more. Oh, Aunt Adelaide, he *will* kiss me when I am dying, won't he? Oh, say you think he will."

"I am *sure* of it, darling," replied Adelaide soothingly, as she bent down and kissed the little feverish cheek; "but we are not going to let you die yet."

"But will you ask papa? will you *beg* him to come?" pleaded the little voice still more eagerly.

"I will, I *have*, darling," replied the aunt; "and I doubt not that he will start for home immediately on receiving my letter."

Day after day the fever raged in Elsie's veins, and when at length it was subdued, it left her very weak indeed; but the doctor pronounced her free from disease, and said she only needed good nursing and nutritious diet to restore her to health; and Mrs. Travilla and Chloe, who had watched day and night by her couch with intense anxiety, wept for joy and thankfulness that their precious one was yet spared to them.

But alas! their hopes faded again, as day after day the little girl lay on her bed, weak and languid, making no progress toward recovery, but rather losing strength.

The doctor shook his head with a disappointed air, and drawing Adelaide aside, said, "I cannot understand it, Miss Dinsmore; has she any mental trouble? She seems to me like one who has some weight of care or sorrow pressing upon her, and sapping the very springs of life. She appears to have no desire to recover; she needs something to rouse her, and revive her love of life. *Is* there anything on her mind? If so, it must be removed, or she will certainly die."

"She is very anxious to see her father," said Adelaide, weeping. "Oh, *how* I wish he would come! I cannot imagine what keeps him. I have written again and again."

"I wish he was here, indeed," replied the doctor, with a look of great anxiety. "Miss Adelaide," he suddenly exclaimed, "if she were ten years older I should say she was dying of a broken heart, but she is so young the idea is absurd."

"You are right, doctor! it is nothing but that. Oh! how I wish Horace would come!" cried Adelaide, walking up and down the room, and wringing her hands. "Do you notice, doctor," she asked, stopping before him, "how she watches the opening of the door, and starts and trembles at every sound? It is killing her, for she is too weak to bear it. Oh! If Horace would only come, and set her mind at rest! He has been displeased with her, and threatened to send her to a convent, of which she has a great horror and dread—and she idolizes him; and so his anger and his threats have had this sad effect upon her, poor child!"

"Write again, Miss Adelaide, and tell him that her *life* depends upon his speedy return and a reconciliation with him. If he would not lose her he must at *once* relieve her of every fear and anxiety," said the physician, taking up his hat. "*That* is the medicine she needs, and the *only* one that will do her much good. Good-morning. I will be in again at noon."

And Adelaide, scarcely waiting to see him off, rushed away to her room to write to her brother exactly what he had told her, beseeching him, if he had any love for his child, to return immediately. The paper was all blistered with her tears, for they fell so fast it was with difficulty she could see to write.

"*She* has spoken from the first as though it were a settled thing that this sickness was to be her last; and now a great, a terrible dread is coming over me that she is right. Oh, Horace, will you not come and save her?"

Thus Adelaide closed her note; then sealing and despatching it, she returned to the bedside of her little niece.

Elsie lay quietly with her eyes closed, but there was an expression of pain upon her features. Mrs. Travilla sat beside her, holding one little hand in hers, and gazing with tearful eyes upon the little wan face she had learned to love so well.

Presently those beautiful eyes unclosed, and turned upon her with an expression of anguish that touched her to the very heart.

"What is it, darling—are you in pain?" she asked, leaning over her, and speaking in tones of the tenderest solicitude.

"Oh! Mrs. Travilla," moaned the little girl, "my sins—my sins—they are so many—so black. 'Without holiness no man shall see the Lord.' God says it; and I—I am *not* holy—I am *vile*—oh, *so* vile, so sinful! Shall I ever see his face? how can I dare to venture into his presence!"

She spoke slowly, gaspingly—her voice sometimes sinking almost to a whisper; so that, but for the death-like stillness of the room, her words would scarcely have been audible.

Mrs. Travilla's tears were falling very fast, and it was a moment ere she could command her voice to reply.

"My precious, *precious* child," she said, "*He* is able to save to the *uttermost*. 'The blood of Jesus Christ cleanseth from *all* sin.' He will wash you in that precious fountain opened for sin, and for all uncleanness. He will clothe you with the robe of his own righteousness, and present you faultless before the throne of God, without spot or wrinkle, or any such thing. *He* has said it, and shall it not come to pass, my darling? Yes, dear child, I am confident of this very thing, that he who has begun a good work in you will perform it until the day of Jesus Christ."

"Oh, yes, he will, I know he will. Precious Jesus! *my* Saviour," murmured the little one, a smile of heavenly peace and joy overspreading her features; and, closing her eyes, she seemed to sleep, while Adelaide, unable longer to control her feelings, stole softly from the room, to seek a place where she might weep without restraint.

An hour later Adelaide sat alone by the bedside, Mrs. Travilla having found it necessary to return to Ion for a few hours, while Chloe had gone down to the kitchen to see to the preparation of some new delicacy with which she hoped to tempt Elsie's failing appetite.

Adelaide had been sitting for some moments gazing sadly at the little pale, thin face, so fair, so sad, yet so full of meekness and resignation. Her eyes filled as she looked, and thought of all that they feared.

"Elsie, darling! precious little one," she murmured in low, tremulous tones, as she leant over the child in tender solicitude.

"Dear Aunt Adelaide, how kind you are to me," said the little girl, opening her eyes and looking up lovingly into her aunt's face.

There was a sound of carriage-wheels.

"Is it my papa?" asked Elsie, starting and trembling.

Adelaide sprang to the window. No, it was only a kind neighbor, come to inquire how the invalid was.

A look of keen disappointment passed over the expressive countenance of the little girl—the white lids drooped over the soft eyes, and large tears stole from beneath the long dark lashes, and rolled silently down her cheeks.

"He will not come in time," she whispered, as if talking to herself. "Oh, papa, I want to hear you say you forgive all my naughtiness. I want one kiss before I go. Oh, take me in your arms, papa, and press me to your heart, and say you love me yet!"

Adelaide could bear it no longer; the mournful, pleading tones went to her very heart. "Dear, *dear* child," she cried, bending over her with streaming eyes, "he *does* love you! I *know* it. *You* are the very idol of his heart; and you must not die. Oh, darling, live for his sake, and for mine. He will soon, be here, and then it will be all right; he will be so thankful that he has not lost you, that he will never allow you to be separated from him again."

"No, oh, no! he said he did not love a rebellious child," she sobbed; "he said he would never kiss me again until I submit; and you know I cannot do that; and oh, Aunt Adelaide, *he never breaks his word!*"

"Oh, Horace! Horace! will you *never* come? will you let her die? so young, so sweet, so fair!" wept Adelaide, wringing her hands.

But Elsie was speaking again, and she controlled herself to listen.

"Aunt Adelaide," she murmured, in low, feeble tones, "I am too weak to hold a pen; will you write something for me?"

"I will, darling; I will do anything I can for you," she replied.

Then turning to the maid, who had just entered the room: "Fanny," she said, "bring Miss Elsie's writing-desk here, and set it close to the bedside. Now you may take that waiter down-stairs, and you need not come in again until I ring for you."

Elsie had started and turned her head on the opening of the door, as she invariably did, looking longingly, eagerly toward it—then turned away again with a sigh of disappointment.

"Poor papa! poor, dear papa!" she murmured to herself; "he will be so lonely without his little daughter. My heart aches for you, my own papa."

"I am quite ready now, Elsie, dear. What do you wish me to write?" asked her aunt.

"Aunt Adelaide," said the little girl, looking earnestly at her, "do you know how much mamma was worth? how much money I would have if I lived to grow up?"

"No, dear," she replied, much surprised at the question, for even in health Elsie had never seemed to care for riches; "I cannot say exactly, but I know it is a great many thousands."

"And it will all be papa's when I am gone, I suppose. I am glad of that. But I would like to give some of it away, if I might. I know I have no *right*, because I am so young—papa has told me that several times—but I think he will like to do what I wish with a part of it; don't you think so, too, Aunt Adelaide?"

Adelaide nodded assent; she dared not trust herself to speak, for she began to comprehend that it was neither more nor less than the last will and testament of her little niece, which she was requesting her to write.

"Well, then, Aunt Adelaide," said the feeble little voice, "please write down that I want my dear papa to support one missionary to the heathen out of my money. Now say that I know he will take care of my poor old mammy as long as she lives, and I hope that, for his little Elsie's sake, he will be very, *very* kind to her, and give her everything she wants. And I want him to do something for Mrs. Murray, too. Mamma loved her, and so do I; for she was very kind to me always, and taught me about Jesus; and so I want papa to give her a certain sum every year; enough to keep her quite comfortable, for she is getting old, and I am afraid she is very poor."

"I have written all that, Elsie; is there anything more?" asked Adelaide, scarcely able to command her voice.

"Yes, if you please," replied the little girl; and she went on to name every member of the family, from her grandfather down—servants included—setting apart some little gift for each; most of them things already in her possession, though some few were to be bought, if her papa was willing. Even Miss Day was not forgotten, and to her Elsie bequeathed a valuable ring. To her Aunt Adelaide she gave her papa's miniature, a lock of her own hair, and a small Testament.

"Are you really willing to part with your papa's picture, Elsie, dear?" asked Adelaide. "I thought you valued it very highly."

"I cannot take it with me, dear Aunt Adelaide," was the quiet reply, "and he will not want it himself, and I believe you love him better than any one else. Oh, Aunt Adelaide, comfort my poor papa when I am gone, and he is left *all alone*!" she exclaimed, the big tears chasing each other down her cheeks. "It is so sad to be alone, with nobody to love you; my poor, poor papa! I am all he has."

"You have given nothing to him, Elsie," said Adelaide, wiping away her tears, and glancing over what she had just written.

"Yes, there is a little packet in my desk directed to him. Please give him that, and my dear, precious little Bible. I can't part with it yet, but when I am gone."

She then mentioned that she had pointed out to her nurse the spot where she wished to be buried, and added that she did not want any monument, but just a plain white stone with her name and age, and a text of Scripture.

"That is all, and thank you very much, dear auntie," she said, when Adelaide had finished writing down her directions; "now, please put the pen in my fingers and hold the paper here, and I think I can sign my name."

She did so quite legibly, although her hand trembled with weakness; and then, at her request, the paper was folded, sealed, and placed in her desk, to be given after her death to her father, along with the packet.

It was evidently a great relief to Elsie to get these things off her mind, yet talking so long had exhausted all her little strength, and Adelaide, much alarmed at the death-like pallor of her countenance, and the sinking of her voice, now insisted that she should lie quiet and try to sleep.

Elsie made an effort to obey, but her fever was returning, and she was growing very restless again.

"I cannot, Aunt Adelaide," she said at length, "and I want to tell you a little more to say to papa, for I may not be able again. I am afraid he will not come until I am gone, and he will be so sorry; my poor, poor papa! Tell him that I loved him to the very last; that I longed to ask him to forgive me for all the naughty, rebellious feelings I have ever had towards him. Twice, since he has been displeased with me, I have rebelled in my heart—once when he refused to give me Miss Allison's letter, and again when he sent mammy away; it was only for a few moments each time; but it was very wicked, and I am very sorry."

Sobs choked her utterance.

"Poor darling!" said Adelaide, crying bitterly. "I don't think an angel could have borne it better, and I know he will reproach himself for his cruelty to you."

"Oh, Aunt Adelaide, *don't* say that; don't *let* him reproach himself, but say all you can to comfort him. I am his child—he had a right—and he only wanted to make me good—and I needed it all, or God would not have permitted it."

"Oh, Elsie, darling, I *cannot* give you up! you *must not* die!" sobbed Adelaide, bending over her, her tears falling fast on Elsie's bright curls. "It is too hard to see you die so young, and with so much to live for."

"It is very *sweet* to go home so soon," murmured the soft, low voice of the little one, "so sweet to go and live with Jesus, and be free from sin forever!"

Adelaide made no reply, and for a moment her bitter sobbing was the only sound that broke the stillness of the room.

"Don't cry so, dear auntie," Elsie said faintly. "I am very happy—only I want to see my father." She added something incoherently, and Adelaide perceived, with excessive alarm, that her mind was again beginning to wander.

She hastily summoned a servant and despatched a message to the physician, urging him to come immediately, as there was an alarming change in his patient.

Never in all her life had Adelaide suffered such anxiety and distress as during the next half-hour, which she and the faithful Chloe spent by the bedside, watching the restless tossings of the little sufferer, whose fever and delirium seemed to increase every moment. Jim had not been able to find the doctor, and Mrs. Travilla was staying away longer than she had intended.

But at length she came, and, though evidently grieved and concerned at the change in Elsie, her quiet, collected manner calmed and soothed Adelaide.

"Oh, Mrs. Travilla," she whispered, "do you think she will die?"

"We will not give up hope yet, my dear," replied the old lady, trying to speak cheerfully; "but my greatest comfort, just at present, is the sure knowledge that she is prepared for any event. No one can doubt that she is a lamb of the Saviour's fold, and if he is about to gather her into his bosom—" She paused, overcome by emotion, then added in a tremulous tone, "It will be a sad thing to *us*, no doubt, but to her—dear little one—a blessed, *blessed* change."

"I cannot bear the thought," sobbed Adelaide, "but I have scarcely any hope now, because—" and then she told Mrs. Travilla what they had been doing in her absence.

"Don't let that discourage you, my dear," replied her friend soothingly. "I have no faith in presentiments, and while there is life there is hope."

Dr. Barton, the physician, came in at that moment, looked at his young patient, felt her pulse, and shook his head sorrowfully.

Adelaide watched his face with the deepest anxiety.

He passed his hand over Elsie's beautiful curls.

"It seems a sad pity," he remarked in a low tone to her aunt, "but they will have to be sacrificed; they must be cut off immediately, and her head shaved."

Adelaide shuddered and trembled. "Is there any hope, doctor?" she faltered almost under her breath.

"There is *life* yet, Miss Adelaide," he said, "and we must use all the means within our reach; but I wish her father was here. Have you heard nothing yet?"

"No, nothing, nothing!" she answered, in a tone of keen distress; then hastily left the room to give the necessary orders for carrying out the doctor's directions.

"No, no, you must not! Papa will not allow it—he will be very angry—he will punish me if you cut off my curls!" and Elsie's little hand was raised in a feeble attempt to push away the remorseless scissors that were severing the bright locks from her head.

"No, darling, he will not be displeased, because it is quite necessary to make you well." said Mrs. Travilla in her gentle, soothing tones; "and your papa would bid us do it, if he were here."

"No, no, don't cut it off. I *will* not, I *cannot* be a nun! Oh, papa, save me! save me!" she shrieked.

"Dear child, you are safe at home, with none but friends around you."

It was Mrs. Travilla's gentle voice again, and for a moment the child seemed calmed; but only for a moment; another wild fancy possessed her brain, and she cried out wildly, "Don't! don't!—take it away! I will not bow down to images! No, no, I will not." Then, with a bitter, wailing cry, that went to the heart of every one who heard it: "Oh, papa, don't be angry! I will be good! Oh, I am all alone, nobody to love me."

"Elsie, darling, we are all here, and we love you dearly, *dearly*," said Adelaide in quivering tones, while her scalding tears fell like rain upon the little hand she had taken in hers.

"My papa—I want my papa; but he said he would never kiss me till I submit;" the tone was low and plaintive, and the large mournful eyes were fixed upon Adelaide's face.

Then suddenly her gaze was directed upward, a bright smile overspread her features, and she exclaimed in joyous accents, "Yes, mamma, yes; I am coming! I will go with you!"

Adelaide turned away and went weeping from the room, unable to bear any more.

"Oh, Horace! Horace, what have you done!" she sobbed, as she walked up and down the hall, wringing her hands.

The doctor came out, but she was too much absorbed in her grief to notice him. He went to her, however, and took her hand.

"Miss Adelaide," he said kindly, "it is true your little niece is very ill, but we will not give up all hope yet. It is possible her father's presence may do something, and surely he will be here ere long. But try to calm yourself, my dear young lady, and hope for the best, or I fear I shall have another patient on my hands. I will stay with the little girl myself to-night, and I wish I could prevail upon you to lie down and take some rest, for I see you need it sadly. Have you had your tea?"

Adelaide shook her head. "I *could* not eat," she said sadly.

"You ought at least to *try*; it would do you good," he urged.

"No, you will not? well, then, you will lie down; indeed, you must; you will certainly be ill."

Adelaide looked the question she dared not ask.

"No," he said, "there's no *immediate* danger, and if there should be any important change I will call you."

And, reassured on that point, she yielded to his persuasions and went to bed.

CHAPTER XII

"I drink
So deep of grief, that he must only think,
Not dare to speak, that would express my woe:
Small rivers murmur, deep gulfs silent flow."

MARSTON'S SOPHONIESA.

It was no want of love for his child that had kept Mr. Dinsmore from at once obeying Adelaide's summons. He had left the place where she supposed him to be, and thus it happened that her letters did not reach him nearly so soon as she had expected.

But when at length they were put into his hands, and he read of Elsie's entreaty that he would come to her, and saw by the date how long she had been ill, his distress and alarm were most excessive, and within an hour he had set out on his return, travelling night and day with the greatest possible despatch.

Strangers wondered at the young, fine-looking man, who seemed in such desperate haste to reach the end of his journey—sat half the time with his watch in his hand, and looked so despairingly wretched whenever the train stopped for a moment.

Elsie was indeed, as Adelaide had said, the very idol of his

Martha Finley

heart; and at times he suffered but little less than she did; but his will was stronger even than his love, and he had fondly hoped that this separation from him would produce the change in her which he so much desired; and had thus far persuaded himself that he was only using the legitimate authority of a parent, and therefore acting quite right; and, in fact, with the truest kindness, because, as he reasoned, she would be happier all her life if once relieved from the supposed necessity of conforming to rules so strict and unbending. But suddenly his eyes seemed to have been opened to see his conduct in a new light, and he called himself a brute, a monster, a cruel persecutor, and longed to annihilate time and space, that he might clasp his child in his arms, tell her how dearly he loved her, and assure her that never again would he require her to do aught against her conscience.

Again and again he took out his sister's letters and read and re-read them, vainly trying to assure himself that there was no danger; that she *could* not be so very ill. "She is so young," he said to himself, "and has always been healthy, it *cannot* be that she will die." He started and shuddered at the word. "Oh, no! it is impossible!" he mentally exclaimed. "God is too merciful to send me so terrible an affliction."

He had not received Adelaide's last, and was therefore quite unprepared to find his child so near the borders of the grave.

It was early on the morning of the day after her fearful relapse, that a carriage drove rapidly up the avenue, and Horace Dinsmore looked from its window, half expecting to see again the little graceful figure that had been wont to stand upon the steps of the portico, ready to greet his arrival with such outgushings of joy and love.

But, "Pshaw!" he exclaimed to himself, "of course she is not yet able to leave her room; but my return will soon set her up again—the darling! My poor little pet!" he added, with a sigh, as memory brought her vividly before him as he had last seen her, and recalled her sorrowful, pleading looks and words; "my poor darling, you shall have all the love and caresses now that your heart can desire." And he sprang out, glancing up at the windows above, to see if she were not looking down at him; but she was not to be seen; yet it did not strike him as strange that all the shutters were closed, since it was the east side of the house, and a warm summer's sun was shining full upon them.

A servant met him at the door, looking grave and sad, but Mr. Dinsmore waited not to ask any questions, and merely giving the man a nod, sprang up the stairs, and hurried to his daughter's room, all dusty and travel-stained as he was.

He heard her laugh as he reached the door. "Ah! she must be a great deal better; she will soon be quite well again, now that I have come," he murmured to himself, with a smile, as he pushed it open.

But alas! what a sight met his eye. The doctor, Mrs. Travilla, Adelaide, and Chloe, all grouped about the bed, where lay his little daughter, tossing about and raving in the wildest delirium; now shrieking with fear, now laughing an unnatural, hysterical laugh, and so changed that no one could have recognized her; the little face so thin, the beautiful hair of which he had been so proud all gone, the eyes sunken deep in her head, and their soft light changed to the glare of insanity. Could it be Elsie, his own beautiful little Elsie? He could scarcely believe it, and a sickening feeling of horror and remorse crept over him.

No one seemed aware of his entrance, for all eyes were fixed upon the little sufferer. But as he drew near the bed, with a heart too full for speech, Elsie's eye fell upon him, and with a wild shriek of mortal terror, she clung to her aunt, crying out, "Oh, save me! save me! he's coming to take me away to the Inquisition! Go away! go away!" and she looked at him with a countenance so full of fear and horror, that the doctor hastily took him by the arm to lead him away.

But Mr. Dinsmore resisted.

Martha Finley

"Elsie! my daughter! it is I! your own father, who loves you dearly!" he said in tones of the keenest anguish, as he bent over her, and tried to take her hand. But she snatched it away, and clung to her aunt again, hiding her face, and shuddering with fear.

Mr. Dinsmore groaned aloud, and no longer resisted the physician's efforts to lead him from the room. "It is the delirium of *fever*," Dr. Barton said, in answer to the father's agonized look of inquiry; "she will recover her reason—if she lives."

The last words were added in a lower, quicker tone.

Mr. Dinsmore covered his face, and uttered a groan of agony.

"Doctor, is there *no* hope?" he asked in a hoarse whisper.

"Do you wish me to tell you precisely what I think?" asked the physician.

"I do! I do! let me know the worst!" was the quick, passionate rejoinder.

"Then, Mr. Dinsmore, I will be frank with you. Had you returned one week ago, I think she *might* have been saved; *possibly*, even had you been here yesterday morning, while she was still in possession of her reason; but now, I see not one ray of hope. I never knew one so low to recover."

He started, as Mr. Dinsmore raised his face again, so pale, so haggard, so grief-stricken had it become in that one moment.

"Doctor," he said in a hollow, broken voice, "save my child, and you may take all I am worth. I cannot live without her."

"I will do all I can," replied the physician in a tone of deep compassion, "but the Great Physician alone can save her. We must look to him."

"Doctor," said Mr. Dinsmore hoarsely, "if that child dies, I must go to my grave with the brand of Cain upon me, for I have killed her by my cruelty; and oh! doctor, she is the very light of my eyes—the joy of my heart! How *can* I give her up? Save her, doctor, and you will be entitled to my everlasting gratitude."

"Surely, my dear sir, you are reproaching yourself unjustly," said the physician soothingly, replying to the first part of Mr. Dinsmore's remark. "I have heard you spoken of as a very fond father, and have formed the same opinion from my own observation, and your little girl's evident affection for you."

"And I *was*, but in *one* respect. I insisted upon obedience, even when my commands came in collision with her conscientious scruples; and she was firm; she had the spirit of a martyr—and I was very severe in my efforts to subdue what I called wilfulness and obstinacy," said the distracted father in a voice often, scarcely audible from emotion. "I thought I was right, but now I see that I was fearfully wrong."

"There is *life* yet, Mr. Dinsmore," remarked the doctor compassionately; "and though human skill can do no more, he who raised the dead child of the ruler of the synagogue, and restored the son of the widow of Nain to her arms, can give back your child to your embrace; let me entreat you to go to *him*, my dear sir. And now I must return to my patient. I fear it will be necessary for you to keep out of sight until there is some change, as your presence seems to excite her so much. But do not let that distress you," he added kindly, as he noticed an expression of the keenest anguish sweep over Mr. Dinsmore's features; "it is a common thing in such cases for them to turn away from the very one they love best when in health."

Mr. Dinsmore replied only by a convulsive grasp of the friendly hand held out to him, and hurrying away to his own apartments, shut himself up there to give way to his bitter grief and remorse where no human eye could see him.

For hours he paced backward and forward, weeping and groaning in such mental agony as he had never known before.

His usual fastidious neatness in person and dress was entirely forgotten, and it never once occurred to his recollection that he had been travelling for several days and nights in succession, through heat and dust, without making any change in his clothing. And he was equally unconscious that he had passed many hours without tasting any food.

The breakfast-bell rang, but he paid no heed to the summons. Then John, his faithful servant, knocked at his door, but was refused admittance, and went sorrowfully back to the kitchen with the waiter of tempting viands he had so carefully prepared, hoping to induce his master to eat.

But Horace Dinsmore could not stay away from his child while she yet lived; and though he might not watch by her bed of suffering, nor clasp her little form in his arms, as he longed to do, he must be where he could hear the sound of that voice, so soon, alas! to be hushed in death.

He entered the room noiselessly, and took his station in a distant corner, where she could not possibly see him.

She was moaning, as if in pain, and the sound went to his very heart. Sinking down upon a seat, he bowed his head upon his hands, and struggled to suppress his emotion, increased tenfold by the words which the next instant fell upon his ear, spoken in his little daughter's own sweet voice.

"Yes, mamma; yes," she said, "I am coming! Take me to Jesus."

Then, in a pitiful, wailing tone, "I'm *all alone*! There's nobody to love me. Oh, papa, kiss me just once! I will be good; but I must love Jesus best, and obey him always."

He rose hastily, as if to go to her, but the doctor shook his head, and he sank into his seat again with a deep groan.

"Oh, papa!" she shrieked, as if in mortal terror, "don't send me there! they will kill me! Oh, papa, have mercy on your own little daughter!"

It was only by the strongest effort of his will that he could keep his seat.

But Adelaide was speaking soothingly to her.

"Darling," she said, "your papa loves you; he will not send you away."

And Elsie answered, in her natural tone, "But I'm going to mamma. Dear Aunt Adelaide, comfort my poor papa when I am gone."

Her father started, and trembled between hope and fear. Surely she was talking rationally now; but ah! those ominous words! Was she indeed about to leave him, and go to her mother?

But she was speaking again in trembling, tearful tones: "He wouldn't kiss me! he said he never would till I submit; and oh! he never breaks his word. Oh! papa, papa, will you *never* love me any more? I love *you* so *very* dearly. You'll kiss me when I'm dying, papa dear, won't you?"

Mr. Dinsmore could bear no more, but starting up he would have approached the bed, but a warning gesture from the physician prevented him, and he hurried from the room.

He met Travilla in the hall.

Neither spoke, but Edward wrung his friend's hand convulsively, then hastily turned away to hide his emotion, while Mr. Dinsmore hurried to his room, and locked himself in.

He did not come down to dinner, and Adelaide, hearing from the anxious John how long he had been without food, began to feel seriously alarmed on his account, and carried up a biscuit and a cup of coffee with her own hands.

He opened the door at her earnest solicitation, but only shook his head mournfully, saying that he had no desire for food. She urged him, even with tears in her eyes, but all in vain; he replied that "he could not eat; it was impossible."

Adelaide had at first felt inclined to reproach him bitterly for his long delay in returning home, but he looked so very wretched, so utterly crushed by the weight of this great sorrow, that she had not the heart to say one reproachful word, but on the contrary longed to comfort him.

He begged her to sit down and give him a few moments' conversation. He told her why he had been so long in answering her summons, and how he had travelled night and day since receiving it; and then he questioned her closely about the whole course of Elsie's sickness—every change in her condition, from first to last—all that had been done for her—and all that she had said and done.

Adelaide told him everything; dwelling particularly on the child's restless longing for him, her earnest desire to receive his forgiveness and caress before she died, and her entreaties to her to comfort her "dear papa" when she was gone. She told him, too, of her last will and testament, and of the little package which was, after her death, to be given to him, along with her dearly loved Bible.

He was deeply moved during this recital, sometimes sitting with his head bowed down, hiding his face in his hands; at others, rising and pacing the floor, his breast heaving with emotion, and a groan of anguish ever and anon bursting from his overburdened heart, in spite of the mighty effort he was evidently making to control himself.

But at last she was done; she had told him all that there was to tell, and for a few moments both sat silent, Adelaide weeping quietly, and he striving in vain to be calm.

At length he said, in a husky tone, "Sister Adelaide, I can never thank you as you deserve for your kindness to her—my precious child."

"Oh, brother!" replied Adelaide, sobbing, "I owe her a debt of gratitude I can never pay. She has been all my comfort in my great sorrow; she has taught me the way to heaven, and now she is going before." Then, with a burst of uncontrollable grief, she exclaimed: "Oh, Elsie! Elsie! darling child! how *can* I give you up?"

Mr. Dinsmore hid his face, and his whole frame shook with emotion.

"My punishment is greater than I can bear!" he exclaimed in a voice choked with grief. "Adelaide, do you not despise and hate me for my cruelty to that angel-child?"

"My poor brother, I am very sorry for you," she replied, laying her hand on his arm, while the tears trembled in her eyes.

There was a light tap at the door. It was Doctor Barton. "Mr. Dinsmore," he said, "she is begging so piteously for her papa that, perhaps, it would be well for you to show yourself again; it is just possible she may recognize you"

Mr. Dinsmore waited for no second bidding, but following the physician with eager haste, was the next moment at the bedside.

The little girl was moving restlessly about, moaning, "Oh! papa, papa, will you never come?"

"I am here, darling," he replied in tones of the tenderest affection. "I *have* come back to my little girl"

She turned her head to look at him. "No, no," she said, "I want my papa."

"My darling, do you not know me?" he asked in a voice quivering with emotion.

"No, no, you shall not! I will never do it—*never*. Oh! make him go away," she shrieked, clinging to Mrs. Travilla, and glaring at him with a look of the wildest affright, "he has come to torture me because I won't pray to the Virgin."

"It is quite useless," said the doctor, shaking his head sorrowfully; "she evidently does not know you."

And the unhappy father turned away and left the room to shut himself up again alone with his agony and remorse.

No one saw him again that night, and when the maid came to attend to his room in the morning, she was surprised and alarmed to find that the bed had not been touched.

Mr. Travilla, who was keeping a sorrowful vigil in the room below, had he been questioned, could have told that there had been scarcely a cessation in the sound of the footsteps pacing to and fro over his head. It had been a night of anguish and heart-searching, such as Horace Dinsmore had never passed through before. For the first time he saw himself to be what he really was in the sight of God, a guilty, hell-deserving sinner— lost, ruined, and undone. He had never believed it before, and the prayers which he had occasionally offered up had been very much in the spirit of the Pharisee's, "God, I thank thee that I am not as other men are!"

He had been blessed with a pious mother, who was early taken from him; yet not too early to have had some influence in forming the character of her son; and the faint but tender recollection of that mother's prayers and teachings had proved a safeguard to him in many an hour of temptation, and had kept him from falling into the open vices of some of his less scrupulous companions. But he had been very proud of his morality and his upright life, unstained by any dishonorable act. He had always thought of himself as quite deserving of the prosperity with which he had been blessed in the affairs of this world, and just as likely as any one to be happy in the next.

The news of Elsie's illness had first opened his eyes to the enormity of his conduct in relation to her; and now, as he thought of her pure life, her constant anxiety to do right, her deep humility, her love to Jesus, and steadfast adherence to what she believed to be her duty, her martyr-like spirit in parting with everything she most esteemed and valued rather than be guilty of what seemed to others but a very slight infringement of the law of God—as he thought of all this, and contrasted it with his own worldly-mindedness and self-righteousness, his utter neglect of the Saviour, and determined efforts to make his child as worldly as himself, he shrank back appalled at the picture, and was constrained to cry out in bitterness of soul: "God be merciful to me, a sinner."

It was the first *real* prayer he had ever offered. He would fain have asked for the life of his child, but dared not; feeling that he had so utterly abused his trust that he richly deserved to have it taken from him. The very thought was agony; but he dared not ask to have it otherwise.

He had given up all hope that she would be spared to him, but pleaded earnestly that one lucid interval might be granted her, in which he could tell her of his deep sorrow on account of his severity toward her, and ask her forgiveness.

He did not go down to breakfast, but Adelaide again brought him some refreshment, and at length he yielded to her entreaties that he would try to eat a little.

She set down the salver, and turned away to hide the tears she could not keep back. Her heart ached for him. She had never seen such a change in a few hours as had passed over him. He seemed to have grown ten years older in that one night—he was so pale and haggard—his eyes so sunken in his head, and there were deep, hard lines of suffering on his brow and around his mouth.

His meal was soon concluded.

"Adelaide, how is she?" he asked in a voice which he vainly endeavored to make calm and steady.

"Much the same; there seems to be very little change," replied his sister, wiping away her tears. Then drawing Elsie's little Bible from her pocket, she put it into his hand, saying, "I thought it might help to comfort you, my poor brother;" and with a fresh burst of tears she hastily left the room and hurried to her own, to spend a few moments in pleading for him that this heavy affliction might be made the means of leading him to Christ.

And he—ah! he could not at first trust himself even to look at the little volume that had been so constantly in his darling's hands, that it seemed almost a part of herself.

He held it in a close, loving grasp, while his averted eyes were dim with unshed tears; but at length, passing his hand over them to clear away the blinding mist, he opened the little book and turned over its pages with trembling fingers, and a heart swelling with emotion.

There were many texts marked with her pencil, and many pages blistered with her tears. Oh, what a pang that sight sent to her father's heart! In some parts these evidences of her frequent and sorrowful perusal were more numerous than in others. Many of the Psalms, the Lamentations of Jeremiah, and the books of Job and Isaiah, in the Old Testament, and St. John's gospel, and the latter part of Hebrews, in the New.

Hour after hour he sat there reading that little book; at first interested in it only because of its association with her—his loved one; but at length beginning to feel the importance of its teachings and their adaptedness to his needs. As he read, his convictions deepened the inspired declaration that "without holiness no man shall see the Lord," and the solemn warning, "See that ye refuse not him that speaketh. For if they escaped not who refused him that spake on earth, much more shall not we escape, if we turn away from him that speaketh from heaven," filled him with fear of the wrath to come; for well he remembered how all his life he had turned away from the Saviour of sinners, despising that blood of sprinkling, and rejecting all the offers of mercy; and he trembled lest he should not escape.

Several times during the day and evening he laid the book aside, and stole softly into Elsie's room to learn if there had been any change; but there was none, and at length, quite worn out with fatigue and sorrow—for he had been several nights without any rest—he threw himself down on a couch, and fell into a heavy slumber.

About midnight Adelaide came and woke him to say that Elsie had become calm, the fever had left her, and she had fallen asleep.

"The doctor," she added, "says this is the crisis, and he begins to have a *little* hope—very faint, indeed, but still a *hope*—that she may awake refreshed from this slumber; yet it might be— he is fearful it is—only the precursor of death."

The last word was almost inaudible.

Mr. Dinsmore trembled with excitement.

"I will go to her," he said in an agitated tone. "She will not know of my presence, now that she is sleeping, and I may at least have the sad satisfaction of looking at her dear little face."

But Adelaide shook her head.

"No, no," she replied, "that will never do; for we know not at what moment she may awake, and the agitation she would probably feel at the sight of you would be almost certain to prove fatal. Had you not better remain here? and I will call you the moment she wakes."

Mr. Dinsmore acquiesced with a deep sigh, and she went back to her post.

Hour after hour they sat there—Mrs. Travilla, Adelaide, the doctor, and poor old Chloe—silent and still as statues, watching that quiet slumber, straining their ears to catch the faint sound of the gentle breathing—a sound so low that ever and anon their hearts thrilled with the sudden fear that it had ceased forever; and one or another, rising noiselessly, would bend over the little form in speechless alarm, until again they caught the low, fitful sound.

The first faint streak of dawn was beginning in the eastern sky when the doctor, who had been bending over her for several minutes, suddenly laid his finger on her pulse for an instant; then turned to his fellow-watchers with a look that there was no mistaking.

There was weeping and wailing then in that room, where death-like stillness had reigned so long.

"Precious, precious child! dear lamb safely gathered into the Saviour's fold," said Mrs. Travilla in quivering tones, as she gently laid her hand upon the closed eyes, and straightened the limbs as tenderly as though it had been a living, breathing form.

"Oh, Elsie! Elsie! dear, *dear* little Elsie!" cried Adelaide, flinging herself upon the bed, and pressing her lips to the cold cheek. "I have only just learned to know your value, and now you are taken from me. Oh! Elsie, darling, precious one; oh! that I had sooner learned your worth! that I had done more to make your short life happy!"

Chloe was sobbing at the foot of the bed, "Oh! my child! my child! Oh! now dis ole heart will break for sure!" while the kind-hearted physician stood wiping his eyes and sighing deeply.

"Her poor father!" exclaimed Mrs. Travilla at length.

"Yes, yes, I will go to him," said Adelaide quickly. "I promised to call him the moment she waked, and *now*—oh, *now*, I must tell him she will never wake again."

"No!" replied Mrs. Travilla, "rather tell him that she has waked in heaven, and is even now singing the song of the redeemed."

Adelaide turned to Elsie's writing-desk, and taking from it the packet which the child had directed to be given to her father as soon as she was gone, she carried it to him.

Her low knock was instantly followed by the opening of the door, for he had been awaiting her coming in torturing suspense.

She could not look at him, but hastily thrusting the packet into his hand, turned weeping away.

He well understood the meaning of her silence and her tears, and with a groan of anguish that Adelaide never could forget, he shut and locked himself in again; while she hurried to her room to indulge her grief in solitude, leaving Mrs. Travilla and Chloe to attend to the last sad offices of love to the dear remains of the little departed one.

The news had quickly spread through the house, and sobs and bitter weeping were heard in every part of it; for Elsie had been dearly loved by all.

Chloe was assisting Mrs. Travilla.

Suddenly the lady paused in her work, saying, in an agitated tone, "Quick! quick! Aunt Chloe, throw open that shutter wide. I thought I felt a little warmth about the heart, and— yes! yes! I was not mistaken; there *is* a slight quivering of the eyelid. Go, Chloe! call the doctor! she may live yet!"

The doctor was only in the room below, and in a moment was at the bedside, doing all that could be done to fan into a flame that little spark of life.

And they were successful. In a few moments those eyes, which they had thought closed forever to all the beauties of earth, opened again, and a faint, weak voice asked for water.

The doctor was obliged to banish Chloe from the room, lest the noisy manifestation of her joy should injure her nursling, yet trembling upon the very verge of the grave; and as he did so, he cautioned her to refrain from yet communicating the glad tidings to any one, lest some sound of their rejoicing might reach the sick-chamber, and disturb the little sufferer.

And then he and the motherly old lady took their stations at the bedside once more, watching in perfect silence, and administering every few moments a little stimulant, for she was weak as a new-born infant, and only in this way could they keep the flickering flame of life from dying out again.

It was not until more than an hour had passed in this way, and hope began to grow stronger in their breasts, until it became almost certainty that Elsie would live, that they thought of her father and aunt, so entirely had their attention been engrossed by the critical condition of their little patient.

It was many minutes after Adelaide left him ere Mr. Dinsmore could think of anything but the terrible, crushing blow which had fallen upon him, and his agonized feelings found vent in groans of bitter anguish, fit to melt a heart of stone; but at length he grew somewhat calmer; and as his eye fell upon the little packet he remembered that it was her dying gift to him, and with a deep sigh he took it up and opened it.

It contained his wife's miniature—the same that Elsie had always worn suspended from her neck—one of the child's glossy ringlets, severed from her head by her own little hands the day before she was taken ill—and a letter, directed in her handwriting to himself.

He pressed the lock of hair to his lips, then laid it gently down, and opened the letter.

"Dear, dear papa," it began, "my heart is very sad to-night! There is such a weary, aching pain there, that will never be gone till I can lay my head against your breast, and feel your arms folding me tight, and your kisses on my cheek. Ah! papa, how often I wish you could just look down into my heart and see how *full* of love to you it is! I am always thinking of you, and longing to be with you. You bade me go and see the home you have prepared, and I have obeyed you. You say, if I will only be submissive we will live there, and be so very happy together, and I cannot tell you how my heart longs for such a life with you in that lovely, lovely home; nor how happy I could be there, or *anywhere* with you, if you would only let me make God's law the rule of my life; but, my own dear father, if I have found your frown so dreadful, so *hard* to bear, how much more terrible would my Heavenly Father's be! Oh, papa, *that* would make me wretched indeed! But oh, I cannot *bear* to think of being sent away from you amongst strangers! Dear, *dear* papa, will you not spare your little daughter this trial? I will try to be so very good and obedient in everything that my conscience will allow. I am so sad, papa, so very sad, as if something terrible was coming, and my head feels strangely. I fear I am going to be ill, perhaps to die! Oh, papa, will I never see you again? I want to ask you to forgive me for all the naughty thoughts and feelings I have ever had towards you. I think I have never disobeyed you in *deed*, papa— except the few times you have known of, when I forgot, or thought you bade me break God's law—but twice I have rebelled in my heart. Once when you took Miss Rose's letter from me, and again when mammy told me you had said she must go away. It was only for a little while each time, papa, but it was very wicked, and I am very, *very* sorry; will you please forgive me? and I will try never to indulge such wicked feelings again."

The paper was blistered with Elsie's tears, and *other* tears were falling thick and fast upon it now.

"*She* to ask forgiveness of me, for a momentary feeling of indignation when I so abused my authority," he groaned. "Oh, my darling! I would give all I am worth to bring you back for one hour, that I might ask *your* forgiveness, on my knees."

But there was more of the letter, and he read on:

"Dear papa," she continued, "should I die, and never see you again in this world, don't ever feel vexed with yourself, and think that you have been too severe with me. I know you have only done what you had a right to do—for am I not your own? Oh, I *love* to belong to you, papa! and you meant it all to make me good; and I needed it, for I was loving you *too* dearly. I was getting away from my Saviour. But when you put me away from your arms and separated me from my nurse, I had no one to go to but Jesus, and he drew me closer to him, and I found his love very sweet and precious; it has been all my comfort in my great sorrow. Dear papa, when I am gone, and you feel sad and lonely, will not *you* go to Jesus, too? I will leave you my dear little Bible, papa. Please read it for Elsie's sake, and God grant it may comfort you as it has your little daughter. And, dear papa, try to forget these sad days of our estrangement, and remember only the time when your little girl was always on your knee, or by your side. Oh! it breaks my heart to think of those sweet times, and that they will never come again! Oh, for one kiss, one caress, one word of love from you! for oh, how *I love* you, my own dear, be loved, precious papa!

"Your little daughter,
"ELSIE."

Mr. Dinsmore dropped his head upon his hands, and groaned aloud. It was his turn now to long, with an *unutterable* longing, for one caress, one word of love from those sweet lips that should never speak again. A long time he sat there, living over again in memory every scene in his life in which his child had borne a part, and repenting, oh, so bitterly! of every harsh word he had ever spoken to her, of every act of unjust severity; and, alas! how many and how cruel they seemed to him now! Remorse was eating into his very soul, and he would have given worlds to be able to recall the past.

CHAPTER XIII

"Joy! the lost one is restored!!
Sunshine comes to hearth and board."

MRS. HEMANS.

"O remembrance!
Why dost thou open all my wounds again?"

LEE'S THEODOSIUS.

"I am a fool,
To weep at what I am glad of."

SHAKS. TEMPEST.

"But these are tears of joy! to see you thus, has filled
My eyes with more delight than they can hold."

CONGREVE.

Mr. Dinsmore was roused from the painful reverie into which
he had fallen by a light rap on his dressing-room door; and,
supposing it to be some one sent to consult him concerning
the necessary arrangements for the funeral, he rose and opened
it at once, showing to the doctor, who stood there, such a
grief-stricken countenance as caused him to hesitate whether
to communicate his glad tidings without some previous

prepartion, lest the sudden reaction from such despairing grief to joy so intense should be too great for the father to bear.

"You wish to speak to me about the—"

Mr. Dinsmore's voice was husky and low, and he paused, unable to finish his sentence.

"Come in, doctor," he said, "it is very kind in you, and—"

"Mr. Dinsmore," said the doctor, interrupting him, "are you prepared for good news? can you bear it, my dear sir?"

Mr. Dinsmore caught at the furniture for support, and gasped for breath.

"What is it?" he asked hoarsely.

"*Good* news, I said," Dr. Barton hastened to say, as he sprang to his side to prevent him from falling. "Your child yet lives, and though her life still hangs by a thread, the crisis is past, and I have some hope that she may recover."

"Thank God! thank God!" exclaimed the father, sinking into a seat; and burying his face in his hands, he sobbed aloud.

The doctor went out and closed the door softly; and Horace Dinsmore, falling upon his knees, poured out his thanks-givings, and then and there consecrated himself, with all his talents and possessions, to the service of that God who had so mercifully spared to him his heart's best treasure.

Adelaide's joy and thankfulness were scarcely less than his, when to her, also, the glad and wondrous tidings were communicated. And Mr. Travilla and his mother shared their happiness, as they had shared their sorrow. Yet they all rejoiced with trembling, for that little life was still for many days trembling in the balance; and to the father's anxiety was also added the heavy trial of being excluded from her room.

Martha Finley

The physician had early informed him that it would be risking her life for him to enter her presence until she should herself inquire for him, as they could not tell how great might be the agitation it would cause her. And so he waited, day after day, hoping for the summons, but constantly doomed to disappointment; for even after she had become strong enough to look about her, and ask questions, and to notice her friends with a gentle smile, and a word of thanks to each, several days passed away, and she had neither inquired for him nor even once so much as mentioned his name.

It seemed passing strange, and the thought that perhaps his cruelty had so estranged her from him that she no longer cared for his presence or his love, caused him many a bitter pang, and at times rendered him so desperate that, but for the doctor's repeated warnings, he would have ended this torturing suspense by going to her, and begging to hear from her own lips whether she had indeed ceased to love him.

Adelaide tried to comfort and encourage him to wait patiently, but she, too, thought it very strange, and began to have vague fears that something was wrong with her little niece.

She wondered that Dr. Barton treated the matter so lightly.

"But, then," thought she, "he has no idea how strongly the child was attached to her father, and therefore her strange silence on the subject does not strike him as it does us. I will ask if I may not venture to mention Horace to her."

But when she put the question, the doctor shook his head.

"No," he said; "better let her broach the subject herself; it will be much the safer plan."

Adelaide reluctantly acquiesced in his decision, for she was growing almost as impatient as her brother. But fortunately she was not kept much longer in suspense.

The next day Elsie, who had been lying for some time wide awake, but without speaking, suddenly asked: "Aunt Adelaide, have you heard from Miss Allison since she went away?"

"Yes, dear, a number of times," replied her aunt, much surprised at the question; "once since you were taken sick, and she was very sorry to hear of your illness."

"Dear Miss Rose, how I want to see her," murmured the little girl musingly. "Aunt Adelaide," she asked quickly, "has there been any letter from papa since I have been sick?"

"Yes, dear," said Adelaide, beginning to tremble a little; "one, but it was written before he heard of your illness."

"Did he say when he would sail for America, Aunt Adelaide?" she asked eagerly.

"No, dear," replied her aunt, becoming still more alarmed, for she feared the child was losing her reason.

"Oh, Aunt Adelaide, do you think he will *ever* come home? Shall I ever see him? And do you think he will love me?" moaned the little girl.

"I am sure he *does* love you, darling, for indeed he mentions you very affectionately in his letters," Adelaide said, bending down to kiss the little pale cheek. "Now go to sleep, dear child," she added, "I am afraid you have been talking quite too much, for you are very weak yet."

Elsie was, in fact, quite exhausted, and closing her eyes, fell asleep directly.

Then resigning her place to Chloe, Adelaide stole softly from the room, and seeking her brother, repeated to him all that had just passed between Elsie and herself. She simply told her story, keeping her doubts and fears confined to her own breast; but she watched him closely to see if he shared them.

He listened at first eagerly; then sat with folded arms and head bent down, so that she could not see his face; then rising up hastily, he paced the floor to and fro with rapid strides, sighing heavily to himself.

"Oh, Adelaide! Adelaide!" he exclaimed, suddenly pausing before her, "are *my* sins thus to be visited on my innocent child? better death a thousand times!" And sinking shuddering into a seat, he covered his face with his hands, and groaned aloud.

"Don't be so distressed, dear brother, I am sure it cannot be so bad as you think," whispered Adelaide, passing her arm around his neck and kissing him softly. "She looks bright enough, and seems to perfectly understand all that is said to her."

"Dr. Barton!" announced Pompey, throwing open the door of the parlor where they were sitting.

Mr. Dinsmore rose hastily to greet him.

"What is the matter? is anything wrong with my patient?" he asked hurriedly, looking from one to the other, and noticing the signs of unusual emotion in each face.

"Tell him, Adelaide," entreated her brother, turning away his head to hide his feelings.

Adelaide repeated her story, not without showing considerable emotion, though she did not mention the nature of their fears.

"Don't be alarmed," said the physician, cheerfully; "she is *not* losing her mind, as I see you both fear; it is simply a failure of memory for the time being; she has been fearfully ill, and the mind at present partakes of the weakness of the body, but I hope ere long to see them both grow strong together.

"Let me see—Miss Allison left, when? a year ago last April, I think you said, Miss Adelaide, and this is October. Ah! well, the little girl has only lost about a year and a half from her life, and it is altogether likely she will recover it; but even supposing she does not, it is no great matter after all."

Mr. Dinsmore looked unspeakably relieved, and Adelaide hardly less so.

"And this gives you one advantage, Mr. Dinsmore," continued the doctor, looking smilingly at him; "you can now go to her as soon as Miss Adelaide has cautiously broken to her the news of your arrival."

When Elsie waked, Adelaide cautiously communicated to her the tidings that her father had landed in America, in safety and health, and hoped to be with them in a day or two.

A faint tinge of color came to the little girl's cheek, her eyes sparkled, and, clasping her little, thin hands together, she exclaimed, "Oh! can it really be true that I shall see my own dear father? and do you think he will *love* me, Aunt Adelaide?"

"Yes, indeed, darling; he *says* he loves you dearly, and longs to have you in his arms."

Elsie's eyes filled with happy tears.

"Now you must try to be very calm, darling, and not let the good news hurt you," said her aunt kindly; "or I am afraid the doctor will say you are not well enough to see your papa when, he comes."

"I will try to be very quiet," replied the little girl; "but, oh! I *hope* he will come soon, and that the doctor will let me see him."

"I shall read to you now, dear," remarked Adelaide, taking up Elsie's little Bible, which had been returned to her some days before; for she had asked for it almost as soon as she was able

Martha Finley

to speak.

Adelaide opened to one of her favorite passages in Isaiah, and read in a low, quiet tone that soon soothed the little one to sleep.

"Has my papa come?" was her first question on awaking.

"Do you think you are strong enough to see him?" asked Adelaide, smiling.

"Oh, yes, Aunt Adelaide; is he here?" she inquired, beginning to tremble with agitation.

"I am afraid you are not strong enough yet," said Adelaide doubtfully; "you are trembling very much."

"Dear Aunt Adelaide, I will try to be very calm; *do* let me see him," she urged beseechingly; "it won't hurt me half so much as to be kept waiting."

"Yes, Adelaide, she is right. My precious, precious child! they shall keep us apart no longer." And Elsie was gently raised in her father's arms, and folded to his beating heart.

She looked up eagerly into his face.

It was full of the tenderest love and pity,

"Papa, papa, my *own* papa," she murmured, dropping her head upon his breast.

He held her for some moments, caressing her silently; then laid her gently down upon her pillow, and sat by her side with one little hand held fast in his.

She raised her large, soft eyes, all dim with tears, to his face.

"Do you love me, my own papa?" she asked in a voice so low

and weak he could scarcely catch the words.

"Better than life," he said, his voice trembling with emotion; and he leaned over her, passing his hand caressingly over her face.

"Does my little daughter love me?" he asked.

"Oh, so very, *very* much," she said, and closing her eyes wearily, she fell asleep again.

And now Mr. Dinsmore was constantly with his little girl. She could scarcely bear to have him out of her sight, but clung to him with the fondest affection, which he fully returned; and he never willingly left her for an hour. She seemed to have entirely forgotten their first meeting, and everything which had occurred since, up to the beginning of her illness, and always talked to her father as though they had but just begun their acquaintance; and it was with feelings half pleasurable, half painful, that he listened to her.

It was certainly a relief to have her so unconscious of their estrangement, and yet such an utter failure of memory distressed him with fears of permanent and serious injury to her intellect; and thus it was, with mingled hope and dread, that he looked forward to the fulfilment of the doctor's prophecy that her memory would return.

She was growing stronger, so that she was able to be moved from her bed to a couch during the day; and when she was very weary of lying, her father would take her in his arms and carry her back and forth, or, seating himself in a large rocking-chair, soothe her to sleep on his breast, holding her there for hours, never caring for the aching of his arms, but really enjoying the consciousness that he was adding to her comfort by suffering a little himself.

Mrs. Travilla had some time since found it absolutely necessary to give her personal attention to her own household, and

Adelaide, quite worn out with nursing, needed rest; and so, with a little help from Chloe, Mr. Dinsmore took the whole care of his little girl, mixing and administering her medicines with his own hand, giving her her food, soothing her in her hours of restlessness, reading, talking, singing to her—exerting all his powers for her entertainment, and never weary of waiting upon her. He watched by her couch night and day; only now and then snatching a few hours of sleep on a sofa in her room, while the faithful old nurse took his place by her side.

One day he had been reading to Elsie, while she lay on her sofa. Presently he closed the book, and looking at her, noticed that her eyes were fixed upon his face with a troubled expression.

"What is it, dearest?" he asked.

"Papa," she said in a doubtful, hesitating way, "it seems as if I had seen you before; have I, papa?"

"Why, surely, darling," he answered, trying to laugh, though he trembled inwardly, "I have been with you for nearly two weeks, and you have seen me every day."

"No, papa; but I mean before. Did I *dream* that you gave me a doll once? Were you ever vexed with me? Oh, papa, help me to think," she said in a troubled, anxious tone, rubbing her hand across her forehead as she spoke.

"Don't try to think, darling," he replied cheerfully, as he raised her, shook up her pillows, and settled her more comfortably on them. "I am not in the least vexed with you; there is nothing wrong, and I love you very, *very* dearly. So shut your eyes and try to go to sleep."

She looked only half satisfied, but closed her eyes as he bade her, and was soon asleep. She seemed thoughtful and absent all the rest of the day, every now and then fixing the same troubled, questioning look on him, and it was quite impossible to interest her in any subject for more than a few moments at a time.

That night, for the first time, he went to his own room, leaving her entirely to Chloe's care. He had watched by her after she was put in bed for the night, until she had fallen asleep; but he left her, feeling a little anxious, for the same troubled look was on her face, as though even in sleep memory was reasserting her sway.

When he entered her room again in the morning, although it was still early, he found her already dressed for the day, in a pretty, loose wrapper, and laid upon the sofa.

"Good-morning, little daughter; you are quite an early bird to-day, for a sick one," he said gayly.

But as he drew near, he was surprised and pained to see that she was trembling very much, and that her eyes were red with weeping.

"What is it, dearest?" he asked, bending over her in tender solicitude; "what ails my little one?"

"Oh, papa," she said, bursting into tears, "I remember it all now. Are you angry with me yet? and must I go away from you as soon as—"

But she was unable to finish her sentence.

He had knelt down by her side, and now raising her gently up, and laying her head against his breast, he kissed her tenderly, saying in a moved tone, in the beautiful words of Ruth, the Moabitess, "The Lord do so to me, and more also, if aught but death part me and thee." He paused a moment, as if unable to proceed; then, in tones tremulous with emotion, said: "Elsie, my dear, my *darling* daughter, I have been a very cruel father to you; I have most shamefully abused my authority; but never again will I require you to do anything contrary to the teachings of God's word. Will you forgive your father, dearest, for all he has made you suffer?"

"Dear papa, don't! oh, *please* don't say such words to me!" she said; "I cannot bear to hear them. You had a right to do whatever you pleased with your own child."

"No, daughter; not to force you to disobey God," he answered with deep solemnity. "I have learned to look upon you now, not as absolutely my own, but as belonging first to him, and only lent to me for a time; and I know that I will have to give an account of my stewardship."

He paused a moment, then went on: "Elsie, darling, your prayers for me have been answered; your father has learned to know and love Jesus, and has consecrated to his service the remainder of his days. And now, dear one, we are travelling the same road at last."

Her happiness was too deep for words—for anything but tears; and putting her little arms around his neck, she sobbed out her joy and gratitude upon his breast.

Aunt Chloe had gone down to the kitchen, immediately upon Mr. Dinsmore's entrance, to prepare Elsie's breakfast, and so they were quite alone. He held her to his heart for a moment; then kissing away her tears, laid her gently back upon her pillow again, and took up the Bible, which lay beside her.

"I have learned to love it almost as well as you do, dearest," he said. "Shall we read together, as you and Miss Rose used to do long ago?"

Her glad look was answer enough; and opening to one of her favorite passages, he read it in his deep, rich voice, while she lay listening, with a full heart, to the dearly loved words, which sounded sweeter than ever before.

He closed the book. He had taken one of her little hands in his ere he began to read, and still holding it fast in a close, loving grasp, he knelt down and prayed.

He thanked God for their spared lives, and especially for the recovery of his dear little one, who had so lately been tottering upon the very verge of the grave—and his voice trembled with emotion as he alluded to that time of trial—and confessed that it was undeserved mercy to him, for he had been most unfaithful to his trust. And then he asked for grace and wisdom to guide and guard her, and train her up aright, both by precept and example. He confessed that he had been all his days a wanderer from the right path, and that if left to himself he never would have sought it; but thanked God that he had been led by the gracious influences of the Holy Spirit to turn his feet into that straight and narrow way; and he prayed that he might be kept from ever turning aside again into the broad road, and that he and his little girl might now walk hand in hand together on their journey to the celestial city.

Elsie's heart swelled with emotion, and glad tears rained down her cheeks, as thus, for the first time, she heard her father's voice in prayer. It was the happiest hour she had ever known.

"Take me, papa, please," she begged, holding out her hands to him, as he rose from his knees, and drawing his chair close to her couch sat down by her side.

He took her in his arms, and she laid her head on his breast again, saying, "I am *so* happy, so *very* happy! Dear papa, it is worth all the sickness and everything else that I have suffered."

He only answered with a kiss.

"Will you read and pray with me every morning, papa?" she asked,

"Yes, darling," he said, "and when we get into our own home we will call in the servants morning and evening, and have family worship. Shall you like that?"

"*Very* much, papa! Oh, how nice it will be! and will we go *soon* to our own home, papa?" she asked eagerly.

"Just as soon as you are well enough to be moved, dearest. But here is Aunt Chloe with your breakfast, so now we must stop talking, and let you eat."

"May I talk a little more now, papa?" she asked, when she had done eating.

"Yes, a little, if it is anything of importance," he answered smilingly.

"I wanted to say that I think our new home is very, very lovely, and that I think we shall be *so* happy there. Dear papa, you were so very kind to furnish those pretty rooms for me! thank you *very* much," she said, pressing his hand to her lips. "I will try to be so good and obedient that you will never regret having spent so much money, and taken so much trouble for me."

"I know you will, daughter; you have always been a dutiful child," he said tenderly, "and I shall never regret anything that adds to your happiness."

"And will you do all that you said in that letter, papa? will you teach me yourself?" she asked eagerly.

"If you wish it, my pet; but if you prefer a governess, I will try to get one who will be more kind and patient than Miss Day. One thing is certain, *she* shall never teach you again."

"Oh, no, papa, please teach me yourself. I will try to be very good, and not give you much trouble," she said coaxingly.

"I will," he said with a smile. "The doctor thinks that in a day or two you may be able to take a short ride, and I hope it will not be very long before we will be in our own home. Now I am going to wrap you up, and carry you to my dressing-room to spend the day; for I know you are tired of this room."

"How pleasant!" she exclaimed; "how kind you are to think of it, papa! I feel as glad as I used to when I was going to take a long ride on my pony."

He smiled on her a pleased, affectionate smile, and bade Chloe go and see if the room was in order for them.

Chloe returned almost immediately to say that all was in readiness; and Elsie was then raised in her father's strong arms, and borne quickly through the hall and into the dressing-room, where she was laid upon a sofa, and propped up with pillows. She looked very comfortable; and very glad she was to have a little change of scene, after her long confinement to one room.

Just as she was fairly settled in her new quarters, the breakfast-bell rang, and her father left her in Chloe's care for a few moments, while he went down to take his meal.

"I have brought you a visitor, Elsie," he said when he returned.

She looked up, and, to her surprise, saw her grandfather standing near the door.

He came forward then, and taking the little, thin hand she held out to him, he stooped and kissed her cheek.

"I am sorry to see you looking so ill, my dear," he said, not without a touch of feeling in his tone—"but I hope you will get well very fast now."

"Yes, grandpa, thank you; I am a great deal better than I was," she answered, with a tear in her eye; for it was the first caress she ever remembered having received from him, and she felt quite touched.

"Have the others come, grandpa?" she asked.

"Yes, my dear, they are all at home now, and I think Lora will be coming to speak to you presently, she has been quite anxious to see you."

"Don't let her come until afternoon, father? if you please," said his son, looking anxiously at his little girl. "Elsie cannot bear much yet, and I see she is beginning to look exhausted already." And he laid his finger on her pulse.

"I shall caution her on the subject," replied his father, turning to leave the room. Then to Elsie, "You had better go to sleep now, child! sleep and eat all you can, and get strong fast."

"Yes, sir," she said faintly, closing her eyes with a weary look.

Her father placed her more comfortably on the pillows, smoothed the cover, closed the blinds to shut out the sunlight, and sat down to watch her while she slept.

It was a long, deep sleep, for she was quite worn out by the excitement of the morning; the dinner-hour had passed, and still she slumbered on, and he began to grow uneasy. He was leaning over her, with his finger on her slender wrist, watching her breathing and counting her pulse, when she opened her eyes, and looking up lovingly into his face, said "Dear papa, I feel so much better."

"I am very glad, daughter," he replied; "you have had a long sleep; and now I will take you on my knee, and Aunt Chloe will bring up your dinner."

Elsie's appetite was poor, and her father spared neither trouble nor expense in procuring her every dainty that could be thought of which was at all suited to her state of health, and he was delighted when he could tempt her to eat with tolerable heartiness. She seemed to enjoy her dinner, and he watched her with intense pleasure.

"Can I see Lora now, papa?" she asked, when Chloe had removed the dishes.

"Yes," he said. "Aunt Chloe, you may tell Miss Lora that we are ready to receive her now."

Lora came in quite gay and full of spirits; but when she caught sight of Elsie, lying so pale and languid in her father's arms, she had hard work to keep from bursting into tears, and could scarcely command her voice to speak.

"Dear Lora, I am so glad to see you," said the little girl, holding out her small, thin hand.

Lora took it and kissed it, saying, in a tremulous tone, "How ill you look!"

Elsie held up her face, and Lora stooped and kissed her lips; then bursting into tears and sobs, she ran out of the room.

"Oh, Adelaide!" she cried, rushing into her sister's room, "how she is changed! I should never have known her! Oh! do you think she can ever get well?"

"If you had seen her two or three weeks ago, you would be quite encouraged by her appearance now," replied her sister. "The doctor considers her out of danger now, though he says she must have careful nursing; and that I assure you she gets from her father. He seems to feel that he can never do enough for her, and won't let me share the labor at all, although I would often be very glad to do it."

"He *ought* to do all he can for her! he would be a *brute* if he didn't, for it was all his doing, her being so ill!" exclaimed Lora indignantly. "No, no; I ought not to say that," she added, correcting herself immediately, "for we were *all* unkind to her; I as well as the rest. Oh, Adelaide! what a bitter thought that was to me when I heard she was dying! I never realized before how lovely, and how very different from all the rest of us she was."

"Yes, poor darling! she has had a hard life amongst us," replied Adelaide, sighing, while the tears rose to her eyes. "You can never know, Lora, what an agonizing thought it was at the moment when I believed that she had left us forever. I would have given worlds to have been able to live the last six years over again. But Horace—oh, Lora! I don't believe there was a more wretched being on the face of the earth than he! I was very angry with him at first, but when I saw how utterly crushed and heartbroken he was, I couldn't say one word."

Adelaide was crying now in good earnest, as well as Lora.

Presently Lora asked for a full account of Elsie's illness, which Adelaide was beginning to give, when a servant came to say that Elsie wanted to see her; so, with a promise to Lora to finish her story another time, she hastened to obey the summons.

She found the little girl still lying languidly in her father's arms.

"Dear Aunt Adelaide," she said, "I wanted to see you; you haven't been in to-day to look at your little patient."

Adelaide smiled, and patted her cheek.

"Yes, my dear," she said, "I have been in twice, but found you sleeping both times, and your father keeping guard over you, like a tiger watching his cub."

"No, no, Aunt Adelaide; papa isn't a bit like a tiger," said Elsie, passing her small, white hand caressingly over his face. "You mustn't say that."

"I don't know," replied Adelaide, laughing and shaking her head; "I think anybody who should be daring enough to disturb your slumbers would find there was considerable of the tiger in him."

Elsie looked up into her father's face as if expecting him to deny the charge.

"Never mind," said he, smiling; "Aunt Adelaide is only trying to tease us a little."

A servant came in and whispered something to Adelaide.

"Mr. and Mrs. Travilla," she said, turning to her brother; "is Elsie able to see them?"

"Oh, yes, papa, please," begged the little girl in a coaxing tone.

"Well, then, for a few moments, I suppose," he answered rather doubtfully; and Adelaide went down and brought them up.

Elsie was very glad to see them; but seeing that she looked weak and weary they did not stay long, but soon took an affectionate leave of her, expressing the hope that it would not be many weeks before she would be able to pay a visit to Ion.

Her father promised to take her to spend a day there as soon as she was well enough, and then they went away.

Elsie's strength returned very slowly, and she had many trying hours of weakness and nervous prostration to endure. She was almost always very patient, but on a few rare occasions, when suffering more than usual, there was a slight peevishness in her tone. Once it was to her father she was speaking, and the instant she had done so, she looked up at him with eyes brimful of tears, expecting a stern rebuke, or, at the very least, a look of great displeasure.

But he did not seem to have heard her, and only busied himself in trying to make her more comfortable; and when she seemed to feel easier again, he kissed her tenderly, saying softly: "My poor little one! papa knows she suffers a great deal, and feels very sorry for her. Are you better now, dearest?"

Martha Finley

"Yes, papa, thank you," she answered, the tears coming into her eyes again. "I don't know what makes me so cross; you are very good not to scold me."

"I think my little girl is very patient," he said, caressing her again; "and if she were not, I couldn't have the heart to *scold* her after all she has suffered. Shall I sing to you now?"

"Yes, papa; please sing 'I want to be like Jesus.' Oh, I *do* want to be like him! and then I should never even *feel* impatient."

He did as she requested, singing in a low, soothing tone that soon lulled her to sleep. He was an indefatigable nurse, never weary, never in the least impatient, and nothing that skill and kindness could do for the comfort and recovery of his little daughter was left undone. He carried her in his arms from room to room; and then, as she grew stronger, down into the garden. Then he sent for a garden chair, in which he drew her about the gardens with his own hands; or if he called a servant to do it, he walked by her side, doing all he could to amuse her, and when she was ready to be carried indoors again, no one was allowed to touch her but himself. At last she was able to take short and easy rides in the carriage—not more than a quarter of a mile at first, for he was very much afraid of trying her strength too far—but gradually they were lengthened, as she seemed able to bear it.

One day he was unusually eager to get her into the carriage, and after they had started, instead of calling her attention to the scenery, as he often did, he began relating a story which interested her so much that she did not notice in what direction they were travelling until the carriage stopped, the foot-man threw open the door, and her father, breaking off in the middle of a sentence, sprang out hastily, lifted her in his arms, and carried her into the house.

She did not know where she was until he had laid her on a sofa, and, giving her a rapturous kiss, exclaimed—

"Welcome home, my darling! welcome to your father's house."

Then she looked up and saw that she was indeed in the dear home he had prepared for her months before.

She was too glad to speak a word, or do anything but gaze about her with eyes brimming over with delight; while her father took off her bonnet and shawl, and setting her on her feet, led her across the room to an easy-chair, where he seated her in state.

He then threw open a door, and there was another pleasant surprise; for who but her old friend, Mrs. Murray, should rush in and take her in her arms, kissing her and crying over her.

"Dear, *dear* bairn," she exclaimed, "you are looking pale and ill, but it does my auld heart gude to see your winsome wee face once more. I hope it will soon grow as round and rosy as ever, now that you've won to your ain home at last. But where, darling, are all your bonny curls?" she asked suddenly.

"In the drawer, in my room at grandpa's," replied the little girl with a faint smile. "They had to be cut off when I was so sick. You were not vexed, papa?" she asked, raising her eyes timidly to his face.

"No, darling, not *vexed* certainly, though very sorry indeed that it was necessary," he said in a kind, gentle tone, passing his hand caressingly over her head.

"Ah, well," remarked Mrs. Murray cheerfully, "we winna fret about it; it will soon grow again, and these little, soft rings of hair are very pretty, too."

"I thought you were in Scotland, Mrs. Murray; when did you come back?" asked the little girl.

"I came to this place only yesterday, darling; but it is about a week since I landed in America."

Martha Finley

"I am so glad to see you, dear Mrs. Murray," Elsie said, holding fast to her hand, and looking lovingly into her face. "I haven't forgotten any of the good things you taught me." Then turning to her father, she said, very earnestly, "Papa, you won't need now to have me grow up for a long while, because Mrs. Murray is such an excellent housekeeper."

He smiled and patted her cheek, saying pleasantly, "No, dear, I shall keep you a little girl as long as ever I can; and give Mrs. Murray plenty of time to make a good housekeeper of you."

"At what hour will you have dinner, sir?" asked the old lady, turning to leave the room.

"At one, if you please," he said, looking at his watch. "I want Elsie to eat with me, and it must be early, on her account."

Elsie's little face was quite bright with pleasure. "I am so glad, papa," she said, "it will be very delightful to dine together in our own house. May I always dine with you?"

"I hope so," he said, smiling. "I am not fond of eating alone."

They were in Mr. Dinsmore's study, into which Elsie's own little sitting-room opened.

"Do you feel equal to a walk through your rooms, daughter, or shall I carry you?" he asked, bending over her.

"I think I will try to walk, papa, if you please," she said, putting her hand in his.

He led her slowly forward, but her step seemed tottering, and he passed his arm around her waist, and supported her to the sofa in her own pretty little boudoir.

Although it was now quite late in the fall, the weather was still warm and pleasant in that southern clime—flowers were blooming in the gardens, and doors and windows stood wide open.

Elsie glanced out of the window, and then around the room.

"What a lovely place it is, papa!" she said; "and everything in this dear little room is so complete, so very pretty. Dear papa, you are very, *very* kind to me! I will have to be a very good girl to deserve it all."

"Does it please you, darling? I am very glad," he said, drawing her closer to him. "I have tried to think of everything that would be useful to you, or give you pleasure; but if there is anything else you want, just tell me what it is, and you shall have it."

"Indeed, papa," she said, smiling up at him, "I could never have thought of half the pretty things that are here already; and I don't believe there is anything else I could possibly want. Ah! papa, how happy I am to-day; so very much happier than when I was here before. Then I thought I should never be happy again in this world. There is your picture. I cried very much when I looked at it that day, but it does not make me feel like crying now, and I am so *glad* to have it. Thank you a thousand times for giving it to me."

"You are very welcome, darling; you deserve it all, and more than all," replied her father tenderly. "And now," he asked, "will you look at the other rooms, or are you too tired?"

"I want to try the piano first, if you please, papa," she said; "it is so long since I touched one."

He opened the instrument, and then picked her up and seated her on the stool, saying, "I am afraid you will find yourself hardly equal to the exertion; but you may try."

She began a little piece which had always been a favorite of his—he standing beside her, and supporting her with his arm —but it seemed hard work; the tiny hands trembled so with weakness and he would not let her finish.

"You must wait until another day, dearest," he said, taking her in his arms; "you are not strong enough yet, and I think I will have to *carry* you through the other rooms, if you are to see them at all. Shall I?"

She assented, laying her head down languidly on his shoulder, and had very little to say, as he bore her along through the dressing-room, and into the bed-room beyond.

The bed looked very inviting with its snowy drapery, and he laid her gently down upon it, saying, "You are too much fatigued to attempt anything more, and must take a nap now, my pet, to recruit yourself a little before dinner."

"Don't leave me, papa! *please* don't!" she exclaimed, half starting up as he turned toward the door.

"No, dearest," he said, "I am only going to get your shawl to lay over you, and will be back again in a moment."

He returned almost immediately, but found her already fast asleep.

"Poor darling! she is quite worn out," he murmured, as he spread the shawl carefully over her. Then taking a book from his pocket, he sat down by her side, and read until she awoke.

It was the sound of the dinner-bell which had roused her, and as she sat up looking quite bright and cheerful again, he asked if she thought she could eat some dinner, and would like to be taken to the dining-room. She assented, and he carried her there, seated her in an easy-chair, wheeled it up to the table, and then sat down opposite to her, looking supremely happy.

The servants were about to uncover the dishes, but motioning them to wait a moment, Mr. Dinsmore bowed his head over his plate, and asked a blessing on their food. It sent a glow of happiness to Elsie's little, pale face, and she loved and respected her father more than ever. She seemed to enjoy her dinner, and he watched her with a pleased look.

"The change of air has done you good already, I think," he remarked; "you seem to have a better appetite than you have had since your sickness."

"Yes, papa, I believe everything tastes good because it is home," she answered, smiling lovingly up at him.

After dinner he held her on his knee a while, chatting pleasantly with her about their plans for the future; and then, laying her on the sofa in her pretty boudoir, he brought a book from his library, and read to her.

It was a very interesting story he had chosen; and he had been reading for more than an hour, when, happening to look at her he noticed that her eyes were very bright, and her cheeks flushed, as if with fever. He suddenly closed the book, and laid his finger on her pulse.

"Oh! papa, please go on," she begged; "I am so much interested."

"No, daughter, your pulse is very quick, and I fear this book is entirely too exciting for you at present—so I shall not read you any more of it to-day," he said, laying it aside.

"Oh! papa, I want to hear it so much; do please read a *little* more, or else let me have the book myself," she pleaded in a coaxing tone.

"My little daughter must not forget old lessons," he replied very gravely.

She turned away her head with almost a pout on her lip, and her eyes full of tears.

He did not reprove her, though, as he once would have done; but seeming not to notice her ill-humor, exerted himself to soothe and amuse her, by talking in a cheerful strain of other matters; and in a very few moments all traces of it had disappeared, and she was answering him in her usual pleasant tone.

They had both been silent for several minutes, when she said, "Please, papa, put your head close down to me, I want to say something to you."

He complied, and putting her little arm around his neck, she said, in a very humble tone, "Dear papa, I was very naughty and cross just now; and I think I have been cross several times lately; and you have been so good and kind not to reprove or punish me, as I deserved. Please, papa, forgive me; I am very sorry, and I will try to be a better girl."

He kissed her very tenderly.

"I do forgive you freely, my little one," he said, "I know it seemed hard to give up the story just there, but it was for your good, and you must try always to believe that papa knows best. You are very precious to your father's heart, Elsie, but I am not going to *spoil* my little girl because I love her so dearly; nor because I have been so near losing her."

His voice trembled as he pronounced the last words, and for a moment emotion kept him silent. Then he went on again.

"I shall never again bid you do violence to your conscience, my daughter, but to all the commands which I *do* lay upon you I shall still expect and require the same ready and cheerful obedience that I have heretofore. It is my duty to require, and yours to yield it."

"Yes, papa, I know it is," she said with a little sigh, "but, it is very difficult sometimes to keep from wanting to have my own way."

"Yes, darling, I know it, for I find it so with myself," replied her father gently; "but we must, ask God to help us to give up our own wills, and be satisfied to do and have what we *ought*, rather than what we would *like*."

"I will, papa," she whispered, hugging him tighter and tighter. "I am so glad you teach me that."

They were quite quiet again for a little while. She was running her fingers through his hair.

"Oh, papa!" she exclaimed, "I see two or three white hairs! I am so sorry! I don't want you to get old. What made these come so soon, papa?"

He did not reply immediately, but, taking her in his arms, held her close to his heart. It was beating very fast.

Suddenly she seemed to comprehend.

"Was it because you were afraid I was going to die, papa?" she asked.

"Yes, dearest, and because I had reason, to think that my own cruelty had killed you."

The words were almost inaudible, but she heard them.

"Dear *dear* papa, how I love you!" she said, putting her arms around his neck again; "and I am so glad, for your sake, that I did not die."

He pressed her closer and closer, caressing her silently with a heart too full for words.

They sat thus for some time, but were at length interrupted by the entrance of Chloe, who had been left behind at Roselands to attend to the packing and removal of Elsie's clothes, and all her little possessions. She had finished her work, and her entrance was immediately followed by that of the men-servants bearing several large trunks and boxes, the contents of which she proceeded at once to unpack and rearrange in the new apartments.

Elsie watched this operation with a good deal of interest, occasionally directing where this or that article should be put; but in the midst of it all was carried off by her father to the tea-table.

Soon after tea the servants were all called together, and Mr. Dinsmore, after addressing a few words to them on the importance of calling upon God—the blessings promised to those who did, and the curses pronounced upon those individuals and families who did not—read a chapter from the Bible and offered up a prayer.

All were solemn and attentive, and all seemed pleased with the arrangement—for Mr. Dinsmore had told them it was to be the regular custom of the house, morning and evening—but Elsie, Mrs. Murray, and Chloe fairly wept for joy and thankfulness.

Elsie begged for another chapter and prayer in the privacy of her own rooms, and then Chloe undressed her, and her father carried her to her bed and placed her in it with a loving good-night kiss. And thus ended the first happy day in her own dear home.

CHAPTER XIV

"Her world was ever joyous;
She thought of grief and pain
As giants in the olden time,
That ne'er would come again."

MRS. HALE'S ALICE RAY.

"Then all was jollity,
Feasting, and mirth."

ROWE'S JANE SHORE.

It was with a start, and a momentary feeling of perplexity as to her whereabouts, followed almost instantly by the glad remembrance that she was indeed at *home*, that the little Elsie awoke the next morning. She sat up in the bed and gazed about her. Everything had a new, fresh look, and an air of simple elegance, that struck her as very charming.

A door on her right, communicating with her father's sleeping apartment, was slightly ajar, and she could hear him moving about.

"Papa!" she called, in her sweet, silvery tones.

"Good-morning, daughter," he said, appearing in answer to her summons. "Why, how bright my little girl is looking

Martha Finley

this morning!"

"Yes, papa, I feel so well and strong I do believe I can walk to the dining-room. Please, may I get up now?"

"Yes; Aunt Chloe may dress you, and call me when you are ready," he replied, bending down to give her a kiss.

Chloe was just coming in from a small adjoining room which had been appropriated to her use, and exclaimed with delight at her darling's bright looks.

"Dress her very nicely, Aunt Chloe," said Mr. Dinsmore, "for I think it is quite possible we may have visitors to-day; and besides, I want her to look her best for my own enjoyment," he added, with a loving look and smile directed toward his little girl.

Chloe promised to do her best; and he seemed entirely satisfied with the result of her labors, as well he might, for Elsie looked very lovely in her simple white dress, and little embroidered pink sacque, which seemed to lend a faint tinge of color to her pale cheeks. She was tired, though, with the dressing, and quite willing to give up her plan of walking to the dining-room, and let her father carry her.

After breakfast he sat with her on his knee for a little while, and then, laying her on the sofa and giving her a kiss, he told her he must leave her with Chloe for an hour or two, as he had some business matters to arrange with her grandfather, after which he would take her to ride.

"I wish you didn't have to go, papa; but please come back as soon as you can," she said coaxingly.

"I will, darling. And now, Aunt Chloe, I leave her in your care; don't let her do anything to tire herself," he said as he went out.

Elsie listened until she heard the sound of his horse's hoofs as he galloped down the avenue, and then turning to her nurse, she exclaimed eagerly,

"Now, mammy, please hand me my work-box and that unfinished slipper."

"You's not fit to sew, darlin' chile," objected the careful old woman, doing as she was asked, nevertheless.

"Well, mammy, I want to try, and I'll stop directly if it tires me," replied the little girl. "Please put me in my rocking-chair. They are for papa, you see, and I want to get them done before Christmas."

"Dere's plenty ob time yet 'fore Christmas, darlin', to do dat little bit," Chloe said; "'tain't comin' dis four or five weeks; better wait till you git stronger."

Elsie was not to be dissuaded, however, from making the attempt; but a very few moments' work satisfied her that she was still too weak for such an employment; and she readily consented to let Chloe put away her work-box and lay her on her sofa again, where she spent the rest of the time in reading her Bible until her father returned. Then came her ride, and then a nap, which took up all the morning until near dinner-time.

She found Mr. Travilla sitting there, talking with her father, when she awoke. She was very glad to see him, and to hear that he was going to stay to dinner; and they had quite a little chat together about the new home and its surroundings.

After dinner, her Aunt Adelaide, Lora, and Walter called to see them and the house; but both they and Mr. Travilla went away early—he promising to bring his mother to see her very soon—and then she was left alone with her father again.

"Would you like now to hear the remainder of the story we

were reading yesterday, daughter?" he asked.

"Very much, papa; I have been wanting it all day."

"Why did you not ask for it, then?" he inquired.

"Because, papa, I was ashamed, after being so naughty about it yesterday," she answered, hanging her head and blushing deeply.

"Well, you shall have it now, daughter," he said luridly, pressing his lips to the little blushing cheek. "I had forgotten about it, or I would have given you the book to read while I was out this morning."

A very pleasant, happy life had now begun for our little Elsie: all her troubles seemed to be over, and she was surrounded by everything that heart could wish. Her father watched over her with the tenderest love and care; devoting the greater part of his time to her entertainment and instruction, sparing neither trouble nor expense to give her pleasure, and though still requiring unhesitating, cheerful obedience to his wishes and commands—yet ruling her not less gently than firmly. He never spoke to her now in his stern tone, and after a while she ceased to expect and dread it.

Her health improved quite rapidly after their removal to the Oaks, and before Christmas came again she was entirely equal to a little stroll in the grounds, or a short ride on her favorite pony.

Her cheeks were becoming round and rosy again, and her hair had grown long enough to curl in soft, glossy little ringlets all over her head, and her father thought her almost prettier than ever. But he was very careful of her still, scarcely willing to have her a moment out of his sight, lest she should become over-fatigued, or her health be injured in some way; and he always accompanied her in her walks and rides, ever watching over her with the most unwearied love. As her health and strength returned he permitted her, in accordance with her own wishes, gradually to resume her studies, and took great pleasure in instructing her; but he was very particular to see that she did not attempt too much, nor sit poring over her books when she needed exercise and recreation, as she was sometimes rather inclined to do.

"Massa, dere's a gentleman wants to speak to you," said a servant, looking in at the study door one afternoon a few days before Christmas.

"Very well, John, show him into the library, and I will be there in a moment," replied Mr. Dinsmore, putting down his book.

He glanced at Elsie's little figure, half buried in the cushions of a great easy-chair near one of the windows, into which she had climbed more than an hour before, and where she had been sitting ever since, completely lost to all that might be going on about her, in the deep interest with which she was following the adventures of FitzJames in Scott's "Lady of the Lake."

"Daughter, I am afraid you are reading more to-day than is quite good for you," he said, looking at his watch. "You must put up your book very soon now, and go out for a walk. I shall probably be down in ten or fifteen minutes; but if I am not, you must not wait for me, but take Aunt Chloe with you."

"Yes, papa," she replied, looking up from her book for an instant, and then returning to it again as he left the room.

She had not the least intention of disobeying, but soon forgot everything else in the interest of her story.

The stranger detained Mr. Dinsmore much longer than he had expected, and the short winter day was drawing rapidly to a close when he returned to his study, to find Elsie—much to his surprise and displeasure—precisely where he had left her.

She was not aware of his entrance until he was close beside her;

Martha Finley

then, looking up with a start, she colored violently.

He gently took the book from her hand and laid it away, then, lifting her from the chair, led her across the room, where he seated himself upon the sofa, and drawing her in between his knees, regarded her with a look of grave, sad displeasure.

"Has my little daughter any idea how long it is since her father bade her put up her book?" he asked in a gently reproving tone.

Elsie hung her head in silence, and a tear rolled quickly down her burning cheek.

"It grieves me very much," he said, "to find that my little girl can be so disobedient! it almost makes me fear that she does not love me very much."

"Oh, papa, don't! oh, don't say that! I can't bear to hear it!" she cried, bursting into an agony of tears and sobs, and hiding her face on his breast. "I do love you *very* much, papa, and I can't bear to think I've grieved you," she sobbed. "I know I am very naughty, and deserve to be punished—but I didn't mean to disobey, only the book was so interesting I didn't know at all how the time went."

He sighed, but said nothing; only drew her closer to him, pulling his arm around her, and stroking her hair in a gentle, caressing way.

There was no sound for some moments but Elsie's sobs.

Then she asked in a half whisper, "Are you going to punish me, papa?"

"I shall take the book from you for a few days; I hope that will be punishment enough to make you pay better attention to my commands in future," he said very gravely.

"Dear papa how kind you are! I am sure I deserve a great deal worse punishment than that," she exclaimed, raising her head and looking up gratefully and lovingly into his face, "but I am very, very sorry for my disobedience; will you please forgive me?"

"I will, daughter," and he bent down and kissed her lips.

"Now go," he said, "and get your cloak and hood. I think we will still have time for a little stroll through the grounds before dark."

Elsie had very little to say during their walk, but moved silently along by her father's side, with her hand clasped in his; and he, too, seemed unusually abstracted.

It was quite dusk when they entered the house again, and when the little girl returned to the study, after Chloe had taken off her wrappings, she found her father seated in an easy-chair, drawn up on one side of a bright wood fire that was blazing and crackling on the hearth.

Elsie dearly loved the twilight hour, and it was one of her greatest pleasures to climb upon her father's knee and sit there talking or singing, or perhaps, oftener, just laying her head down on his breast and watching the play of the fire-light on the carpet, or the leaping of the flame hither and thither.

Mr. Dinsmore sat leaning back in his chair, apparently in deep thought, and did not hear Elsie's light step.

She paused for one instant in the doorway, casting a wistful, longing look at him, then, with a little sigh, walked softly to the other side of the fire-place, and seated herself in her little rocking-chair.

For several minutes she sat very quietly gazing into the fire, her little face wearing a very sober, thoughtful look. But she was startled out of her reverie by the sound of her father's voice.

"Why am I not to have my little girl on my knee to-night?" he was asking.

She rose instantly, in a quick, eager way, and ran to him.

"If you prefer the rocking-chair, stay there, by all means," he said.

But she had already climbed to her accustomed seat, and, twining her arms around his neck, she laid her cheek to his, saying, "No, indeed, papa; you know I don't like the rocking-chair half so well as your knee; so please let me stay here."

"Why did you not come at first, then?" he asked in a playful tone.

"Because I was afraid, papa," she whispered,

"*Afraid*!" he repeated, with an accent of surprise, and looking as if he felt a little hurt.

"Yes, papa," she answered in a low tone, "because I have been so very naughty this afternoon that I know I don't deserve to come."

"Did you not hear me say I forgave you?" he asked.

"Yes, papa."

"Very well, then, if you are forgiven you are taken back into favor, just as if you had not transgressed; and if you had quite believed me, you would have come to me at once, and claimed a daughter's privilege, as usual," he said very gravely.

"I do believe you, papa; I know you always speak the truth and mean just what you say," she replied in half-tearful tones, "but I know I don't deserve a place on your knee to-night."

"What you *deserve* is not the question at present; we are talking about what you can *have*, whether you *deserve* it or not.

"Ah!" he continued in a low, musing tone, more as if thinking aloud than speaking to her, "just so it is with us all in reference to our Heavenly Father's forgiveness; when he offers us a full and free pardon of all our offences, and adoption into his family, we don't more than half believe him, but still go about groaning under the burden of our sins, and afraid to claim the privileges of children.

"It hurts and displeases me when my child doubts my word, and yet how often I dishonor my Father by doubting his. 'He that believeth not God, maketh him a liar.' 'Without faith it is impossible to please him.'"

He relapsed into silence, and for some moments neither of them spoke.

He was passing his hand caressingly over her hair, and she resting in his arms and gazing thoughtfully into the fire.

"What is my little one thinking of?" he asked at last.

"I was thinking what a very naughty girl I have been this afternoon, and what a dear, kind papa I have," she said, looking up lovingly into his face. "You were so kind, papa, not to punish me as I deserved. I was afraid you would send me directly to bed, and I should miss my pleasant evening with you."

"I hope, my darling," he answered gently, "that you do not think, when I punish you, it is from anything like a feeling of revenge, or because I take pleasure in giving you pain? Not at all. I do it for your own good—and in this instance, as I thought you were sorry enough for having grieved and displeased me to keep you from repeating the offence, I did not consider any further punishment necessary. But perhaps I was mistaken, and it was only fear of punishment that caused your tears," he added, looking keenly at her.

"Oh, no, papa! no indeed!" she exclaimed earnestly, the tears rushing into her eyes again; "it is worse than any punishment to know that I have grieved and displeased you, because I love you so very, *very* dearly!" and the little arm crept round his neck again, and the soft cheek was laid to his.

"I know it, darling," he said, "I fully believe that you would prefer any physical suffering to the pain of my displeasure."

"Papa," she said, after a few moments' silence, "I want to tell you something."

"Well, daughter, I am ready to listen," he answered pleasantly; "what is it?"

"I was looking in my desk to-day, papa, for a letter that I wrote to you the evening before I was taken sick, and I couldn't find it. Did Aunt Adelaide give it to you?"

"Yes, dear, I have it, and one of your curls," he said, pressing her closer to him.

"Yes, papa, *that* was what I wanted to tell you about. I am afraid I was very naughty to cut it off after all you said about it last Christmas; but everything was so strange that night—it seems like a dreadful dream to me now. I don't think I was quite in my right mind sometimes, and I thought I was going to die, and something seemed to tell me that you would want some of my hair when I was gone, and that nobody would save it for you; and so I cut it off myself. You do not mind about it, papa, dear, do you? You don't think it was *very* naughty in me?" she asked anxiously.

"No, darling, no; it was very right and kind, and much more than I deserved," he answered with emotion.

"I am glad you are not angry, papa," she said in a relieved tone, "and, indeed, I did not mean to be naughty or disobedient."

John was just bringing in the lights, and Mr. Dinsmore took a note from his pocket, saying, "I will read this to you, daughter, as it concerns you as well as myself."

It was an invitation from Mrs. Howard—the mother of Elsie's friend, Caroline—to Mr. Dinsmore and his little girl, to come and spend the Christmas holidays with them.

"Well, my pet, what do you say to it? would you like to go?" he asked, as he refolded the note and returned it to his pocket.

"I don't know, papa; it seems as if it would be pleasant, as we are both invited; but home is so sweet, and I am so happy just alone with you that I hardly want to go away; so if you please, papa, I would much rather just leave it all to you."

"Well, then, we will stay quietly at home," he said, with a gratified look; "and I think it will be much the better plan, for you are not strong enough yet for gayety, and it would be very little pleasure for you to be there while unable to join in the sports, and obliged always to keep early hours.

"But we might have a Christmas dinner at home, and invite a few friends to help us eat it. Whom would you like to have?"

"Mr. and Mrs. Travilla, and Aunt Adelaide, and Lora, if you please, papa, and anybody else you like," she replied, looking very much pleased. "I should like to have Carry Howard, but of course I can't—as she is going to have company of her own; and I believe nearly all the little girls I am acquainted with are to be there."

"Yes, I suppose so. Well, we will ask those you have mentioned, and I hope they will come. But there is the tea-bell, and I shall carry my dolly out to the dining-room," he said, rising with her in his arms.

"Papa," she said, when they had returned to their seats by the study fire, "may I give mammy a nice present this Christmas?"

"Yes," he replied kindly, "I supposed you would want to give some presents, and I have just been thinking how it might be managed, as you are not fit to shop for yourself. As you have not had any pocket-money for several months, I will allow you now to spend as much as you choose—provided you keep within tolerably reasonable bounds," he added, smiling; "so you may make out a list of all the articles you want, and I will purchase them for you. Will that do?"

"Oh, nicely, papa!" she cried, clapping her hands with delight, "it was very good of you to think of all that."

"De slippers is come, darlin'; Bill, he fotched 'em from de city dis afternoon," remarked Chloe, as she was preparing her little charge for bed that night.

"Oh, have they, mammy? let me see them!" was Elsie's eager exclamation.

Chloe went to her room and was back again in a moment with a bundle in her hand, which Elsie immediately seized and opened with eager haste.

"Oh, how pretty!" she cried, capering about with them in her hands, "aren't they, mammy? Won't papa be pleased?"

Then starting at the sound of his step in the adjoining room, she threw them into a drawer which Chloe had hastily opened for the purpose.

"Elsie," said her father, opening the door and putting in his head, "why are you not in bed, my daughter? you will take cold standing there half undressed. Go to bed immediately."

"Yes, papa, I will," she replied submissively; and he drew back his head again and shut the door.

"Mighty narrow 'scape dat," remarked Chloe, laughing; "ef Massa had come jes a minute sooner, de cat been out de bag sure 'nough."

Elsie made out her list the next day, with the help of some suggestions from her father, and by Christmas eve all the purchases had been made, and one of the closets in her bedroom was quite filled with packages of various sizes and shapes.

The little girl was all excitement, and did not want to go to bed when the hour came.

"Please, papa, let me stay up a little longer," she pleaded coaxingly. "I am not a bit sleepy."

"No, my daughter; you must go at once," he said; "early hours are of great importance in your present state of health, and you must try to put away all exciting thoughts, and go to sleep as soon as you can. You will try to obey me in this?"

"Yes, papa; I am sure I ought to be very good when you are so kind and indulgent to me," she replied, as she put up her face for the usual good-night kiss.

"God bless and keep my little one, and give her many happy returns of this Christmas eve," said Mr. Dinsmore, folding her to his heart.

Elsie had intended to stay awake until her father should be in bed and asleep, and then to steal softly into his room and take away the slippers he usually wore, replacing them with the new ones which she had worked. But now she engaged Chloe to do this for her, and in obedience to his directions endeavored to put away all exciting thoughts and go to sleep, in which she succeeded much sooner than she could have believed possible.

She was up and dressed, and saying "Merry Christmas!" at her papa's door, quite early the next morning.

"Come in," said he, "and tell me what fairy has been here, changing my old slippers to new ones."

"No fairy at all, papa; but just dear old mammy," she cried, springing into his arms with a merry, ringing laugh.

"Ah, but I know very well it wasn't Aunt Chloe's fingers that worked them," he said, kissing her first on one cheek, then on the other. "I wish you a very merry Christmas, and a *very happy* New Year, my darling. Thank you for your gift; I like it very much, indeed; and now see what papa has for *you*."

And opening a pretty little box that stood on his dressing-table, he took from it a beautiful pearl necklace and bracelets, and clasped them round her neck and arms.

"Oh, how beautiful! dear papa, thank you very much," she exclaimed, delighted.

"Your Aunt Adelaide thought you didn't care much for ornaments," he remarked, looking much pleased.

"I do when *you* give them to me, papa," she answered, raising her eyes to his face with one of her sweet, loving smiles.

"I am very glad my present pleases you," he said, "but for fear it should not, I have provided another," and he placed in her hand a very handsomely bound volume of Scott's poems.

"I don't deserve it, papa," she said, coloring deeply, and dropping her eyes on the carpet.

"You shall have it, at any rate," he replied, laying his hand gently on her drooping head; "and now you can finish the 'Lady of the Lake' this afternoon, if you like. His prose works I may perhaps give you at some future day; but I do not choose you should read them for some years to come. But now we will lay this book aside for the present, and have our morning chapter together."

They had finished their devotions, and she was sitting on his knee, waiting for the breakfast-bell to ring.

"When did you find an opportunity to work these without letting me into the secret?" he asked, extending his foot, and turning it from side to side to look at his slipper. "It puzzles me to understand it, since I know that for weeks past you have scarcely been an hour out of my sight during the day—not since you were well enough to sew," he said, smiling down at her.

There was an expression of deep gravity, almost amounting to sadness, on Elsie's little face, that surprised her father a good deal.

"All, papa!" she murmured, "it makes me feel sad, and glad, too, to look at those slippers."

"Why, darling?" he asked in a tender tone.

"Because, papa, I worked almost the whole of them last summer, in those sorrowful days when I was all alone. I thought I was going to die, papa, for I was sure I could not live very long without you to love me, and I wanted to make something for you that would remind you of your little girl when she was gone, and perhaps convince you that she did really love you, although she seemed so naughty and rebellious,"

The tears were streaming down her cheeks, and there was a momentary struggle to keep down a rising sob; and then she added—

"I finished them since I came here, papa, a little at a time, whenever you were not with me."

He was deeply moved. "My poor darling!" he sighed, drawing her closer to him, and caressing her tenderly, "those were sad days to us both, and though I *then* persuaded myself that I was doing my duty toward you, if you had been taken away from me I could never have forgiven myself, or known another happy moment. But God has treated me with undeserved mercy."

After breakfast the house-servants were all called in to family worship, as usual; and when that had been attended to, Elsie uncovered a large basket which stood on a side-table, and with a face beaming with delight, distributed the Christmas gifts—a nice new calico dress, or a bright-colored hand-kerchief to each, accompanied by a paper of confectionery.

They were received with bows and courtesies, broad grins of satisfaction, and many repetitions of "Tank you, Miss Elsie! dese berry handsome—berry nice, jes de ting for dis chile."

Mr. Dinsmore stood looking on highly gratified, and coming in for a share of the thanks.

An hour or two later, Elsie's little pony, and her father's larger but equally beautiful steed, were brought up to the door, and they rode down to the quarter, followed by Jim and Bill, each carrying a good-sized basket; and there a very similar scene was gone through with—Elsie finishing up the business by showering sugar-plums into the outstretched aprons of the little ones, laughing merrily at their eagerness, and highly enjoying their delight.

She half wished for an instant, as she turned her horse's head to ride away again, that she was one of them, so much did she want a share of the candy, which her father refused to let her taste, saying it was not fit for her when she was well, and much less now while she had yet hardly recovered from severe illness.

But it was a lovely morning, the air pure and bracing, and everything else was speedily forgotten in the pleasure of a brisk ride with her father. They rode several miles, and on their return were overtaken by Mr. Travilla, who remarked that Elsie had quite a color, and was looking more like herself than he had seen her since her sickness. He was on horseback, and his mother arrived a little later in the carriage, having called at Roselands on the way, and picked up Adelaide. Lora did not come, as she had accepted an invitation to spend the holidays at Mr. Howard's, where a little girl about her own age, a cousin of Carry's, from the North, was spending the winter.

Mr. Travilla put a beautiful little pearl ring on Elsie's finger, which she gracefully thanked him for, and then showing it to her father, "See, papa," she said, "how nicely it matches the bracelets."

"Yes, daughter, it is very pretty," he replied, "and one of these days, when you are old enough to wear it, you shall have a pin to match."

Mrs. Travilla and Adelaide each gave her a handsome book—Adelaide's was a beautifully bound Bible—and Elsie was delighted with all her presents, and thought no little girl could be richer in Christmas gifts than herself.

The day passed very pleasantly, for they were quite like a family party, every one seeming to feel perfectly at home and at ease.

The negroes were to have a grand dinner at the quarter, and Elsie, who had been deeply interested in the preparations—cake-baking, etc.—was now very anxious to see them enjoying their feast; so about one o'clock she and her father invited their guests to walk down there with them to enjoy the sight.

"*I*, for one, would like nothing better," said Mr. Travilla, offering his arm to Adelaide, while Mr. Dinsmore took Mrs. Travilla, Elsie walking on the other side and keeping fast hold of his hand.

They found it a very merry scene; and the actors in it scarcely enjoyed it more than the spectators.

Their own dinner was served up somewhat later in the day, and with appetites rendered keen by their walk in the bracing air, they were ready to do it full justice.

Adelaide, at her brother's request, took the head of the table, and played the part of hostess very gracefully.

"Ah, Dinsmore," remarked Travilla, a little mischievously, glancing from one to the other, "you have a grand establishment here, but it still lacks its chief ornament. Miss Adelaide fills the place *to-day*, most gracefully, it is true; but then we all know she is only borrowed for the occasion."

Mr. Dinsmore colored a little and looked slightly annoyed.

"Elsie will supply that deficiency in a few years," he said, "and until then, I think I can depend upon the kindness of my sisters. Besides, Travilla," he added laughingly, "you must not forget the old proverb about people who live in glass houses."

"Ah," replied Travilla, looking affectionately at his mother, "*I have* a mistress for my establishment, and so can *afford* to wait for Elsie."

The child looked up quickly, with a slight flush on her face.

"You needn't, Mr. Travilla!" she said, "for I am *never* going to leave my father; and you know he promised not to give me away, so if you want a little girl you will have to look somewhere else."

"Ah! well, I will not despair yet," he replied laughingly, "for I have learned that ladies, both little and large, very often change their minds, and so I shall still live in hopes."

"You know I like you very much indeed, Mr. Travilla—next best to papa—but then I couldn't leave him for *anybody*, you see," Elsie said in a deprecating tone, and looking affectionately up into his face.

"No, my dear, that is quite right, and I don't feel at all hurt," he answered with a good-natured smile, which seemed to relieve her very much.

Tea was over, the guests had returned to their homes, and Mr. Dinsmore sat by the fire, as usual, with his little girl upon his knee.

"We have had a very pleasant day, papa, haven't we?" she remarked.

"Yes, darling, I have enjoyed it, and I hope you have, too."

"Very much indeed, papa; and I do like all my presents so much."

"If I should ask you to give me something of yours, would you be willing to do it?" he inquired in a grave tone.

"Why, papa!" she said, looking up quickly into his face, "doesn't everything I have belong to you?"

"In some sense it does, certainly," he replied, "and yet I like you to feel that you have some rights of property. But you did not answer my question."

"I can't think what it can be, papa; but I am sure there is nothing of mine that I wouldn't be very glad to give you, if you wanted it," she said earnestly.

"Well, then," said he, "your aunt gave you a new Bible to-day, and as you don't need two, will you give the old one to me?"

A slight shade had come over the little girl's face, and she sat for a moment apparently in deep thought; then, looking up lovingly into his face, she replied, "I love it very much, papa, and I don't know whether any other Bible could ever seem *quite* the same to me—it was mamma's, you know—and it has been with me in all my troubles, and I don't think I could be quite willing to give it to anybody else; but I am very glad to give it to you, my own dear, dear papa!" and she threw her arms around his neck.

"Thank you very much, my darling. I know it is a very strong proof of your affection, and I shall value it more than its weight in gold," he said, pressing her to his heart, and kissing her tenderly.

CHAPTER XV

"Wide flush the fields; the softening air is balm;
Echo the mountains round; the forest smiles;
And every sense, and every heart, is joy."

THOMSON.

It was spring again; early in April; the air was filled with the melody of birds, and balmy with the breath of flowers. All nature was awaking to renewed life and vigor; but not so with our little friend. She had never fully recovered her strength, and as the season advanced, and the weather became warmer she seemed to grow more languid.

Her father was very anxious about her, and sending for Dr. Barton one morning, held a long consultation with him, the result of which was a determination on Mr. Dinsmore's part that he would take his little girl travelling for some months. They would go North immediately; for the doctor said it was the best thing that could be done; in fact the only thing that would be likely to benefit her.

When the doctor had gone, Mr. Dinsmore went into Elsie's little sitting-room, where she was busily engaged with her lessons.

"I am not quite ready yet, papa," she said, looking up as he entered; "isn't it a little before the time?"

"Yes, a little," he replied, consulting his watch, "but you needn't mind that lesson, daughter; I'm afraid I have been working you too hard."

"Oh, no, papa! and if you please, I would rather finish the lesson."

"Very well, then, I will wait for you," he said, taking up a book.

She came to him in a few moments, saying that she was quite ready now, and when he had heard her recitations, and praised her for their excellence, he bade her put her books away and come and sit on his knee, for he had something to tell her.

"Is it good news, papa?" she asked, as he lifted her to her accustomed seat.

"Yes, I hope you will think so: it is that you and I, and mammy, and John are about to set out upon our travels. I am going to take you North to spend the summer, as the doctor thinks that is the best thing that can be done to bring back your health and strength."

Elsie's eyes were dancing with joy. "Oh, how delightful that will be!" she exclaimed. "And will you take me to see Miss Rose, papa?"

"Yes, anywhere that you would like to go. Suppose we make out a list of the places we would like to visit," he said, taking out pencil and paper.

"Oh, yes, papa," she answered eagerly; "I would like to go to Washington, to see the Capitol, and the President's house, and then to Philadelphia to see Independence Hall, where they signed the Declaration, you know, and then to New York, and then to Boston; for I want to see Bunker Hill, and Faneuil Hall, and all the places that we read so much about in the history of the Revolution, and—but, papa, may I *really* go *wherever* I want to?" she asked, interrupting herself in the midst of her rapid enumeration, to which he was listening with an amused expression.

"I said so, did I not?" he replied, smiling at her eagerness.

"Well, then, papa, I want to see Lakes Champlain and Ontario; yes, and all those great lakes—and Niagara Fails; and to sail up or down the Hudson River and the Connecticut, and I would like to visit the White Mountains, and—I don't know where else I would like to go, but—"

"That will do pretty well for a beginning, I think," he said, laughing, "and by the time we are through with all those, if you are not ready to return home, you may be able to think of some more. Now for the time of starting. This is Wednesday—I think we will leave next Tuesday morning."

"I am glad it is so soon," Elsie said, with a look of great satisfaction, "for I am in such a hurry to see Miss Rose. Must I go on with lessons this week, papa?"

"With your music and drawing; but that will be all, except that we will read history together for an hour every day. I know a little regular employment will make the time pass much more quickly and pleasantly to you."

Elsie could now talk of very little but her expected journey, and thought that time moved much more slowly than usual; yet when Monday evening came and she and her father walked over the grounds, taking leave of all her favorite haunts, everything was looking so lovely that she half regretted the necessity of leaving her beautiful home even for a few months.

They started very early in the morning, before the sun was up, travelling to the city in their own carriage, and then taking the cars.

They visited Baltimore and Washington, staying just long

enough in each place to see all that was worth seeing; then went on to Philadelphia, where they expected to remain several weeks, as it was there Miss Rose resided. Mr. Allison was a prosperous merchant, with a fine establishment in the city, and a very elegant country-seat a few miles out of it.

On reaching the city Elsie was in such haste to see her friend, that she entreated her father to go directly to Mr. Allison's, saying she was certain that Miss Rose would wish them to do so.

But Mr. Dinsmore would not consent. "It would never do," he said, "to rush in upon our friends in that way, without giving them any warning; we might put them to great inconvenience."

So John was sent for a carriage, and they drove to one of the first hotels in the city, where Mr. Dinsmore at once engaged rooms for himself, daughter, and servants.

"You are looking tired, my child," he said, as he led Elsie to her room and seated her upon a sofa; "and you are warm and dusty. But mammy must give you a bath, and put on your loose wrapper, and I will have your supper brought up here, and then you must go early to bed, and I hope you will feel quite bright again in the morning."

"Yes, papa, I hope so; and then you will take me to see Miss Rose, won't you?" she asked coaxingly.

"I will send them our cards to-night, my dear, since you feel in such haste," he replied in a pleasant tone, "and probably Miss Rose will be here in the morning if she is well, and cares to see us."

John and the porter were bringing up the trunks. They set them down and went out again, followed by Mr. Dinsmore, who did not return until half an hour afterwards, when he found Elsie lying on the sofa, seeming much refreshed by her bath and change of clothing. "You look better already, dearest," he said, stooping to press a kiss on her lips.

"And you, too, papa," she answered, smiling up at him. "I think it improves any one to get the dust washed off. Won't you take your tea up here with me? I should like it so much."

"I will, darling," he said kindly; "it is a great pleasure to me to gratify you in any harmless wish." And then he asked her what she would like for her supper, and told Chloe to ring for the waiter, that she might order it.

After their tea they had their reading and prayer together; then he bade her good-night and left her, telling Chloe to put her to bed immediately. Chloe obeyed, and the little girl rose the next morning, feeling quite rested, and looking very well and bright.

"How early do you think Miss Rose will come, papa?" was the first question she put to him on his entrance into her room.

"Indeed, my child, I do not know, but I certainly should not advise you to expect her before ten o'clock, at the very earliest."

"And it isn't eight yet," murmured Elsie, disconsolately. "Oh, papa, I wish you would take me to see her as soon as breakfast is over."

He shook his head. "You must not be so impatient, my little daughter," he said, drawing her towards him. "Shall I take you to Independence Hall to-day?"

"Not until Miss Rose has been here, if you please, papa; because I am so afraid of missing her."

"Very well, you may stay in this morning, if you wish," he replied in an indulgent tone, as he took her hand to lead her down to the breakfast-table.

So Elsie remained in her room all the morning, starting at every footstep, and turning her head eagerly every time the door opened: but no Miss Rose appeared, and she met her father at dinner-time with a very disconsolate face. He sympathized in her disappointment, and said all he could to raise her drooping spirits.

When dinner was over, he did not ask if he should take her out, but quietly bade her go to Chloe and get her bonnet put on. She obeyed, as she knew she must, without a word, but as he took her hand on her return, to lead her out, she asked, "Is there no danger that Miss Rose will come while we are gone, papa?"

"If she does, my dear, she will leave her card, and then we can go to see her; or very possibly she may wait until we return," he answered in a kind, cheerful tone. "But at any rate, you must have a walk this afternoon."

Elsie sighed a little, but said no more, and her father led her along, talking so kindly, and finding so many pretty things to show her, that after a little she almost forgot her anxiety and disappointment.

They were passing a confectioner's, where the display of sweetmeats in the window was unusually tempting. Elsie called his attention to it.

"See, papa, how *very* nice those candies look!"

He smiled a little, asking, "Which do you think looks the most inviting?"

"I don't know, papa, there is such a variety."

"I will indulge you for once—it isn't often I do," he said, leading her into the store; "so now choose what you want and I will pay for it."

"Thank you, papa!" and the smile that accompanied the words was a very bright one.

When they returned to their hotel Elsie eagerly inquired of Chloe if Miss Rose had been there, and was again sadly disappointed to learn that she had not.

"Oh, papa!" she said, bursting into tears, "what *can* be the reason she doesn't come?"

"I don't know, darling," he answered soothingly; "but never mind; she is probably away from home, and perhaps will return in a day or two."

The next morning Mr. Dinsmore would not hear of staying in to wait for a call that was so uncertain, but ordered a carriage immediately after breakfast, and had Elsie out sight-seeing and shopping all day. One of their visits—one which particularly pleased and interested the little girl—was to Independence Hall, where they were shown the bell which in Revolutionary days had, in accordance with its motto, "Proclaimed liberty throughout all the land, to all the inhabitants thereof."

"I am so glad to have seen it, papa," Elsie said. "I have always felt so interested in its story, and shall never forget it so long as I live."

"Yes," he said, with a pleased smile, "I was sure you would enjoy seeing it; for I know my little girl is very patriotic."

Other historical scenes were visited after that, and thus several days passed very pleasantly. Still there were no tidings of Miss Allison, and at last Elsie gave up expecting her; for her father said it must certainly be that the family had left the city for the summer, although it was so early in the season; so he decided that they would go on and visit Boston, and the White Mountains; and perhaps go up the Hudson River, too, and to Niagara Falls, and the lakes, stopping in Philadelphia again on their return; when their friends would probably be in the

Martha Finley

city again.

It was on Saturday morning that he announced this decision to Elsie, adding that they would remain where they were over the Sabbath, and leave for New York early Monday morning.

Elsie sighed at the thought of giving up for so long a time all hope of seeing Miss Rose, and looked very sober for a little while, though she said nothing.

"Well, I believe we have seen all the sights in this city of Brotherly Love, so what shall we do with ourselves to-day?" her father asked gayly, as he drew her towards him, and playfully patted her cheek.

"I should like to go back to the Academy of Fine Arts, if you will take me, papa; there are several pictures there which I want very much to see again."

"Then get your bonnet, my pet, and we will go at once," he said; and Elsie hastened to do his bidding.

There were very few other visitors in the Academy when Mr. Dinsmore and his little girl entered. They spent several hours there, almost too much absorbed in studying the different paintings to notice who were coming or going, or what might be passing about them. They themselves, however, were by no means unobserved, and more than once the remark might have been heard from some one whose eyes were turned in that direction, "What a very fine-looking gentleman!" or, "What a lovely little girl!"

One young lady and gentleman watched them for some time.

"What a very handsome and distinguished-looking man he is," remarked the lady in an undertone, "His face looks familiar, too, and yet I surely cannot have met him before."

"Yes, he is a fine, gentlemanly looking fellow," replied her companion in the same low tone, "but it is the little girl that attracts my attention. She is perfectly lovely! his sister, I presume. There, Rose, now you can see her face," he added, as at that moment Elsie turned toward them.

"Oh, it is a dear little face! But can it be? no, surely it is impossible! yes, yes, it *is*, my own little Elsie!"

For at that instant their eyes met, and uttering a joyful exclamation, the little girl darted across the room, and threw herself into the lady's arms, crying, "Oh, Miss Rose! dear, dear Miss Rose, how glad I am!"

"Elsie! darling! why, where did you come from?" and Rose's arms were clasped about the little girl's waist, and she was showering kisses upon the sweet little face.

"I did not even know you were in the North," she said presently, releasing her from her embrace, but still keeping fast hold of her hand, and looking down lovingly into her face. "When did you come? and who is with you? but I need scarcely ask, for it must be your papa, of course."

"Yes, ma'am," replied Elsie, looking round, "there he is, and see! he is coming toward us. Papa, this is Miss Rose."

Rose held out her hand with one of her sweetest smiles. "I am very glad to see you, Mr. Dinsmore, especially as you have brought my dear little friend with you. This is my brother Edward," she added, turning to her companion. "Mr. Dinsmore, Edward, and little Elsie, of whom you have so often heard me speak."

There was a cordial greeting all around; then questions were asked and answered until everything had been explained; Mr. Dinsmore learning that Mr. Allison's family were out of the city, passing the summer at their country-seat, and had never received his cards; but that to-day, Rose and her brother had come in to do a little shopping, and finding that they had an hour to spare, had fortunately decided to pay a visit to the Academy.

When these explanations had been made, Edward and Rose urged Mr. Dinsmore to return with them to their home and pay them a long visit, saying that they knew nothing else would at all satisfy their parents, and at length he consented to do so, on condition that they first dined with him at his hotel, to which they finally agreed.

Elsie was delighted with the arrangement, and looked happier, her father laughingly affirmed, than she had done for a week.

She was seated by Miss Rose at dinner, and also in the carriage during their ride, which was a beautiful one, and just long enough to be pleasant.

They had passed a number of very handsome residences, which Rose had pointed out to Elsie, generally giving the name of the occupant, and asking how she liked the place. "Now, Elsie, we are coming to another," she said, laying her hand on the little girl's arm, "and I want you to tell me what you think of it. See! that large, old-fashioned house built of gray stone; there, beyond the avenue of elms."

"Oh, I like it so much! better than any of the others! I think I should like to live there."

"I am very glad it pleases you," Rose answered with a smile, "and I hope you will live there, at least for some weeks or months."

"Oh, it is your home? how glad I am!" exclaimed the little girl as the carriage turned into the avenue.

"This is a very fine old place, Miss Allison," remarked Mr. Dinsmore, turning toward her; "I think one might well be content to spend his days here."

Rose looked gratified, and pointed out several improvements her father had been making. "I am very proud of my home," she said, "but I do not think it more lovely than Roselands."

"Ah! Miss Rose, but you ought to see the Oaks—papa's new place," said Elsie, eagerly. "It is much handsomer than Roselands, I think. Miss Rose must visit us next time, papa, must she not?"

"If she will, daughter, Miss Allison, or any other member of her father's family, will always find a warm welcome at my house."

Rose had only time to say "Thank you," before the carriage had stopped, and Edward, springing out, was ready to assist the others to alight.

Mr. Dinsmore and Elsie were left standing upon the piazza, looking about them, while Edward was engaged for a moment in giving some directions to the coachman, and Rose was speaking to a servant who had come out on their approach.

"Mamma is lying down with a bad headache, Mr. Dinsmore, and papa has not yet returned from the city," said Rose, turning to her guests; "but I hope you will excuse them, and Edward will show you to your room, and try to make you feel at home."

Mr. Dinsmore politely expressed his regret at Mrs. Allison's illness, and his hope that their arrival would not be allowed to disturb her.

Miss Allison then left him to her brother's care, and taking Elsie's hand, led her to her own room. It was a large, airy apartment, very prettily furnished, with another a little smaller opening into it.

"This is my room, Elsie," said Miss Rose, "and that is Sophy's. You will sleep with her, and so I can take care of you both, for though Chloe can attend you morning and evening as usual, she will have to sleep in one of the servants' rooms in the attic."

She had been taking off Elsie's bonnet, and smoothing her hair as she spoke, and now removing her own, she sat down on a low seat, and taking the little girl on her lap, folded her in her arms, and kissed her over and over again, saying softly, "My darling, darling child! I cannot tell you how glad and thankful I am to have you in my arms once more. I love you very dearly, little Elsie."

Elsie was almost too glad to speak, but presently she whispered, "Not better than I love you, dear Miss Rose. I love you next to papa."

"And you are very happy now?"

"Very, very happy. Do you like my papa, Miss Rose?"

"Very much, dear, so far," Rose replied with simple truthfulness; "he seems to be a very polished gentleman, and I think is extremely handsome; but what is best of all, I can see he is a very fond father," she added, bestowing another kiss upon the little rosy cheek.

"I am so glad!" exclaimed the little girl, her eyes sparkling with pleasure. Then she added, in a deprecating tone, "But he doesn't spoil me, Miss Rose; indeed he does not. I always know I must obey, and promptly and cheerfully, too."

"No, dearest, I did not think you had been spoiled; indeed, I doubt if it would be possible to spoil you," Rose answered in a tone of fondness.

"Ah! you don't know me, Miss Rose," said Elsie, shaking her head. "If papa were not very firm and decided with me, I know I should be very wilful sometimes, and he knows it, too; but he is too really kind to indulge me in naughtiness. My dear, dear papa! Miss Rose, I love him so much."

"I am so glad for you, my poor little one," murmured Rose, drawing the little girl closer to her. "It seemed so sad and lonely for you, with neither father nor mother to love you. And you were very ill last summer, darling? and very unhappy before that? Your Aunt Adelaide wrote me all about it, and my heart ached for my poor darling; oh, how I longed to comfort her!"

"Yes, Miss Rose, that was a dreadful time; but papa only did what he thought was right, and you cannot think how kind he was when I was getting better." Elsie's eyes were full of tears.

"I know it, darling, and I pitied him, too, and often prayed for you both," said Rose. "But tell me, dearest, was Jesus near to you in your troubles?"

"Yes, Miss Rose, very near, and very precious; else how could I have borne it at all? for oh, Miss Rose, I thought sometimes my heart would break!"

"It was a bitter trial, dearest, I know; and certain I am that you must have had much more than your own strength to enable you to be so firm," said Rose, tenderly.

"Ah, there is Sophy!" she added quickly, as a mass of flaxen curls, accompanied by a pair of dancing blue eyes, appeared for an instant at the door, and then as suddenly vanished. "Sophy! Sophy, come here!" she called, and again the door opened and the owner of the blue eyes and flaxen ringlets—a little girl about Elsie's age, came in, and moved slowly towards them, looking at the stranger in her sister's lap with a mingled expression of fun, curiosity, and bashfulness.

"Come, Sophy, this is Elsie Dinsmore, whom you have so often wished to see," said Rose. "Elsie, this is my little sister Sophy. I want you to be friends, and learn to love one another dearly. There, Sophy, take her into your room, and show her all your toys and books, while I am changing my dress; that will be the way for you to get acquainted."

Sophy did as she was desired, and, as Rose had foreseen, the first feeling of bashfulness soon wore off, and in a few moments they were talking and laughing together as though they had been acquainted as many months. Sophy had brought out a number of dolls, and they were discussing their several claims to beauty in a very animated way when Rose called to them to come with her.

"I am going to carry you off to the nursery, Elsie, to see the little ones," she said, taking her young visitor's hand; "should you like to see them?"

"Oh, so much!" Elsie exclaimed eagerly; "if Sophy may go, too."

"Oh, yes, Sophy will come along, of course," Miss Rose said, leading the way as she spoke.

Elsie found the nursery, a beautiful, large room, fitted up with every comfort and convenience, and abounding in a variety of toys for the amusement of the children, of whom there were three—the baby crowing in its nurse's arms, little May, a merry, romping child of four, with flaxen curls and blue eyes like Sophy's, and Freddie, a boy of seven.

Harold, who was thirteen, sat by one of the windows busily engaged covering a ball for Fred, who with May stood intently watching the movements of his needle.

Elsie was introduced to them all, one after another.

Harold gave her a cordial shake of the hand, and a pleasant "Welcome to Elmgrove," and the little ones put up their faces to be kissed.

Elsie thought Harold a kind, pleasant-looking boy, not at all like Arthur, Fred and May, dear little things, and the baby perfectly charming, as she afterwards confided to her father.

"May I take the baby, Miss Rose?" she asked coaxingly.

Miss Rose said "Yes," and the nurse put it in her arms for a moment.

"Dear, pretty little thing!" she exclaimed, kissing it softly. "How old is it, Miss Rose? and what is its name?"

"She is nearly a year old, and we call her Daisy."

"I'm sure your arms must be getting tired, miss, for she's quite heavy," remarked the nurse presently, taking the child again.

Miss Rose now said it was time to go down-stairs, and left the room, followed by Elsie, Harold, and Sophy, the last-named putting her arm around Elsie's waist, saying what a delightful time they would have together, and that she hoped she would stay all summer.

They had not quite reached the end of the hall when Elsie saw her father come out of the door of another room, and hastily releasing herself from Sophy's arm, she ran to him, and catching hold of his hand, looked up eagerly into his face, saying, "Oh, papa, do come into the nursery and see the dear little children and the baby! it is so pretty."

He looked inquiringly at Miss Allison.

"If you care to see it, Mr. Dinsmore," she said, smiling, "there is no objection; we are very proud of our baby."

"Then I should like to go," he replied, "both to gratify Elsie and because I am fond of children."

Rose led the way and they all went back to the nursery, where Mr. Dinsmore kissed the little folks all round, patted their heads and talked kindly to them, then took the babe in his arms, praising its beauty, and tossing it up till he made it laugh and crow right merrily.

"I often wish I had seen my baby," he remarked to Rose, as he returned it to the nurse. Then laying his hand on Elsie's head, "Do you know, Miss Allison," he asked, "that I never saw my little girl until she was nearly eight years old?"

"Yes," she replied, "I knew her before you did, and sympathized strongly in her longing for a father's love."

"Ah! we both lost a good deal in those years, and if I could live them over again it should be very different," he said, with a loving glance at his daughter's face; "nothing should keep me from my child. Though no doubt it has all been for the best," he added, with a slight sigh, as he thought of the worldly wisdom he would have taught her.

They all now went down to the parlor, where Mr. Dinsmore and Elsie were introduced to Richard Allison, a wild boy full of fun and frolic, between Rose and Harold in age.

Edward was the eldest of the family, and quite sober and sedate.

Richard took a great fancy to Elsie from the first moment, and very soon had coaxed her out to the lawn, where he presently engaged her in a merry game of romps with Sophy, Harold, and himself, which was finally brought to a conclusion by the arrival of the elder Mr. Allison, almost immediately followed by the call to supper.

Mr. Allison had a pleasant face, and was a younger looking man than might have been expected in the father of such a family. He welcomed his guests with the greatest cordiality, expressing the hope that they intended paying a long visit to Elmgrove, which he said they owed him in return for Rose's lengthened sojourn at Roselands.

Mrs. Allison also made her appearance at the tea-table, saying that she had nearly recovered from her headache; although she still looked pale and languid.

She had a kind, motherly look, and a gentle, winning address that quite took Elsie's fancy; and was evidently pleased at their arrival, and anxious to entertain them in the most hospitable manner.

Mr. Dinsmore and his little girl were the only guests, and all the children, excepting the baby, were allowed to come to the table.

They seemed to be well-bred children, behaved in a quiet, orderly way, and asked politely for what they wanted, but were rather too much indulged, Mr. Dinsmore thought, as he observed that they all ate and drank whatever they fancied, without any remonstrance from their parents.

Elsie was seated between her father and Miss Rose.

"Will your little girl take tea or coffee, Mr. Dinsmore?" asked Mrs. Allison.

"Neither, thank you, madam: she will take a glass of milk if you have it; if not, cold water will do very well,"

"Why, Elsie, I thought I remembered that you were very fond of coffee," Rose remarked, as she filled a tumbler with milk and set it down beside the little girl's plate.

"Elsie is a good child, and eats and drinks just whatever her father thinks best for her, Miss Allison," said Mr. Dinsmore, preventing Elsie's reply. "No, no; not any of those, if you please," for Rose was putting hot, buttered waffles upon Elsie's plate; "I don't allow her to eat hot cakes, especially at night."

"Excuse me, Mr. Dinsmore, but are you not eating them yourself?" asked Rose, with an arch smile.

"Yes, Miss Rose; and so may she when she is my age," he answered in a pleasant tone, accompanied by an affectionate glance and smile bestowed upon his little daughter.

"I think you are quite right, Mr. Dinsmore," remarked Mrs. Allison. "I know we pamper our children's appetites entirely too much, as I have often said to their father; but he does not agree with me, and I have not sufficient firmness to carry out the reform by myself."

"No, I like to see them enjoy themselves, and whatever I have, I want my children to have, too," said Mr. Allison, bluntly.

"It would seem the kindest treatment at first sight, but I don't think it is in the end," replied Mr. Dinsmore. "To buy present enjoyment at the expense of an enfeebled constitution is paying much too dear for it, I think."

"Ah! young people are full of notions," said the elder gentleman, shaking his head wisely, "and are very apt to be much more strict with the first child than with any of the rest. You are bringing this one up by rule, I see; but mark my words: if you live to be the father of as many as I have, you will grow less and less strict with each one, until you will be ready to spoil the youngest completely."

"I hope not, sir; I am very sure I could not possibly love another better than I do this," Mr. Dinsmore said with a smile, and coloring slightly, too; then adroitly changed the subject by a remark addressed to Edward.

Immediately after tea the whole family adjourned to the sitting-room, the servants were called in, and Mr. Allison read a portion of Scripture and prayed; afterwards remarking to Mr. Dinsmore that it was his custom to attend to this duty early in the evening, that the younger children might have the benefit of it without being kept up too late.

Mr. Dinsmore expressed his approval, adding that it was his

plan also.

"Papa," whispered Elsie, who was close to him, "I am to sleep with Sophy."

"Ah! that will be very pleasant for you," he said, "but you must be a good girl, and not give any unnecessary trouble."

"I will try, papa. There, Sophy is calling me; may I go to her?"

"Certainly;" and he released her hand, which he had been holding in his.

"I want to show you my garden," said Sophy, whom Elsie found in the hall; and she led the way out through a back door which opened into a garden now gay with spring flowers and early roses.

Sophy pointed out the corner which was her especial property, and exhibited her plants and flowers with a great deal of honest pride.

"I planted every one of them myself," she said. "Harold dug up the ground for me, and I did all the rest, I work an hour every morning pulling up the weeds and watering the flowers."

"Oh? won't you let me help you while I am here?" asked Elsie, eagerly.

"Why, yes, if you like, and your papa won't mind I think it would be real fun. But he's very strict, isn't he, Elsie? I feel quite afraid of him."

"Yes, he is strict, but he is very kind, too."

"Let's go in now," said Sophy; "I've got a beautiful picture-book that I want to show you; and to-morrow's Sunday, you know, so if you don't see it to-night, you'll have to wait till Monday, because it isn't a Sunday book."

"What time is it?" asked Elsie. "I always have to go to bed at half-past eight."

"I don't know," said Sophy, "but we'll look at the clock in the dining-room," and she ran in, closely followed by her little guest.

"Just eight! we've only got half an hour; so come along. But won't your papa let you stay up longer?"

"No," Elsie answered in a very decided tone; and they hurried to the parlor, where they seated themselves in a corner, and were soon eagerly discussing the pictures in Sophy's book.

They had just finished, and Sophy was beginning a very animated description of a child's party she had attended a short time before, when Elsie, who had been anxiously watching her father for the last five minutes, saw him take out his watch and look at her.

"There, Sophy," she said, rising, "I know papa means it is time for me to go to bed."

"Oh, just wait one minute!"

But Elsie was already half way across the room.

"It is your bedtime, daughter," said Mr. Dinsmore, smiling affectionately on her.

"Yes, papa; good-night," and she held up her face for the accustomed kiss.

"Good-night, daughter," he replied, bestowing the caress. Then laying his hand gently on her head, he said softly, "God bless and keep my little one."

Rose, who was seated on the sofa beside him, drew Elsie to her, saying, "I must have a kiss, too, darling."

"Now go, daughter," said Mr. Dinsmore, as Rose released her from her embrace, "go to bed as soon as you can, and don't lie awake talking."

"Mayn't I talk at all, after I go to bed, papa?"

"No, not at all."

Seeing that Elsie was really going, Sophy had put away her book, and was now ready to accompany her. She was quite a talker, and rattled on very fast until she saw Elsie take out her Bible; but then became perfectly quiet until Elsie was through with her devotions, and Chloe had come to prepare her for bed. Then she began chatting again in her lively way, Elsie answering very pleasantly until she was just ready to step into bed, when she said gently, "Sophy, papa said, before I came up, that I must not talk at all after I got into bed, so please don't be vexed if I don't answer you, because you know I *must* obey my father."

"Pshaw! how provoking. I thought we were going to have such a good time, and I've got ever so much to say to you."

"I'm just as sorry as you are, Sophy, but I can't disobey papa."

"He'd never know it," suggested Sophy in a voice scarcely above a whisper.

Elsie started with astonishment to hear Miss Rose's sister speaking thus.

"Oh, Sophy! you can't mean to advise me to deceive and disobey my father?" she said. "God would know it, and papa would soon know it, too, for I could never look him in the face again until I had confessed it."

Sophy blushed deeply. "I didn't think about its being deceitful. But would your papa punish you for such a little thing?"

"Papa says disobedience is never a little thing, and he always punishes me when I disobey him; but I wouldn't care so much for that, as for knowing that I had grieved him so; because I love my papa very dearly. But I must not talk any more; so good-night;" and she climbed into bed, laid her head on the pillow, and in a very few moments was fast asleep.

CHAPTER XVI

"Hail, Holy Day! the blessing from above
Brightens thy presence like a smile of love,
Smoothing, like oil upon a stormy sea,
The roughest waves of human destiny—
Cheering the good, and to the poor oppresse'd
Bearing the promise of their heavenly rest."

MRS. HALE'S PRIME OF LIFE.

When Chloe came in to dress her young charge the next morning, she found her already up and sitting with her Bible in her hand.

"Don't make a noise, mammy," she whispered; "Sophy is still asleep."

Chloe nodded acquiescence, and moving softly about, got through the business of washing and dressing her nursling, and brushing her curls, without disturbing the sleeper. Then they both quietly left the room, and Elsie, with her Bible in her hand, rapped gently at her father's door.

He opened it, and giving her a kiss and a "Good-morning, darling," led her across the room to where he had been sitting by a window looking into the garden. Then taking her on his knee, and stroking her hair fondly, he said with a smile, "My little girl looks very bright this morning, and as if she had had a good night's rest. I think she obeyed me, and did not lie awake talking."

"No, papa, I did not, though I wanted to very much," she answered with a slight blush.

"We did not have our chapter together last night," he said, opening the Bible, "but I hope we will not miss it very often."

Their plan was to read verse about, Elsie asking questions about anything she did not understand, and her father explaining and making remarks, he having read it first in the original, and generally consulted a commentator also. Then Elsie usually had one or two texts to recite, which she had learned while Chloe was dressing her; after that they knelt down and Mr. Dinsmore prayed. They never read more than a few verses, and his prayer was always short, so that there was no room for weariness, and Elsie always enjoyed it very much. They had still a little time to talk together before the breakfast-bell rang, of which Elsie was very glad, for she had a great deal to say to her father.

"It is such a sweet, sweet Sabbath-day, papa," she said, "is it not? and this is such a nice place, almost as pretty as our own dear home; and are they not pleasant people? I think they seem so kind to one another, and to everybody."

"Which must mean you and me, I suppose; there is no one else here," he answered smilingly.

"Oh! the servants, you know, papa, and the people at the hotel: but don't you think they are kind?"

"Yes, dear, they certainly seem to be, and I have no doubt they are."

"And the baby, papa! isn't it pretty, and oh, papa, *don't* you like Miss Rose?"

"I hardly know her yet, daughter, but I think she is very sweet looking, and seems to be gentle and amiable."

"I am glad you like her, papa; and I knew you would," Elsie said in a tone of great satisfaction.

The church the Allisons attended was within easy walking distance of Elmgrove, and service was held in it twice a day; the whole family, with the exception of the very little children and one servant, who stayed at home to take care of them, went both morning and afternoon, and Mr. Dinsmore and Elsie accompanied them.

The interval between dinner and afternoon service Elsie spent in her father's room, sitting on a stool at his feet quietly reading. When they had returned from church Miss Allison gathered all the little ones in the nursery and showed them pictures, and told them Bible stories, until the tea-bell rang; after which the whole family, including children and servants, were called together into the sitting-room to be catechized by Mr. Allison; that was succeeded by family worship, and then they sang hymns until it was time for the children to go to bed.

As Elsie laid her head on her pillow that night, she said to herself that it had been a very pleasant day, and she could be quite willing to live at Elmgrove, were it not for the thought of her own dear home in the "sunny South."

The next morning her father told her they would be there for several weeks, and that he would expect her to practise an hour every morning—Miss Rose having kindly offered the use of her piano—and every afternoon to read for an hour with him; but all the rest of the day she might have to herself, to spend just as she pleased; only, of course, she must manage to take sufficient exercise, and not get into any mischief.

Elsie was delighted with the arrangement, and ran off at once to tell Sophy the good news.

"Oh! I am ever so glad you are going to stay!" exclaimed Sophy joyfully. "But why need your papa make you say lessons at all? I think he might just as well let you play all the time."

"No," replied Elsie, "papa says I will enjoy my play a great deal better for doing a little work first, and I know it is so. Indeed, I always find papa knows best."

"Oh, Elsie!" Sophy exclaimed, as if struck with a bright thought, "I'll tell you what we can do! let us learn some duets together."

"Yes, that's a good thought," said Elsie; "so we will."

"And perhaps Sophy would like to join us in our reading, too," said Mr. Dinsmore's voice behind them.

Both little girls turned round with an exclamation of surprise, and Elsie, taking hold of his hand, looked up lovingly into his face, saying, "Oh, thank you, papa; that will be so pleasant."

He held out his other hand to Sophy, asking, with a smile, "Will you come, my dear?"

"If you won't ask me any questions," she answered a little bashfully.

"Sophy is afraid of you, papa," whispered Elsie with an arch glance at her friend's blushing face.

"And are not you, too?" he asked, pinching her cheek.

"Not a bit, papa, except when I've been naughty," she said, laying her cheek lovingly against his hand.

He bent down and kissed her with a very gratified look. Then patting Sophy's head, said pleasantly, "You needn't be afraid of the questions, Sophy; I will make Elsie answer them all."

Elsie and her papa stayed for nearly two months at Elmgrove, and her life there agreed so well with the little girl that she became as strong, healthy and rosy as she had ever been. She and Sophy and Harold spent the greater part of almost every day in the open air—working in the garden, racing about the grounds, taking long walks in search of wild flowers, hunting eggs in the barn, or building baby-houses and making tea-parties in the shade of the trees down by the brook.

There was a district school-house not very far from Elmgrove, and in their rambles the children had made acquaintance with two or three of the scholars—nice, quiet little girls—who, after a while, got into the habit of bringing their dinner-baskets to the rendezvous by the brook-side, and spending their noon-recess with Elsie and Sophy; the dinner hour at Mr. Allison's being somewhat later in the day.

Sophy and Elsie were sitting under the trees one warm June morning dressing their dolls. Fred and May were rolling marbles, and Harold lay on the grass with a book in his hand.

"There come Hetty Allen and Maggie Wilson," said Sophy, raising her head. "See how earnestly they are talking together! I wonder what it is all about. What's the matter, girls?" she asked, as they drew near.

"Oh, nothing's the matter," replied Hetty, "but we are getting up a party to go strawberrying. We've heard of a field only two miles from here—or at least not much over two miles from the school-house—where the berries are very thick. We are going to-morrow, because it's Saturday, and there's no school, and we've come to ask if you and Elsie and Harold won't go along."

"Yes, indeed!" exclaimed Sophy, clapping her hands; "it will be such fun, and I'm sure mamma will let us go."

"Oh, that's a first-rate idea!" cried Harold, throwing aside his book; "to be sure we must all go."

"Will you go, Elsie?" asked Maggie; adding, "we want you so very much."

"Oh, yes, if papa will let me, and I think he will, for he allows me to run about here all day, which I should think was pretty much the same thing, only there will be more fun and frolic with so many of us together, and the berries to pick, too; oh, I should like to go very much indeed!"

Hetty and Maggie had seated themselves on the grass, and now the whole plan was eagerly discussed. The children were all to meet at the school-house at nine o'clock, and proceed in a body to the field, taking their dinners along so as to be able to stay all day if they chose.

The more the plan was discussed, the more attractive it seemed to our little friends, and the stronger grew their desire to be permitted to go.

"I wish I knew for certain that mamma would say yes," said Sophy. "Suppose we go up to the house now and ask."

"No," objected Harold, "mamma will be busy now, and less likely to say yes, than after dinner. So we had better wait."

"Well, then, you all ask leave when you go up to dinner, and we will call here on our way home from school to know whether you are going or not," said Hetty, as she and Maggie rose to go.

Harold and Sophy agreed, but Elsie said that she could not know then, because her father had gone to the city and would not be back until near tea-time.

"Oh, well, never mind! he'll be sure to say yes if mamma does," said Harold, hopefully. And then, as Hetty and Maggie walked away, he began consulting with Sophy on the best plan for approaching their mother on the subject. They resolved to wait until after dinner, and then, when she had settled down to her sewing, to present their request.

Mrs. Allison raised several objections; the weather was very warm, the road would be very dusty, and she was sure they would get overheated and fatigued, and heartily wish themselves at home long before the day was over.

"Well, then, mamma, we can come home; there is nothing to prevent us," said Harold.

"Oh, mamma, do let us go just this once," urged Sophy; "and if we find it as disagreeable as you think, you know we won't ask again."

And so at last Mrs. Allison gave a rather reluctant consent, but only on condition that Mr. Dinsmore would allow Elsie to go, as she said it would be very rude indeed for them to go and leave their little guest at home alone.

This conversation had taken place in Mrs. Allison's dressing-room, and Elsie was waiting in the hall to learn the result of their application.

"Mamma says we may go if your papa says yes," cried Sophy, rushing out and throwing her arms round Elsie's neck. "Oh, aren't you glad? Now, Elsie, coax him hard and make him let you go."

"I wouldn't dare to do it; I should only get punished if I did, for papa never allows me to coax or tease, nor even to ask him a second time," Elsie said, with a little shake of her head.

"Oh, nonsense!" exclaimed Sophy, "I often get what I want by teasing. I guess you never tried it."

"My papa is not at all like your father and mother," replied Elsie, "and it would be worse than useless to coax after he has once said no."

"Then coax him before he has a chance to say it," suggested Sophy, laughing.

"Perhaps that might do if I can manage it," said Elsie, thoughtfully. "I wish he would come!" she added, walking to the window and looking out.

"He won't be here for an hour or two, at any rate, if he dined in the city," said Sophy. "Oh, how warm it is! let's go to our room, Elsie, and take off our dresses and have a nap. It will help to pass away the time until your papa comes."

Elsie agreed to the proposal, and before long they were both sound asleep, having tired themselves out with romping and running.

When Elsie awoke she found Chloe standing over her. "You's had a berry good nap, darlin', an' you's berry warm," she whispered, as she wiped the perspiration from the little girl's face. "Let your ole mammy take you up an' give you a bath an' dress you up nice an' clean, 'fore Miss Sophy gits her blue eyes open."

"Oh, yes, that will make me feel so much better," agreed the little girl, "and you must make me look very nice, mammy, to please papa. Has he come yet?"

"Yes, darlin'; master's been home dis hour, an' I 'specs he's in de parlor dis minute talkin' 'long of Miss Rose an' de rest."

"Then hurry, mammy, and dress me quickly, because I want to ask papa something," Elsie said in an eager whisper, as she stepped hastily off the bed.

Chloe did her best, and in half an hour Elsie, looking as sweet and fresh as a new-blown rose in her clean white frock and nicely brushed curls, entered the parlor where her father, Mrs. Allison, Miss Rose, and her elder brother were seated.

Mr. Dinsmore was talking with Edward Allison, but he turned his head as Elsie came in, and held out his hand to her with a proud, fond smile.

She sprang to his side, and, still going on with his conversation, he passed his arm around her waist and kissed her cheek, while she leaned against his knee, and with her eyes feed lovingly upon his face waited patiently for an opportunity to prefer her request.

Miss Rose was watching them, as she often did, with a look of intense satisfaction, for it rejoiced her heart to see how her little friend revelled in her father's affection.

The gentlemen were discussing some scientific question with great earnestness, and Elsie began to feel a little impatient as they talked on and on without seeming to come any nearer to a conclusion: but at last Edward rose and left the room in search of a book which he thought would throw some light on the subject; and then her father turned to her and asked, "How has my little girl enjoyed herself to-day?"

"Very much, thank you, papa; but I have something to ask you, and I want you to say yes. Please, papa, *do!* won't you?" she pleaded eagerly, but in a low tone only meant for his ears.

"You know I love to gratify you, daughter," he said kindly, "but I cannot possibly say yes until I know what you want."

"Well, papa," she replied, speaking very fast, as if she feared he would interrupt her, "a good many little girls and boys are going after strawberries to-morrow: they are to start from the school-house, at nine o'clock in the morning, and walk two miles to a field where the berries are very thick; and they've asked us to go—I mean Harold and Sophy and me—and we all want to go *so much*; we think it will be such fun, and Mrs. Allison says we may if you will only say yes. Oh, papa, *do please* let me go, *won't* you?"

Martha Finley

Her tone was very coaxing, and her eyes pleaded as earnestly as her tongue.

He seemed to be considering for a moment, and she watched his face eagerly, trying to read in it what his answer would be.

At length it came, gently, but firmly spoken, "No, daughter, you cannot go. I do not at all approve of the plan."

Elsie did not utter another word, of remonstrance or entreaty, for she knew it would be useless; but the disappointment was very great, and two or three tears rolled quickly down her cheeks.

Her father looked at her a moment in some surprise, and then said, speaking in a low tone, and very gravely, "This will never do, my daughter. Go up to my room and stay there until you can be quite cheerful and pleasant; then you may come down again."

Elsie hurried out of the room, the tears coming thick and fast now, and almost ran against Edward in the hall.

"Why, what is the matter, my dear?" he asked in a tone of surprise and alarm, laying his hand on her shoulder to detain her.

"Please don't ask me, Mr. Edward. Please let me go," she sobbed, breaking away from him and rushing up the stairs.

He stood for an instant looking after her, then turning to go back to the parlor, encountered Rose, who was just coming out.

"What ails her?" he asked.

"I don't know. Something that passed between her and her father. I rather suspect he sent her upstairs as a punishment."

"Pshaw! I've no patience with him. The dear little thing! I don't believe she deserved it."

Rose made no reply, but glided up-stairs, and he returned to the parlor to finish the discussion with Mr. Dinsmore.

In the meantime Elsie had shut herself into her father's room, where she indulged for a few moments in a hearty cry, which seemed to do her a great deal of good. But presently she wiped away her tears, bathed her eyes, and sat down by the window.

"What a silly little girl I am," she said to herself, "to be crying just because I can't have my own way, when I know it will not alter papa's determination in the least; and when I know, too, that I have always found his way the best in the end! Oh, dear, I have quite disgraced myself before Miss Rose and her mother, and the rest, and vexed papa, too! I wish I could be good and then I might be down-stairs with the others, instead of alone up here. Well, papa said I might come down again as soon as I could be pleasant and cheerful, and I think I can now, and there is the tea-bell."

She ran down just in time to take her place with the others. She raised her eyes to her father's face as he drew her chair up closer to the table. The look seemed to ask forgiveness and reconciliation, and the answering smile told that it was granted; and the little heart bounded lightly once more, and the sweet little face was wreathed in smiles.

Sophy and Harold were watching her from the other side of the table, and their hopes rose high, for they very naturally concluded from her beaming countenance that she had carried her point, and they would all be allowed to go to the strawberry party next day.

Their disappointment was proportionally great, when, after supper, Elsie told them what her father's answer had really been.

"How provoking!" they both exclaimed; "why, you looked so pleased we were sure he had said yes; and we had quite set our hearts on it."

"What is the matter?" asked Richard, who had just come up to them.

They explained.

"Ah! so that was what you were crying about this afternoon, eh?" he said, pinching Elsie's cheek.

"Did you really, Elsie?" asked Sophy, in surprise.

Elsie blushed deeply, and Richard said, "Oh, never mind; I dare say we've all cried about more trifling things than that in our day. Let's have a good game of romps out here on the lawn. Come, what shall it be, Elsie?"

"I don't care," she replied, struggling to keep down an inclination to cry again.

"Puss wants a corner," suggested Harold; "trees for corners."

"Here goes, then!" cried Richard. "Sophy, you stand here; Elsie, you take that tree yonder. Here, Fred and May, you can play, too. One here and another there: and now I'll be the puss."

So the game commenced, and very soon every disappointment seemed to be forgotten, and they were all in the wildest spirits.

But after a while, as one romping game succeeded another, Elsie began to grow weary, and seeing that her father was sitting alone upon the piazza, she stole softly to his side, and putting her arm round his neck, laid her cheek to his.

He passed his arm around her waist and drew her to his knee.

"Which was my little daughter doubting this afternoon," he asked gently, as he laid her head against his breast; "papa's wisdom or his love?"

"I don't know, papa; please don't ask me. I'm very sorry and ashamed," she said, hanging her head and blushing deeply.

"I should be very happy," he said, "if my little girl could learn to trust me so entirely that she would always be satisfied with my decisions—always believe that my reasons for refusing to gratify her are good and sufficient, even without having them explained."

"I do believe it, papa, and I am quite satisfied now," she murmured. "I don't want to go at all. Please forgive me, dear papa."

"I will, daughter; and now listen to me. I know that you are not very strong, and I think that a walk of two miles or more in this hot June sun, to say nothing of stooping for hours afterwards picking berries, exposed to its rays, would be more than you could bear without injury; and if you want strawberries to eat, you may buy just as many as you please, and indeed you can get much finer ones in that way than you could find in any field. You need not tell me it is the fun you want, and not the berries," he said, as she seemed about to interrupt him, "I understand that perfectly; but I know it would not be enough to pay you for the trouble and fatigue.

"And now to show you that your father does not take pleasure in thwarting you, but really loves to see you happy, I will tell you what we have been planning. Miss Rose and her brothers tell me there is a very pretty place a few miles from here where strawberries and cream can be had; and we are going to make up a family party to-morrow, if the weather is favorable, and set out quite early in the morning in carriages. Mrs. Allison will provide a collation for us to carry along—to which we will add the berries and cream after we get there—and we will take books to read, and the ladies will have their work, and the little girls their dolls, and we will spend the day in the woods. Will not that be quite as pleasant as going with the school-children?"

The little arm had been stealing round his neck again while he was telling her all this, and now hugging him tighter and tighter, she whispered: "Dear papa, you are very kind to me, and it makes me feel so ashamed of my naughtiness. I always find in the end that your way is best, and then I think I will never want my own way again, but the very next time it is just the same thing over. Oh, papa, you will not get out of patience with me, and quit loving me, and doing what is best for me, because I am foolish enough to wish for what is not?"

"No, darling, never. I shall always do what seems to me to be for your good, even in spite of yourself. I who have so often been guilty of murmuring against the will of my heavenly Father, who, I well know, is infinite in wisdom and goodness, ought to be very patient with your distrust of a fallible, short-sighted earthly parent. But come, darling, we will go up-stairs; we have just time for a few moments together before you go to bed."

On going to their bedroom after leaving her father, Elsie found Sophie already there, impatiently waiting to tell her of the plan for the morrow, which she had just learned from Richard.

She was a little disappointed to find that it was no news to Elsie, but soon got over that, and was full of lively talk about the pleasure they would have.

"It will be so much pleasanter," she said, "than going berrying with those school-children, for I dare say we would have found it hot and tiresome walking all that distance in the sun; so I'm right glad now that your father said no, instead of yes. Aren't you, Elsie?"

"Yes," Elsie said with a sigh.

Sophy was down on the floor, pulling off her shoes and stockings. "Why, what's the matter?" she asked, stopping with her shoe in her hand to look up into Elsie's face, which struck her as unusually grave.

"Nothing, only I'm so ashamed of crying when papa said I shouldn't go," Elsie answered, with a blush. "Dear papa! I always find he knows best, and yet I'm so often naughty about giving up."

"Never mind, it wasn't much. I wouldn't care about it," said Sophy, tossing away her shoe, and proceeding to pull off the stocking.

Chloe whispered in Elsie's ear, "Massa not vexed wid you, darlin'?"

Elsie smiled and shook her head. "No, mammy, not now."

The little girls were awake unusually early the next morning, and the first thing they did was to run to the window to ascertain the state of the weather. It was all they could desire; a little cooler than the day before, but without the slightest appearance of rain; so the young faces that surrounded the breakfast table were very bright and happy.

The carriages were at the door very soon after they left the table. It did not take many minutes to pack them, and then they set off all in high glee; more especially the little ones.

Everything passed off well; there was no accident, all were in good humor, the children on their best behavior, and they found the strawberries and cream very fine; so that when the day was over, it was unanimously voted a decided success.

A few days after this the children were again in their favorite spot down by the brook. They were sitting on the grass talking, for it was almost too warm to play.

"How nice and cool the water looks!" remarked Sophy, "Let's pull off our shoes and stockings, and hold up our dresses and wade about in it. It isn't at all deep, and I know it would feel so good and cool to our feet."

"Bravo! that's a capital idea!" cried Harold, beginning at once to divest himself of his shoos and stockings; then rolling his pantaloons up to his knees he stepped in, followed by Sophy, who had made her preparations with equal dispatch.

"Come, Elsie, aren't you going to get in, too?" she asked, for Elsie still sat on the bank making no movement towards following their example.

"I should like to, very much; but I don't know whether papa would approve of it."

"Why, what objection could he have? it can't do us any harm, for I'm sure we couldn't drown if we tried," said Harold. "Come now, Elsie, don't be so silly. I wouldn't ask you to do anything your papa had forbidden, but he never said you shouldn't wade in the brook, did he?"

"No, he never said anything about it," she answered, smiling, "for I never thought of doing such a thing before."

"Come, Elsie, do," urged Sophy; "it is such fun;" and at length Elsie yielded, and was soon enjoying the sport as keenly as the others.

But after a while they grew tired of wading, and began to amuse themselves by sailing bits of bark and leaves on the water. Then Harold proposed building a dam; and altogether they enjoyed themselves so thoroughly, that they quite forgot how time was passing until the lengthening shadows warned them that it was long past their usual hour for returning home.

"Oh, we must make haste home," exclaimed Harold suddenly; "it can't be very far from tea-time, and mamma won't like it if we are late."

They hurried out of the water, dried their feet as well as they could, put on their shoes and stockings, and started on a run for the house.

But they had not gone more than half-way when Elsie cried out that she had lost her rings.

"Those beautiful rings! Oh, dear! where did you lose them?" asked Sophy.

"I don't know at all; I just missed them this minute, and I am afraid they are in the brook;" and Elsie turned and ran back as fast as she could; followed by the others.

"We'll all hunt," said Harold, kindly, "and I guess we'll find them; so don't cry, Elsie;" for the little girl was looking much distressed.

"O Elsie, I'm afraid your papa will be very angry; and perhaps whip you very hard," exclaimed Sophy; "they were such pretty rings."

"No, he won't whip me; he never did in his life," replied Elsie quickly, "and he has often told me he would never punish me for an accident, even though it should cost the loss of something very valuable. But I am very sorry to lose my rings, because, besides being pretty, and worth a good deal of money, they were presents, one from papa, and the other from Mr. Travilla."

"But, Elsie, I thought your papa was awfully strict, and punished you for every little thing,"

"No; for *disobedience*, but not for accidents."

They searched for some time, looking all about the part of the stream where they had been playing, and all over the bank, but without finding the rings; and at last Elsie gave it up, saying it would not do to stay any longer, and they could look again to-morrow.

"O Elsie!" cried Sophy, as they were starting again for home, "you must have got your dress in the water, and then on the ground, for it is all muddy."

"Oh, dear!" sighed Elsie, examining it, "how very dirty and slovenly I must look; and that will vex papa, for he can't bear to see me untidy. Can't we get in the back way, Sophy? so that I can get a clean dress on before he sees me? I don't mean to *deceive* him. I will tell him all about it afterwards, but I know he wouldn't like to see me looking so."

"Yes, to be sure," Sophy said in reply; "we can go in at the side door, and run up the back stairs."

"And we may be in time for tea yet, if papa is as late getting home as he is sometimes," remarked Harold; "so let us run."

Mr. Allison was late that evening, as Harold had hoped, and tea was still waiting for him, as they learned from a servant whom they met in passing through the grounds: but when they reached the porch upon which the side door opened, they found, much to their surprise and chagrin, that the ladies were seated there with their work, and Mr. Dinsmore was reading to them.

He looked up from his book as they approached, and catching sight of his little girl's soiled dress, "Why, Elsie," he exclaimed, in a mortified tone, "can that be you? such a figure as you are! Where have you been, child, to get yourself in such a plight?"

"I was playing in the brook, papa," she answered in a low voice, and casting down her eyes, while the color mounted to her hair.

"Playing in the brook! that is a new business for you, I think.

Well, run up to Aunt Chloe, and tell her I want you made decent with all possible haste or you will be too late for tea. But stay," he added as she was turning to go, "you have been crying; what is the matter?"

"I have lost my rings, papa," she said, bursting into tears.

"Ah! I am sorry, more particularly because it distresses you, though. But where did you lose them, daughter?"

"I don't know, papa, but I am afraid it was in the brook."

"Ah, yes! that comes of playing in the water. I think you had better keep out of it in the future: but run up and get dressed, and don't cry any more; it is not worth while to waste tears over them."

Elsie hurried upstairs, delivered her father's message, and Chloe immediately set to work, and exerting herself to the utmost, soon had her nursling looking as neat as usual.

Rose had followed the little girls upstairs, and was helping Sophy to dress.

"Dere now, darlin'; now I tink you'll do," said Chloe, giving the glossy hair a final smooth. "But what's de matter? what my chile been cryin' 'bout?"

"Because, mammy, I lost my rings in the brook, and I'm afraid I will never find them again."

"No such ting, honey! here dey is safe an' sound," and Chloe opened a little jewel-box that stood on the toilet-table, and picking up the rings, slipped them upon the finger of the astonished and delighted child; explaining as she did so, that she had found them on the bureau where Elsie must have laid them before going out, having probably taken them off to wash her hands after eating her dinner.

Martha Finley

Elsie tripped joyfully downstairs. "See, papa! see!" she cried holding up her hand before him, "they were not lost, after all. Oh, I am so glad! aren't you, papa?"

"Yes, my dear, and now I hope you will be more careful in future."

"I will try, papa; but must I never play in the brook any more? I like it so much."

"No, I don't like to forbid it entirely, because I remember how much I used to enjoy such things myself at your age. But you must not stay in too long, and must be careful not to go in when you are heated with running, and always remember to dip your hands in first. And another thing, you must not stay out so late again, or you may give trouble. You must always be ready at the usual hour, or I shall have to say you must sup on bread and water."

"Oh! I think that would be rather too hard, Mr. Dinsmore," interposed Mrs. Allison, "and I hope you will not compel me to be so inhospitable."

"I hope there is not much danger that I shall ever have to put my threat into execution, Mrs. Allison, for it is not often that Elsie is twice guilty of the same fault; one talking generally does her," he answered with an affectionate glance at his little daughter.

"Then I call her a very good child," remarked the lady emphatically; "it is no unusual thing for mine to require telling half a dozen times. But walk in to tea," she added, folding up her work. "Ah! Sophy, I am glad to see you looking neat again. I think you were in no better plight than Elsie when you came in."

For some time after this, the young people were very careful to come in from their play in good season; but one afternoon they had taken a longer walk than usual, going farther down their little brook, and establishing themselves in a new spot where they imagined the grass was greener, and the shade deeper. The day was cloudy, and they could not judge of the time so well as when they could see the sun, and so it happened that they stayed much later than they should have done.

Elsie was feeling a little anxious, and had once or twice proposed going home, but was always overruled by Harold and Sophy, who insisted that it was not at all late. But at length Elsie rose with an air of determination, saying she was sure it *must* be getting late, and if they would not go with her, she must go alone.

"Well, then, we will go, and I guess it's about time," said Harold; "so come along, Soph, or we'll, leave you behind."

Elsie hurried along with nervous haste, and the others had to exert themselves to keep up with her, but just as they reached the door the tea-bell rang.

The children exchanged glances of fright and mortification.

"What shall we do?" whispered Elsie.

"Dear! if we were only dressed!" said Sophy. "Let's go in just as we are; maybe no one will notice."

"No," replied Elsie, shaking her head, "that would never do for me; papa would see it in a moment and send me away from the table. It would be worse than waiting to dress."

"Then we will all go upstairs and make ourselves decent, and afterwards take the scolding as well as we can," said Harold, leading the way.

Chloe was in Sophy's room, waiting to attend to her child. She did not fret the little girl with lamentations over her tardiness, but set about adjusting her hair and dress as quickly as possible.

Elsie looked troubled and anxious.

"Papa will be very much vexed, and ashamed of me, too, I am afraid," she said with tears in her eyes. "And, Sophy, what will your mamma say? Oh! how I wish I had come in sooner!"

"Never mind," replied Sophy; "mamma won't be very angry, and we'll tell her the sun wouldn't shine, and so how were we to know the time."

Elsie was ready first, but waited a moment for Sophy, and they went down together. Her first sensation on entering the room and seeing that her father's chair was empty, was certainly one of relief. When her eye sought Mrs. Allison's face, it was quite as pleasant as usual.

"You are rather late, little girls," she said in a cheerful tone, "but as you are usually so punctual, we will have to excuse you this once. Come, take your places."

"It was cloudy, you know, mamma, and we couldn't see the sun," said Harold, who was already at the table.

"Very well, Harold, you must try to guess better next time. Rose, help Elsie to some of that omelet and a bit of the cold tongue."

"No, thank you, ma'am; papa does not allow me to eat meat at night," said the little girl resolutely, turning her eyes away from the tempting dish.

"Ah! I forgot, but you can eat the omelet, dear," Mrs. Allison said; "and help her to the honey, and a piece of that cheese, Rose, and put some butter on her plate."

It cost Elsie quite a struggle, for she was as fond of good things as other children, but she said firmly, "No, thank you, ma'am,

I should like the omelet, and the honey and the cheese too, very much, but as I was late to-night, I can only have dry bread, because you know my papa said so."

Harold spoke up earnestly. "But, mamma, it wasn't her fault; she wanted to come home in time, and Sophy and I wouldn't."

"No, mamma, it wasn't her fault at all," said Sophy, eagerly, "and so she needn't have just bread, need she?"

"No, Elsie dear, I think not. Do, dear child, let me help you to something; here's a saucer of berries and cream; won't you take it? I feel quite sure your papa would not insist upon the bread and water if he were here, and I am sorry he and Edward happen to be away to tea."

"As it was not your fault, Elsie dear, I think you might venture," said Rose, kindly. "I wouldn't want you to disobey your papa, but under the circumstances, I don't think that it would be disobedience."

"You are very kind, Miss Rose, but you don't know papa as well as I do," Elsie replied, a little sadly. "He told me I must always be in in time to be ready for tea, and he says nothing excuses disobedience; and you know I could have come in without the others; so I feel quite sure I should get nothing but bread for my supper if he were here."

"Well, dear, I am very sorry, but if you think it is really your duty to sup on dry bread, we will all honor you for doing it," Mrs. Allison said.

And then the matter dropped, and Elsie quietly ate her slice of bread and drank a little cold water, then went out to play on the lawn with the others.

"Did you ever see such a perfectly conscientious child?" said Mrs. Allison to Rose. "Dear little thing! I could hardly stand it to see her eating that dry bread, when the rest were enjoying all the luxuries of the table."

"No, mamma, it fairly made my heart ache. I shall tell her father all about it when he comes in. Don't you think, mamma, he is rather too strict and particular with her?"

"I don't know, Rose, dear; I'm afraid she is much better trained than mine; and he certainly is very fond of her, and quite indulgent in some respects."

"Fond of her! yes, indeed he is, and she loves him with her whole heart. Ah! mamma, you don't know how glad it makes me to see it. The poor little thing seemed to be literally famishing for love when I first knew her."

When Elsie had done anything which she knew would displease her father, she never could rest satisfied until she had confessed it and been forgiven. Through all her play that evening she was conscious of a burden on her heart; and every now and then her eyes were turned wistfully in the direction from which she expected him to come. But the clock struck eight, and there were no signs of his approach, and soon it was half-past, and she found she must go to bed without seeing him. She sighed several times while Chloe was undressing her, and just as she was about leaving her, said, "If papa comes home before I go to sleep, mammy, please ask him to let me come to him for one minute."

"I will, darlin'; but don't you try for to stay awake; kase maybe massa ain't gwine be home till berry late, an' den he might be vexed wid you."

It was nearly ten o'clock when Mr. Dinsmore returned, and he was talking on the piazza with Mr. and Miss Allison for nearly half an hour afterwards; but Chloe was patiently waiting for him, and meeting him in the hall on the way to his room, presented Elsie's request.

"Yes," he said, "see if she is awake, but don't disturb her if she is not."

Chloe softly opened the door, and the little girl started up, asking in an eager whisper, "Did he say I might come, mammy?"

"Yes, darlin'," said Chloe, lifting her in her arms and setting her down on the floor. And then the little fairy-like figure in its white night-dress stole softly out into the hall, and ran with swift, noiseless steps across it, and into the open door of Mr. Dinsmore's room.

He caught her in his arms and kissed her several times with passionate fondness. Then sitting down with her on his knee, he asked tenderly, "What does my darling want with papa to-night?"

"I wanted to tell you that I was very naughty this afternoon, and didn't get home until just as the tea-bell rang."

"And you were very glad to find that papa was not here to make you sup upon bread and water, eh?"

"No, papa, I didn't eat anything else," she said in a hurt tone; "I wouldn't take such a mean advantage of your absence."

"No, dearest, I know you would not. I know my little girl is the soul of honor," he said, soothingly, pressing another kiss on her cheek; "and besides, I have just heard the whole story from Miss Rose and her mother."

"And you *wouldn't* have let me have anything but bread, papa, would you?" she asked, raising her head to look up in his face.

"No, dear, nothing else, for you know I must keep my word, however trying it may be to my feelings."

"Yes, papa; and I am so glad you do, because then I always know just what to expect. You are not angry with me

Martha Finley

now, papa?"

"No, darling, not in the very least; you are entirely forgiven. And now I want you to go back to your bed, and try to get a good night's sleep, and be ready to come to me in the morning. So good-night, my pet, my precious one. God bless and keep my darling. May He ever cause His face to shine upon you, and give you peace."

He held her to his heart a moment, then let her go: and she glided back to her room, and laid her head on her pillow to sleep sweetly, and dream happy dreams of her father's love and tenderness.

She was with him again the next morning, an hour before it was time for the breakfast-bell to ring, sitting on his knee beside the open window, chatting and laughing as gleefully as the birds were singing on the trees outside.

"What do you think of this?" he asked, laying an open jewel-case in her lap.

She looked down, and there, contrasting so prettily with the dark blue velvet lining, lay a beautiful gold chain and a tiny gold watch set with pearls all around its edge.

"Oh, papa!" she cried, "is it for me?"

"Yes, my pet. Do you like it?"

"Indeed I do, papa! it is just as lovely as it can be!" she said, taking it up and turning it about in her hands. "It looks like mamma's, only brighter, and newer; and this is a different kind of chain from hers."

"Yes, that is entirely new; but the watch is the one she wore. It is an excellent one, and I have had it put in order for her daughter to wear. I think you are old enough to need it now, and to take proper care of it."

"I shall try to, indeed. Dear, darling mamma! I would rather have her watch than any other," she murmured, a shade of tender sadness coming over her face for a moment. Then, looking up brightly, "Thank you, papa," she said, giving him a hug and a kiss; "it was so kind in you to do it. Was that what you went to the city for yesterday?"

"It was my principal errand there."

"And now how sorry and ashamed I should be if I had taken advantage of your absence to eat all sorts of good things."

"I think we are never sorry for doing our duty," her father said, softly stroking her hair, "and I think, too, that my little girl quite deserves the watch."

"And I'm *so* glad to have it!" she cried, holding it up, and gazing at it with a face full of delight. "I must run and show it to Sophy!"

She was getting down from his knee; but he drew her back. "Wait a little, daughter; I have something to tell you."

"What, papa?"

"We have paid our friends a very long visit, and I think it is time for us to go, if we would not have them grow weary of us: so I have decided to leave Elmgrove to-morrow."

"Have you, papa? I like to travel, but I shall be so sorry to leave Sophy, and Miss Rose, and all the rest; they are so kind, and I have had such a pleasant time with them."

"I have told you the bad news first," he said, smiling; "now I have some good. We are going to take a trip through New England and the State of New York; and Miss Rose and Mr. Edward have promised to accompany us: so you see you will not have to part with them just yet."

Elsie clapped her hands at this piece of good news.

"O papa, how pleasant it will be! Dear, *dear* Miss Rose; I am so glad she is going."

"And Mr. Edward?"

"Yes, papa, I like him too, but I love Miss Rose the best of all. Don't you, papa?"

Her father only smiled, and said "Miss Rose was very lovely, certainly."

The breakfast-bell rang, and she ran down, eager to show her watch. It was much admired by all; but there was great lamentation, especially amongst the younger members of the family, when it was announced that their guests were to leave them so soon.

"Why couldn't Elsie stay always?" they asked. "Why couldn't she live with them? they would only be too glad to have her."

Mr. Dinsmore laughed, and told them he could not possibly spare Elsie, for she was his only child, and he had no one else to share his home.

"But you may stay too, Mr. Dinsmore," said Sophy; "there's plenty of room, and mamma and Rose like to have you read to them."

Rose blushed, and shook her head at Sophy, and Mr. Dinsmore replied that it would be very pleasant to live at Elmgrove, but that Elsie and he had a home of their own to which they must soon return, and where she would be very glad to receive a visit from any or all of them.

CHAPTER XVII

"Have you arranged your plans in regard to what places you will visit and in what order you will take them?" asked Mr. Allison, addressing Mr. Dinsmore.

"We have not," he replied; "that is, not very definitely; only that we will visit New England and New York."

"Elsie looks as if she could make a suggestion," remarked Miss Rose, with a smiling glance at the bright, animated face of the little girl.

"I should like to if I were old enough," said the child, dropping her eyes and blushing as she perceived that at that moment she was the object of the attention of every one at the table.

"We will consider you so, my dear," laughed Mr. Allison. "Come, give us the benefit of your ideas."

Still Elsie hesitated till her father said pleasantly, "Yes, daughter, let us have them. We can reject or adopt them as we see fit."

"Yes, papa," she returned. "I was just thinking that Valley Forge and Paoli are both in this State, and I should like very much to see them both."

"I call that a very good idea," said Mr. Edward Allison. "I have always intended to visit those historical places, but have never

Martha Finley

done so yet."

"Then let us go," said Rose, "for I, too, should like very much to see them; if the plan suits you, Mr. Dinsmore," she added, giving him a smiling glance.

"Perfectly," he said; "it will be a new and interesting experience to me, as I have never visited either spot, though quite familiar with their history, as doubtless you all are."

"Then we may consider that matter as settled," remarked Edward with satisfaction.

Elsie hardly knew whether to be more glad or sorry when the time came for the final leave-taking; but the joyful thought that Miss Rose was to accompany them fairly turned the scale in favor of the former feeling; and though she brushed away a tear or two at parting from Sophy, she set off with a bright and happy face.

They spent several weeks most delightfully in travelling about from place to place, going first to Valley Forge—a little valley so called because a man named Isaac Potts had a forge there on a creek which empties into the Schuylkill River. He was an extensive iron manufacturer. The valley is a deep, short hollow, seemingly scooped out from a low, rugged mountain.

The Americans had their camp on a range of hills back of the village, Washington his quarters at the house of Isaac Potts. It was a stone building standing near the mouth of the creek. Our friends were invited in by a cheerful old lady living there, and shown Washington's room. It was very small, but they found it interesting. The old lady took them into it, and, leading the way to an east window, said: "From here Washington could look to those slopes yonder and see a large part of his camp." Then, lifting a blue sill, she showed a little trap-door and beneath it a cavity, which she said had been arranged by Washington as a hiding place for his papers.

On leaving that house, our little party went to view the ruins of an old flour-mill near by.

"This was going in those revolutionary days," said the old lady, who was still with them, "and soon after the battle of Brandywine, before the encampment in this valley, the Americans had a large quantity of stores here in this mill. Washington heard that the British General Howe had sent troops to destroy them, and he sent some of his men, under Alexander Hamilton and Captain Henry Lee, to get ahead of the British; which they did. Knowing there was danger of a surprise, they had a flat-bottomed boat ready to cross the river in, and two videttes out on the hill to the south yonder"— pointing with her finger. "Well, the soldiers had crossed the river and were just going to begin the work they had come to do, when the guns of the videttes were heard, and they were seen running down the hill with the British close after them. Lee, the videttes, and four of the other men ran across the bridge—the enemy sending a shower of bullets after them— while the others, with Hamilton, took to the boat. They were fired upon too, but got away safely. The two parties had got separated, and neither one knew just how the other had fared. Lee sent a note to Washington telling his fears for Hamilton and his men; and while Washington was reading it Hamilton rode up with a face full of distress, and began telling the general his fears for Lee; then Washington relieved him by handing him Lee's note to read."

Our party thanked the old lady for her story, and Mr. Dinsmore asked what more there was to see.

"There's an observatory over yonder on that south hill," she said, pointing to it. "It was there a large part of the American army was quartered—on the hill, I mean. If you go up to the top of the building you can see a good deal of the camping ground from it."

"Thank you," he returned, slipping a silver dollar into her hand. "We are all greatly obliged for your kindness in showing us about this interesting place and refreshing our memories in regard to its history."

The others thanked her also; then taking a carriage they drove to the observatory she had pointed out.

They were told that it stood on the spot where Washington's marquee was placed on his arrival at Valley Forge. It was a neat octagonal structure about forty feet high, with a spiral staircase in the centre leading up to an open gallery on the top. They went up, and found it gave them a fine view of the greater part of what had been the camping ground. "Our troops came here from Whitemarsh, if my memory serves me right," said Edward Allison.

"Yes," assented Mr. Dinsmore. "It was Washington's decision that they should do so, as here he would be near enough to watch the movements of the British army, then in possession of Philadelphia. He wished, for one thing, to keep the foraging parties in check, protecting the people from their depredations."

"Wasn't it in the winter they were here, papa?" asked Elsie.

"Yes; and the poor fellows found it terribly cold; especially for men so poorly provided as they were with what are esteemed by most civilized people as the barest necessities of life—food, clothing, shoes, and blankets."

"Yes, I remember reading about it—how their poor feet bled on the ground as they marched over it, with neither shoes nor stockings," said Elsie, tears springing to her eyes as she spoke. "And didn't they suffer from hunger too, papa?"

"Yes, they did, poor fellows!" he sighed. "They endured a great deal in the hope of winning freedom for themselves, their children, and their country. They had not even material to raise their beds from the ground, and in consequence many sickened and died from the dampness."

"It is really wonderful how they bore it all," said Edward. "They certainly must have been true and ardent patriots."

"We were told that Washington's marquee stood just here in that time," said Elsie. "What did he want with it when he had a room in Mr. Potts' house?"

"He occupied the marquee only while his men were building their huts," explained her father, "then afterward took up his quarters in that house."

Our party now returned to their carriage and drove to Paoli— some nine miles distant. They were told that the place of the massacre was about a quarter of a mile from the highway, and leaving their vehicle at the nearest point, they followed a path leading through open fields till they came to the monument. They found it a blue clouded marble pedestal, surmounted by a white marble pyramid, standing over the broad grave in which lie the remains of the fifty-three Americans found in that field the morning after the massacre, and buried by the neighboring farmers.

"Papa," said Elsie, "won't you please go over the story?"

"If a short rehearsal will not be unpleasant to our friends," he answered kindly.

Both Rose and Edward assured him they would be glad to listen to it, and he at once began.

"It was but a few days after the battle of Brandywine that Wayne was here with about fifteen hundred men and four pieces of cannon, Washington having given him directions to annoy the enemy's rear and try to cut off his baggage train. This place was some two or three miles southwest of the British lines, away from the public roads, and at that time covered with a forest.

"But for the treachery of a Tory the British would have known nothing of the whereabouts of these patriots who were struggling to free their country from unbearable oppression. But Howe, learning it all from the Tory, resolved to attempt to surprise and slaughter the Americans. He despatched General Grey (who was afterwards a murderer and plunderer at Tappan and along the New England coast) to steal upon the patriot camp at night and destroy as many as he could.

"Wayne heard that something of the kind was intended, but did not believe it. Still, he took every precaution; ordered his men to sleep on their arms with their ammunition under their coats—to keep it dry I suppose, as the night was dark and stormy.

"Grey and his men marched stealthily on them in the night, passing through the woods and up a narrow defile. It was about one o'clock in the morning that they gained Wayne's left. Grey was a most cruel wretch, called the no-flint general because of his orders to his soldiers to take the flints from their guns; his object being to compel them to use the bayonet; his orders were to rush upon the patriots with the bayonet and give no quarter. In that way, in the darkness and silence, they killed several of the pickets near the highway.

"The patrolling officer missed these men, his suspicions were aroused, and he hastened with his news to Wayne's tent. Wayne at once paraded his men, but unfortunately in the light of his fires, which enabled the enemy to see and shoot them down. Grey and his men came on in silence, but with the fierceness of tigers; they leaped from the thick darkness upon the Americans, who did not know from which quarter to expect them. The Americans fired several volleys, but so sudden and violent was the attack that their column was at once broken into fragments, and they fled in confusion. One hundred and fifty Americans were killed and wounded in this assault. It is said that some of the wounded were cruelly butchered after surrendering and asking for quarter. But for Wayne's coolness and skill his whole command would have been killed or taken prisoners. He quickly rallied a few companies, ordered Colonel Humpton to wheel the line, and with the cavalry and a part of the infantry successfully covered a retreat."

"Then did all who had not already been killed get away from the British, papa?" asked Elsie.

"Not quite all; they captured between seventy and eighty men, taking, besides, a good many small arms, two pieces of cannon, and eight wagon-loads of baggage and stores."

"Weren't some of the British killed?" she asked.

"Only one captain and three privates; and four men were wounded."

The story was finished, and having seen all there was to see in connection with it, our travellers went on their way and pursued their journey, not feeling at all hurried, seeing all they wanted to see, and stopping to rest whenever they felt the need of it. Elsie enjoyed it all thoroughly. There was no abatement of the tender, watchful care her father had bestowed upon her in their former journey, and added to that was the pleasant companionship of Miss Rose and her brother.

Mr. Edward was very kind and attentive to both his sister and Elsie, always thinking of something to please them or add to their comfort; and both he and Rose treated the little girl as though she were a dear, younger sister.

Elsie was seldom absent from her father's side for many minutes, yet sometimes in their walks she found herself left to Mr. Edward's care, while Rose had Mr. Dinsmore's arm. But that did not trouble the little girl; for loving them both so dearly, she was very anxious that they should like each other; and then she could leave Mr. Edward and run to her papa whenever she pleased, sure of being always received with the same loving smile, and not at all as though they felt that she was in the way.

Choose from Thousands of 1stWorldLibrary Classics By

A. M. Barnard
Ada Leverson
Adolphus William Ward
Aesop
Agatha Christie
Alexander Aaronsohn
Alexander Kielland
Alexandre Dumas
Alfred Gatty
Alfred Ollivant
Alice Duer Miller
Alice Turner Curtis
Alice Dunbar
Allen Chapman
Alleyne Ireland
Ambrose Bierce
Amelia E. Barr
Amory H. Bradford
Andrew Lang
Andrew McFarland Davis
Andy Adams
Angela Brazil
Anna Alice Chapin
Anna Sewell
Annie Besant
Annie Hamilton Donnell
Annie Payson Call
Annie Roe Carr
Annonaymous
Anton Chekhov
Archibald Lee Fletcher
Arnold Bennett
Arthur C. Benson
Arthur Conan Doyle
Arthur M. Winfield
Arthur Ransome
Arthur Schnitzler
Arthur Train
Atticus
B.H. Baden-Powell
B. M. Bower
B. C. Chatterjee
Baroness Emmuska Orczy
Baroness Orczy
Basil King
Bayard Taylor
Ben Macomber
Bertha Muzzy Bower
Bjornstjerne Bjornson

Booth Tarkington
Boyd Cable
Bram Stoker
C. Collodi
C. E. Orr
C. M. Ingleby
Carolyn Wells
Catherine Parr Traill
Charles A. Eastman
Charles Amory Beach
Charles Dickens
Charles Dudley Warner
Charles Farrar Browne
Charles Ives
Charles Kingsley
Charles Klein
Charles Hanson Towne
Charles Lathrop Pack
Charles Romyn Dake
Charles Whibley
Charles Willing Beale
Charlotte M. Braeme
Charlotte M. Yonge
Charlotte Perkins Stetson
Clair W. Hayes
Clarence Day Jr.
Clarence E. Mulford
Clemence Housman
Confucius
Coningsby Dawson
Cornelis DeWitt Wilcox
Cyril Burleigh
D. H. Lawrence
Daniel Defoe
David Garnett
Dinah Craik
Don Carlos Janes
Donald Keyhoe
Dorothy Kilner
Dougan Clark
Douglas Fairbanks
E. Nesbit
E. P. Roe
E. Phillips Oppenheim
E. S. Brooks
Earl Barnes
Edgar Rice Burroughs
Edith Van Dyne
Edith Wharton

Edward Everett Hale
Edward J. O'Biren
Edward S. Ellis
Edwin L. Arnold
Eleanor Atkins
Eleanor Hallowell Abbott
Eliot Gregory
Elizabeth Gaskell
Elizabeth McCracken
Elizabeth Von Arnim
Ellem Key
Emerson Hough
Emilie F. Carlen
Emily Bronte
Emily Dickinson
Enid Bagnold
Enilor Macartney Lane
Erasmus W. Jones
Ernie Howard Pie
Ethel May Dell
Ethel Turner
Ethel Watts Mumford
Eugene Sue
Eugenie Foa
Eugene Wood
Eustace Hale Ball
Evelyn Everett-green
Everard Cotes
F. H. Cheley
F. J. Cross
F. Marion Crawford
Fannie E. Newberry
Federick Austin Ogg
Ferdinand Ossendowski
Fergus Hume
Florence A. Kilpatrick
Fremont B. Deering
Francis Bacon
Francis Darwin
Frances Hodgson Burnett
Frances Parkinson Keyes
Frank Gee Patchin
Frank Harris
Frank Jewett Mather
Frank L. Packard
Frank V. Webster
Frederic Stewart Isham
Frederick Trevor Hill
Frederick Winslow Taylor

Friedrich Kerst
Friedrich Nietzsche
Fyodor Dostoyevsky
G.A. Henty
G.K. Chesterton
Gabrielle E. Jackson
Garrett P. Serviss
Gaston Leroux
George A. Warren
George Ade
Geroge Bernard Shaw
George Cary Eggleston
George Durston
George Ebers
George Eliot
George Gissing
George MacDonald
George Meredith
George Orwell
George Sylvester Viereck
George Tucker
George W. Cable
George Wharton James
Gertrude Atherton
Gordon Casserly
Grace E. King
Grace Gallatin
Grace Greenwood
Grant Allen
Guillermo A. Sherwell
Gulielma Zollinger
Gustav Flaubert
H. A. Cody
H. B. Irving
H.C. Bailey
H. G. Wells
H. H. Munro
H. Irving Hancock
H. R. Naylor
H. Rider Haggard
H. W. C. Davis
Haldeman Julius
Hall Caine
Hamilton Wright Mabie
Hans Christian Andersen
Harold Avery
Harold McGrath
Harriet Beecher Stowe
Harry Castlemon
Harry Coghill
Harry Houidini

Hayden Carruth
Helent Hunt Jackson
Helen Nicolay
Hendrik Conscience
Hendy David Thoreau
Henri Barbusse
Henrik Ibsen
Henry Adams
Henry Ford
Henry Frost
Henry James
Henry Jones Ford
Henry Seton Merriman
Henry W Longfellow
Herbert A. Giles
Herbert Carter
Herbert N. Casson
Herman Hesse
Hildegard G. Frey
Homer
Honore De Balzac
Horace B. Day
Horace Walpole
Horatio Alger Jr.
Howard Pyle
Howard R. Garis
Hugh Lofting
Hugh Walpole
Humphry Ward
Ian Maclaren
Inez Haynes Gillmore
Irving Bacheller
Isabel Cecilia Williams
Isabel Hornibrook
Israel Abrahams
Ivan Turgenev
J.G.Austin
J. Henri Fabre
J. M. Barrie
J. M. Walsh
J. Macdonald Oxley
J. R. Miller
J. S. Fletcher
J. S. Knowles
J. Storer Clouston
J. W. Duffield
Jack London
Jacob Abbott
James Allen
James Andrews
James Baldwin

James Branch Cabell
James DeMille
James Joyce
James Lane Allen
James Lane Allen
James Oliver Curwood
James Oppenheim
James Otis
James R. Driscoll
Jane Abbott
Jane Austen
Jane L. Stewart
Janet Aldridge
Jens Peter Jacobsen
Jerome K. Jerome
Jessie Graham Flower
John Buchan
John Burroughs
John Cournos
John F. Kennedy
John Gay
John Glasworthy
John Habberton
John Joy Bell
John Kendrick Bangs
John Milton
John Philip Sousa
John Taintor Foote
Jonas Lauritz Idemil Lie
Jonathan Swift
Joseph A. Altsheler
Joseph Carey
Joseph Conrad
Joseph E. Badger Jr
Joseph Hergesheimer
Joseph Jacobs
Jules Vernes
Julian Hawthrone
Julie A Lippmann
Justin Huntly McCarthy
Kakuzo Okakura
Karle Wilson Baker
Kate Chopin
Kenneth Grahame
Kenneth McGaffey
Kate Langley Bosher
Kate Langley Bosher
Katherine Cecil Thurston
Katherine Stokes
L. A. Abbot
L. T. Meade

L. Frank Baum
Latta Griswold
Laura Dent Crane
Laura Lee Hope
Laurence Housman
Lawrence Beasley
Leo Tolstoy
Leonid Andreyev
Lewis Carroll
Lewis Sperry Chafer
Lilian Bell
Lloyd Osbourne
Louis Hughes
Louis Joseph Vance
Louis Tracy
Louisa May Alcott
Lucy Fitch Perkins
Lucy Maud Montgomery
Luther Benson
Lydia Miller Middleton
Lyndon Orr
M. Corvus
M. H. Adams
Margaret E. Sangster
Margret Howth
Margaret Vandercook
Margaret W. Hungerford
Margret Penrose
Maria Edgeworth
Maria Thompson Daviess
Mariano Azuela
Marion Polk Angellotti
Mark Overton
Mark Twain
Mary Austin
Mary Catherine Crowley
Mary Cole
Mary Hastings Bradley
Mary Roberts Rinehart
Mary Rowlandson
M. Wollstonecraft Shelley
Maud Lindsay
Max Beerbohm
Myra Kelly
Nathaniel Hawthrone
Nicolo Machiavelli
O. F. Walton
Oscar Wilde
Owen Johnson
P.G. Wodehouse
Paul and Mabel Thorne

Paul G. Tomlinson
Paul Severing
Percy Brebner
Percy Keese Fitzhugh
Peter B. Kyne
Plato
Quincy Allen
R. Derby Holmes
R. L. Stevenson
R. S. Ball
Rabindranath Tagore
Rahul Alvares
Ralph Bonehill
Ralph Henry Barbour
Ralph Victor
Ralph Waldo Emmerson
Rene Descartes
Ray Cummings
Rex Beach
Rex E. Beach
Richard Harding Davis
Richard Jefferies
Richard Le Gallienne
Robert Barr
Robert Frost
Robert Gordon Anderson
Robert L. Drake
Robert Lansing
Robert Lynd
Robert Michael Ballantyne
Robert W. Chambers
Rosa Nouchette Carey
Rudyard Kipling
Saint Augustine
Samuel B. Allison
Samuel Hopkins Adams
Sarah Bernhardt
Sarah C. Hallowell
Selma Lagerlof
Sherwood Anderson
Sigmund Freud
Standish O'Grady
Stanley Weyman
Stella Benson
Stella M. Francis
Stephen Crane
Stewart Edward White
Stijn Streuvels
Swami Abhedananda
Swami Parmananda
T. S. Ackland

T. S. Arthur
The Princess Der Ling
Thomas A. Janvier
Thomas A Kempis
Thomas Anderton
Thomas Bailey Aldrich
Thomas Bulfinch
Thomas De Quincey
Thomas Dixon
Thomas H. Huxley
Thomas Hardy
Thomas More
Thornton W. Burgess
U. S. Grant
Upton Sinclair
Valentine Williams
Various Authors
Vaughan Kester
Victor Appleton
Victor G. Durham
Victoria Cross
Virginia Woolf
Wadsworth Camp
Walter Camp
Walter Scott
Washington Irving
Wilbur Lawton
Wilkie Collins
Willa Cather
Willard F. Baker
William Dean Howells
William le Queux
W. Makepeace Thackeray
William W. Walter
William Shakespeare
Winston Churchill
Yei Theodora Ozaki
Yogi Ramacharaka
Young E. Allison
Zane Grey

www.ingramcontent.com/pod-product-compliance
Lightning Source LLC
Chambersburg PA
CBHW020436270626
47155CB00022B/494